Praise for *The Schooling of*

D0287482

"A sumptuous, life-affirming treat."

"Janis Owens's haunting characters will stay with you, like a quiet song playing in your memory, long after you have finished the novel."
 —Loraine Despres, author of *The Scandalous Summer of Sissy LeBlanc*

"Atmospheric and teeming with memorable characters, *The Schooling of Claybird Catts* delivers a powerful message about the ties of love and the meaning of family . . . in Claybird the author has created one of the most endearing narrators since Scout in *To Kill a Mockingbird*."
 —*Curled Up with a Good Book* (www.curledup.com)

"Janis Owens possesses one of the freshest and most original literary voices I have read of late. Claybird Catts is a mesmerizing narrator: honest and funny and wise beyond his years. He is also exquisitely naïve, which makes us root for him all the more. This is a wonderful novel. Readers will find themselves laughing through their tears as Claybird uncovers the time-hewn universal truths that bind family and friends in the bumpy but un-broken circle we call love."
 —Connie May Fowler, author of *Before Women Had Wings*

"The Southern-born and -bred Owens laces the poignant narrative with an appealing combination of humor, pathos, and down-home wisdom."
 —*Booklist*

"Embracing all the contradictions of a Southern childhood, Janis Owens's novel achieves a life-affirming vision. In a voice of remarkable originality and freshness, young Claybird narrates his wayward journey from denial to consolation."
 —Sena Jeter Naslund, author of *Ahab's Wife* and *Four Spirits*

"Warm and affirming."                                        —*Kirkus Reviews*

## *About the Author*

JANIS OWENS was born in Marianna, Florida, in 1960, the last child and only daughter of an Assembly of God preacher who later became a salesman for the Independent Life Insurance Company. As a child, she lived in Louisiana and Mississippi, but her heart and her literary roots can be traced to west Florida, to the old mill neighborhood where her mother was raised, which the old-timers call Magnolia Hill. A graduate of the University of Florida, Ms. Owens lives in rural north Florida with her husband and three daughters.

ALSO BY JANIS OWENS

*My Brother Michael*

*Myra Sims*

# The Schooling of Claybird Catts

## A NOVEL

## JANIS OWENS

 Perennial
*An Imprint of* HarperCollins*Publishers*

*For my goofball brothers:*
*the millionaire and the rocket scientist*

*Pretty good ol' boys, both*

Excerpts from "Childhood Is the Kingdom Where Nobody Dies," "Pity Me Not Because the Light of Day," and "What Lips My Lips Have Kissed," by Edna St. Vincent Millay. From *Collected Poems*, HarperCollins. Copyright © 1923, 1951, 1962, Edna St. Vincent Millay and Norma Millay Ellis. All rights reserved. Reprinted by permission of Elizabeth Barnett, literary executor.

A hardcover edition of this book was published in 2003 by HarperCollins Publishers.

HarperCollins books may be purchased for educational, business, or sales promotional use. For information please write: Special Markets Department, HarperCollins Publishers Inc., 10 East 53rd Street, New York, NY 10022.

First Perennial edition published 2004.

*Designed by Joy O'Meara Battista*

The Library of Congress has catalogued the hardcover edition as follows:
Owens, Janis.
    The Schooling of Claybird Catts / by Janis Owens.— 1st ed.
       p.   cm.
   ISBN 0-06-009062-6
     1. Fathers—Death—Fiction. 2. Florida—Fiction. 3. Uncles—Fiction.
   4. Boys—Fiction. I. Title.
PS3565.W5665 S68 2003
813'.54—dc21

                               2002068479

ISBN 0-06-009063-4 (pbk.)

      07 08 ❖/RRD 10 9 8 7 6 5 4

# PART ONE

*Childhood is not from birth to a certain age and at a certain age*
*The child is grown, and puts away childish things.*
*Childhood is the kingdom where nobody dies.*

EDNA ST. VINCENT MILLAY

# CHAPTER ONE

To be perfectly honest, the day my father Michael died really wasn't the worst day of my life.

Of course, it has panned out to be the worst, but at the time, it was just the last day in a week of one fun thing after another, all part of what I later learned was a carefully constructed plot to distract us children from the inevitable. Every night my brother Simon and my sister Missy and me were wined and dined by different friends and kin, making for a fast, hectic week that peaked on Saturday, when my best friend Kenneth's Uncle Lou, who is full-blooded Italian (like Kenneth wishes he was) and very sympathetic to Daddy's plight, took Kenneth and me to Busch Gardens as he works for Anheuser-Busch and gets free tickets.

We left early that morning, before five, and got there just as the gates opened, and had a heck of a time except that I puked on the Scorpion, or just after. We'd eaten breakfast at the IHOP outside the park and I must have eaten one chocolate-chip pancake too many, for I got sick as a dog on the first loop, but was man enough to hold my bile till I made it to the bathroom. Other than that, we had a big time. Uncle Lou even bought each of us a copy of the picture they take when you come in the park that Daddy always said was such a rip-off (fifteen bucks) though maybe he (Uncle Lou, that is) got an employee discount.

In any case, I have the picture on my nightstand to this day and have to say that yes, I look quite the happy boy, not a clue in the world that my father was lying on his deathbed four hundred miles away fighting for his last breath. Just me and that idiot Kenneth grinning like possums, Uncle Lou between us, his arms draped loosely around our necks, very Italian and all, like a good-natured mafioso with his two favorite Godsons.

By the time we started home, it was nearly dark, all the little tourist towns along US 19 decorated for Christmas, each with its own entice- ment: mermaids and alligator farms and manatee crossings. We even stopped at some of them as Uncle Lou is divorced and kind of lonely, and all the billboards had these well-matured women in bikinis urging you to drop by. At least, I *think* that's why we stopped. It was too dark to see much at any of them, and as the gray December evening gave way to a cold, clear night, I began to get a little antsy with how late it was getting, and Daddy being sick at home.

I kept thinking about Mama and how worried she'd be if I was late, how she always paced around when Daddy was late from Waycross. It started eating at me, made me curse the traffic lights and silently rejoice when it got late enough that they were turned off for the night, blinking yellow through the little towns in the Big Bend till we finally made Perry, where Uncle Lou stopped for coffee and let me call home on his credit card.

It must have been something like two o'clock in the morning by then, not the perfect time for a call home, but I didn't pause for a second because for one thing, with Daddy so sick, our household routine had be- come hopelessly upended, and for another: my mother never sleeps any- way. I mean, hardly ever. It's one of her strange old *vampire* things that we'd all grown used to, never gave a second thought to knocking on her bedroom door at midnight, or calling home at odd hours of the night.

Sure enough, she answered on the second ring, not at all upset or sleepy, just her calm, matter-of-fact self, asking me where we were; if I'd had fun.

I told her it was big fun, though I'd almost puked on the Scorpion, and she was the soul of comfort. "Did it make you feel better?"

I had to admit that it did and she said good, at least it hadn't spoiled my day, then gave the phone to Daddy, said he wanted to talk to me. I could make out a rustling of sheets and the faint sound of Mama's voice on the line, calm and rock-solid, catching Daddy up on what I'd just told her, then his own voice, weak but familiar, which was a relief, as everything else about him had become so strange lately.

I mean, if he wasn't lying in his own bedroom in his own bed when I left that morning, I wouldn't even recognize him, he was so awful looking, his face so thin you could count the bones, his hair almost completely gray, and he was only forty-three. Aunt Candace (Daddy's older sister), who is a nurse, said that's what pain will do to you, age you, but still, it was very strange, and I was almost glad I couldn't actually see him, because over the phone he sounded perfectly fine, just a little tired and hoarse.

"Hey, Clayman," he said in his thin, kindly voice, for Daddy was the kind of old-school redneck who was constantly churning out terms of affection for the people he loved. He called Simon *Sim* or *Simbo,* called our sister Missy *Mimi* or *Red* (because of her red hair), and though I was technically named after my great-grandfather Clayton, he seldom (if ever) called me by my given name, but *Claybird* most of the time, along with *Clayman* and *Big Man* and all sorts of variations therein.

"Hey, Daddy," I replied, then I stood there at the counter and gave him a fast travelogue of the day, telling him the same things I'd just told Mama—about how I'd eaten too many pancakes before I got on the Scorpion, but didn't realize it till that first loop; how Uncle Lou had his picture taken with a mermaid.

"Good for Lou," Daddy said with his old dry laugh, then asked to speak to him.

I called Uncle Lou to the phone then sat at the counter with Kenneth and drank whatever they'd ordered for me—a milkshake, I think—

not paying much attention to their conversation, though I wished I would have now, because I think Daddy told him to get me home fast so he could see me one last time, before they sent him to the hospital.

He must have, for Uncle Lou didn't even finish his coffee, just tossed a ten on the counter, then loaded us up and hauled butt down the four-lane through the flat woods. He didn't even bother to bypass downtown Tallahassee, but just cruised down the parkway doing sixty, slowing down for the lights, but not coming to a full stop, which made for an eerily silent, fast little spin through town.

I kept thinking a cop would see us and pull us over, but nothing stirred or impeded our progress, Highway 90 winding empty and gray through the tobacco barns and old plantation houses in Gretna and Quincy and finally over the Apalachicola that was high on its banks that time of year, smoking and silent in the darkness of the early dawn.

I don't remember much of the trip after the river. After that, I was busy packing my stuff and doing my thanks and giving directions to the various back roads and cutoffs that made for the shortcut home. In no time at all we were turning off the highway into our drive, the woods that lead up to the house pitch black till the motion detectors went off, flickering on just ahead of us, one after another, bringing to light the trees and gravel and frost-stiffened grass till we made it around back to the garage.

Uncle Lou dropped me off there, as planned, I guess, as Mama was waiting at the back door (or maybe she'd seen the lights and come downstairs). She was wearing the same thing she'd had on when I left that morning, her white winter robe, her face unmade and vampire-pale, her dark red hair kind of spiky and wild, like she'd been in bed, though she didn't seem sleepy at all, just glad to see me as she let me in with one of her big Mama-hugs. There was no indication—not a smell, not a wink—that Daddy's illness was reaching what Missy would call *critical mass*, the house kind of tousled like it always got around Christmas, not as many presents under the tree as usual, Mama too busy nursing Daddy to do much shopping.

But other than that, everything was just as it should be, and after my hug, I plunked my stuff on the floor and gave her the Busch Gardens picture that she turned over in her hands, smiling at it a moment before she thanked Uncle Lou with the particular graciousness that Gabe would later call her good Louisiana manners. She would have walked him to his car if he'd have let her, but he insisted it was too cold and made his departure at the French door with many profuse thanks and offers of money on Mama's part, and an equal number of steadfast refusals (for the money) and offers of assistance on his.

It was like a battle of good Louisiana manners and good Sicilian manners, which made for a lot of vehement protest and proclamations of undying gratitude that I didn't join in or make much of, hit by a wall of sleepiness the moment I walked in the door. I hadn't been home much the past week, what with all the wining and dining and gallivanting around. Now that I was back in my own living room with its own familiar smells—coffee and Pine-Sol and damp wood (old-house smells, Daddy used to call them), I was suddenly dead on my feet, overtaken by a fit of yawning.

With no further ado, I headed up to my bedroom, wanting to climb in bed, clothes and all, though Mama stopped me on the stairs and called that Daddy was awake; that he wanted to see me.

"I'm taking him back to the hospital," she said aside to Mr. Lou, then, to me: "The ambulance'll be here in a minute, baby. Run show him your picture."

I just nodded, then headed up the stairs, not at all upset by the news that he was going back to the hospital. He'd been in and out of the hospital two or three times by then, for tests and operations and different little procedures that everyone said were a success, though he hadn't gotten any better as far as I could see. But the hospital was okay; it was cool. Aunt Candace worked there, and all the nurses knew us and were always teasing me about how I peed in Dr. Winston's face when I was a baby because this is a small town and a small hospital and everybody remembers every little embarrassing thing you ever did and loves to bring it up.

So hearing that Daddy was being readmitted wasn't such a big deal. I just took the steep stairs two at a time, the high-ceilinged old hallway pitch-black that time of morning, and drafty, too, smelling of Lysol and astringent, their bedroom door open, sending out a pale little triangle of light. That's where Daddy was waiting, sitting up in bed as usual, dressed to go to town in the shiny, satin pajamas Mama had bought him for his first surgery—his *hospital pajamas,* we called them, because he never wore them anywhere else. He didn't look any better or worse than he had when I'd left that morning, though he was kind of slumped over, one hand pressed flat against his chest as if he was having a hard time breathing.

But he smiled when he saw me, called: "Hey, Big Man," then: "Where's your mama?" which was also not unusual.

I'd noticed that in the past few weeks, whenever she left the room, he'd get worried and nervous, so different than he used to be, so unlike him. I knew why: he was scared when she was gone, afraid he couldn't breathe; afraid he'd die, and nobody could understand that better than me. I mean, I cried for a year when they sent me to kindergarten, I really did. I remember my teacher finally just telling everyone to ignore me while I sat there in my little desk every morning and broke all my pencils into pieces and cried and cried because I wanted to be back home with Mama and not out in that cold cruel world, and there was just nothing anyone could do about it.

"She's thanking Mr. Lou," I told Daddy, crawling in bed beside him and handing him the picture. "Says you're going back to the hospital."

"I am," he breathed, taking the picture and glancing at it, though he was really too agitated to focus on it, kept looking up at the door, waiting for Mama.

He was so worried that I shimmied back off the bed, went to see what was keeping her, but she'd finally managed to out-thank Uncle Lou and met me at the door, came back to the bed with no complaint, which was a great blessing. I mean, after six weeks, a lot of women would say:

*Oh, quit being such a sissy,* but not Mama. She's not one of the reproachers of the world and just climbed back under the covers, robe and all. Once she was there beside him, Daddy was himself again, holding the Busch Gardens picture at arm's length and regarding it with his old nearsighted squint.

"My *gosh,* Kenneth's getting tall," he murmured aside to Mama, "his arms are a yard long. Susan needs to git thet boy in baseball." (Which was what he said of any child out of diapers who wasn't actually wheelchair-bound: that their parents should get them into baseball, or basketball or *something.* For Daddy was an athlete by inclination and a competitor by nature, who couldn't imagine a life that didn't involve some form of sweating and straining or require the purchase of a protective cup.)

"I think Kenneth's more the poet type," Mama answered with a fond little smile, because Kenneth is my best friend, and everyone, she says, should have a best friend.

Daddy just made one of his thoughtful little grunts in reply (he was a great grunter, my father was, able to communicate a wide expression of emotion in his various grunts: disgust, regret, bemused agreement) though he didn't say anything else. He just kept staring at the picture with this quiet, reflective intensity like he was really moved by it, unintentionally creating my last, most vivid memory of him, sitting there in the dim light of the bedside lamp, his face not as bloated and weird as it had been before his last surgery, but thin now.

Terribly, cadaverously thin, all bones and bright eyes when he seemed to come to himself and remember that I was sitting next to him. "Well, I'm glad you had fun, baby," he said, reaching over and gripping my knee. "It was nice of Lou to take you. Didju thank him?"

Now, around the Catts house, there was nothing as sniveling as an ingrate, and I went to some lengths to assure him I had. I went on to tell him about the picture and how much it cost, all to underscore what a prince of a guy Uncle Lou was, a sly maneuver on my part as he had offered to take me and Kenneth to Atlanta to see the Braves next summer.

Given his reputation for barhopping, Mama was not likely to agree unless Daddy came down big on our side, so I laid it on pretty thick, till Mama quietly interrupted me.

"They're here," she said, lifting her face to a flicker of red light that blinked in a quick little beat against the far wall, signaling the arrival of the ambulance.

She must have told them that it wasn't an emergency because they didn't have their siren on, just that voiceless blink of red that lit the dark wall, unexpectedly striking me with the same undertow of unease I had been touched with on that fast, silent drive through Tallahassee. It wasn't overwhelming or anything, just this nervous belly-drop of awareness that for all the assurance of Mama's low-key manner, something quite out of the ordinary was afoot as she maneuvered herself off the bed and went back downstairs.

Daddy's breath quickened accordingly, though he tried to make light of it for my sake, his attention back on the Busch Gardens picture he was still holding in his hand. I just lay there against him, too tired to talk, though after a moment, I did ask when I could come see him, because Aunt Candace wasn't so hot about taking us up to intensive care. It was always good to get an appointment so that if she started making excuses, I could say: "*Daddy* said I could come on Monday," or whatever, and then she'd take me.

But he didn't answer; I'm not sure now that he heard me. Downstairs, you could hear Mama letting in the paramedics and bringing them up the stairs, not an easy prospect as the staircase was as old as the rest of the house, steep-cut and creaky, with a sharp angle at the landing that made for a lot of commotion and instruction ("Higher, Jim—no, lean in. There we go—").

Daddy didn't pay them any mind, just sat there staring at my picture with that tired resignation till they finally made it upstairs, and began rolling the gurney down the hallway toward us with a mighty rattle of rubber on wood. That's when he finally looked up and spoke to me,

everything about him—his color, his hair, even the whites of his eyes—
so weirdly and quickly changed, though his voice was his own: "You keep
having fun, Claybird," he said with all his old bossy sureness. "You don't
let this bother you, me getting sick. Don't let it get you down. You and
that fool Kenneth just keep living. Keep having fun. 'Kay?"

Which, as it turned out, was the only thing my father ever planned
or asked of me. I mean, with Sim and Missy, he spent *months* agonizing
over their futures, what they'd do when they grew up, where they'd go
to college. But with me, he never said *go to school* or *stay home* or anything.
He just told me to live, to have fun. To *keep* having fun, as much fun as
we were having when they snapped that picture of us at Busch Gardens
that day.

At the time, I saw no reason to deny him and just yawned—"Sure,
Daddy"—and that was about the end of it.

Almost immediately, the paramedics were at the door, two men and
a woman, who shooed me into the hallway while they prodded around
on him awhile, took his blood pressure and checked his pulse, then transferred him to the gurney in one quick lift. With a minimum of fuss and
bother, they strapped him in and rolled him out the door and down the
hallway to the narrow staircase, lifting him like a king on a royal litter a
foot or so above the rails, everything smooth till they made the sharp corner, where they by God would have lost him if he hadn't been secured
at the chest and legs.

But he just tilted a little to the side, and once they got him to
ground level, they made good time, rolling him quickly down the hall to
the front door, that I ran ahead to open. They slid by with professional
briskness, nobody paying me any mind till Mama went past, her purse in
hand, as if she was going to town, when I had to break in and ask: "Aren't
you getting dressed?"

Because she was still in her old winter robe, her hair wild and upended, and no makeup at all, which in Mama's case makes for a ghostly
pale. She was also barefoot, which was odd as it was stinking cold there

on the porch, the puddles from an afternoon rain crinkled with a thin ice, though she didn't seem to notice.

"Candace'll bring me something," she answered distractedly, her eyes on the ambulance. "Sim and Missy are at your grandmother's—I'll call from the hospital, see if she can pick you up for church—"

"I'm okay," I assured her, and right about then, when I might have taken the opportunity to run across that icy porch and duck my head in the ambulance and kiss my father good-bye for the very last time, I just begged, "Can I sleep in yawl's bed?"

Now, I have to take a moment to defend this idiotic lapse by pointing out that I *was* terribly sleepy and *had* been up a long time—and anyway, this isn't any ordinary bed we're talking about, but a king-size wrought-iron canopy, draped with tulle and tassels and even a few peacock feathers, with a squashy feather mattress on top (Mama's contribution) and an insanely expensive Posturepedic beneath (for Daddy's bad back). To lie there was to be happy, to sleep there, a living dream, and indeed I did, as often as I could, at least until Daddy got sick. Since then, their bedroom had become the hub of life in the house and I'd been exiled to my room next door, and my own little bunk beds that even then weren't as wide and accommodating as they used to be.

So I was quick to take this opportunity to get back in clover and Mama didn't argue. "Sure, baby," she said as she backed across the porch, "but turn on the alarm and leave Sim a note or it'll go off when he gets home."

I nodded quickly, didn't even wait around to watch them leave, just shut the door and hightailed it to the laundry room and set the alarm, then painstakingly wrote Sim a note telling him to disengage it or be prepared for a blast from on high. Then I scampered upstairs and took my time ordering my little nest, meticulously straightening the top sheet and big fluffy comforter, even arranging the pillows into an inviting half circle before.I stripped off and dove in with a happy little sigh, just as the first tendrils of daylight were lightening the eastern sky.

I didn't even lie there and savor the moment, just went right to sleep, right where Daddy had been lying a few minutes before, the feather mattress still warm, so comfortable that I didn't wake till much later than I'd expected, almost four in the afternoon, when Sim finally came home. As it turned out, he and Missy had been stranded at Grannie's for the better part of two days, not having such a hot time of it, what with all our Catts and Tierney relations circling like buzzards, so morbid and weepy that Sim finally had enough of it and came home to get dressed to go to the movies.

He even let me go for once and we had a big time, saw *Witness* with Harrison Ford and Kelly McGillis, who you got to see topless before it was over, always a treat. And, you know, that's really about all I remember from those last few days when Daddy was wasting away in the hospital, out of sight and out of mind. I remember the day at Busch Gardens and almost puking on the Scorpion, and later, watching Kelly McGillis standing there topless, taking a sponge bath, and thinking Harrison Ford was an idiot for not going in. I remember that so clearly, in every detail, but not much else till Tuesday morning, when Aunt Candace woke me up early, just after dawn, and hurried me downstairs to the living room, where Brother Sloan told us that Daddy had died that morning in the hospital, "peaceful in the end," which was what Grannie kept telling everyone at the funeral.

But I never got to see him again, and it wasn't till much later—maybe March—that one of the nurses on the ICU found the picture of me and Kenneth tucked away in a spare drawer in the nurses' station and sent it home by Aunt Candace. Apparently, Daddy had taken it with him to the hospital that night in the ambulance, had kept it taped to his bed rails those last two days in intensive care, showed it to all the nurses; talked about how tall Kenneth and me were getting; how we both needed to be in baseball.

Indeed, if you looked closely, you could see the tape marks on the back of it—you still can, to this day. Like I say, I keep it here on my bedside table at Aunt Candace's and I look at it a lot, for it is one of the few pieces of actual physical evidence I have here in Exile that can take me back to the old house and the old life and the day that, contrary to what it might have seemed at the time, has truly and everlastingly turned out to be the worst day of my life: December 19, 1987. The day my father Michael died.

He was forty-three. I was eleven.

# CHAPTER TWO

Now, when I say that my mother is a vampire, I'm not being intentionally cruel or resentful or casting any aspersions on her character. She and I have gone our separate ways these days, but I still love her a lot, I always will. I mean, I know it's a wimpy thing to say and maybe I'm as fairy as I once thought Gabe was, but there it is. Though I live with Aunt Candace now, I still catch an occasional glimpse of her tooling around town in her big old Mercedes, all sunglasses and stiff hair, and from this angle, from the outside, I can see why people tend to look at her with such distant respect: the rich woman in the big house; unapproachable, not among us.

It used to puzzle me when I lived at home, for there was nothing particularly remote or distant about her back then. She was just Mama: the center of our lives, or eye of the hurricane, if you will. Around her blew Daddy's chaotic business life, the day-to-day operations of two thriving furniture factories (Sanger Manufacturing here in town, and the South Georgia Furniture Company in Waycross) and Simon and Missy's sports and science projects and two dozen best friends. Nothing about her ever struck me as unusual or scary back then; if I'd had to liken her to any supernatural creature, it'd have been Casper, the Friendly Ghost.

Come to think of it, I wasn't the one who came up with the Vampire Theory to begin with, but that doofus Kenneth. He was the one who began to detect echoes of the supernatural around our house sometime in the spring of what? First grade? Second? One of the lower grades, when you still sit at tables, when this know-it-all black kid named Reggie Hines informed the rest of the class that I lived in a haunted house, which, in fact, I do (or did, before I moved into town with Aunt Candace, who is so stinking hygienic that no self-respecting ghost would come within a mile of the place or he'd be put to work scrubbing tile).

But at the time I did, one that was old enough to have a name: *The Clarence Thurmon House.* That's how it's listed on the National Register of Historic Places, not because it's haunted, of course, but because it's old, built in 1903 by a rich old banker who once owned half the county. Who, when it came time to build his new country house, bypassed twenty thousand acres of pristine Florida woodland to situate it smack-dab on top of an old slave graveyard, an insult the local black folk have never forgiven him.

Their offspring faithfully warned us Catts children of the dangers of living on top of such hallowed ground, said there used to be a church there, too, that he not only tore down, but incorporated into the structure of the house. According to them, the windows in our front parlor (the bow ones) were once the front windows of the church, an insult the Lord duly avenged when the Old Man was struck down by a heart attack just seven months after he moved in. As legend had it, he fell out right in the front yard, dead as a hammer, though his ghost wasn't the one that supposedly haunted the place, but the dozen or so slaves buried in the old graveyard beneath the foundation. They were the ones who had sent Old Man Thurmon to his untimely death, and after that, no one would live there for a long time.

"Not till *yo* people moved in," Reggie noted with a sniff, as if such a foolhardy move was just the kind of thing he'd expect from the likes of me.

I didn't argue the matter, for like I say, I was just in second grade at the time and still brokenhearted over leaving the sanctuary of my sagging old house, haunted or not. Furthermore, I was kind of shy of the black folk and had no intention of disputing anything with any of them, as Lincoln Park is about 60 percent black, and not middle-class *Cosby Show* black, either, but homegrown, don't-need-to-listen-to-noner-yo-crap black.

So I just shrugged, as I'd actually heard the story before, grown up with it, familiarity wearing away the Stephen King aspects of living on top of a graveyard, though Kenneth, it fascinated him. *Obsessed* him. Until then, we had just been playground buddies, the lukewarm kind who'd wave to each other in the grocery store, but after that, he pursued me, spending the rest of the school year nagging me to sit with him in the lunchroom, or on the bus, where he'd always work the conversation around to our house.

"You ever noticed any, like, sunken places in the yard?" he pressed. "Or corners of coffins? You know, poking up out of the dirt?"

"I don't thank there are any," I told him flatly. "Mama would have dug 'em up with her roses. Reggie's just talking."

But that didn't satisfy Kenneth, who is the kind of person naturally drawn to the supernatural, always watching *The Outer Limits* and *The Twilight Zone,* reading horror comics. I really don't know why, for there's nothing particularly haunted about *his* family. God knows Miss Susan isn't a vampire, she's too doggone busy. Maybe it's because he's Catholic—or was when he was born, way up north in New York, though he only lived there a few years before his parents divorced and his mother moved him and his brothers Kemp and Keith (who are identical twins) to Ft. Walton, looking for a better life. Unfortunately, all she found there was yet another husband (and a sorry one at that) and another divorce that left her crapped out at thirty with three children and no education and not many prospects. It was a burden a lot of women would have wilted under, but not Miss Susan, who, despite her sorry taste in men, is probably the best mother I know, or at least the most energetic (even more than Aunt Candace). Instead of lying down and admitting defeat, she just packed up her sons and moved inland, where she took on any job that paid, working at convenience stores, gas stations, what-have-you, till she finally found her niche cleaning houses for the rich folk at Indian Springs. By then she'd nosed out the cheapest rent in America in the form of a ratty old single-wide trailer a mile or so east of Sinclair, the tiny black crossroads just down the road that supplies most of the population of Lincoln Park Elementary/Middle.

That's how Kenneth came to be the Yankee minority student amongst us, though Miss Susan is full-blooded Italian (actually, Sicilian), making him curly-haired and kind of dark. When we were little he was sometimes mistaken for an oreo (that is, mulatto), which used to annoy him, though since we've started high school in town, I've noticed he's better about it, even subtly fosters this image of a cool, light-skinned black dude, wearing starter jackets and gold chains and stuff.

But anyway, that was him in second grade: small and dark and quiet around adults, though he's a great schemer and chatterer on the sly, and soon had me begging Mama to let him spend Memorial Day with us. This didn't take much persuading because I've never had the truckload of friends Sim and Missy have and Mama was always afraid I'd grow up a loner like her, was just pleased as punch I had me a friend. When we got home that day, she had the house all clean and sparkling, had even made M&M cookies, as if she was afraid Kenneth would get mad if there wasn't anything fit to eat and storm home, leaving me friendless.

To tell you the truth, I think she might have overdone it a little, for even aside from its haunted reputation, our house can be kind of overwhelming on first impression, with the marble pool and the draped palms and the high-ceilinged rooms, all full of shining floors and antiques and (in Kenneth's honor) even fresh flowers on the mantel. Poor Kenneth seemed kind of shell-shocked by it all, just sat there at the kitchen table, gnawing cookies and glancing around with these scared, furtive little looks, hardly able to answer Mama's solicitous questions about where he was from and what his daddy did for a living.

It was just her good Louisiana manners asserting themselves, but Kenneth is kind of sensitive about where he's from, because he catches a lot of grief at school about being a Yankee, and his father has always been a sore spot that he doesn't like to talk about much. And to be honest, Mama can be intimidating in her own right when she's trying to make a good impression, for she is doggone close to six foot tall, and red-haired and attractive in an old-timey way, kind of a hick Maureen O'Hara. She's also part Cajun (though she doesn't like to talk about it) and just this *inspired* cook, her M&M cookies not the recipe on the bag, but this pleasing combination of butter and brown sugar, chocolate and pecans, all colorful and crunchy, better than anything you can find at the bakery or the mall.

Between her and the house and the cookies, poor Kenneth didn't have much to say, though once I got him shook loose of Mama's good manners, he regained a little spunk and color as we spent the afternoon poking fishing poles in the dirt, searching for coffins. We didn't have any luck but still had fun, and after another day spent nosing around the house, under the staircase and down in the cellar, he announced positively that for once in his young life, Reggie Hines was right: I most certainly did live in a haunted house.

"We ain't *found* nothing," I argued, though he was insistent.

"Gosh, Clay, who cares what we *found*? Ghosts aren't like *dogs*. They just don't come out when you *whistle*. But they're here, all right. I can *feel* 'em."

Now, I believe I've mentioned that Kenneth can be a great persuader when he wants to be, and in the light of his absolute certainty I began to study our house with a different eye and had to admit that from certain angles and in certain lights, it certainly *looked* haunted. Partially because of its age and partially because of my mother's love of trees and the fact she never cuts any of them down, even if they are half-dead and hollow to the core. She just lets them stand, especially the live oaks, and won't even clear out the scrub beneath them, so that our narrow gravel driveway curves through thirty acres of moss-draped wilderness till our old house suddenly appears, standing silent in the half-light of the canopy. It really does look gloomy on cold days, big and old-timey and spooky, with gables and a deep porch and three different chimneys, all with different angles and caps.

So I had to admit that maybe Kenneth was on to something, and when school ended in June, ghost-busting quickly became our hobby. In the morning, Miss Susan sent him to day care in town, but as soon as he got home every afternoon, he'd pedal his bike over and we'd resume our investigation, poking the soft ground under the live oaks for graves or thumping the parlor walls, searching for secret passages. He'd sometimes bring along horror comics to fuel the fire, once brought along a Ouija board so we could have a séance and clear the air once and for all, but when we went to Mama to borrow candles, she strictly forbid it.

"Leave them to their sorrows," she said of our household ghosts with this half-joking, half-serious resignation that just infuriated me.

"One of these days you'll come upon one, at night, when Daddy's at work," I predicted, hoping to scare her. "*Then* what'll you do?"

But Mama, particularly resistant to this kind of challenge, just crossed her arms and smiled. "Well, baby, I'll probably sit him down, fix him a cup of hot tea, ask why they planted the century oak so close to the house. Your daddy says it's upending the foundation."

Coming from anyone but Mama, this would have sounded like rank sarcasm, but the heck of it was: she really meant it. I mean, she wouldn't let us use the Ouija board because she *didn't* believe our house was haunted, but because she *did*, and didn't think we had any business disturbing our ghosts' rest.

It was just the kind of nonsense you'd expect from someone with a drop of French Louisiana blood, and try as I might, I couldn't convince her otherwise. I pouted, I begged, I even went to Daddy to plead our case, though he took Mama's side, which was odd, for Daddy was usually the voice of reason in the Catts household. He was the one you went to when you wanted to watch a suspect movie or spend the night with someone who didn't go to the church or go fishing with Uncle Case (who would sometimes get drunk and do goofy things, like run the boat aground, which was the reason Mama didn't like us going with him). As a rule, Daddy never forbid *anything*, or hardly anything, and would even talk Mama around. ("Oh, Myra, let 'em go. Quit your worrying. My gosh, they're only young once.")

But on the matter of the summoning up the spirits of our unquiet dead, he was as adamant as Mama, a great disappointment, for by then, I was as convinced as Kenneth that we did indeed live in a haunted house. Maybe even *more* convinced, for I actually lived there seven days a week, and slept there, too, and over the course of the summer had begun to detect whispers of the supernatural all around me: doors that would shut by themselves, windows left mysteriously opened. The stairs especially creaked a lot at night, though when I asked Daddy about it, he said it was nothing more sinister than a cracked foundation.

"The real mystery is that it ain't ever fallen down around our ears," he said with a grunt, as our stylish old house was really nothing but a thorn in his overworked flesh, always requiring time and money and Uncle Case's expertise to shore up the sagging floors and dry rot and shifting beams. He claimed to have spent ten times more money in renovation than he'd paid for it, though he never complained too much because the house was Mama's, the forty acres around it, her kingdom.

I mean, I'm sure they owned the deed jointly, but Mama was the one who found it, who'd stripped the floors and opened the fireplaces and dug out the apron of lawn and coaxed the St. Augustine grass and camellia and fern. She was the one who'd reclaimed the marble pool and surrounded it in this lush, Louisiana splendor, with phoenix palms and mondo grass and a marble urn that dribbled water like a fountain.

When I was very small, I hardly remember her ever leaving the house except to attend church or go to the grocery store or cart Sim and

Missy around to their endless rounds of ball games. Aside from those out-
ings, she stayed strictly inside, obsessively cleaning and polishing and
restoring till the sun began to dip behind the tree line, when she would
finally emerge on the front porch, trowel in hand, and spend the next few
hours tending her roses in the gray half-light of the long summer night.

I really never gave it much thought, at least not until that fool Kenneth came into the picture, when, after a month's worth of fruitless digging for any sign of a coffin, he began to look further afield for the source
of our old house's haunting, would occasionally pose these delicately
worded questions to me.

"Why doesn't your mother do her gardening in the morning?" he
asked late one Friday evening from the perch of the attic window, where
we were secretly reading a horror comic, keeping a weather eye on her
as she deadheaded roses in the garden below. "Does she work nights?"

I told him no, she didn't work at all, and he was thoughtful. "She
doesn't go out much during the day, does she?"

Well, no, she wasn't social in any sense of the word back then, but
shy and retiring, which didn't strike me as so terribly odd, though apparently it did Kenneth, who, as the summer progressed, began to watch
Mama even more closely, put even more subtle questions to me: Why
didn't she eat? Why didn't she sleep? Why didn't she go to the beach or
the movies or join the PTA like everyone else's mom?

I just shrugged in reply, for my mother was kind of like my house:
so familiar that I never thought to question the fact that though she spent
an hour each and every afternoon conjuring up these breathtaking suppers, once all that fried chicken and macaroni and cheese was buttered
and peppered and set on the table, she'd usually just sip tea while the rest
of us dove in. It was just Mama: she didn't eat.

She also didn't sleep, or at least not the way everyone else did, taking catnaps during the day, but staying wide-awake at night, the lamp in
her bedroom lit where she was sitting up in bed reading book after book
while Daddy snored peacefully at her side. When I was little, if I was ever

wakened by a nightmare or got up to pee, there she'd be, or sometimes I'd find her downstairs, standing at the French doors sipping hot tea, or even folding laundry or cleaning windows. She wouldn't look particularly startled or guilty; would just ask why I was up; ask if I was all right.

I never thought to ask if *she* was all right; never thought much about her bizarre sleeping patterns one way or another till Kenneth brought the matter to a head sometime in July, when one of the networks was doing a rerun of *Salem's Lot* and he simply *insisted* that Sim and me spend the night with him and his brothers and watch it.

"It's the best vampire movie *ever*," he assured me with one of his nutty, knowing looks. "I think you'll find it *very* interesting."

He kept at us till Mama finally allowed us to go over and spend the night, even though Miss Susan was working that night, and we'd all be on our own. I must say we had a big time running around the woods playing War till nine o'clock, when we all snuggled down on their old foldout couch, Pepsi and popcorn in hand, ready to be scared, and in that, at least, we were not disappointed. For another of Mama's peculiarities is that she's never allowed us to watch anything weird or violent or otherwise distressing on any screen, big or small, leaving me and Sim ill-prepared for our first night alone in the woods with nothing but the doofus Brown brothers and Stephen King for company.

Twenty minutes into the thing, I kept having to get up to pee, I was so scared, and when it came to the part where those vampire boys stick their faces to the window, I screamed like a woman, I really did. I mean, I would have run through the woods in my underwear all the way home, screaming as I ran, if Sim hadn't shamed me into staying, telling me what a *chicken* I was; how Mama wouldn't let us do sleepovers anymore if I told. Kemp and Keith sided with him, and after they barricaded the door and brought me a crucifix to clutch in my sweating little hand, I made it to the teeth-chattering end, though I couldn't sleep for the rest of the night, I was so scared.

Fortunately, Kenneth couldn't either, and as we lay there on their little sofa bed, sprinkled with garlic salt and clutching our crucifix, we fell to discussing vampires, the reality and the myth, Kenneth bringing the conversation back to my mother, who was beginning to obsess him as much as our house.

"Have you ever noticed that she turns off the light when she does her hair?" he asked, for he'd come over so much that summer that he'd gotten to know our household routines.

I had to admit that yes, she did. I mean, the upstairs bathroom had a big window, not a frosted one, and if you came in and turned on the overhead light while Mama was standing at the sink, brushing her teeth, or her hair, she'd switch it right back off. ("I can see," she'd say.)

It was just another of her Mama-things that I didn't take much notice of, though Kenneth must have found it mighty peculiar, for he offered in this light, suggestive voice: "It's almost as if she doesn't want you to *see* her *reflection*."

Now, I've never been what you might call fast on the uptake, and didn't get his drift, just offered: "She doesn't like to get her picture taken either."

Kenneth made a noise of interest at that, and it was right about then that I finally realized what he was hinting at, and sat up on my elbow. "You thank Mama's a vampire?" I asked in this tone of gigantic disbelief.

"No, *no,*" he said, quick to make sure I hadn't taken offense, though when he saw I hadn't, he was equally quick to make his point: "It's just— well, think about it, Clay: she doesn't come out till dark, doesn't eat, doesn't sleep. Never goes to town. Doesn't want anyone to *take* her picture, or *see* her *reflection*."

In reply, I just made one of Daddy's skeptical little grunts, then lay back down, not particularly insulted or appalled, as I knew in my heart that *whatever* my mother was, it wasn't a vampire. For one thing, she was too afraid of blood. I mean, it flipped her out if one of us so much as smashed a finger or got a bloody nose. When Sim cracked his head on the diving board that time, Grannie had to come out and drive him to the hospital because Mama was too stinking hysterical, curled up on the couch with her hands pressed to her ears, as if someone was dropping bombs on the backyard.

So I had a pretty good idea that Kenneth was off base, though it took me a while to come up with a few more concrete bits of evidence in her defense, the most glaring being that to my knowledge, she didn't sleep in a coffin, had never drunk anyone's blood, and most importantly: she wasn't afraid of crosses. I even took him to church that Sunday to demonstrate Mama's ability to park in the parking lot of Welcome Baptist and walk right in under the shadow of a big old ten-foot cross without a flinch or a glare.

"She's a *Christian*," I argued. "She teaches *Sunday school,* for crying out loud."

Kenneth just shook his head thoughtfully, for he's not a hardheaded know-it-all like Missy, but more of a puzzler and a muser on the great parade of life. He never went so far as to *insist* that Mama was one of the Unquiet Dead, but he didn't back down either, and over the course of the summer would occasionally hit upon some other piece of evidence, like how thin Mama got that summer; how she'd sit wrapped in an electric blanket sometimes, her teeth chattering like she was freezing to death, even on the hottest day of the year.

Even her insistence that we not use the Ouija board began to seem kind of suspect. What was she so scared of? Afraid we'd push around the little pointer and *her* name would come up?

I mean, we never got scared of her or anything; never went after her with a silver bullet or a stake through the heart, though we did talk about it, muse on it as the summer ended and a new school year was upon us, when in small, peculiar ways, Mama became even stranger, pacing the house every night like a tiger while she waited for Daddy to come home from work, back and forth, back and forth. When she'd hear his car in the drive she'd run out to the garage and stay close to him all night, pieces of their hushed conversation drifting up the stairwell. "It's just rebound—

no, I slept, from two to five. Just jumpy. Jittery. I yelled at Sim——could you talk to him? I couldn't go to his game today, I hurt his feelings, I know."

There would be a fast rush of tears then, strange in Mama as she had never been much of weeper before, not excitable in any sense, but calm and levelheaded, her passion seen, if anywhere, in her lush gardens and ornate designs. It was only that autumn that she began to be overtaken by these jagged emotional outbursts, Daddy having to call one or another of us aside every few days to apologize for something she'd done, some snap of temper, some flash of anger that she bitterly regretted and asked him to explain.

"Why is she so, like, *sensitive* all of a sudden?" I remember Missy asking him one night after she'd made one of her typical Missy remarks, accurate but tactless, to the effect that Mama was getting weirder by the day, causing Mama to burst into tears.

"Oh, baby, she's just having a rough time," Daddy replied with a weary rub of his neck. "Thet fool Candace talked her into going off her medicine. But it'll be all right. It'll pass."

We accepted his explanation easily enough, for Mama took a pill every morning of her life, all of us knew that, even me. I even knew what it was called: *lithium,* a name so common that it was part of our household routine, Mama having to go to Dr. Williams every month for a blood test, then a stop by the pharmacy to pick up the little bottle of white pills that she was just frantically afraid we'd get into, kept locked in a drawer in the kitchen, as if it was a loaded gun.

I couldn't really understand why taking or not taking it would be such a big deal, but it clearly was, her and Daddy discussing it when he came home from work every night, him always asking what the doctor said, Mama nervous but determined, and as the autumn passed into the early days of winter, increasingly triumphant.

"I slept six hours last night," she'd tell him at breakfast in this voice of great *achievement,* as if it were just the coolest thing in the world, sleeping.

Daddy would indeed seem impressed, with Mama suddenly more confident, suddenly the expert. "I'm only taking Pamelor now, and it's down to fifty and I'll just have to stay on that till Christmas, or maybe Easter."

"Don't go so fast," he'd warn her, though by Christmas it was clear that she was much improved, eating more and even sleeping while the sun was down, the door to their bedroom dark if you got up in the middle of the night, the hallway lit by a night-light. And though she was still overprotective to a fault, and still paced the floor when Daddy was late coming home from Waycross, and still (till this day) turns off the light if you come in the bathroom while she's doing her hair, she's never been as isolated as she was that summer, so much the stranger. I doubt anyone would mistake her for a vampire these days, even a doofus kid like Kenneth, who long ago moved on to other obsessions (girls, mostly) and pretty much abandoned his Vampire Theory, except maybe to laugh about it, and how dumb we were when we were little.

So in the end, you might say that I am the last true believer, for I don't think I've ever really looked at my mother in exactly the same light as I did before that summer. I mean, Gabe used to hammer us about the power of image, the power of *myth*. It was one of his *things* that he used to warn us about, and how the South was filled with all these loaded symbols, like the plantation house, the rebel flag, and how powerful they were; how they had formed our identity, shaped our history.

At the time I never really understood what the *heck* he was talking about, but maybe I'm beginning to see his point. Because even now, when all Mama's secrets have been so thoroughly explored with Aunt Candace's cut-and-dried precision, and the mystery of the pills and the paleness and the aversion to mirrors is so easily explained—still, whenever I think of her, and her life and her sadness, I never think in terms of manic depression or Chattahoochie or *One Flew Over the Cuckoo's Nest*. Nothing like that occurs to me at all——nothing but a sad, familiar image that must date back to that summer when I first perceived her difference, of her wandering through her roses at twilight: my tired old vampire mother, converted to Christ and condemned to time, tired and haunted, unable to sleep.

# CHAPTER THREE

That's how I came to understand and accept the fact that I did indeed live in a bona fide moss-draped haunted house, though it wasn't until Daddy died that our household spirits began to rattle their chains, demand their freedom—or maybe it all started a couple of years before that.

I guess you could say the earliest stirrings—unrecognized by few and certainly not me—began the weekend of my ninth birthday, on a fairly ordinary March afternoon that stands in infamy as the first time in my life that I remember my father ever breaking a promise or getting sick, or so much as uttering the name of the man who would so quickly, so completely, change my life: his brother Gabe.

Now, Gabe, Gabe, Gabe, I am of two minds on how to approach him. On one hand, I would just as soon leave him out of my history completely, pretend he didn't exist—but that would never be easy, for he is the kind of personality that it doesn't pay to ignore. I figure I might as well introduce him here, cleanly and aboveboard, otherwise he'll creep in, quote by quote, shadowy and pale, and haunt my story like my poor old mother—not that any of us ever thought *he* was a vampire.

God, I wish we had. Then, maybe I would have kept him at arm's length, with a crucifix and a stake handy in case he got too close. But no,

Gabe is slick. As a matter of fact, that's what Bobo and Darius and all the black kids at Lincoln Park used to call him: *Slick*. They said it with great affection, for they really did come to love their old teacher, recognized him *on sight,* a heck of a lot sooner than I did, I really don't know why. Maybe it was a black thing—a *migration* thing, as Gabe would say (see what I mean about him creeping in?). Maybe they all have uncles just like him, poor boys who'd hopped the bus north first chance they got, looking for a better life: an education; a job that paid. Who'd kept up with their old hometown at first, returning home Christmas or Thanksgiving to show off a new car or a good-looking wife, though over the years they'd gradually lost touch and drifted away, become nothing more than faded ink on old letters; someone for the old folks to brag about, which is all Gabe ever was to me.

He was just Uncle Gabe: the brother who got out, who headed north and never looked back. He went to Harvard. He was real smart. He was a genius. Those were the rumors I heard growing up, a snip of oral history to support the only actual physical evidence I ever saw of Daddy's younger brother: a handful of tiny black-and-white photos in Grannie's big picture box of a grinning little towheaded boy standing next to Daddy and Aunt Candace in different Easter ensembles, and a head-and-shoulders graduation photograph of the same little boy, now grown into a somber-faced man, that had sat on top of Grannie's television for time out of mind. Daddy's graduation photograph occupied the opposite side of the double frame, their faces only alike in their very lack of expression, their hair cut back in severe flattops like they wore back then, though the front of Uncle Gabe's hair didn't poke up as stiffly as Daddy's, but curled forward a little, giving him a softer, more melancholy look.

But that was all I really knew about him; nothing very exciting when you compared him with Mama's brother, Uncle Ira, who I bragged about all the time, as Lincoln Park is the kind of school that has a prematurely jaded student population that is doggoned hard to impress, let me tell you. I mean, nobody ever gave a flip that my father owned two factories or was a millionaire, or that Mama was a master gardener who could make roses thrive, even in the shade and humidity of a West Florida oak hammock. Nobody gave a diddle about any of that; the only flicker of respect I ever got from anyone was due to my close blood ties to a man doing time in *The Joint,* though to be perfectly honest, the *close* part was a little stretch of the truth.

For technically speaking, I've hardly ever seen Uncle Ira except when I was little, when he used to come and visit sometimes. Even then, he wasn't a real people person, nothing like my favorite uncle or anything (that would be Grannie's brother, my great-uncle Case), but kind of distant and big, really big, which is what I remember most about him. He also smoked (Camels, I think), and filled the house with the smell of tobacco, which I found very pleasant, though it used to aggravate Daddy, who really did have this, like, *pathological* horror of being connected to trash in any form. And though Uncle Ira was borderline respectable back then, he still had the makings of a pretty trashy life, with a different woman every time he came (and a wife, too, somewhere out there, who Mama would always ask about). He also had a lot of tattoos, of dragons and eagles and things, some of which dated back to when he was stationed in Saigon, that I thought pretty cool, a sentiment Daddy didn't share in the least. He only put up with him out of respect for Mama, at least till he (Uncle Ira, that is) was arrested in Orange Park for a crime (a murder, I knew that much) so bad that Mama wouldn't talk about, though Sim knew all about it, but wouldn't discuss it either. ("Spare yourself the details" is what he used to tell Missy and me.)

But anyway, that was Uncle Ira, who was a drill instructor in the Marines and now in prison, two qualities I (secretly) found kind of attractive and certainly brag-worthy, much more than the Mystery Genius, who never favored us with so much as a phone call, much less a Christmas card or a visit. In my mind's eye I pictured him as balding and nearsighted, kind of like the old guy on *My Favorite Martian,* though if I'd have thought about it, I'd have realized that he was too young for that, younger than Daddy, even.

Like I say, I never really gave it much thought, at least not till that landmark weekend I turned nine, a day that started innocently enough, out by the pool, where everything in this family begins. The reason I was out there that day was because I had been begging Mama to let me and Kenneth swim early, when the water was still cold, and somehow in the wheeling and dealing had agreed to clean the pool, which was my first mistake of the day.

For I believe I've mentioned that my mother has a great affection for trees; the only problem is that she has an equal aversion to aluminum and refuses to even consider defiling her marble pool with anything as tacky as a screened enclosure. This means that practically speaking, someone ends up with the thankless job of skimming leaves about five times a week, especially in March when the live oaks are shedding at a rate of about a pound a minute. It really is enough to try a saint's patience, and I had finally burst into tears that afternoon as I had worked and worked to remove the floaters, when a burst of March wind sent down a shower of leaves, ruining an hour's hard work.

Missy, who was busy packing for a weeklong French Club field trip to Paris and in a rare obliging mood, came out to see what the fuss was all about and with her usual take-charge sureness, informed me that I was going about it the wrong way.

"Do the bottom first," she told me, "then the floaters."

I didn't argue as she took the skimmer in hand and proceeded to demonstrate, giving me a little breathing space to sit there with my feet in the shallow end and curse Mama and her trees, too, when there was the sound of a car in the drive, pulling in so fast it skidded a little in the gravel.

Something in the force of it was portentous, making Missy pause in her skimming long enough to lift her face, though before she could speak, our cousin Lori came tearing around the corner of the garage in bare feet and a pair of old cheerleading sweats, her blond hair limp, her face white-lipped and haggard.

"Aint Myra?" she asked Missy in a trembling little voice. "Is she home?"

Now, Lori is Aunt Candace's one and only princess of a daughter, a Farrah Fawcett look-alike (though not as tall and skinny) who won't leave the house until she's spent some quality time with her hot-rollers and makeup mirror. Seeing her in public with flat hair and white lips was really kind of a shock, and I stood there and frankly stared as Missy tipped her head toward the house to indicate that Mama was inside.

Lori didn't even nod, just went straight in, calling for Mama, who met her just inside the French door, Lori handing her a slip of paper that she glanced at curiously, then looked up with a face of stone-cold surprise.

"What is it?" Missy hissed, as if I had X-ray vision or something.

I just shrugged, though it was clear something very heavy was coming down, Mama leading Lori to the kitchen with a protective arm around her shoulder, both of them looking at whatever Lori had handed her, a bad piece of news by the look of it.

Missy and me just stood there gawking, polite enough to give them a thirty-second buffer before we tired of the suspense. "Be back in a sec," she said, handing me the skimmer and gingerly opening the French door to go inside. She was only gone for a matter of seconds before she came back outside with a face of disgust.

"What is it?" I whispered, though Missy just took the skimmer and started on the leaves again.

"Nothing. I don't know. Mama said for us to stay outside. Said we're going over to *Grannie's*." She rolled her eyes when she said it because we were always being shuffled off to Grannie's when something interesting was afoot. "But something *mighty* fishy's going on. Mama called Daddy at *work*."

This was surely a premonition of evil if there ever was one, for

Daddy was an unashamed workaholic who only left work early for reasons of national emergency. After that, Missy and I were a little rebuffed, watched in silence as Aunt Candace came screeching up in her little Subaru, then Daddy, who drove us to Grannie's little house on the far side of town, in a West End neighborhood the old-timers call Magnolia Hill. Originally built around the same factory Daddy started working in when he was fifteen (and by dint of hard work and good luck, eventually bought from the original owners, lock, stock, and barrel), Magnolia Hill is just a tiny remnant of what was once the thriving working-class section of town.

Now reduced to only three or four streets wide, it's mostly made up of ancient little row houses intermixed with cheap prefabs and one or two mobile homes, the trailers flat-roofed double-wides with garden tubs and central air (that attract a lot of envy), the older houses with not much to offer in the way of modern comfort, though they have a lot of native charm, each with its own little yard and porch and potted begonia. But the Hill's best feature, far and away, is that it's within easy walking distance of all the landmarks of modern civilization: the Piggly Wiggly and the church and a McDonald's, and comparatively close to the high school, so that it acts as our official home-away-from-home when we're in town. I spend most of my Sunday afternoons there (watching wrestling with Grannie), while Missy and Sim practically live there during softball and basketball seasons, sometimes only coming home three or four nights a week.

As a matter of fact, Sim was already there that day when Daddy dropped us off, just home from some practice or another—probably basketball, that time of year. For like Missy, Sim's an all-around athlete, though unlike Missy, he's not a born prodigy, just a solid, plodding player, the kind of four-year letterman who plays three different sports a year, but is never offered anything at graduation but small, low-dollar scholarships to no-name community colleges. He never complains, for in that and in most ways, he is truly the Perfect Southern Son, heir to the best of the Catts-Sims clans, as polite as Mama, as ambitious as Daddy, the kind of multicultural phenomenon who would be equally comfortable at Augusta National or the Winston Cup in Atlanta.

When we got to Grannie's that day, he came out as soon as he heard the car door and met us on the porch. "What's up?" he asked Missy, who didn't answer right away, just gave him a little glance over my head.

"Don't know," she said. "Nobody's talking. But something is *up*. Something has *hit* the *fan*."

That's all she would offer with me standing there, for she and Sim have always had this annoying habit of keeping secrets to themselves and not letting me in on them. That meant that around the Catts house, the Official Family Grapevine went from Mama to Daddy, to Sim to Missy, and there it ended, with me completely out of the loop. I never really knew why at the time, maybe because I was the baby of the family, or because I'd been known to blow their cover occasionally, or pass on information they'd just as soon I'd kept to myself.

I was sure they knew something I didn't, though when I went to Grannie for details, she didn't pay me any mind, just concentrated on cooking supper (which is what Grannie does when she's nervous: Mama gardens, Grannie cooks), filling her tiny little kitchen with the delectable smell of fried pork.

"It'll be all right," she kept murmuring in this distracted little voice as she shifted pots around on her old gas stove, "it'll work out."

I could get nothing more out of her, finally wandered back to the living room and spent the afternoon building a Lego city on the coffee table till just before dark, when there was a commotion in the drive, then the sound of many feet coming up the porch steps. Soon a whole chattering crowd spilled into the living room, Mama and Daddy and Uncle Ed and Aunt Candace, and finally Curtis and Lori, who were all smiles now, holding hands and announcing they had some big news: they were getting married.

"I knew thet already," I said, for they'd been engaged since Christmas, though Mama clarified things.

"They're getting married next weekend, baby," she told me. "In the front yard, in the rose garden."

There was an immediate flurry of excitement and hugging, Grannie moved to tears at the wondrous news, till something suddenly occurred to me. "*Wait* a minute," I cried. "You cain't get married next week! We're going fishing, me and Daddy. It's all planned."

Because it was. That was my birthday present, a bass expedition to Lake Eufaula, just me and Daddy. We were going all out, borrowing Mr. Sam's bass boat and spending two nights at the Holiday Inn on the river. We'd had reservations since Christmas, and wedding or not, I wasn't letting go so easily, making my way to Lori and telling her flat out: "You'll just have to wait till June. Thet's what the invitations say, anyway. Why d'you wanta mess it up? Nobody gets married in *March*."

"Oh, hush," was Lori's truly blond reply, all my protests drowned out as Grannie's living room is kind of small and gets filled pretty quickly.

Within minutes, it was packed with Curtis's sisters and parents, a regular hillbilly love fest, with me running around like a little white rabbit, tugging at people's sleeves, saying: "But they *cain't*. It's my *birthday*. Me and Daddy are going *fishing*. It's all *planned*."

"Oh, Clay, give it up," Missy told me, as it was easy for her, she was going to *Paris France* on Monday, she could afford to be generous. I was the one getting the short end of the stick, and finally collapsed at the dining-room table in a torrent of tears, right there at the end where Grannie was sure to see me.

Sure enough, she took one look at me and waded back into the living room, returned with Daddy in tow, though everyone was making such a racket that he could hardly be heard.

"Settle down, Claybird!" he raised his voice to shout. "What's all this fuss about?"

"They *cain't* get married next weekend!" I told him. "We're going fishing! You PROMISED!"

I had to positively *holler* this last, as it was the clincher and I wanted to make sure he heard me. Apparently he did, for he rubbed his face a moment, then made a grunt of impatience at the noise, gestured for me to follow him to Grannie's spare bedroom, where he closed the door behind us, slightly muffling the roar.

"Good *God,* what a bigmouthed bunch they are," he said of his future nephew-in-law's relations, for to be honest, I don't think Daddy was ever real impressed with Curtis's larger family, though he thought Curtis was nice enough. I mean, they weren't like Uncle Ira, absolute abominations, but they weren't much to write home about either, just *pure-dee* country, as they used to say; 100 percent pure *Saltine.*

But that was all he said of them as he sat me down on the edge of the bed and tried to reason with me in this kind, patient voice: "Son, I know what I promised, but——"

That was about as far as he got before I gave into complete despair, bursting into a fresh wave of tears, as it was clear that by some jinx of fate, Lori's idiotic whim was taking precedence over MY BIRTHDAY! Me, Clayton Michael Catts! Who never even got to go to Atlanta, much less Paris, France! Who was the baby of the family and by God, dyslexic! Who couldn't even read, though I tried and tried!

The horror of the thing was just about more than I could bear, and for some time, Daddy sat there and tried to reason with me, promised me all kinds of things: that he'd take me to Waycross with him the next Friday, or buy me a new bike; that we'd plan another fishing trip, this one bigger and better than before.

"To Eufaula?" I managed in a sniffly little voice.

For a moment, he just sat there, then said: "Well, baby, I was thinking that maybe we'd do something a little closer to home. You know, wait till the river's down in July, then call and see if Gabe could take off a few days, and we could all go out to Uncle Case's like we used to when we were boys, set some trout lines, gig the stumps."

Now, of all the strange, misplaced, straight-out-of-left-field notions my father ever entertained, this had to be the strangest. I just looked at him in the purest amazement, breathed, "*What?*"

He repeated himself levelly and you could tell he'd given it some thought, though I just sat there, thinking: Who cares? I mean, what was that by way of barter? Give up my golden trip to Eufaula with the custom-built bass boat and the Holiday Inn in favor of a weekend at Uncle Case's dinky little trailer with seven hundred flea-bitten hounds and *My Favorite Martian* for company?

I'd just as soon have a tooth pulled and my face must have shown it, for Daddy backed off after a moment, and went on to other options, other promises, though I just wouldn't be consoled, kept bringing him back to my original argument: "But they weren't supposed to get married till June! The invi*t*ations!"

Daddy finally gave up then and stood, and for one desperate moment I thought I'd talked him around to my side and he was going to the living room to inform the larger household. But he just stood there a moment, arms crossed resolutely on his chest, then sighed and told me the real reason that Lori and Curtis had changed their wedding date: Lori was pregnant.

"But she *cain't* be," I argued. "She ain't married."

Daddy just scratched his ear on that, commented in a wry little voice: "Well, son, you don't have to be married to get pregnant, you know."

By the blank look on my face, he must have realized that I by gosh *didn't* know, for he sighed another big sigh, then sat back down on the edge of the bed and began talking to me in this patient, fatherly voice about how we were all *human* and made *mistakes* and how that sometimes, your emotions could get away with you, and all kinds of nutty, irrelevant stuff.

I just sat there and stared at him, was wondering what the *heck* he was talking about, when he suddenly dispensed with the morality of the situation and dived in the deep end, explained how you could indeed get pregnant, married or not, as long as you performed a few necessary functions. Then, without even pausing for a breath, he went into a little blunt, country detail about those functions, about which I'd heard a lot of snickering and rumors before, but never stated so baldly right there on my sainted Grannie's chenille bedspread in a house full of chattering relations.

I don't believe I've ever been so truly disgusted in my life, and my face must have shown it, for Daddy stood again abruptly and began pacing around the little room like he did when he was nervous. He finally paused and asked if I had any questions, which I certainly did not, though I did lower my pillow to ask in a trembling voice: "Daddy, *you* ain't ever done anything like that, have you?"

This brought him to a complete halt there at the foot of the bed, his arms crossed on his chest, his face amazed and a little exasperated, though he tried to be kind.

"Well, Claybird?" he asked. "*Son?* Where d'you think I got you childrun?"

And I tell you what: the horror of that remark just about made me swoon, it really did, till an even more hideous thought occurred to me, making me lift three trembling fingers, whisper: "You did it *three times?*"

For a moment, Daddy just stood there staring at me, arms crossed on his chest, his face much like Mama's had been when Lori handed her that mysterious slip of paper, kind of stunned and blank, then he just dropped forward to the bed, as if he'd been shot. I didn't know if he'd fainted or what, and really didn't care, just buried my face in my pillow, while he lay there beside me, laughing so hard he couldn't speak.

"Claybird, Claybird, *Claybird,*" he finally wheezed. "What are we gonna do with you, son?"

But I was too numb to join in the hilarity, just lay there thinking: *My gosh,* Curtis and Lori did *that?* No wonder they were always traipsing off to the drive-in—at least that was *dark.* How could they come waltzing into Grannie's living room in front of God and everybody when everyone *knew* what they'd been up to? Had they no taste? Had they no *shame?*

I don't know how long we lay there, till Uncle Case gingerly opened the door and checked us out, clearly curious about Daddy's laughter, though he only asked, "Claybird? You wanta run uptown with me? Yo Grannie's out of rock salt, wanting to make some ice cream. You kin ride in the back."

Now, I've never turned down an opportunity to ride in the back of a pickup if I can help it, and left easily enough, needing a little fresh air to clear my head of the fumes of Daddy's hideous revelation. We didn't go far, just up to the Jiffy, though by the time I got back to Grannie's, I had a feeling Daddy hadn't been too discreet about the details of our little talk, for I could detect a snickering at my back wherever I went, especially among the men on the porch.

Even Grannie looked suspiciously amused whenever our paths crossed, though she was at some pains to hide it, and even let me lick the bowls when she was done mixing her famous peach custard. By the time it was all packed in rock salt and rattling around the churn, the evening that had begun so ominously ended up nothing more than a routine family gathering, the men all congregated on the back porch, the women in the living room, where my shameless cousin was perched in the middle of the room on Grannie's old ottoman, going on and on about her wedding, and moreover, her magnificent honeymoon.

"Curtis wants to go to Gatlinburg, but I want a go to New Orleans. Remember, Aint Myra, when we stopped there on the way to your cousin's? It was so romantic, with all the verandas."

"I remember more drag queens than verandas," Mama countered, as she was trying, without much success, to steer Lori into spending her wedding money in a more practical vein.

But Lori was having none of it, just went on and on about the French Quarter and how *romantic* it was till I'd finally had about enough of her and her shameless ways and told her plainly, "Well, why don't yawl just save your money and run down to the drive-in. Sounds like you been having pretty good luck down there already."

For a blink of a moment, I thought I had actually achieved the miraculous and caused Lori a flicker of remorse, her face losing its excitement as Curtis's sisters allowed themselves a snicker or two that I appreciated as the room had suddenly become so quiet. I didn't know why and was just sitting there, still a little steamed, till I realized that Mama was slowly coming to her feet, her eyes on me, and I'll tell you what: I've only gotten about three whippings in my life and saw every one of them coming.

I mean, Mama is not the kind of mother who does much threatening or much whipping, either, for that matter, though she does draw a clear line on one point: intentional cruelty, which she had somehow misinterpreted my innocent little jibe to be.

"But *Mama! Mama!*" I cried immediately. "I didn't mean it! *I will be good!*"

This last was an actual wail as she yanked me up and dragged me to the porch, ripped a switch off the closest crepe myrtle, and let me have it, leaves and all. I was hopping around, yelping like a dog, my situation not made any easier by the fact that Sim and Missy had climbed on the cedar chest in the bedroom for ringside seats, with Mama giving them their money's worth, all right, chewing me out the whole time she switched in this furious little voice: "—doan you *ever* let me heah you *talk* thet way agin—" Which is the way Mama sounds when she's good and mad, lapsing into this awful swamp-running, hillbilly brogue that was kind of hard to understand, not that I was listening.

I was too busy trying to get clear of her, though it didn't last long, it never did. When it was over, she just stood there and continued her lecture with a furious shake of the switch: "—doan you think thet chile'll have a hard enough time without your little *smart-ass* remarks?"

I didn't venture a reply, just collapsed on the porch steps, my head in my hands, about crapped out by then: no trip to Eufaula, no Holiday Inn. No illusions left about the nature of true love. Nothing. All gone in one sorry afternoon, and whipped on top of that, and Mama cussing, which always made me feel kind of weenie, anyway.

I just sat there, my head in my hands, and would have cried except that I had cried myself out when I was trying to talk Daddy out of postponing our fishing trip. There was nothing left now but black despair, Mama's breath still kind of fast and labored, though after a moment, she asked in a small voice, "You all right?"

Well, no, I *by gosh* wasn't. I was forever changed and just sat there on the step till Daddy came around and tried to rouse me, with little result. Even after all the relations cleared out and I apologized (under the threat of another whipping) to Lori, and Grannie gave me a bowl of peach ice cream to take home, even then I couldn't shake the horror of the day, going straight to bed when I got home and staring at the underside of my top bunk, drowning in a sea of despair. I was thinking what a relatively simple life Kenneth had, with two brothers and a mother who worked all the time. I was wishing I was him when the door opened and Mama came in and stood by my bed, still in her town clothes, though she was barefoot.

"Claybird?" she asked quietly. "Are you all right? I didn't hurt you, did I?"

There was an old Mama-concern in her voice that I steeled myself against, for I was the one who'd been humiliated; dragged out of a roomful of women and publicly whipped. My reply was a cold silence, though Mama wasn't so easily rebuffed, just felt around in the darkness till she found my hand.

"Baby, you just cain't treat people that way," she told me in a quiet little voice. "You have to be careful about your words. Words can hurt. I know you're disappointed about your trip, but you hurt Lori tonight and she's needing our support, not our—smart remarks."

I didn't argue, but just lay there, trying to be the Big Man, though a few traitor tears began to seep out and roll down the sides of my face.

"But he *promised*," I finally managed, as that was the heart of the mat-

ter: that who cared what kind of mess Lori and Curtis had gotten themselves into? Daddy *promised*.

"Well, I know he did," Mama agreed, for she hated Daddy's busy
schedule, was always harassing him about it. "And I know it ain't fair," she
allowed, which was a comfort, that someone was finally on my side.

"I'll tell you what," she began, and I braced myself for another wonderful option, like going to Uncle Case's with a stranger, but Mama can
be the soul of comfort when she wants to be and really hit upon a worthy substitution: "When the wedding's over, we'll all go to the beach afterward. We can rent a condo, take everyone, Uncle Ed and Aunt
Candace. The Miracle Strip'll be open, we can buy a family pass. It'll do
Candace good to get away a few nights. This hasn't been easy for her, either, you know."

Now, I cared not at all for Aunt Candace and her worries, but was
immediately intrigued by the part about the Miracle Strip—a little
amusement park on Front Street that was just the funnest place in the
world before it got too hot in June. Spring was the perfect time to go,
and after a moment, I asked in a weenie little voice, "Can Kenneth go?"

"Sure," Mama said easily. "I'll call Susan tonight."

"And Daddy'll be there? All weekend?"

"All weekend," she said with another little squeeze to my hand.
"We'll get Lori and Curtis down the aisle and run 'em through the rice,
be there in time for supper. We'll all eat at Captain Anderson's, go out
on the boat."

This was sounding better by the minute; I could feel a corresponding loosening in my chest, and a wash of happy relief, thinking how
flipped out Kenneth would be when he heard about Captain Anderson's,
because he was too stinking poor to eat at McDonald's, much less a big
old ship.

Once Mama saw that she had me hooked, she kissed the back of my
hand. "Go to sleep, Big Man," she said. "We've got a big week ahead of
us. Lori's shower, then Missy leaves on her trip. You'll have to help me."

Right on the tail end of my wash of happy relief came a corresponding rise of guilt, and just as she made the door, I sat up and offered in this weenie little voice, "I'm sorry I was mean to Lori. Tell Daddy."

Mama just paused in the doorway, smiled. "I already have. Sleep tight. Don't let the bed bugs bite." Which is what she and Grannie always used to say when we were little: *Don't let the bed bugs bite*.

As predicted, the next week did fly by, first the bridal shower, then we had to take Missy to the airport in Tallahassee, then we had to get the house fixed up for the wedding. For five straight days, me and Mama and Kenneth worked like dogs, stuffing crabs and stringing lights and picking up cakes and tuxes and florist flowers, even having to transplant two little magnolias that were in the way of the outdoor altar, that Mama didn't want to lose.

We were about pooped out by the day of the wedding, though Mama was as good as her word about the weekend in Panama City, except in one small respect: Daddy didn't get down there on Friday night as promised, neither did she. They didn't come till the next day, for Daddy had been struck down after the wedding by a particularly nauseating stomachache that he originally thought was food poisoning. He was afraid Mama had gotten ahold of some bad oysters, but it passed quickly, both of them showing up bright and early the next morning, so that we were able to do all the things she'd promised: the Miracle Strip and the roller coaster and the swings and the log ride. We even rented a pontoon boat on Sunday and went snorkeling off Shell Island, saw some dolphins and jumped right in with them, though Mama wouldn't let us touch them, said they looked too much like sharks. All in all it turned out to be just the funnest weekend of my life, with only one unexpected twist, courtesy of my sister, who had managed to squeeze in a weeklong trip to Paris while the rest of us were working like dogs, returning from France the night before the wedding with tidings of something even more exotic than smoked eel or edible snails: news of Uncle Gabe.

# CHAPTER FOUR

She'd met him at an airport in New York while she was waiting for her plane, a visit of less than an hour, I later learned, though to hear her talk, you'd have thought that she'd never left his side the whole week she was gone. I mean, she would just not shut up about him; all weekend long, it was Gabe-this-and-Gabe-that-and-Gabe-killed-the-yeller-cat (rhyme of my Grannie's). I personally couldn't see what all the fuss was about, though Daddy seemed spellbound by every detail, asked her how he looked, where he lived.

"Well, I don't know about *thet,*" Missy said. "I just called him from the airport when the plane was late, just like you said, and he came right over, still wearing his pajama top, and I said, 'Gosh, Uncle Gabe, I said the plane was late, not on *fire* —'"

"Is he still teaching?" Daddy pressed, though Missy just shrugged.

"Don't know thet, either. Didn't ask. I guess he is. Mostly we just talked about us. I showed him all the pictures in my wallet and give him one—you know, the Olan Mills one where Mama has big hair—and he was nice about it, said we all looked good. I wanted him to come down for the wedding, but he wouldn't, I don't know why. I mean, it's not like we live on another *planet* or something. Why don't you call him, Daddy? I know he'd come if you called."

Now, I wish I could remember Daddy's reply to all her nagging, but I had bigger fish to fry that weekend and didn't much care that Missy had inexplicably fallen in love with her own uncle, though I did tell her to quit going on and on about him, that it was *embarrassing*.

"You're just jealous," she snapped. "You hate it when I know people you don't. You're still mad about that stupid fishing trip."

I told her to *hush,* didn't think much about it, for Missy is the kind of person who always has to be in the superior position, which in fact, she usually is: president of Beta Club, champion debater, star of the girls' softball team. I figured that meeting the Genius Uncle was just another feather in her cap, though even Sim seemed kind of fascinated by his appearance, listening to Missy's unending recital with considerable interest, even offering his own contribution: how Uncle Gabe had stayed with us one summer; had taught him to swan dive.

*"When?"* Missy asked, outraged that Sim had one-upped her. "Where was *I?*"

Sim thought back. "You couldn't have been more than two or three. Remember? He was writing a book, lived upstairs in the old apartment."

"All that junk is *his?*" Missy asked in amazement, meaning the ratty old maps that were pinned around the walls of the apartment, and had been, as long as I could remember.

"Sure," Sim said with great confidence, suddenly the expert. "That's all his stuff. He used to work on it in the morning and swim with us in the afternoon—remember?"

"How old was *I?*" I interrupted to ask, though Sim seemed kind of taken back by the question, just blinked at me a moment, then looked away.

"I don't know," he answered vaguely. "It was a long time ago. Before you were born."

He said no more about it, though sometime that weekend—it must have been the drive home, when it was just me and him and Kenneth—he brought up Gabe once again, asked me if I'd ever thought about meeting him. That wasn't I *curious?*

"No," I told him plainly, "and I don't get why you and Missy are so, like, *obsessed* with him. He don't care about us. He don't even come see Grannie."

Simon just lifted his face at that, offered mysteriously: "Well, maybe he *cain't*. Maybe Grannie won't *let* him."

I simply couldn't believe this; couldn't imagine anyone so low that Grannie wouldn't welcome them home. Why, even Uncle Ira found protection under her maternal wing. He and Mama had lived across the fence from her when they were children, and to this day, no one could mention Uncle Ira being in *The Joint* without Grannie snorting and saying, "Well, there's two sides to every hoecake, even if one of them's burnt," meaning that there was two sides to every story, and maybe Uncle Ira's side hadn't been told.

So I couldn't imagine her cutting off her own son, and the next Sunday after dinner when everyone else had left and she and I were alone, I broached the subject of Uncle Gabe, asked why he never came home. I was standing in the kitchen when I asked it, helping her do the dishes like I always did, her washing and me standing on a footstool rinsing. She didn't answer right away, just stared out the window at her backyard that was in full bloom that time of year, full of giant azaleas and hydrangeas and six or seven camellias. They weren't planted like Mama's in a careful design, but just stuck in the ground any old way, Grannie's eyes on them when she answered: "Oh, baby—Gabe—he's a long way from home. Way up north."

Which sounded like the very definition of sorry to me: a man who raced off north first chance he got, made it big, and forgot where he came from. It made me feel very sorry for my poor old grannie, standing there doing dishes in her rickety old kitchen, though when I asked her if it was true that she wouldn't *let* him come home, her face lost its wistfulness in a instant.

"Who told you *thet*?" she snapped.

When I told her Sim, she made a little noise of annoyance in her throat, the feminine counterpart to one of Daddy's grunts. "Well, Sim is just wrong, is all. My childrun are free to come and go as they please. Gabe," she began, then paused again and sighed, "he knows where I live."

But her eyes were back on her azaleas when she said it, thoughtful and sad, her usual confidence cut by a note of regret so palpable that I backed off quickly and changed the subject, though that wasn't the end of it. For Grannie has never been one to politely overlook an offense and must have straightened Sim out the first chance she got—probably in the parking lot that night after church, because he came straight home in a rush of ill temper and cornered me in the kitchen like a wild dog.

"You are just such a *blabbermouth*," he said to my face in this furious little whisper. "I cain't *believe* you told Grannie about Uncle Gabe. Now she's all mad and it's all your fault—*shhhh!*" he hissed as Mama came to the door. "Don't you say a word or I'm *telling Daddy!*"

"You can tell anybody you want to," I informed him stoutly, for I'm actually less afraid of Sim than Missy, as Sim isn't a fighter. I mean, if you push him too far, he'll get in your face and holler like a crazy man, eyes bulging and spit flying, but unlike Missy, he'll never take a swing.

So I didn't see any reason to mince words and told him plainly: "I don't even know what you're talking about."

"—about what?" Mama asked, as she had heard the commotion and come in on the tail end of it.

Sim straightened up when he saw her, said, "Nothing," very quickly, and would have ended it at that.

But I didn't much like being cornered and spit at, and wasn't letting go so easy. "He came in here *yelling* and *spitting* in my *face* 'cause Grannie's mad at him."

Mama looked surprised, as Grannie has never been known to have a cross word with any of us, but is our protector and shield, the cooker of cakes and the churner of ice cream. She's the kind of grannie who slips you gum in church and affixes your coloring projects to her refrigerator and never a word of criticism does she voice, even when you're caught flat-footed, hand in the cookie jar.

So she was rightly concerned to hear that Sim had offended her, asked, "Well, Sim? What in the world's wrong with you and Cissie?"

Sim looked truly murderous by then, for he's the kind of person who'd rather have his arm amputated than admit he was wrong. "Nothing," he repeated, and would have backed off, if Mama hadn't folded her arms and leaned against the counter like she was preparing for a long siege.

"Simon," she repeated levelly. "I think you heard me."

He rolled his eyes at that, then exhaled this huge breath and told her, very quickly: "It's just something *stupid* Clay told her I said about Uncle Gabe. Grannie just misunderstood and Clay's got to go running his mouth to her about every *stinking* thing like he was three *stinking* years old."

Now, is it my imagination or do I remember Mama looking a little stunned at the mention of Gabe's name? Do I remember a flicker of concern, a fast cut of her eyes to me? It's hard to say, for I really wasn't paying her much attention, was too thrilled that I'd caught the Perfect One in a lie, rebounding in an instant, shouting, "Did *not*! *Liar!*"

Mama silenced me with one look and a finger to the face (which was all she had to do; around our house, Daddy was the one who had to raise his voice) then turned back to Sim, asked in a small curious voice, "Well, Sim? What did you say about Gabriel that made her so upset?"

I think the reason I remember this part so clearly is that even then it struck me funny that she called him that: Ga*briel*. Something in the way she said it—drawn out, three syllables—made me understand just that quickly that Mama knew him. She knew Uncle Gabe. She had a history with him. She called him Ga-*bri-el*.

But I didn't ponder it too much, for Sim was trying his best to wiggle out of this thing, lying like a dog, telling Mama: "I doan remember," and me: "*Shut up,* you little *snot!*"

Because I was back in action, jumping on my toes, shouting, "*Do, too!* He said Grannie wouldn't *let* him come home and she *does! Liar-liar-pants-on-fire!*"

Sim actually went for me then and might have landed a few licks, except that Mama got between us and sent us to our rooms, and as far as I can remember, that was about the end of it. There was no more discussion, no more spitting and shouting, though Simon was so mad he wouldn't *look* at me for a whole week, much less speak, and even got Missy on his side about it.

"You really *are* a blabbermouth," she told me that night with this look of just absolute disgust.

I simply couldn't understand what all the fuss was about, but have never been able to withstand Sim and Missy when they gang up on me. After that, I backed off the subject of the precious Uncle Gabe and never mentioned him again to anyone. He just became a taboo subject, like Uncle Ira's conviction or Uncle Case's drinking or Mama's vampire things, one that you took a wide berth around if you could help it, which wasn't too much of a strain, as I had plenty of other things to occupy me those days.

For that was not only the year that Lori and Curtis married, but shortly thereafter, Ryan was born and I finally demonstrated a skill that made me invaluable in any Southern family: I could calm a baby. The reason it proved so valuable is that though Lori seemed to have learned the mechanics of how to *make* a baby, nobody ever taught her the means of *caring* for one, especially not a preemie like Ryan, who had all these allergies to formula and plastic diapers, even to Lori's milk. He was always screaming from some rash or another, and between Lori and Curtis's first year of college, and various part-time jobs, they had a hard pull, always arguing over money and begging me to baby-sit. I never minded because they did pay (a little) and always let Kenneth come, too, and by summer, we had a standing date every Friday night.

I must say I looked forward to it, for in true redneck fashion, though Lori and Curtis could barely make their trailer or their hospital

payments, they *had* managed to finance a big-screen TV and a huge satel-
lite system that got HBO, MTV, the works. Since Mama hadn't quite gotten around to sniffing out this channel of corruption, Kenneth and me
were able to watch whatever we wanted, a real education, I can grant you
that, and one that went a long ways toward making me lose my disgust
for the baby-making process, though I really preferred the war movies
to the skin ones. I mean, on the weeks Kenneth got to pick, we'd watch
*Halloween,* or *Porky's,* or the like. On my weeks it'd be *Rambo* or *Platoon,*
though our favorite show, hands down, was *Miami Vice.*

We watched it every week, knew all the characters, wished we had
the wherewithal to grow out a five-o'clock shadow like Don Johnson—
and to tell you the truth, that's really what I remember most about that
last summer Daddy was alive. Sometimes I'll hear a song on the radio—
one of Madonna's early hits, or the theme song of *Miami Vice*—and for a
moment, will just sit there, transfixed, and remember it so clearly: living at home with Mama and Daddy, Sim in baseball, Missy still carless,
stuck at home with her entourage of four thousand girlfriends. I can almost hear their laughter around the pool, am magically transported back
to the summer of 1987, to this clear-cut, carefree world where Daddy's
still alive, seldom home, but momentarily expected, so close I can almost
smell his cologne.

I used to live for such moments, used to channel-surf MTV, waiting
for the right video that could take me back, though I never do anymore.
The rebound is just too fast, too bitter. Now days I'd just as soon forget I
ever had a childhood. I mean, it was happy and loving and fun, but it just
passed too fast, too casually, came to too abrupt an end the last week in
September, when Daddy finally gave in to Mama's nagging and made
plans to have surgery and get rid of his gallstones once and for all. For
that's what the doctor had finally pinpointed as the cause of his nightly
bellyaches: routine gallstones, the kind you had to have surgically removed, with a couple of nights' stay in the hospital.

None of us were particularly worried, for compared to the drama of Curtis and Lori's troubles, Daddy's stuff seemed so middle-aged and routine. There was nothing life-and-death about it at all, no family squabbles or tears or threats of divorce, Daddy just making an appointment with a surgeon friend of Aunt Candace's and going to the hospital that morning like he was having a tooth pulled. Mama went with him, and after a lot of begging on our part, decided that we were old enough to stay home by ourselves, though she must have had a change of heart once she got to the hospital, for she sent Carlym (our Youth Pastor at Welcome) to pick us up the next morning and take us to Grannie's. Try as we might, we couldn't talk him out of it, and when we went to see Daddy at the hospital that night, Missy told him all about it.

"Mama treats us like *babies*," she said indignantly, though Daddy just looked at her sadly.

"You *are* babies," he said, though he didn't argue it too much, just called Grannie and told her that we could go home if we wanted, that he'd be discharged Saturday, or maybe Monday morning.

I was vaguely (very vaguely) aware that this wasn't part of the master plan—that he was only supposed to have stayed in the hospital for two, maybe three days, but didn't think much of it, as Miss Susan insisted that I spend the weekend with them, even took us over to Tallahassee to see *Top Gun,* which, at the time, I thought was just the coolest movie in the universe. Me and Kenneth stayed up all night talking about it, plotting to see it again when Sim and Kemp went on Monday—and that's really how I spent the last evening of my childhood, with no inkling it was about to all come to an end.

The only possible hint I remember of anything being out of the ordinary was when Miss Susan was dropping me off at the house the next morning, when we came across a half-dozen cars parked in the drive, more than there should have been on a Saturday. I didn't know what was up, just gathered my backpack and went inside to the living room that was full of people, not just Sim and Missy and Mama, but Aunt Candace

and Uncle Ed, even our preacher Brother Sloan, all of them drinking coffee and chatting, very casual.

Daddy was there, too, just home from the hospital, still wearing the
shiny new pajama-and-robe set Mama had brought him for his operation
that for the first time in his life, made him look like the millionaire he
was. He smiled when he saw me, and waved me over for a kiss, then sent
me to the kitchen in search of something to eat while Mama walked Miss
Susan to her car, which always took a little time because Mama always insisted on reimbursing her for having me over because she really couldn't
afford it, and Miss Susan always puts up a fight.

I'd made my way back to the living room, Pop-Tart in hand, was sitting on the edge of the coffee table telling Daddy and Brother Sloan about
*Top Gun* and how cool it was, when Mama finally made it back inside and
sat down next to Daddy, and he took a breath and told us he had cancer.

"Of where?" I asked, as Kenneth's Uncle Lou had once had cancer,
too, of the lung, though he'd had part of it removed and was doing fine
now, coming down in a few months for Christmas.

But Daddy's cancer wasn't the same kind. His was harder to pro-
nounce and harder to explain, Aunt Candace jumping in and trying to
give the technical details, though the whole process was complicated by
the fact that Missy started crying, and Sim did, too. I was the only one
who didn't quite get it, remember just sitting there, munching a Pop-
Tart, wondering why they were making such a *deal* over it, kind of annoyed by all their blubbering, afraid it would upset Mama. It made me
even quicker to reassure everyone that I was okay, that I was fine, which,
in fact, I was. I mean, I was more interested than scared; kind of pumped
up and excited, as if Daddy had announced that we were going on a big
vacation out west—to, say, the Grand Canyon or Las Vegas. Somewhere
you heard other people went, saw their snapshots and videos, but had
never actually gone yourself.

I don't know why it struck me that way, for it was clear that everyone else was just flipped out and grieved and devastated, Aunt Candace

having us pray like she always did, telling us to have faith in God, that *nothing was impossible to those who believe.* She went on to talk about faith and healing, told us straight up that if we had faith Daddy would be healed (which is what charismatics are big on), though Brother Sloan was too Baptist to let that pass unchallenged and jumped in and started talking about the Lord knowing best and *not my will but Thy will be done* (which is what the Baptists are big on).

Back and forth they went in this polite little scripture-quoting war that didn't convince anyone of anything, though it did kind of defuse all the tears and emotion, helped Sim and Missy get a grip on themselves. By the time they all left, everything was back to normal, Missy catching a ride to town with Brother Sloan for softball practice, Daddy lying on the couch in his new pajamas and watching TV since it was baseball season, and what with TBS, Atlanta played all the time.

They weren't any dang good back then, but that didn't bother Daddy, who was a Braves fan from a way back and followed every play, the day turning hot, then muggy, Mama opening all the French doors for the breeze. She even let Kenneth come over to swim, and we had a good time, rigged up a swing from the eaves of the apartment that we used to swing off into the deep end of the pool.

Every once in a while Daddy would hobble to the French door and stand there in his new robe and watch us, warn us not to let go too soon or we'd crash to the marble. We'd wave and reassure him, and he'd go back inside to his game, so that what had started out as such an earth-shaking morning had once again flattened out into just another routine late-summer afternoon, and to tell you the truth, that's the way it went, all the way to the end.

There was no more hysteria or tears, no gruesome operations or amputations or radiation: just Daddy at home with Mama, getting thinner and grayer by the week, their bedroom soon the hub of the household, Mama's vanity cluttered with brown bottles and vials of alcohol and pharmacy bottles full of white pills. By Halloween, the whole house smelled of Lysol, though Mama put out her jack-o'-lantern like usual and a Tupperware bowl of Snickers bars that Kenneth and I ended up eating, for the local kids would just as soon spend the night in a funeral home as to brave our front yard on the spookiest night of the year.

But Mama didn't seem to mind. In fact, she seemed fairly content in those days, easily slipping back into her old vampire ways, hardly eating or sleeping so she could stay by Daddy's side, occasionally taking him to town, to the doctors or lawyers, though by Thanksgiving, he was too weak to take the stairs, and they mostly just stayed in bed. That's where I'd find them every day when I came home from school, both of them looking up when I came in with these faces of great and glowing love, as if I'd been gone for forty years.

I'd kick off my shoes and lie there on the foot of the bed and tell them about my day, happy as a dog to have their undivided attention, especially Daddy, who was usually too busy to sit around the house and make small talk. With Sim and Missy, he spent those last few months hammering them about their futures—where they'd go to college and who they'd marry and what they'd do for a living. But he never went into all that stuff with me, just told me that I was smart as anyone; that I'd do well in life, dyslexia or not, because I was a hard worker, and had faith and good sense, attributes that Daddy valued above all the books and schooling in the world.

And sometimes, there toward the end, he'd tell me about his brother Gabe.

He did it so carefully that even then I understood there was still a mystery here, if for no other reason than he never talked about him when Mama was around, but when she was making a run to the drugstore, or downstairs cooking supper.

"Why doesn't he ever come home to see Grannie?" I remember asking him, for that was one thing about Uncle Gabe that still annoyed me, him abandoning Grannie.

In reply, Daddy was thoughtful, choosing his words carefully. "Well, baby, Mama and Gabe, they're just too much alike for their own good—

hardheads, both of them, the Hardheads of the World. And Gabe's kind of a strange personality. Not *bad* strange, you understand. Just——*diffrent*. But I want you to get to know him, give him a chance. He'll come back, one day. He'd have come already, if I'd have let him."

"Why won't you *let* him?" I asked, as something in his words recalled Sim's speculation long ago (could it only be the summer before?) that Grannie wouldn't *let* Uncle Gabe come home.

For a long moment, Daddy didn't answer, then sighed. "Well, he'd cry too much for one thing, and it'd kill him, too, seeing me this way." He paused again, as if unable to find the right words, then settled for the obvious. "Anyway, I want him to remember me like I was. Not like this."

Because by then——by December——he really was kind of pathetic looking, and the heck of it was, it happened so fast. I mean, one week, he was thin and sallow, but still himself, then *boom,* a week later he was this puffy-eyed skeleton who had to go back to the hospital for yet another operation, a *routine procedure,* Aunt Candace called it, though they wouldn't let me see him afterward. This really steamed me, for Sim got to go by that day after school while I had to ride the bus home like usual, then hang around the house by myself, with no one to talk to and nothing to do.

I got so bored that I finally went out and watered Mama's roses, was wrestling with the hose when I heard the phone ringing inside, dim and hollow under the trees. I threw down the hose and charged inside, thinking it was Mama; that she'd had a change of heart and was calling to tell me she'd sent Carlym over to pick me up.

But when I answered, a distant, unfamiliar voice asked to speak to Daddy; said he was his brother. Now, I believe I've mentioned that I'm kind of slow on the uptake, and even then, I didn't connect him with the Mystery Genius and told him plainly, "He ain't here."

"Well, *shit,*" he breathed, and I must say I was little shocked at his language, though he rolled along without turning a hair. "Can I leave a message?"

I just stared at the phone in my hand, for it had suddenly occurred to me who I was speaking with so casually: the Mysterious Uncle Gabe. It was kind of intriguing, talking to him in person, and I put the phone back to my ear and carefully offered: "He's at the hospital. I don't know when he'll be back. They won't let me see him."

I don't know why I unbent enough to confess such a thing to a stranger, but there is something about Gabe, some priestly aura, that makes him easy to confide in. And anyway, like Missy and Sim are always saying, I really am a blabbermouth. I mean, if spilling my guts gets me my way, then spill I will, and indeed, Uncle Gabe took the bait nicely, his voice suddenly not so pressing and impatient. "Well, he probably doesn't want you to see him like this," he explained. "He's got ascites."

Which, of course, meant nothing to me. "What's thet?" I asked.

"Ah, fluid in the peritoneal cavity. It can be pretty nasty."

He sounded just like Aunt Candace, who was so weird about me going to the hospital, as if seeing my own father in a hospital gown, hooked to an IV, would warp my mind or something, turn me into a serial killer. It was truly the stupidest thing I'd ever heard in my life and I told him plainly, "Well, I ain't going up there to ask him to the prom. I just want to see him. Simon got to."

I braced myself for a volley of excuse and argument and explanation, but there was just a small silence on the line, then a quiet: "Well, I'll mention it when I call the hospital."

I remember thinking it so strange that he'd given in so easily, for around our house, you have to fight to the death for every inch in an argument, and here he was, immediately taking my side. Just that quickly, I recognized him as an ally, and was very grateful, told him in a fast rush of gratitude: "Yeah, and tell 'em—tell 'em I'm fine. That I won't cry, I swear to God."

Which was the other reason Aunt Candace didn't want me to go: she was afraid I'd flip out and start bawling and upset Daddy—and why she was afraid of that, I'll never know, because Missy and Sim were the crybabies who tuned up the day he told us about the cancer. I was the strong one. I hadn't cried yet and didn't intend to, and somehow, my unseen uncle seemed to perceive my strength, for he added in that quiet, level voice: "Well. It was nice talking to you. You must be Clayton."

"Yeah." I smiled. "Clayton Michael Catts, Missy's little brother. You don't know me," I added, in case he was trying in vain to put a face to my name.

For a moment, there was another silence on the line, then he offered in that same quiet voice: "Well. Maybe we can remedy that sometime soon. You take care of yourself, *Clayton Michael Catts*. Tell your sister I said hey."

And that was it. He just hung up, leaving me alone in the hallway, the open door letting in a brilliant slant of late-afternoon sun that brought to life the shining oak floor, turning it to gold at my feet. After a moment, I quietly replaced the phone on the cradle and went outside and finished my watering, and I'll be just perfectly honest here, though it galls me to admit it: that even though I didn't go around running my mouth like Missy, but pretty much kept our conversation to myself—just like that, just that quickly, I was as carried away and besotted and infatuated with Uncle Gabe as she.

# CHAPTER FIVE

Maybe even more fascinated, for at least Missy had been able to vent her curiosity about Gabe aloud, pose a few questions, and once Daddy came home from the hospital, he simply never mentioned his brother again. He was just too sick by then, on oxygen part of the time and all these different medicines, so weak he hardly got out of bed anymore, even to go to the bathroom. But as long as Mama was with him, he was fine, all safe and sound and content, which is just where the rest of us wanted him, Sim and Missy and me farmed out to friends and relations who wined and dined us every night of the week.

Sim practically moved in the parsonage with Brother and Sister Sloan, while Missy stayed with Joanna Chapin (her best friend) and I was shuttled around between different people—Daddy's partner, Mr. Sam, and his family, and Curtis and Lori—though I mostly stayed with Kenneth, who lived so close that I could still ride the bus to school. I couldn't complain, for Uncle Lou had flown in for the holidays, and every night would present us with some new Italian delicacy: antipasto and hand-made cannolis, fried squid and fresh spinach swimming in garlic and olive oil. I think he was trying to feed me out of my misery, though to tell you the truth, I had gotten caught up in the whirlwind of activities and the hugs and pity and being the center of attention and really wasn't as heart-broken as everyone thought.

I mean, sure, it was tough seeing Daddy so thin and weak, but he and Mama were so low-key and coolheaded about it all. Whenever he wasn't actually sleeping, they would pass the afternoons sitting up in bed planning his funeral, fussing like they always did, Daddy wanting to go first class, Mama more practical, wondering aloud at the luxury of a polished cherry coffin when the pine ones looked good to her.

"You'll be in a vault," she reasoned, making Daddy (who was just the pickiest person in the world on matters of quality assurance) rise up from his bed of affliction long enough to shout: "Pine? Slash *pine?* It's particle-board, Myra! Why don't you just pitch me in the ground and be done with it?"

"Oh, hush," Mama would reply, not very moved by his outburst, but kind of tired and drugged herself, as Dr. Williams had put her back on medication—not lithium, but something else. Something for her nerves, she said, the first she had taken in years.

Whatever it was, it made her sleep about as much as Daddy, so that if you dropped by the house to see them those first few weeks in December, chances were you'd find them snuggled up under an electric blanket like two little twins in a mother's womb, the bed strewn with sports pages and get-well cards and florist brochures. I'd just leave them a note and a kiss before I was swooped off on another fun trip, to the beach with Sim or mullet fishing with Uncle Case, or there, the first Saturday of Christmas break, to Busch Gardens with Kenneth and his uncle Lou, who'd fought the good fight with cancer himself, and was very sympathetic to Daddy's plight.

It all went so quickly, so painlessly, that even after Daddy went back to the hospital that night, I wasn't too worried. I just hung out with Sim, went to the movies, really didn't understand that the end was upon us, because, well, it had never been upon us before. Even when Aunt Candace woke me up early Tuesday morning and told me to get dressed, that Brother Sloan needed to talk to me, I didn't get too upset. I just pulled on some sweats and followed her to the living room, where in a scene almost identical to the one in September, he sat us down on the couch and told us that Daddy had died that morning in the hospital, just before dawn.

This time, there was no hysteria or crying, just a lot of closed eyes and deep breaths, and it was only then that I realized what a burden Daddy's quiet, stoic decline had been on all of us. I mean, when they'd sat us down four months ago and given us the news about the cancer, there'd been tears and disbelief and fake courage. Now there was only a bone-deep relief that it was finally over: the thinness and the shots and the morphine and the Lysol smell, all of it echoed in Brother Sloan's assurance that Daddy hadn't suffered, but died in his sleep, peaceful in the end.

Only Aunt Candace seemed truly rattled, jumping in and giving us this bright-eyed lecture about how we had to *stick together* and *have faith in God,* before she finally fell apart and sobbed like a schoolgirl against Brother Sloan's shoulder. He patted her on the back and told her all his little Baptist things, leaving me and Missy and Sim to sit there in our pajamas in an embarrassed little silence, glancing at one another out of the corners of our eyes and getting kind of weird about it when there was a rattle at the door, and Mama came in for the first time in three days.

Just that quickly, the weirdness was gone, for she was just her tired old Mama-self, disheveled and exhausted and vampire-pale. But she had a kiss for all of us, even Brother Sloan, before she plopped down in one of the wing chairs and answered Aunt Candace's sniffling inquiries about where she'd been. That wasn't she supposed to go to Mama's? (Aunt Candace's Mama, which would be Grannie.)

"I've already come and gone," she said with a yawn.

Somebody—Brother Sloan—asked how Grannie was holding up, and Mama answered with her eyes closed: "You know Cissie. Solid as a rock. Sent me home to sleep, I don't know why. That's all I do anymore."

"Where's Daddy?" I asked, bringing on a round of these fast, strange looks, as if everyone thought I hadn't caught it, that he was dead, though all I meant was: Where was his body?

Only Mama understood and answered with that same tired, un-emotional levity that had taken her through his illness: "Being fitted for that fine cherry coffin, I guess. Twelve thousand dollars and gold-plated fittings. He *will* be pleased."

It was so unexpected, so calm and assured, that suddenly everything was cool again, all of us bursting into laughter, even Aunt Candace, who quickly regrouped and ordered Mama to bed, then spent the rest of the day working out her grief by bossing us around like a drill instructor. I mean, you'd think the day your father died would be one of peace and introspection, but with Aunt Candace in charge, it wasn't exactly a day of rest, Missy and me having to do laundry and strip our beds and even vacuum the pool.

By the time Mama woke up that afternoon, the house was restored to a semblance of its old holiday cheer, the Christmas tree twinkling in the living room, the kitchen sparkling, the late-December chill barely cool enough for a fire. You'd never know anything had happened at all except for the constant baying of the phone and the carloads of food that began to arrive around supper: whole hams and smoked turkey, fried chicken and sweet corn, cakes and pies and a gigantic pan of homemade lasagna from Mr. Lou. I think in that way, Sicilians and Southerners are alike: they think gluttony a good cure for grief, and far from spending that little two-day interval between Daddy's death and funeral in mourning, I mostly spent it in feasting, hanging around the kitchen, Styrofoam plate in hand, chatting with the hundred thousand visitors who dropped in to pay their respects.

To tell you the truth, I don't think some of them even *knew* Daddy, but had just seen his obituary in the paper and dropped by out of sheer curiosity, as rumor of Mama's magnificent house and garden had circulated around town for years, but if you didn't attend Welcome Baptist, chances are you never got a peek. At least none of the mourners seemed too overwhelmed by grief, but just wandered around, plate in hand, going on and on about the marble pool and the palms, asking all kinds of questions about the fireplaces and the mantels and the acres of shining wood floor.

"—white oak downstairs, yellow pine above," I heard Mama explain a dozen times in answer to a dozen inquiries, and of her roses: "The red are *Louie-Philippe*, the white, *Clotilde Soupert*."

You'd think she was a guide on a tour of homes instead of a grieving widow, though I much preferred her levelheaded, gray-eyed hospitality to the cloud of just inconsolable despair that had settled at Grannie's, where Daddy's people had gathered in this strange Baptist-Irish wake that was just too creepy for words. Mama made us go over that first night to show ourselves to our aunts (great-aunts, that is, Grannie's sisters), who kept grabbing me every time I passed in these rib-crushing hugs, telling me things like: "He picks the loveliest flowers for His bouquet" (meaning, I suppose, that Jesus had picked Daddy for his centerpiece—and a strange notion it was).

Even the men on the porch were subdued, Uncle Case slumped in a corner, chin to his chest, not joining in the stories the other men told about Daddy, but just staring into space, so pathetic that I offered him different things to cheer him up: cake, tea, even a stick of gum, all of which he refused with a polite: "No, baby. Wouldn't care for it."

Compared to that, I much preferred Mama and her historic tour that lasted till Thursday afternoon when her relatives began to trickle in from Birmingham and Slidell. And though they were pretty Irish themselves, with flaming red hair and majorly hick voices, they were naturally less heartbroken than Daddy's kin, and seemed to look on his demise as an opportunity to take a cheap trip to Florida, most of them having plans to go on to Disney or the beach once Daddy was properly put away. I didn't begrudge them their holidays, though their sheer numbers made for a lot of dirty dishes and loud talk and commotion, the house filled with a cloud of cigarette smoke that made me think of Uncle Ira, who couldn't come, of course, though he did call Grannie and offer his condolences.

By the afternoon of the viewing, Uncle Gabe was the only official relation still unaccounted for, and a source of some anxiety to Missy, as the general feeling among the Louisiana kin was that he wouldn't show.

"Why not?" she was bold enough to ask one of the old men on the porch, a great-uncle from Slidell, who regarded her levelly over his cigarette, drawled: "Well, shug, same reason the skeleton wouldn't cross the road."

He let us reflect on this nonsense a moment, then supplied the punch line with a wink: "Didn't have the *guts*."

The other old men burst into laughter, prompting Missy to later ask Mama (in the privacy of her bedroom): "Why are your relatives so weird?"

Mama, who was sitting at her vanity, trying to camouflage her Dracula-paleness with a Estée Lauder compact, just sighed: "Oh, baby, I don't know. It's a *Louisiana thing*."

Which was how Mama explained most of the intricacies of life. Daddy's unbridled ambition was a *compulsion thing*. Uncle Ira's tattoos were a *rejection thing*. Sim's 3.9 average was a *perfection thing*. It was as if she grasped the essence of all of them; she just didn't have the words to break them down into clear-cut explanation.

By then, Missy was positively desperate for news of Uncle Gabe, and tried to pin her down. "Well, why are they so *nasty* about Uncle Gabe?" she asked. "What's he ever done to *them*?"

Mama had not so much as mentioned Uncle Gabe since me and Sim had our little run-in last year, but has always gone to great lengths to satisfy Missy's boundless curiosity. She paused a moment, compact in hand, and tried to offer a halting explanation: "Well, baby—your uncle—he tends to, kind of, get on people's nerves."

"*How?*" Missy insisted. "He's like the *nicest* guy in the world. He's *hilarious*."

Mama just blinked at that, murmured: "Well, he would be, to you."

Missy, who has never had much patience with Mama and her strange Mama-ways, was truly exasperated by then. "How can he be the *nicest* guy in the world and get on everybody's nerves, too?" she demanded, and for a moment, Mama faced her in the mirror, then bowed to the inevitable.

"I don't know, baby," she said, returning to her compact. "It's a *Gabe thing*."

Which didn't offer much hope that he'd show up that night at the viewing, me and Missy spending most of the evening in the foyer of the funeral home, Missy running to the door every time a car pulled in the parking lot, thinking it was Uncle Gabe.

"He ain't coming," I told her at eight, when the early-comers had begun to leave, making Missy gnaw her lip in a way that made her look amazingly like Daddy.

"Well, it's not *his* fault," she reasoned. "He probably doesn't even *know*. I mean, Aint Candace couldn't find a home number, just left a message at work—oh, and Clay," she added, her eyes still on the parking lot, "listen—if he *does* come, don't stare at his hand or anything, okay? I mean, it'll just embarrass the crud out of me if you do."

My reputation as an unabashed starer was legendary in the Catts household, nothing I could deny, though the news about his hand was new to me, making me gape at her, ask, "What's wrong with his hand?"

"Nothing," she said. "It's just messed up. He can't use it, so don't try to shake it or anything, or put the old X-ray vision on it." (Which is what Missy called it when I gave something a particularly potent stare.)

As you can imagine, this just weirded the heck out of me. It was like telling me he had a glass eye or something; I knew as soon as I saw him I'd be staring at his bad hand like a big old goober and he'd be humiliated and never come back. That's really how I felt, which is kind of strange when you think about it, that even then, when Daddy was hardly cold and Mama in shock and Uncle Gabe still sight unseen, I was already making plans for him, wondering what I'd say to him; wondering where he'd stay.

Even with all of Mama's kin piling in, there were still a few empty couches at our house and one bed: the bottom bunk in my bedroom that wasn't what you might call a luxury accommodation, but cheaper than a motel (which is why Grannie said all Mama's people were staying with us: too cheap to rent a room). I'd kept it there, saved, in case he wanted to stay with us, but he never showed that night, Missy finally going inside at nine-thirty and sitting beside Uncle Case in a dejected slump on a love seat in the hallway, both of them red-eyed and desolate, the very picture of grief.

She continued to hold out a faint hope that he'd fly in that night, though when morning dawned the next day, we were too busy to give it much thought, as it wasn't any small task, getting ready for a funeral in a house that for all the splendor of the wood floors and marble pool, only had one shower. Everyone had to line up and take their turn, a minor crisis erupting when I couldn't find my dress shoes, though by the time the funeral home limousine pulled up at ten-thirty, I was the only one who was dressed and ready and got the best seat, next to the window.

Sim had spent the night with Grannie, and at the last minute Mama had insisted on taking her own car to the church, so Missy and me had to ride in alone with all the out-of-towners, Missy weepy and withdrawn while I was overcome by this silly nervousness that made me laugh a lot and just chatter my head off, all the way to town. I mean, it wasn't that I was happy I was going to my father's funeral, it was just so new, the limousine and the attention, everyone slipping me Certs and promising me things—to take me to Disney World that summer, or the Superdome in New Orleans.

It was like I was suddenly the Cinderella of the Ball, the only note of weirdness Missy's tears that were profuse and unending, and Sim's stony silence when he met us at the church and I bragged about the limousine and how cool it was. You could tell by his expression that it was exactly the *wrong* thing to say, though he didn't tell me I was an idiot or anything, just told me to sit still during the service and BE QUIET.

Then he turned me over to a funeral-home usher, who led me through the double doors into the sanctuary that was packed to the gills with people all dressed up in suits and hats and gloves, though I didn't pay them much mind. I only had eyes for the front of the church that was as familiar to me as the back of my hand, though on that day it was hardly recognizable, the altar and pulpit transformed by a strange, glittering *forest* of flowers that were jammed in around an open coffin in a wild profusion of color. They were nothing that Mama could grow in her yard, but enormous carnations and orchids and hothouse lilies, their size and very perfection almost dwarfing Mama's sole contribution to the day: a simple oval arrangement of green spidery fern dotted with ten dozen tiny pink roses that covered the foot of the shining cherry coffin.

They were *Cecile Brunner,* an antique rose that had just lately become her passion, one that Daddy used to bemoan (because they were so expensive), though even he would have admitted that these were a great success, delicate and fragile against the waxy flamboyance of the other flowers, a quiet, intimate message that for the first time that day, brought a heaviness to my heart, a sudden nervous pounding. ("*Sweetheart* roses," Mama had told him in bed last week when she ordered them, "because you are my sweetheart.")

Just that quickly, my happy little rise of excitement was replaced by a clammy tightness in my chest that made it hard to breathe as the usher pushed past the edge of the flowers and seated me smack in the middle of the family pew, right across from the coffin, next to Mama. She must have realized I was having a hard time of it, for she took my hand immediately, gave it a little squeeze for courage, then held it tight throughout the service that was actually kind of boring. There were just too many speakers, the preachers all saying the same things they'd been telling us in private for the past two days: *that in my Father's house are many mansions,* and so on, things I'd been hearing all my life, though I didn't much understand how they applied (because my father already had a mansion, out in the woods, that he and Mama had spent a fortune fixing up and restoring and what good would it do him now, lying there in that shining cherry box?).

When they finally finished, Mr. McQuaig got up last of all and didn't try to preach, but just reminisced about Daddy, about growing up with him on Magnolia Hill and what a hard worker he was and finicky and neat; how much he loved baseball. It was all well and good, just that he went on *forever,* and kept crying and snorting back snot in a way that nearly drove me crazy. I was about nuts by the time they finally handed the service back to Brother Sloan, who prayed a final prayer, then had us stand and sing Daddy's favorite hymn ("Amazing Grace") that for some reason, we sang without an accompaniment. It was the first (and only) time we'd ever done it that way, the familiar old hymn echoing back eerily hollow to my ears and just heart-wrenchingly sad.

Between that and the smell of the hothouse flowers, I could feel the pressure in my chest again as the ushers began herding the congregation forward for their final glimpse of Daddy, who was lying there not six feet in front of me, looking weirdly unlike himself in the big old coffin, I couldn't have told you why. Maybe it was something in the color and plushness of the velvet lining that brought out the awful pallor in his skin—or maybe I'd forgotten how thin he'd become, after not seeing him in a week.

In any case, it was nothing I cared to ruminate on, then or ever, and just stood there in my new black suit, trying to keep my eyes on the carpet or the ceiling or anywhere but the coffin, when the muted funeral hush was cut with a sharp little gasp of surprise. We all looked up at the same time, at Missy, who was standing at the other end of the family row, staring at Daddy's coffin with this red-eyed, red-nosed face of absolute *wonder*. I didn't know what to think—thought maybe he'd *moved* or something—had glanced back at the coffin when Grannie by gosh took off after one of the mourners, a short, broad man in a big winter coat that she hit in an embrace so hard that it would have sent a smaller man over backwards.

He didn't recoil, just caught her evenly in a tight embrace, then turned and hugged Missy, of all people, long and sincerely, before he began making his way down the family row, offering his hand to Sim—his left one, the wrong one for shaking. It finally came to me then that *my gosh,* it was *Uncle Gabe,* though I was too shocked to make much of it, just stood there next to Mama as he came upon me next, not offering his hand, but just standing there in that big coat, returning my stare with one of his own, and I swear to God, it was like I knew him.

It wasn't just a family resemblance, either, for he didn't favor Daddy at all, but was fairer in coloring and a tiny bit taller and altogether stockier—but something in the way he looked out of his eyes, piercing and concerned. Why, they weren't a stranger's eyes at all, but immediately close and familiar, as if he'd lived around us all his life. I almost said: *"Hey,"* right there in front of Daddy's casket, right at his funeral, but he'd glanced aside to Mama by then, to stare at her with that same potent concern. Five seconds passed, then ten, and I don't know what would have happened if Grannie hadn't have been there to grip the sleeve of his coat and turn him back to Daddy, who was lying there in the splendor of his shining cherry coffin, oddly shrunken in death, just a small man in a big suit, dwarfed by all those stinking flowers.

I still didn't want to look at him, much preferred concentrating on the slumped back of his Mysterious Brother, who stood a long moment posed over the coffin before he finally spoke in a clear, carrying voice: *"God,* he looks like Daddy."

Standing there, not four feet behind him, I misunderstood him at first and almost answered aloud: "He *is* Daddy." Then I realized what he meant: that he looked like *their* daddy, Granddaddy Catts, who I never knew except through Grannie's pictures and all the stories Mama told about him; about how kind he was to her when she was a little girl; how she wanted me and Sim to grow up and be just like him.

So I understood he was paying Daddy a compliment with his flat, heartfelt comparison, but couldn't make much of it, too distracted by Mama, who'd dropped noiselessly to the pew at the sound of his voice, like her legs had gone out from under her. It happened so quickly that I didn't know what to do, just glanced around, a little panicked, catching Carlym's eye on the platform, who jerked his head toward Mama, motioned for me to sit down next to her and wait.

I did as he instructed, sat down next to her and waited till Gabe finally turned and led Grannie to the side door, to the pale December sun. Once they were gone, the line of mourners began moving again, an endless, weeping stream, Miss Susan and her brood among them, all emotional and Italian, as if they'd been crying for a hundred years, that doofus Kenneth even giving me a *hug.* I mean, I'm sure it was well intended, but it just made a weird day seem weirder, and I was doggoned stinking glad when the sanctuary finally emptied and I could get the heck out of there and into the waiting limousine.

Mama rode with us to the graveyard, though she didn't say a word, just stared at the white winter sky with vacant eyes that never looked away, never blinked, throughout the graveside service that was really just a rehash of the church one. This time, only Brother Sloan spoke, then there were more prayers and a lot of hugs and handshaking and a return to Grannie's house, where the after-funeral crowd went for dinner.

Compared to the haste and hurry of the morning, this gathering was kind of tired and jaded, the atmosphere not made any cheerier by a cold, gray rain that began to fall around four, or the fact that the Wonderful Uncle Gabe had chosen to snub us all and leave without a word. At first there had been great hopes he'd show up at Grannie's, everyone, even Aunt Candace, looking up at the door at the sound of every car.

But as the short winter afternoon drew on to a wet, chill dusk, they finally gave up and admitted the naysayers had won the day, the women making light of it for Missy's sake, all of them offering different explanations on why he should leave so abruptly (maybe he was sick, or had a plane to catch). At one point, Missy even accused me of unnecessary staring, that I hotly denied.

"I didn't even *see* his stinking hand," I lied.

But in the end, no one could really explain why he left so abruptly, his dismissal just deepening the mystery and making a dreary day even drearier, Mama's people all leaving that afternoon for funner destinations than our own, Grannie's kin likewise scattering, a few of them offering to stay the night, though Mama turned them down.

"We'll be fine," she assured them, and we were, getting through the coming weeks in much the same way we'd come this far, with the support of the church and all our friends, who kept the good times rolling through Christmas and the New Year and the cold January nights that followed. They took us shopping, took us to dinner, took us (or Sim, anyway) to the Super Bowl, and I'd be a liar if I said I really suffered much those first few months Daddy was gone, for there was so much to do, so much to see.

I don't think the reality of his death really sank in for a long time—two months, at least—till sometime in February, on one of those iron-gray winter afternoons that we don't often see in Florida, the house cold and drafty, me home from school with a sore throat that had turned out to be strep. When the throat swab had come back positive, I had naturally rejoiced as it meant I'd miss a whole week of school, though once home, I was quickly bored, because Mama was so drugged out that she seemed to sleep around the clock.

I mean, she'd get up in the morning and send Sim and Missy off to school and set me up with my medicine and Gatorade, but then she'd go back to bed, and there she'd stay, all day long. By Friday afternoon, I was sure enough stir-crazy, tired of TV and wandering around the house, bored and restless, looking for something to do. I pulled out Matchbox cars and tried Legos, but nothing distracted me, the house filled with this hollow, stuffy smell, the rooms dusty and unused, the pool full of dead leaves.

If Daddy had been there, it was a state that wouldn't have lasted long, for he'd have had us jumping, shouting, "Myra! Thet pool's full of leaves! It'll ruin the pump! Git Sim out to skim it! Melissa Anne? Is thet your uniform on the floor? D'you remember how to use a washing machine? Were you raised in a barn?" And so on, as for all Daddy's many undeniable virtues, anyone who knew him understood that at the center of his obsessive little soul there beat the heart of an unrepentant nagger who would go after you like a wild dog about cleaning your bedroom, taking care of your bike, even clipping your toenails.

Under his energizing influence, Mama had kept things pumping, but now that he was gone, we had sunk into an unkempt decline, our old house smells of Pine-Sol and oil soap gradually replaced by the musty stuffiness of piled laundry and old garbage, and still, faintly, the cursed smell of Lysol that had creeped in the curtains and rugs to reassert itself on humid days. It was a sad little reminder of his illness that didn't do much to cheer me up, and for some reason, when dusk finally fell that afternoon, Mama never got up at all, and Missy and Sim didn't come home either.

At six, I tried to call Kenneth, but he'd gone to the skating rink, and when I called Lori's to see how Ryan was doing (he was the one who'd given me strep), no one was home. I finally gave up then and began wandering around again, room to room, till full dark, when I found myself at one of the French doors downstairs, the one closest to the kitchen that we used for a back door.

I stood there listlessly, watching the wet pool, the scatter of leaves, till it suddenly came to me, why I was standing there: because this was Friday night, the night Daddy always came home from Waycross. That's why I'd spent the afternoon circling the house so restlessly: I was waiting for the shine of his headlights, for the run across the cold deck to the garage, and his exasperated greeting: "Claybird? Thet your bicycle I nearly ran over in the drive? Run out and git it, baby. You got to take care of things—"

Once I realized what I was doing, I gave it up and returned to the television, where I spent the rest of the evening watching *Miami Vice* as I had every other Friday night of the year. Except this time, when that lively little theme song came on, instead of the perky lighting of Lori and Curtis's little trailer and the roar of the big-screen TV, I found myself alone, curled up on an overstuffed couch in a moss-hung haunted house, wondering how it could be that my father had died.

Could it really be so? Could it really be that I'd never see him again?

The idea was just preposterous, beyond comprehension, and I shrugged it off, didn't shed a tear, didn't tell a soul, though after that night I knew in my heart that Daddy was dead; that he wasn't coming back, ever again. I also knew that no matter how *vampire* Mama might become, or how many disembodied slaves might rattle our stairs at midnight, the ghost that would haunt me for the rest of my days would be a kindlier one, even closer to home: the ghost of my father Michael.

# PART TWO

*Pity me that the heart is slow to learn*
*What the swift mind beholds at every turn.*

EDNA ST. VINCENT MILLAY

# CHAPTER SIX

When I look back over that long, boring year between Daddy's death and the Great Second Coming, I can think of no single event that stands out as meaningful or historic: nothing but a lifeless gray winter that was short but unusually bitter, with ice storms and temperatures so low that Mama lost a couple of her phoenix palms and a few roses, frozen root to tip on one cold night. Even the pipes froze before it was over, flooding the laundry room and cracking a section of the pool, so that we woke up one morning in early March to the bizarre sight of a smoking, empty marble hole in our backyard, ice-glazed and weirdly beautiful, like a gigantic inverted mausoleum.

I guess you might call 1988 the year I learned to hate winter, though living in Florida, it wasn't as bitter a hate as it might have been, there wasn't enough time. Before I could work up any true resentment, April was upon us, and once the danger of frost had passed, life immediately improved, Mama rallying as she usually does in the spring, emerging like a bear to stand on the front porch every evening, trowel in hand, to survey the winter's damage. This year was no different, though as the weeks passed, the close humidity giving way to real, stinging heat, there were no grand projects begun, no new roses to be imported and painstakingly dug, no corner of the woods transformed into tropical bowers or perennial beds. This year was a holding action, the roses cut back on time and the Osmocote spread, but nothing added or subtracted inside or out, the pool filling with leaves, the laundry piling up so high that Missy told everyone at church about it, christened it *Mount Myra*.

When Mama heard of it, she was not so pleased that Missy was (literally) airing our dirty laundry, and worked for two straight days sorting and bleaching and folding, covering every table in the house with stacks of laundry and making many promises. But without Daddy's energizing influence, she couldn't stay on top of it, and as the weeks creeped into summer, Mount Myra reappeared in all its glory, and the last time I looked, there it remained.

But we survived, and that was the main thing, all of us adjusting to Daddy's absence in different ways: Sim and Missy spending a lot of time with friends in town, me mostly hanging out with Mama, for her comfort or mine, I really don't know. I even took to going to the cemetery with her on Saturday mornings—the only morning she went after dawn—to visit Daddy's grave that was situated very pleasantly beneath a grove of old gray-green cedars, his tombstone kind of plain, I thought, though I'd come up with the inscription myself: He Walks With God.

Everyone was always telling me what a stroke of genius it was, how touching, though to be honest, there was nothing genius about it at all: I'd swiped the line from *Witness*, the movie me and Sim saw the night Daddy went back in the hospital. It was what the Amish guy told Kelly McGillis at her husband's funeral, and as soon as I heard it, I knew that's what I'd tell Mama to put on Daddy's marker, because it was so fitting, so true.

She agreed, and it looked very nice there, though not as impressive as some of his neighbors', for the Riverside is one of those old antebellum cemeteries with live oaks even older than our own, and ornate monuments and marble statues, all ancient and crumbly and weather-stained. True to her vampire origins, Mama seemed very much at home there, not so gray-eyed and listless, but oddly comforted, even cheerful as we strolled along the winding paths.

She was never in much of a hurry to leave; after we finished visiting Daddy, she'd take me around like a tour guide and show me all the various points of interest: the crumbling, scrolled plaques of the slave section, the low hills where the Confederate soldiers were buried; even the paupers' ground, a deep green vale sided by a drainage ditch and the river where poor people were buried at the county's expense. It was maybe the saddest part of the whole cemetery, treeless and bare, only a few of the graves marked with these temporary metal things the county provided, the paper inscriptions turned to pulp by the weather, unreadable and forsaken. I didn't much like going down there, though Mama surprised me one morning by casually mentioning that she'd almost been buried there, once.

*"When?"* I asked, as Mama was popularly believed to be the richest woman in town, with her Mercedes, her factories, her big old house. Even her kindly aloofness added to the myth, for she acted just like you'd expect a moneyed old heiress to act: distant and artsy, kind of eccentric.

"When I was twelve," she said, scanning the lowlands through a pair of dark sunglasses, "the last winter I lived in Florida—you know, next door to your grannie. I almost died that winter and Mama didn't have any money. She'd have had to turn me over to the county, and there I'd be to this day, unmarked and forgotten, but just down the hill from your father—which is ironic, when you think of it."

It sure didn't sound too *ironic* to me; it sounded sadder than *heck*. For a moment, we just stood there squinting into the morning sun, then I tried to tie it up with a happy ending: "*Grannie* would have bought you a tombstone," I told her, my stout sureness making her smile.

"And so she would have," she agreed with a kiss to the top of my head, "and she'd have told everybody about it, too: that poor little Sims girl what died next door. Bless her heart, she was only twelve."

She even laughed when she said it, she and I both did, because that's *exactly* what Grannie would have said. Or at least I *thought* that's what Grannie would have said, though when I asked her about it after church the next Sunday, her face took on that same clouded foreboding it had when I mentioned Uncle Gabe. "Your mama told you *thet?*" she asked.

Then, before I could answer, "Good Lord, what a thang to tell a chile."

"I told her *you'd* have put a marker there," I inserted quickly, afraid Grannie would go after Mama like she'd gone after Sim.

But Grannie just gave one of her little snorts. "Well, I don't know about *thet*," she said. "And I don't know about you two spendin' sa much time at the Riverside, neither. It's in a *bad* part of *town*, and it ain't *safe*, and it needs to *stop*."

"It's all right," I offered nervously, "it ain't haunted or anything." (Which was what I was always telling Kenneth, who wouldn't go within a mile of the place without a priest and a crucifix in hand.) And though I spent the rest of the afternoon trying to appease her, even describing her own funeral, and what a blowout we'd have when her time came, nothing I said seemed to hit the mark, Grannie's face protracted and drawn, clearly worried.

I had a feeling that me and Mama's pleasant little graveyard jaunts would soon be a thing of the past and I was right. Bright and early the next morning, Aunt Candace dropped by the house and passed along Grannie's concern with considerable relish, for Aunt Candace has never cared much for Mama's vampire ways, had never visited Daddy's grave as far as I knew.

It wasn't that she didn't love him, just that Aunt Candace is one of those forward thinkers, always moving, who has never planned a funeral or stripped a floor or worried herself too much with gardening, twilight or otherwise. I guess you could describe her as a career woman, who lived with Uncle Ed in a sparkling tract house in a neat little neighborhood three blocks from the high school, her color schemes all pastel, her house plants all silk. Though in addition to being her sister-in-law she is Mama's best friend, in that and in most things, she is her opposite in every way: petite and fair-haired and energetic, only alike in their devotion to the Lord, though Mama is very open and accepting of diverse beliefs, while Aunt Candace is a fire-breathing charismatic who basically thinks all of us Baptist Catts are going to hell in a handbasket for our trifling, uncommitted ways.

She's always been after Mama to (and this is just a sampling): fire Dr. Williams; make Sim quit driving so fast; put Missy in private school; put me in private school; quit Welcome Baptist and join her at Living Water Assembly. In short, become just like her.

When Daddy was alive, he kept her meddling in line, but now that he was gone, poor Mama had a hard time resisting her, caving in like pressed aluminum on the matter of the graveyard visits, coming to my bedroom when she left and apologizing in a contrite little voice: "Baby, I didn't mean to—you know—*scare* you, with the pauper thing. I don't want to be an unnecessary burden to you children."

I assured her she hadn't been and got kind of cross with Grannie myself, for always keeping such a line on Mama, always trying to run her life. I wouldn't go over to her house to watch wrestling the next Sunday, which might not sound like much of a boycott, but was, Grannie getting my message loud and clear, staring at me in church that night with this sad, forsaken little look and passing me a whole pack of gum (usually she only passes it by the stick). I didn't even unwrap it or chew any, just handed it to Mama to put in her purse, and poor Grannie, it was like a knife in her heart.

After that, she let up on Mama and never criticized her openly, even when spring gave way to a hot, humid summer and the men started calling, all kinds of men, all suddenly very concerned about our welfare, wanting to see how we were holding up under the strain of our grievous loss. Mama told them we were holding up very well, and didn't return their calls, so I didn't think much of it—at least not till late June, when Kenneth casually mentioned that Uncle Lou was flying in for Fourth of July, wondered if me and Mama wanted to go to the beach with them for the fireworks.

I was thinking about it, picturing all of us on a blanket on the sand, when he dropped his bombshell with his customary calm: "I mean, face it, Clay: if you're gonna have a stepfather, you might as well have one you like."

I just stared at this, thinking poor Kenneth had finally gone 'round the bend. "What d'you mean, *stepfather*?" I asked. "I don't have a stepfather."

"Not *yet*," he offered with a knowing little look, "but brace yourself."

I had found over the years that the best way to deal with Kenneth was bald interrogation, and asked him plainly: "What the *heck* are you talking about?"

"Stepfathers," he repeated. "You know: the man who takes your real father's place—your mother's new husband. The guy she starts dating, then talking about all the time, telling you what a great guy he is and how you need to be friends—then, if all goes according to plan, marries."

Finally, he'd hit upon a word that connected. "You think Mama'll get *married*?" I asked with exactly the same disbelief I'd once asked if he thought she was a vampire.

"Sure," he said. "Why not? She's a good-looking woman—for a mother," he added quickly, lest I start suspecting him of untoward motives, "and a good wife, too, and cooks and goes to church, which nobody does anymore. Mom says she'd be perfect for Uncle Lou, because he cooks, too, and has had cancer and all, and can relate to her grief."

I didn't have an answer to this, just sat there and tried to imagine Mama and Uncle Lou, but it was a hard match. Aside from the fact they were both inspired cooks and had good manners, there wasn't much to go by, as Uncle Lou was gray-haired and about fifty and wore a gold chain, and that chain alone knocked him out of Mama's orbit. That chain said: *I ain't from around here,* and furthermore, her old redneck uncles would eat him for breakfast the first time she took him home to Louisiana, run him over with a tractor or something.

I think Kenneth could see that I wasn't taking too much to the notion as he tried to go to bat for Uncle Lou in a sly way, going on to tell me about stepfathers and how awful they could be. How they were all nice at first, when they were after your mother, then, once the honeymoon was over, they slowly got exasperated, then, finally, tired and ready to be rid of you.

"It's your mother they're in love with," he explained with a shrug, not particularly bitter, just matter-of-fact. "You're just a kid to them. Another mouth to feed."

Gabe would later identify this air of tired resignation as Premature Cynicism, but at the time, I took Kenneth's unemotional speculation as the honest truth, and a chilling one at that. I was so shook up about it that Kenneth took pity on me and backed off, though he continued to drop hints about Uncle Lou all summer long, and how much he liked children, how Italians were big on family; how much money he made with Anheuser-Busch. How he had a retirement. I had a feeling that Miss Susan was somewhere in the background feeding this thing, and in less kind moments wondered if they had their eye on planting Uncle Lou upstairs in Daddy's magnificent bed and the rest of them in a trailer out back, with all our family furniture and fortune to be shared.

I must say I wasn't too keen on the idea, not that it did much good, for by then, by Labor Day, everyone at Welcome was full of speculation over who would marry the Widow Catts and become part owner of her Mercedes and big old mansion. With the official Year of Mourning almost over, all kinds of men had begun to call, not just Uncle Lou, but Brother Kennard and James Lee's granddaddy (who was old as the hills and kind of funny about it), even Carlym, who was a lot younger than Mama but probably willing to overlook a few crow's-feet for the chance to move out of the cramped little parsonage and into Mama's magnificent bed (so said Missy).

Mama herself seemed to find the whole subject kind of tasteless and didn't like talking about it, and I finally ended up going to Missy to discuss it, as she is my second-choice confider, less sympathetic than Grannie, but slightly more confidential. I tracked her to her bedroom one night in late September, a year and a month to the day that Daddy had his first surgery, found her sitting up in bed working her way through her usual mountain of homework, the bedspread and surrounding floor strewn with notebook paper and calculators and Norton anthologies.

"We need to talk," I told her, shutting the door behind me.

She was used to me coming to her with my little problems and didn't even ask why, just laid her book facedown on her chest and listened grimly to the news that Kenneth had passed on that afternoon: that Uncle Lou was coming down for Thanksgiving, was wanting to know Mama's favorite flower so he could send her a Thanksgiving arrangement. Missy didn't need any more explanation than that, just chewed her lip a moment, asked: "Does Grannie know?"

I assured her she didn't (or if she did, she hadn't heard it from me) and Missy was thoughtful. "Maybe we ought to tell her," she offered.

I nodded, was about to say something else when she added, from right out of the blue: "Uncle Gabe needs to get his *butt* home where it belongs."

For a moment, I didn't think I'd heard her correctly, breathed: *"What?"*

"Uncle Gabe," she repeated casually, as if we discussed him every night of our life. "He needs to come home."

*"Why?"* I pressed, as Missy had gotten kind of quiet on the subject of Uncle Gabe the last few months, with none of her earlier enthusiasm, carefully sidestepping the subject if I brought him up. Over the course of the summer I'd tried to feel her out a few times, find out why she was suddenly so distant about him, but she was resistant to all my hints and comments, simply wouldn't be drawn out, as elusive and mysterious as Sim had been back when Daddy first mentioned him the weekend I turned nine.

I was naturally curious at her sudden thawing, though Missy just shrugged, answered simply: "'Cause he's the obvious choice."

"Choice of *what?*" I begged, for being the token idiot in a family of child geniuses has always been a burden to me. With Missy especially, I'm always running along a few yards behind, peppering questions at her back that she's too impatient to answer.

"For second husband," she replied, a little line of annoyance creeping into her forehead, as if I'd missed an obvious truth here. I was sure enough speechless at that and just sat there dumbfounded while she went on to bemoan the fact that Aunt Candace had somehow lost his number in a moving mishap. "——And nobody can find him anymore. It's like he's fallen off the *face* of the *earth*."

"But *why* Uncle *Gabe?*" I had to break in and ask, making Missy repeat herself with great exasperation.

"Because he's the *obvious choice,* Clay. You want Carlym moving in here, walking around in his underwear, making us go to church every time the doors open? Or Uncle Lou, or some *stranger* from the *grocery store?*"

"Well, why does Mama have to marry *anyone?*" I countered, my sincerity making Missy back off a little and actually look at me, as if, for once, I'd made a point worthy of consideration.

"Well, you're right, of course," she allowed. "I mean, chances are, she'll just stay holed up in this mausoleum of a old house, sipping tea and reading Sherlock Holmes till she dies. Ever read 'A Rose for Emily'?"

I shook my head wordlessly, though Missy didn't belabor it, just sighed again, hugely, then fixed me with a level eye. "I tell you Clay: Uncle Gabe *must* return. He's the missing link, the only one who can bring Mama back. He would, too, if he thought Grannie was cool with it. That's why he hasn't come back. He's afraid she's still mad about——*you know*——"

She paused then, as if waiting for a reply, though I just sat there, taken aback by the fanatical ring in her voice that kind of reminded me of the way Brother Sloan talked about the Rapture in church. I half expected her to say: *The trump would sound and the dead in Christ would rise first,* though she wouldn't go any further without me, just insisted: "What about you?"

"What about *what?*" I caged, making Missy roll her eyes.

"What about *Uncle Gabe? Marrying Mama?* I mean, you're cool with it, aren't you?"

I shrugged, for I wasn't cool with it as much as perplexed. "Well, I don't know," I offered hesitantly. "I'm not sure it'll, you know, *work*."

I said this very carefully, for we were embarking on sensitive waters here, even I knew that, and a misstep or a wrong comment could bring on the wrath of Missy and Sim and Grannie, too. For in the intervening year since I'd last discussed Uncle Gabe with Missy, I'd had a conversation of my own with an informed source who'd given me a very private, very enlightening bit of insight about our Absent Uncle, whose mystery had turned out to be a very tricky mystery, indeed.

Missy, who has a radar like Grannie, immediately picked up on my hesitancy and pinned me with a level eye. "Did Daddy ever—you know—talk to you about him? About Uncle Gabe?"

We were drifting into even trickier waters here, my reply very careful. "Well, he said, you know, that he'd be back. That I should, give him a chance."

When I didn't offer anything else, she pressed me further: "Is that all? He didn't tell you anything else? Anything kind of"—she paused a moment, then offered—"*weird?*"

I immediately knew what she was talking about and told her plainly: "Not him, but I know. I *heard*."

"*Ah,*" she said with a wry smile. "Who told? Surely not Grannie."

"Miss Cassie," I said, meaning Cassie Campbell, our family beautician.

"Might have guessed," Missy muttered with another roll of her eyes, then: "Well, are you okay with it? I mean, it must have been weirder than *heck,* finding out at the *beauty parlor*—good gosh, don't tell Grannie. She'll have Miss Cassie's *head*."

This was aside, as if speaking to herself, then, more directly: "I didn't even know myself till after the funeral, when I kept wanting to call him. Mama sat me down and had this little gruesome little mother-daughter talk. I think Daddy meant to tell you himself, when he was sick, but everything happened so fast, there at the end, and I don't think he wanted you to—you know—think *badly* of him. Of Uncle Gabe, I mean."

"I don't," I assured her, though I did have to ask: "What about Carlym? And Brother Sloan?" For that was my first concern, that Brother

Sloan or Carlym would find out and be all up in arms about it, have Grannie cut from her Sunday-school class, I shouldn't think.

But Missy didn't seem particularly worried, just gave a little shrug. "Well, what about 'em?" she asked. "They probably don't even know. Or Carlym doesn't. Brother Sloan, maybe."

"What about *Mama?*" I had to ask, meaning: What was her take on all this? I mean, as far as I could see, she'd be the one making the great sacrifice by marrying Uncle Gabe, though Missy just rolled her eyes in exasperation like she always did when speaking of Mama and her nutty vampire ways.

"Well, who knows? You know Mama: the Sphinx Woman. She won't talk about it, even to Aunt Candace. But she'll be cool with it if he comes back. She loves him, you know."

"Uncle *Gabe?*" I exclaimed for maybe the fifth time that night, though Missy was very nonchalant and matter-of-fact.

"Sure. You know, they grew up together on the Hill, were like childhood sweethearts, or something. Her father's the one who messed up his hand."

"Granddaddy *Sims?*" I breathed, though Missy just gave another shrug.

"Apparently so. That's why Grannie hates him so much—because of what he did to Uncle Gabe. Messed him up, like, emotionally. Aunt Candace says that everything that happened was because of him."

I just blinked at that, wondered how Granddaddy Sims could be thought responsible for something as weird as Uncle Gabe's proclivities, though Missy didn't give me much time to ponder it, but brought me back to earth with an impatient: "So? Are we in agreement here? About Uncle Gabe? No throwing your weight behind any *outside* contenders?"

She was speaking of Uncle Lou, of course, and for a moment, I hesitated, weighing the possibilities, then offered without much conviction: "I guess."

She smiled then, a quick, unthinking smile of genuine affection that was always a shock in my redheaded sister, who only favored Daddy in two ways: her grand slams and the sudden, infectious grin that occasionally lit her fair, freckled face, transforming it eerily into his image.

"Then we're cool here," she announced with a fond little slap to my leg. "And I must say, Clay, that you've just surprised the *crud* out of me, taking this so well. I mean, everybody—Aunt Candace and Grannie— they all thought you'd *flip out* or something, and here you are, cool as a cucumber, acting like you practically have good sense."

I just grunted at her good-natured insult, flattered despite myself, though as was usual with Missy, I had the feeling that maybe 60 percent of the conversation had passed a foot over my head. But at the moment was just glad to be on the winning side and stood and went on to bed; I didn't have anything better to do. Sim was at the movies with his girlfriend Sondra, Mama asleep (also as usual), the night hot for October and very still, the summer crickets gone by then, though the owls were out and about, mating in the trees with a racket that wasn't to be believed.

I remember lying in bed that night and listening to them, their frantic cluck-cluck-cluck-CLUCK-*CLUCK* rising to this *shriek* of passion, just unbelievably loud, like flocks of horny chickens had taken over the earth. Between them and my stepfather worries, I stayed up half the night, though I did finally come to some sort of peace about it, figured that Missy was right: if Uncle Gabe could be talked into doing the right thing and coming home to raise his brother's children, then I'd be cool with it, even it meant getting kicked out of Welcome, or becoming the laughingstock of Lincoln Park Middle.

Because that was the real snag, even then. I mean, it was bad enough that I was the token rich white kid in a poor black school, the only kid in class who lived in a haunted house, who could barely read. Now, chances are, I'd be the only kid in North America with a vampire for a mother and a fag for a stepfather. And boy, I knew even then that if word got out, I'd never hear the end of it.

# CHAPTER SEVEN

Now, the notion that Gabe was gay never would have come into my head unassisted, though once the possibility lodged itself there, it became as real and sure to me as the idea that Mama was a converted Baptist vampire. It just answered a lot of questions, solved the Mystery of the Missing Uncle in a most satisfactory manner, sometime right after the funeral when Gabe and his abrupt departure was still the talk of the town, everyone—Lori and Curtis, Brother Sloan, even Uncle Case—pulling me aside, asking if he'd said anything to me while he stood there in front of Daddy's coffin and stared me down.

They usually backed off at my quick shake of the head, my obvious reluctance to discuss it, though not Miss Cassie, who is just the prototype of the nosy beautician, the kind caught in a fashion time warp, still wearing stretch pants and frosted pink lipstick and eternally blond hair. Once she had you caped and imprisoned in her chair, you were at the mercy of her battery of questions that were personal and unending, mostly about Daddy and Sanger Furniture, though that day she was more keyed to family gossip, not beating around the bush with preliminaries, but going straight to the heart of the matter.

"So what's old Gabe Catts up to these days?" she asked as soon as I sat down, in this tone of great familiarity, for she had grown up at Welcome, had known Daddy before he came into any great bucks, a fact she was always bringing up, maybe to prove that their friendship wasn't mere sucking up to the rich, but old and historic.

I shrugged in reply, indicating that I didn't know Gabe or anything about him, though Miss Cassie wasn't to be drawn off the scent, Velcroing the cape at the back of my neck and regarding my head with a professional eye.

"Well, he was home for the funeral," she said, tilting my chin this way and that. "I saw him in the parking lot—didn't get a chance to speak." Then, "How short d'you want this?"

"Real short," I told her, for I was still in my Redneck Stage back then, back before the Gabe Revolution, wearing Wranglers and Ropers, keeping my hair high and tight, crew-cut if Mama would let me.

"Doing that Redneck *Thang*," Miss Cassie murmured as she rifled around her console for her electric shears, then returned to the matter at hand. "Well, he looked kind of *disoriented* to me. Was he drunk?"

I just shrugged again, offered no opinion, though there had been a certain amount of speculation among Mama's kin that he had been just that. *Knee-walking* drunk, they called him, out of earshot of Grannie, of course (who would have thrown them off the porch if she'd have heard it).

A more sensitive soul would have realized that I didn't care to discuss the matter, though Miss Cassie just plowed on ahead, plugging in her electric shears and raising her voice to be heard over the buzz: "Yeah, old Gabe—me and him go back a long way. *Too long,* if you know what I mean."

I didn't, but she didn't pause for a reply anyway, just took long, even swipes at my head with the shears, talking the whole time. "Went to school together, you know, graduated the same year. He was valedictorian and what an *idiot* speech he made. Hightailed it north first chance he got, never saw much of him after that." She finished with the shears and turned them off, added with a contemptuous snort: "Wore a *ponytail* to his daddy's funeral."

For a few minutes she busied herself shaping what was left of my sideburns, then stood back to survey her handiwork. She must have found it satisfactory, for she tossed her scissors on the console, concluded in a flat, sure voice: "Yeah, none of us ever thought he'd amount to much. Old Gabe was a big talker, but when it come right down to it, he wasn't nothing but a smart-mouthed little *faggot*—all he's ever been, you ask me."

"A *what?*" I breathed, though Miss Cassie just glanced around to make sure Mama hadn't strayed within earshot, then whipped me around to the mirror so I could check out my new hairdo.

"Too short?" she asked brightly, and I knew that was the end of it. That no matter how much of a *history* they had together, Miss Cassie wouldn't dare cross Grannie on such a thing and who could blame her?

"No ma'am," I answered, staring in the mirror at my newly shorn head, my fat little face wide-eyed and a tiny bit smug, because now it all made sense: Uncle Gabe was gay. That's why he took off north first chance he got, why he never came home. That's why Mama's old redneck uncles were so hostile about him, why she was so reluctant to discuss him. She was being discreet and protective, as was Daddy, with his careful words, his halting deathbed description ("—kind of a strange personality. Not *bad* strange, you understand. Just—*diffrent*").

I mean, I didn't really know what *gay* was back then, just that it meant he was—you know—sissy and sensitive and into garden design and *House Beautiful* and wearing clothes that matched, maybe have a lisp. I also knew that in the Baptist circles we traveled in, it was just the secretest, most shameful thing, which would explain Grannie's face that day in the kitchen when I'd first brought him up, her pensive, grieving words. ("Gabe—he knows where I live.")

So I was more smug than shocked when Miss Cassie dropped her bombshell, and long after that day, in the face of just a truckload of evidence to the contrary, my perception of Gabe was colored by this sense of his difference, of him being the unwilling bearer of a secret, painful burden, a powerful moral dilemma that was maybe beyond his power to control. Someone to be pitied, really; to be lovingly sheltered, protected from the Pharisees and the intolerant—the Miss Cassies of the world.

Which is all to explain why Missy's hints and nods went straight over my head that night in September, leaving me with more than a little trepidation on the cold December morning, not six weeks later, when Uncle Gabe did indeed return. Not with the parting of the eastern skies and the sound of the trumpet, but in the lowest key possible, just walking into my life at, of all places, the Riverside Cemetery.

It was coincidence I was even there that day, for I hardly ever visited Daddy's grave anymore. Maybe Grannie's disapproval had squelched my enthusiasm, or maybe I'd finally realized that for all the charm of the ancient cedars and the history of the old tombs, basically everyone at the Riverside was dead and there just wasn't much anyone could do about it. I mean, a few things changed over the course of the year: the Seven Sister roses Mama planted took hold and bloomed profusely, and almost every week another grave was dug somewhere down the hill, and the striped funeral-home tent was pitched and the site covered in flowers, but even that small glimmer of life didn't last long.

Soon, the tent would be struck and the flowers would wilt and the family would come and get the plastic vases and stuff them in the garbage barrels at the gate. Then a shiny new tombstone would be erected and new grass would fill in the orange dirt, and it wouldn't look much different from any of the other graves that spotted the hill, unless you knew who they were, of course. Unless you knew their stories.

Only a creature of the twilight like Mama could continue to be entertained down there, day in and day out; I only went on special occasions, for say, a holiday or an anniversary, or on that particular morning, a combination of both. For it was the Saturday before Christmas, a year to the day I'd last seen my father alive, though I didn't realize it at the time, our whole household overtaken by a sudden flurry of holiday plans, Missy leaving that morning for a four-day trip to north Georgia with the Chapins, Sim packing up his tent and sleeping bag and going on a camping trip with a group of men from Welcome. Carlym had made a point of inviting me, too, but I didn't much like the idea of camping in the cold, preferred to sleep in my own little bed and go fishing locally with Curtis, who only got off Lori's leash once a week, and had promised to pick me up at the house at ten for a quick run to the Dead Lakes.

So I wasn't particularly paralyzed by grief or anything, but percolating a little holiday high, rolling out of bed at seven and getting my fishing stuff together before I piled in the car with Mama, who stopped by Hardee's on the way to town and bought biscuits for me, coffee for herself, to wake her up, she said, which was strange, because she still slept a lot, all the time. You'd think she'd be rested by now, after a year in the sack, but she wasn't, her eyes gray-ringed and exhausted as she made her way up the winding path through the cedars, stopping at a little marble bench halfway up, letting me go the rest of the way alone like we always did. It was just too sad to go up there together and look at each other across the grave, alive and well, with Daddy there between us, not growing and never changing, his tombstone already losing its glitter, lines of weathering beginning to streak the marble, giving it a sad, forsaken look.

I never stayed long, and didn't that day, just pulled a few weeds, maybe cried a little, though not much, my mind on my fishing trip and how late it was getting; how the fish wouldn't be biting if we didn't get a move on. I finally kissed the tombstone good-bye (which is another reason I liked to go alone: I always kissed him good-bye) then headed back down the hill a little quicker than usual because it was kind of nippy that day. Not frostbitten, but clear and breezy and sharply cold, the kind of day that creeps up on you in Florida, catches you outside in your shirt-sleeves—and that's basically how I met Gabe.

He didn't walk into my life, as they say, but I walked into his, beating my way down the path in a chilled little gallop when I heard the un-mistakable sound of voices below—a woman's, which would be Mama—and a man, who for a sharp, strange moment sounded amazingly like Daddy. Just like that, I slowed my gallop instinctively and broke into the circle of cedars to find Mama sitting arm in arm with a stocky man in a big winter coat, who I recognized on sight, though he didn't seem to recognize me. Or at least his face didn't light up with welcome or anything, but was kind of blunted and grief-stricken, red-nosed and red-eyed, blinking like an owl as he came to his feet.

Mama stood, too, and introduced us with her good Louisiana manners: "Clay? Baby, this is your uncle Gabe. D'you remember him? From the funeral?"

I hastily made the adjustment when he offered his left hand for a shake, kind of speechless and weirded out, though Mama acted like it was the most normal thing in the world, coming upon a family ghost in the graveyard on a bright December morning. Once she'd made her introductions, she left almost immediately to go up to the grave, and I must say I hated to see her go, for it left me standing there at his side, racking my brain for something intelligent to say. With Missy's warning about his hand still ringing in my ears, I was trying like heck not to look at it, or seem to *want* to look at it, or get within a *mile* of it, my arms across my chest, my hands under my armpits, my eyes anyplace in the universe but his hand, which, as you can imagine, was pretty stifling as far as conversation went.

I was also flipped out by the strange and unavoidable fact that this man was gay. This was my *gay* uncle *Gabe,* though in what furtive little glances I managed to shoot at him, he didn't look particularly feminine or well dressed, everything about him dwarfed by that big gray overcoat, the same one he'd been wearing at the funeral. I'd never seen such a coat on anyone but the low-riding pimps you see on *Hill Street Blues*, and really and truly, that was my first impression of Uncle Gabe: as a con man, a pimp, a foreigner from the North and nothing remotely related to me and Mama and the Riverside, and Daddy's grave on the top of the hill.

Only in his grief did he seem connected to us at all—that and a strange, familiar fatigue about him that reminded me of Mama for some reason; had the flavor of her old vampire exhaustion. It made them seem very much akin from the beginning, Mama coming back from the grave almost immediately, looping her arm through his and smiling at him with an abandon that was rare in most people, practically nonexistent in my mother.

"Well, Gabriel?" She laughed. "What's got into you? You used to tease me all the time."

He just blew his nose on a handkerchief, muttered something about losing his sense of humor, though I didn't have a clue in the world to what they were talking about, just tagged along behind them to the car and climbed in the backseat, wishing to God that Missy was home. I was thinking that if he'd just wait around till Wednesday, then she'd be home from the mountains and could take charge of this thing, but when I finally got up the nerve to ask how long he was staying, he just glanced in the rearview mirror, said: "I don't know. Depends, I guess."

He didn't say what it depended on, and to my annoyance, Mama didn't ask, just kept chattering on about Grannie and how much she'd missed him. I didn't want to sound pushy, just nodded politely and turned back to the window, though Gabe apparently wasn't finished with me. "So where are you going fishing?" he added.

Being the youngest child in a family of talkers, I wasn't used to being plucked out for attention, didn't realize he was speaking to me at first. I kept looking out the window at the shops around the courthouse that were all decorated for Christmas, the streetlights hung with red bells, the bank festooned with garland, when I realized there was a pause in the conversation, that he was waiting on my response.

"Dead Lakes," I hastened to answer, turning and meeting his eye: "Curtis has a boat."

He didn't say anything for a moment, just met my eye evenly, much as he had at the funeral, his face absorbed and intent and strangely familiar. After a moment, he must have realized he was staring, for he dropped his eyes, murmured: "Oh, yeah, the Dead Lakes. We used to go there when we were little—me and Daddy and Michael. Had to rent a boat."

I just nodded, then returned to the window, struck by the way he said *Michael* with such close familiarity, such casual ease. To tell you the truth, I don't think I really believed Daddy even *had* a brother till that moment, then I knew it just *absolutely*—knew that they'd grown up together on the Hill, walked down to church every Sunday at Welcome, shared a bedroom, maybe as close as Missy and me.

I had never in my life thought of Daddy in such a way, was sitting there trying to fit the pieces of the puzzle together when suddenly, with no warning at all, Gabe let out this sharp little bark of laughter, then turned and faced me again, his voice no longer dim with grief, but suddenly alive.

"And one time"—he laughed—"one time when I was eight, Daddy somehow got a week off work, got it into his head that it was time we had us a vacation, like *real* Americans had, like people on TV. God, I don't know how he came up with the money, but he was set on it, took me and Michael down to the Dead Lakes and rented a cabin. Boy, we thought we were *special*."

Just like that, Daddy was conjured before my eyes as a child on the Hill: poor, but ambitious; proud in the same goofy way he was when he was grown. The very familiarity made me grin, suddenly and sincerely, which was all the encouragement Gabe needed to press ahead, his eyes alive with his story, hypnotizing in their intensity: "Trouble was, we went down there in the middle of August, hadn't ever been on a vacation before, didn't know no better, and hot? Was it hot? *Gawd,* I bet it was a hundred and three in the shade, and the mosquitoes—there were scads of them. You could hold out your arm and count fifty, but there was nothing you could do. There weren't any air conditioners—hell, I don't think the place had *screens,* just a dirt floor and a refrigerator and a sink, and something was running that week, I don't remember what. Maybe reds—"

He paused, as if it was important that he remember the *exact* name of the fish, then shook it off and returned to his story: "—anyway, we must have caught forty pounds of fish that first night, filled up the freezer, then slept all day and went out the next night and they were running again, but there was no place to put 'em. The freezer was full, and there was nobody to give them to, so we had to throw 'em back, then go back to that hot, stinking cabin and try to sleep. Well, I was already foreseeing a week of horror, but Daddy knew I was a whiner, had made me swear on a Bible I wouldn't say a word. By Tuesday, I was about to lose my mind, so was Michael. He was this skinny little runt back then, covered in spots, looked like he had the measles—"

He threw his head back and laughed at the memory, we all did, able to see him as clearly as if he was standing before us: skinny and perplexed and determined. And covered in spots.

"—but he was a fighter, Michael was, didn't say a word, kept going out there night after night, and baiting them hooks, catching them reds and tossing them back, till *finally*—it must have been Thursday morning, right in the middle of the day—we were all laid out in our underwear, trying to sleep, when Daddy suddenly sat on his pallet and looked at his arm—" Gabe paused then, laughing too hard to speak, finally wheezed: "—and I bet there were *fifty* damn mosquitoes lighting there. He just stared at them a minute, and God, his face—it was like: the Death of the American Dream. Finally, he looked up, said: 'Pack it up, boys, we're heading home.'"

We laughed all the way to the house, for it was impossible to resist the spell of one of Gabe's stories: the snapping eyes, the sharp, nutty glances aside to make sure you're following him; the bursts of hilarious, unexpected laughter when he comes upon some just-remembered absurdity, so infectious that you're laughing your butt off before he even gets to the punch line. Mama calls it his magic, his *Gabe magic,* so powerful and affecting that by the time we got to the house that morning, I was no longer conscious of his bad hand, hardly remembered he had one.

I wasn't even flipped out about him being gay anymore, or the least bit aggravated when a nail in the trailer tire ended me and Curtis's fishing trip before it had hardly begun. I was just too keyed to Mama and Gabe and wanting him to stay and worried he wouldn't, and God in heaven, I wasn't any good with this sort of thing. How and oh, how could I keep him entertained till Missy came home Wednesday night?

So I just played the part of the mature adult with Curtis, assured him it was all right that he didn't have a spare, had him drop me off at Grannie's when we got back to town, where I took her porch steps two at a time, bursting into her living room, shouting: "Grannie! *Grannie!*"

She immediately appeared at the kitchen door in her usual Saturday-morning attire: curlers and an old housecoat, a half-peeled potato in one hand and a paring knife in the other.

"Uncle Gabe's here!" I announced in a big, ringing voice. "He come back this morning! He's with Mama, I *saw* him!"

Grannie didn't so much as blink at this extraordinary news, just made a little noise of interest in her throat, then went back to the kitchen sink that was piled high with red potatoes, me following behind.

"Well, he ain't there no more," she informed me in a dry little voice as she went back to peeling her potato. "He's laid out in the front bedroom, sound asleep."

*"Here?"* I asked in the purest amazement, though Grannie just offered a little sigh.

"Yessir—come strolling up this morning like he never was gone a day. Got him a *good* job in New York teaching school, driving a *nice car*." She pointed the tip of her knife to the window, where, sure enough, a square-shaped, silvery car was parked under the sweet gum tree.

"Well, where's Mama?" I asked, hoisting myself to the counter for a better look.

Grannie didn't answer for a moment, just concentrated on her potato, then let go another sigh. "Well, they must of had a fight," she confided in a low, sorrowful voice. "She was always one to pick a fight, was Myra, with men. Got thet from her deddy. Thet *red* hair."

She said this with a regretful little shake of the head, as if it summed up the whole thing in a nutshell. I must say I was annoyed, and my face must have shown it, for when Grannie happened to glance at me, she was quick to make amends. "And Gabriel," she added, "well, he can be an aggravation, I'll grant you thet. Everbody always said I spoiled thet boy," she admitted with another shake of her head. "I'm beginning to b'lieve they'se *right*."

It was so strange, hearing her talk about him with such exasperated affection, as much a shock as it had been when Gabe said *Michael* with that casual ease, that illuminating love. I knew then why Missy was so intent on bringing Gabe home: because no matter what other strange and alien things he had become up north, he was also *family,* he was kin. But at that point, I wasn't at all sure that her fairy-tale scenario of him marrying Mama and living happily ever after would play out, neither was Grannie.

She said no more about it, but you could tell she was worried, taking to the stove and cooking like she always did, all kinds of stuff, more than Gabe could eat in a year, while I sat on the counter, shelling pecans and licking bowls and chewing my fingernails to the quick, trying to think of ways to make him stay. As the afternoon wore on, I kept thinking he'd get up, even thought up a few pleasantries to call out when he walked into the kitchen. ("So, how was your trip from New York?" or "So, what kind of car is that you drive?")

But he never got up, not even to pee, and by morning, my nerves were about shot, annoyed as heck with Mama, who hadn't so much as called or come by, though she knew Gabe was at Grannie's, I'd called her the afternoon before and asked permission to spend the night. She had let me stay, hadn't tried to talk me out of it, but had taken on this air of complete indifference, not at all interested when I went down to the church early the next morning to get my clothes and told her about Gabe sleeping straight through the morning, not waking up at all. She just sent me to the bathroom to change, her face tired, her hair kind of poofy and big, attractive if you were trying to snag a redneck, but probably not so effective on New York geniuses of the gay persuasion.

It made it awfully hard to concentrate on the sermon that morning from some missionary to the Congo who just went on *forever* about these nasty diseases they have over there—worms that would crawl up into your joints and wrap around them like a violin string, stuff like that. Grannie seemed very taken with him, though, even invited him to lunch at the Steakhouse, so that by the time we got back to her house, it was late, after two, Mama's car already in her drive, though she usually didn't pick me up on Sundays, just met me at the evening service at church. Me and Grannie didn't know what to make of it, and hurried inside to find Mama and Gabe sitting quietly at the kitchen table, him drinking coffee, her eating a slice of the Lane cake Grannie had baked the day before.

"Baby, you'll ruin your dinner," Grannie told her with this face of beaming affection, just so pleased to have them talking, though they didn't look the least bit in love, but kind of pale and nervous, Mama coming to her feet immediately, asking if they could speak to me in the living room.

Now, the last time I'd been summoned to the living room by an adult was when Brother Sloan sat me down and told me Daddy died, so I knew something big was coming down, though I didn't know exactly what. I just followed Mama to Grannie's tiny living room that was kind of crowded that time of year, with dangling tinsel and two different manger scenes and a big old Christmas tree that took up half the room. Mama sat next to me on the couch, though Gabe was too nervous to sit still, just leaned against the mantel in the same rumpled shirt and pants he'd worn the day before, his light hair tousled and upended where he kept taking swipes at it with his good hand in this crazy, agitated way.

Mama was a lot calmer, taking my hand like a palm reader and launching into this formal speech about how much she loved me and how that life sometimes took unexpected twists and if I didn't like the way those twists were leading, I could say so without fear of *offending* anyone. I, of course, didn't know what the *heck* she was leading up to, was kind of afraid she was outing Gabe, to tell you the truth, thought she was about to say: *And now that your father is gone, his brother will be your guardian, and Clay, he is gay and we must accept it, blah, blah,* and if she did, I was going to just drop dead of embarrassment for me and Gabe, both.

I mean, I had accepted him for what he was, I just couldn't believe that Mama, in all her old vampire inhumanness, didn't understand that these situations called for tact and discretion and not this let-it-all-hang-out Oprah crap. I was steeling myself against it, hoping Grannie would figure out what Mama was up to and run in and save us, when I realized Mama had spoken those old familiar words "—getting married."

*"What?"* I blurted out, though before she could answer, Gabe straightened up and took a step forward, recapped her rambling explanation with a halting summation of his own: "We're just thinking of getting married, Clay. But your mother, she wants it to be cool with you and Simon and Missy. And if you don't think it's cool, then that'll be, cool, with us."

I'd kind of gotten lost in all his *cools* and just stared at him a moment, then realized the deal here: that he was asking for Mama's hand in marriage, like I was her father or something. I didn't quite get it and just looked back and forth between them, waiting for the other shoe to drop: the confession about Uncle Gabe; the plea for mercy, for understanding. When it didn't come, I finally just shrugged or something to give my assent, said the first thing that came to mind: "Mama's last name will still be Catts."

At that, Gabe's face just magically cleared and he laughed his big Gabe laugh, that was, like I say, infectious, bringing Grannie from the dining room in a storm of tears and congratulations and hugging, Mama's red hair no longer the irritant it had been, Grannie kissing it and her both. I just sat there on the couch, feeling somehow responsible for it all, and happily so, proud that I, Clayton Michael Catts, alone and unaided, had snagged the choicest stepfather of them all; the closest thing to Daddy that we'd ever come upon on this old earth: same name, same voice, same mother. *Perfect.*

# CHAPTER EIGHT

Once the big announcement was made public, I thought we'd enter into a week of wedding festivities—you know, bridal showers and trips to the mall to buy lingerie and a wedding dress and maybe new suits for me and Sim. But to mine and Grannie's great annoyance, Mama refused to do anything further till she'd talked it over with her remaining children, and though Missy was easy enough to find (and positively ecstatic about the whole thing), Simon was camping down in the wilds of St. Joseph's, and simply unreachable till Friday night. So everything was put on hold till he could be located, and in the meanwhile, Mama wouldn't do anything you'd expect an engaged woman to do: dress up when she went to town or ask Gabe over to supper or buy so much as a ring or a veil. Mostly, she spent the week laid up in bed in her oldest, rattiest gown, staring at the ceiling, and if you so much as hinted that maybe it was time for a soak in the old tub or a trip to Miss Cassie's for a haircut, she'd bite your head off or go off on a long, tearful tangent about the importance of making the right choices and knowing your own mind and how she never had.

Over at Grannie's, Gabe wasn't much better, still stalking around in the clothes he'd drove down from New York in that were about as wrinkled as Mama's old gown. Grannie kept at him to let her wash them or run up to Dothan and buy something new, but he shrugged her off, spent most of his time on the phone to New York trying to get his life in order over long distance, or walking down to McDonald's, where he took up his morning residence at a booth in the back, reading the paper and drinking cup after cup of coffee, or sitting stock-still, staring into space like an inmate on death row waiting for the governor's call.

It sure didn't make for the most romantic engagement of the decade, the only really happy note on Wednesday night when Missy finally came home from Georgia, bursting out of the Chapins' Explorer and tearing up Grannie's steps to embrace Gabe with this enviable ease, shouting: "*Yes! Yes!* I knew it! It's fate!"

That left Sim as the final holdout, and a source of considerable anxiety to me and Missy till he finally made his way home on Friday in the middle of a freezing December night, hoarse from camping in the cold. I guess Daddy had prepared him for the eventuality of Gabe's return, for he didn't so much as blink at the big news that me and Missy shouted down the stairs the moment he walked in: "Uncle Gabe's here! They're gitting married, him and Mama, they really are!"

He just dropped his duffel bag in the hallway and hugged Mama, told her congratulations in this creaky little voice, then went over to Grannie's bright and early the next morning and shook Gabe's hand like a grown man. "I remember you," he told him in a rasping little whisper. "You taught me to swan-dive," filling me with this sharp jab of jealousy that I didn't have some communal bit of history to share with him, some pleasant childhood memory.

But once that hurdle was cleared, the wedding plans fell into place with amazing speed, the date set for the very next afternoon at Welcome, not in the sanctuary where everyone else got married, but in Brother Sloan's office, kind of plain and boring to my way of thinking and just another way I thought Mama was letting down the team. I mean, even after Lori and Aunt Candace talked her into going on a honeymoon, her plan to run down to Panama City for a couple of days just galled me because Mama is too white to be a real beachgoer and just refuses to do anything fun, won't even go on the roller coaster at the Miracle Strip. ("Not without a sports bra," she used to say.)

I just couldn't see the point of trekking down there in the dead of winter with nothing to do, was sure that she was getting her wifely duties off on exactly the wrong foot and Gabe would be bored to death.

"Why doan yawl go up to Calloway Gardens?" I suggested to her; then, from a faint memory of an old dream, "Or fishing on Eufaula?"

But no, Panama City it was, much to my disgust, and when I went to Missy to beg her to persuade Mama to go *anywhere* else, she just laughed. "Oh, I'm sure they'll find *something* to do down there. It is a *honeymoon,* you know."

Well, sure I knew it was a honeymoon; I just didn't think Mama could pull it off, and spent the day of the wedding compensating where I could, getting dressed an hour early and going down to the church to help Missy decorate Gabe's car with balloons and shaving cream. As five o'clock approached, I got too impatient to hang around back and went around to the front of the church to wait for Mama there, kind of afraid that she wouldn't show up, to tell you the truth. No one was there yet, so I just took a seat on one of the big old cement pillars by the front steps and waited *forever,* getting madder by the minute because Mama was late and Grannie had insisted I wear the same dress pants I'd worn to Daddy's funeral that were a year old now, and so short in the legs they made me look like Jethro Bodeen.

I sat there on that pillar for what seemed like an hour, till *finally,* at like, one second till five, the Mercedes pulled up and Mama and Simon got out, Mama wearing, of all things, a navy-blue *pants suit*. I had never in my life heard of a bride wearing such a thing to a wedding, felt like standing up and pointing to the car, saying: *Young lady, just turn around and go back to the house this instant, put on a nice dress.*

I couldn't help but think that Gabe would be mighty disappointed, and indeed, he didn't look too enthused with the job, but still kind of pale and nervous as we all gathered in Brother Sloan's tiny office and he took his place next to Mama in front of the desk, repeating his vows in this flat, mechanical monotone. Brother Sloan had been unexpectedly felled with the flu that morning, so Carlym had to do the honors with none of the old man's style or humor, just rattling through the service with absolutely no emotion, coming to the end abruptly and slapping shut his book, pronouncing them man and wife.

He paused then, waiting for the official kiss, though Gabe just reached across the desk and offered him his hand like he was concluding the end of a business deal or something. Carlym looked kind of surprised, though Mama didn't seem to notice the omission, and I guess they would have packed it in right then, left without a kiss, if not for Missy, who prodded her on the shoulder, said: "Gosh, Mama, aren't you gonna kiss your groom?"

Mama just blinked at her a moment, as if she didn't understand the request, then said, "Oh," and turned back to Gabe, who obediently dipped his head and kissed her lightly on the mouth, a kiss I couldn't quite figure at the time. I mean, it wasn't one of those awful *tonsillectomies* some people do at weddings these days, but they didn't part right away, either, connecting for a moment with a poignancy that *did* something to me, hit me in the belly with this unexpected *flip* of reaction, so real that I actually glanced around the room, wanted to ask someone: *What was* that? *Did you see* that?

But no one else seemed to have caught it, the ceremony ending in a flurry of handshakes and backslaps and hugging, the whole wedding party moving down the hall to the church steps, where Mama said her good-byes, told us to behave for Aunt Candace, for me and Missy not to bicker. Then she kissed us in our turn and left with Gabe, Aunt Candace watching them leave with a face of wry amusement, commenting after a moment in a dry little voice: "So Peter Pan ended up marrying Wendy after all. I always wondered."

Everyone laughed (except Grannie, who told her to hush), though

I didn't get it, of course, just stood there on the bottom step, staring after the car, when Missy added in this teasing little voice: "Clay's all worried about 'em going to the beach. Thinks Gabe'll be *bored,* won't have anything to *do.*"

There was even more laughter at that, though I didn't pay them any mind, just kept standing there on the bottom step, still in the tail end of the shock from that kiss, still muttering in this pained little undertone: "What the *heck* was *that?*"

It was a riddle that wouldn't be answered for many months, one I wasn't particularly worried with solving at the time, too enamoured with Gabe myself, and still pretty much convinced that this was a marriage of convenience, the kind they used to make movies about in the old days. You know, starring someone like Katharine Hepburn and Spencer Tracy as this odd, impossible couple who started out as strangers at first, maybe for the sake of an adorable child (say, Shirley Temple), then after some tragedy or setback, wake up one morning and find themselves in love.

At least that's what I *hoped* would happen, and more than hoped: worked hard to bring about, me and Missy both did, spending the weekend of their honeymoon sitting around Aunt Candace's kitchen table, eating Christmas fudge and discussing ways to make Uncle Gabe happy as a clam in his new role as stepfather. Simon sometimes joined us, but he was a senior that year, already working part-time at Sanger in his one year's apprenticeship with Sam McRae before he went to FSU for a degree in business, a plan he'd made long ago with Daddy's blessing.

So he wasn't as worried with our domestic arrangements as me and especially Missy, who talked Aunt Candace into taking us home early on Christmas Eve so we could prepare the house for the newlyweds' triumphant return, though we got in a fight the moment Aunt Candace dropped us off over who had to clean the pool. After a lot of shouts and threats and name-calling, she finally agreed to do the outside stuff, left the house to me, and I must say I did a decent job, even dust-mopped all the wood floors with Liquid Gold so that we were slipping and sliding around for weeks to come.

When everything was finally in place, I even brought in camellias for the table, for they were the only flowers blooming that time of year and easy to arrange. It must have been somewhere in the back of my mind that some-one with Gabe's proclivities would appreciate fresh flowers, and he did seem mighty impressed when they came in that night, actually halting just inside the French door, taking in the blinking Christmas tree, the flowers, and the shining floors with a face of true wonder. "This is the most beautiful house in Florida," he proclaimed after a moment in a small, sincere voice.

"The pool is *marble*," I heard myself bragging like a big old goober, I couldn't help it.

It was just so important for me to impress him, to keep the good times rolling. Indeed, he looked considerably more relaxed than he had stalking around Grannie's all week, still in khaki pants and a rumpled but-ton-down shirt (his *uniform,* Mama called it), though his hair was less in-sane, flatter and more subdued. Mama herself seemed little changed, maybe not as tense and snappy, but still preoccupied and worried, kiss-ing me and Missy in turn and looking at us eye to eye, asking when Sim was due home (he was hosting the company Christmas party in Way-cross); if we'd behaved ourselves; if we'd had fun at Aunt Candace's.

"Except that we've been starved," Missy told her, and she wasn't ly-ing, either.

For Aunt Candace, this Queen of Family Values, doesn't cook, and I'm talking never, nothing, nil. It's always been something of a mystery to Sim and Missy and me, how a daughter of Cissie Catts could be so lacking in this respect, so different from Mama, who didn't even change clothes or put up her suitcase, just kicked off her shoes and set about making supper. It wasn't anything extravagant, just bisque from the fresh crab she'd bought at Port St. Joe on the way home, though to hear Gabe talk, you'd have thought she was creating a feast of exotic proportions.

"Where'd you learn to make *bisque?*" he asked as he followed her around the kitchen, watching her prepare the iron pan and melt the butter for the roux.

"In Louisiana," Mama answered in a distracted little voice, her eyes on the pan that she shook with a practiced hand, "when I was about three. Go put up the suitcases," she told him. "I cain't talk, it'll burn."

After a little more shooing, Gabe left the kitchen, though he seemed uneasy when he wasn't with Mama, wandering around downstairs with his hands in his pockets, checking out the pictures in the hallway, the bow windows in the parlor (the ones that used to be part of the church). He kind of reminded me of Kenneth, the first day he came over as a child, struck silent by the opulence of it all, finally making his way up the stairs with me tagging along to help, lugging the garment bag he'd had sent down from New York that was tagged with all these strange names: Logan and LaGuardia, places I'd never heard of.

He was telling me about them as we went down the hall, how they were airports in New York and Boston and what a pain it was to get in and out of either of them, when we got to Mama's bedroom and he came to another of his dead halts. He didn't say anything, just stood there in the doorway, looking around at the room in silence: the shining floor, the carved vanity and ornate bed, the tarnished-brass ceiling fan that stirred a lazy breeze year-round.

"New bed," he finally observed, dropping his bags at the door and hesitantly strolling in with an air of quiet curiosity, like a tourist in a museum, pausing by the vanity to pick up a silver brush, then an oval perfume bottle that he read with a little grunt of recognition.

"Obsession," he murmured. "How *appropriate.*"

He didn't elaborate, just carefully returned it to the vanity top, then wandered over to the bed and sat down with a little *poof* on the feather mattress and gave it a little jiggle. "What *is* this?" he asked. "A *feather* mattress?"

"Feather on top," I told him, inching closer to the bed. "A regular mattress underneath, for Daddy's back. It cost a lot, like a *thousand* dollars," I added, though Uncle Gabe didn't look too disgusted with my unashamed bragging. He just gave another of his little Daddy-grunts of interest, then fell back on the bed, not saying anything else, just lying there rubbing his eyes, quiet so long I finally asked: "Are you all right?" making him blink back to life.

"Oh. Sorry," he answered, sitting up a little and sending me a wan smile. "I'm fine. Kind of bowled over here. It's been so long, I'd forgotten—"

But he let the sentence hang, didn't say what he'd forgotten, just tucked his hands under his head and began in a brisker, more conversational voice: "This house is incredible. Who did the yard?"

"Mama," I answered shyly, taking a seat on the foot of the bed. "She did it all. She works on it all the time. It's like her *kingdom*."

He glanced up at the word with a look I would come to know well over the next few months, his old teacher's look of approbation, of hearing an answer he liked. "That's a very astute observation, Clayton," he told me. "That's *exactly* what this place is: Myra's kingdom. *Huh*. Thirty-seven years and she's finally got to be queen of *something*."

He shook his head at that, then announced in another conversation leap: "Well, it's stunning, I must say. Kind of hard to take in, that it's my new home. I mean, it's not like I've *earned* it or anything—though I haven't lived a totally morally bankrupt life, you know. I mean, I've given to United Way, four dollars a paycheck, rain or shine. And I've gone to church, every Easter and Ash Wednesdays, too, and Christmas, even if it was just Mass. And given money and never a voice of criticism have I raised, even in Indiana, where the priest was queer as a three-dollar bill."

I was a little shocked at the casual way he said *queer*, wondered if we were on the brink of a little confession here, though he just rolled right along in that same level voice: "But I never raised a stink, never—you know—refused to shake a hand. Had many friends, never a racist joke have I spoken, quit saying *nigger* the moment I stepped off the Hill. And never took a job just for the money and never ducked a bar tab or dodged a bet—which is, you know, saying a lot these days."

Indeed, he was looking more pleased by the moment, no longer so intimidated by Mama's feathers and drapes, his face amused and a tiny bit mocking, not at them or me, but at his own conceit as he concluded in that same self-congratulatory voice: "All and all, I've been a good boy. The Lord has been pleased. I mean, *obviously* pleased. I mean, face it, Clay: I've been His favorite all along—*who knew?*"

I just nodded politely, not really *getting* Gabe back then, but still captivated enough to pretend I did, having no inkling that this was just the first of a hundred such conversations—or not conversations, really. More like one-sided streams of consciousness, with him doing the pondering, me acting as the concrete wall he bounced his thoughts off.

"So, what would you call this *style* your mother has so skillfully adapted to her little *kingdom?*" he asked in another of his abrupt conversational leaps, lifting a hand to indicate the draped tulle and tassels, the drooping peacock feathers, the low hum of the old ceiling fan. I just shrugged, for I had no earthly idea what he was talking about, though he didn't seem to mind my silence, just rolled along with that same easy pitch: "What? *Florida Gothic? Plantation Gothic?* Or, no—I know: *Storyville Gothic.*"

He intoned the phrase with deep satisfaction, repeated, "That's it exactly: *Storyville Gothic Splendor.* That's what the feather bed and tulle and the *bisque* is all about."

The potency of this bizarre revelation seemed to just stun him, for he didn't say anything else for a long time, just lay there in silence till Mama called us down to a Christmas Eve supper that was relatively simple, just the bisque and little cheese biscuits she makes by adding cheddar cheese and cayenne pepper to Grannie's old buttermilk-and-Crisco recipe. The beauty of them is that they are so small that you can eat two dozen without anyone counting or raising an eyebrow (at least not at

Mama's table). Sim got there before I could work my way up to an even dozen, and ate his fair share, and once supper was done, we all went to the living room to pick out our early present, a family tradition around the Catts house: on Christmas Eve you can only unwrap one present, leave the rest for the morning.

This was always a tricky business, as you would sometimes pick one that would turn out to be a disappointment, like shoes or underwear, and then you'd have to whine and cry and beg to open more and more till the tree was almost empty. Daddy was usually the holdout who made us save a few for Christmas morning, though Gabe didn't seem to mind, just sat there on the couch eating divinity, urging us on, telling Mama, "Oh, Myra, who cares, let's get the stuff from the car. We all may die in our sleep tonight. Eat, drink, and be merry, I always say."

Mama didn't need any more prodding than that, as she is the world's worst about keeping presents, and before long, the living room was strewn with makeup and a new CD player and a mountain of clothes for Missy, and Legos and a skateboard and a real .22 for me, plus a lot of boring grown-up stuff for Sim, like clothes and cologne and new mats for his truck. The only real toy he got was a shared present for all of us, a Nintendo set and the original Mario Brothers game that we played till midnight, me and Missy and Sim and Gabe, while Mama retired to the kitchen to work on her share of the food for the family feast at Grannie's the next day.

Back then, Nintendo was just the coolest thing around, positively addicting, and me and Sim and Missy laughed our butts off when Gabe had the controls because he kept making Mario fall through the same little crack, time after time, to bursts of just *awful* profanity that finally brought Mama from the kitchen to stand in the door and ask: "Gabriel? Did I hear you say what I *think* I heard you say?"

It was so funny because that doofus Gabe just didn't get it. I mean, he didn't apologize or anything, just jumped up and pointed at the TV, said, "Myra, this game is f—ed. I was pushing the button and he didn't jump. He jumps for Missy—"

Which doesn't sound as hilarious as it was at the time; we were just so relieved to find that Gabe wasn't some sly impostor who'd sneaked in and married Mama for her money, but a real Catts, who hated to lose. And anyway, it wasn't like we'd never heard profanity before, though Daddy just used the old hick standards, and there at first, Gabe didn't use anything but the f-word, and that casually and continually. He'd positively *shout* it when Mario would leap into the abyss, at least till Mama marched him off to the kitchen and gave him his little spanking, when he returned, chastised and sad, and apologized for using *that* word.

But aside from that, the only other hint of the great Catts Wars to come was a little later upstairs after Missy and Sim went to bed, when I'd gone in to try and talk my way into Mama's bed (being twelve at the time, and not such a bright twelve at that). They still had the light on and didn't shoo me out immediately, but let me lie there on the edge of the bed and talk about Christmas and how Gabe was going to finally get to see Ryan the next day at Grannie's.

At some point, lying there talking, I remember Gabe complimenting Mama on the house and its remarkable style, though he couldn't seem to recall the name he'd come up with earlier in the evening that I fortunately remembered.

"Storyville Gothic," I told him, though as soon as I said it, I wished I hadn't. For he immediately tensed, glancing aside at Mama, who just lay there between us, staring thoughtfully at the ceiling.

"Storyville Gothic," she murmured. "What *is* Storyville? I've heard that name somewhere, I can't remember where——"

"Not Story*ville*," he corrected in a quick, casual little jump. "Sto-ry*time*. *Storytime Gothic*——you know——like Hansel and Gretel or Flannery O'Connor. Depraved, but——innocent."

I didn't say a word, though I knew he was lying and he knew it, too, casting me this guilty little glance over Mama, who didn't catch it, just yawned, "Why *Gothic*? I've never understood the term *Southern Gothic*."

Well, that's all the opening Gabe ever needed to launch into an involved treatise about God-knows-what—repression and moral decay and William Faulkner, and God knows what else, for I was getting mighty sleepy before it was over, full of all those biscuits, finally just fell dead asleep.

When I came to, I was lying in my own bed, awakened by Gabe, who had apparently just laid me down, and was tiptoeing toward the door.

"Gabe?" I whispered, making him turn in the half-light, dressed in some shiny, familiar pajamas that I recognized with a little jolt were Daddy's hospital pajamas.

"Those are Daddy's," I said without thinking, though he just glanced down at them, gave one of his Daddy-grunts.

"So I figured. The only ones your mother could find and *God forbid* that I should walk around unclothed in my own house—or my brother's house—" he corrected, though he didn't pursue it. He just came a little closer to the bed, close enough I could make out his face in the half-light. "Listen, Clay," he said, "I want to apologize for that little lie I slid past your mother in there."

"That's all right." I yawned, as we in the Catts household intimately understood the truth of the saying *What Mama don't know won't hurt her.*

My eyes had adjusted to the light by then, and I could see him clearly now, standing a few feet away, his hair upended as usual, his hands shoved deep in the pockets of the robe. "Well, I just wanted to—you know—assure you, that I'm not a pathological liar or anything. I won't make a habit of it. 'Kay?"

"Sure," I said, kind of amazed at all this explaining, though it did give me the opportunity to apologize for Mama in a sly way; to let him know I was on his side.

"I hope, this, marriage and all, works out," I told him, and he seemed amazed in his own turn by my sincerity, standing there in the half-light like he was very moved by it.

"Well, that's very kind of you, Clay," he said in this level, honest voice. "You have your mother's kindness, you know that? You remind me of her, when she was a little girl."

It was funny how he said it, talking about Mama being little in a way that no one ever did, the same way he'd talked about Daddy the week before. It woke me up a little, made me seem kind of close to him, close enough to ask: "What was she like?"

"Your mother?" he asked, and at the quick nod of my head, he stood there a moment with his hands in his pockets, rocking lightly on his feet as if thinking of the right answer. "Well, she was quiet, and kind, and loyal to a fault—and very, very beautiful, just stunning. All of us little snots on the Hill were stone in love with her, to a man."

"Was Daddy?" I grinned, and the question seemed to break his reverie, bring him back to the present with a little jolt.

"No," he murmured, "no, Michael—he was older. Six years older than me. He was already working at the mill by then. He was already gone."

The invisible door he'd opened between us seemed to close at that, but I wasn't quite ready to let him go, sat up even straighter and asked the only other question that came to mind: "Well, what's Storyville?"

*"What?"* he said quickly in a manner which I would later recognize as a sly little maneuver on his part: asking you to repeat yourself to provide him with a few more seconds of thinking and excusing time.

"Storyville," I repeated carefully. *"Storyville Gothic Splendor."*

"Good *God,*" he murmured, then shot me this pained little look in the half-light. "You really wanta know?"

Well, I certainly did now and nodded quickly, making him sigh again, hugely, then explain: "Well, Storyville was the name of a famous—infamous—red-light district, in New Orleans, at the turn of the century."

"A *what?*"

"A—how-would-you-say-it? A district frequented by, ah—prostitutes."

*"Oh,"* I said, as it was suddenly perfectly clear.

Gabe lifted a finger to his lips. "Tell no one," he said. "Especially your mother."

This seemed like a perfectly reasonable request and I nodded again, a little too eagerly, I guess, as he paused a moment to clarify his instructions. "Well, I wouldn't be so quick about—you know—keeping things from your mother. I mean, you hardly know me. I might be this raging *pedophile* for all you know."

I didn't know what a pedophile was, so I just nodded again, though he seemed satisfied and started to the door, when I interrupted one more time. "Well, what's *Gothic*?" I asked, then added quickly, so not to hurt his feelings, "I just fell asleep when you were explaining to Mama. Just tell it shorter this time. I don't pick up things real quick like Simon and Missy. I'm kind of—slow."

He looked at me with even more interest then. "You mean the dyslexia?" he asked.

That's exactly what I meant, though I was shocked he even knew I had it. I mean, it wasn't something we went shouting from the rooftops, that I was dumb as a post, even if that dumbness had a fancy neurological name: *Primary Moderate Dyslexia*. But there was nothing accusing about him when he asked, no hint of condescension, so I nodded quickly, my assent making him stand there a moment, no longer afraid of Mama, but all teacher now, rocking back and forth on his toes, trying to think of a good answer.

"Gothic, Gothic," he murmured, then finally inhaled this great breath, said: "Well, Clay, the *clearest* illustration that comes just *immediately* to mind is standing right here before you: a thirty-eight-year-old man creeping around his late brother's sagging old mansion in a pair of satin pajamas, trying to convince his Baptist widow that the tulle and tassels she's draped around her feather bed looks like something out of 'Hansel and Gretel,' because if she finds out he compared it to a whorehouse, she won't let him sleep with her tonight. *That,* son," he concluded with a sly little smile, "is *Storyville Gothic Splendor*."

I nodded as if I'd understood every word, and he lifted his finger to his lips again, repeated: "Tell no one." Then, in a final aside: "And listen, Clay, don't worry about the dyslexia. I'm ordering your records Monday from the school board, see what I can do about getting you punted from that piece-of-shit Varying Exceptionalities portable to the Gifted class where you belong. 'Kay?"

I just stared at that, wondered how the heck he even *knew* about the special-ed portable at Lincoln Park, and furthermore, how in God's name did he ever in a million years think a doofus like me would ever be placed with Kenneth and the other Masters of the Universe in the *Gifted* program inside?

He must have seen the doubt on my face, for he met my eye, told me in this solemn, righteous little voice: "Clay, just because you're a right-brain thinker doesn't mean you're slow, or *stupid*. It just means you're *different,* and there's nothing wrong with being different," he assured me with a level eye that I took to be an unspoken acknowledgment of his own strange differences. "Different is a welcome change of pace. Different is *good*."

He turned to leave on that strange, dramatic note, though one last point must have occurred to him, for he paused at the door, his finger raised like a wise old prophet. "Albert Einstein," he informed me gravely, "was dyslexic."

Now, I didn't know Albert Einstein from Adam's house cat back then, but such was the ringing authority in his voice that I nodded again, said something like "Cool," then let him go without argument, just lay there in the darkness of a cold Christmas morning without an inkling in the world that a very important threshold had just been crossed in my life. That I had just heard the opening volley of what Missy would later call *The Gabe Revolution*.

# CHAPTER NINE

Missy used the term to describe the wild and nutty way he swept into Lincoln Park, upending the history department and pretty much transforming the whole school, a revolution that never would have come about if me and Kenneth hadn't have been lazing around the school office that day Mr. Nair got in his wreck; if we hadn't jumped at the chance to get Gabe a job and save his marriage.

Because the fact of the matter is, there at first, Gabe's position as resident stepfather was on mighty shaky ground, no one taking any bets he'd last through the holidays, much less till spring. He and Mama just got into too many fights, most of them connected to the godless Yankee ways he'd picked up in New York that Mama was just frantically afraid he'd contaminate her children with, like a bad case of smallpox, leaving us morally pockmarked, scarred for life.

The early signs of trouble were on Christmas Eve, with the f-word, and the Storyville thing, though the real battle lines were drawn that first Sunday when Gabe wouldn't go to church with the rest of us, but stayed home to work on his *magnum opus,* he called it, the book on the Civil War he'd left upstairs in the old apartment a dozen years before. I never even knew it was up there, seldom visited the creaking old rooms above the garage that we'd never used for anything but storage, a final resting place for spare plywood and pool supplies and broken lamps, the only sign of life a teeming colony of banana spiders who'd draped the walls and windows in ghostly webs.

By their handiwork, it looked more like a suite in the Haunted Mansion at Disney World than a servants' quarters (which is what it was in Old Man Thurmon's day), though Gabe seemed fascinated by the place from the very beginning. On his first Saturday home, he offered me and Kenneth the princely sum of twenty dollars apiece to help him clean it out, hauling load after load of junk to the garage below, till we finally unearthed the nasty old furniture that was buried beneath the rubble: a rickety old desk and chair, and in the corner under the window, a narrow, lumpy little bed.

"My God," he muttered when we found it. "I can't believe it. I'm damned if this isn't the same *spread*."

"Well, no one comes up here very much," I said by way of apology, though he just peeled back the nubby spread that was perfectly gray with dust and peered at the underside like an archaeologist opening a tomb.

"By God, it *is* the same spread," he murmured, then lifted his face and gazed around the dirty, cobwebby room in wonder. "*Jeez*, that's weird. I can't believe my maps are still up—it's like time travel."

Me and Kenneth just looked around at the faded old maps that covered the walls like peeling, cracked wallpaper, always had, for as long as I could remember.

"How long have they been here?" Kenneth asked, as they looked ancient, antebellum, at least, though Gabe said they weren't that old, but the same age as me.

"That's right," I said, suddenly remembering what Simon had told me the weekend of Lori's wedding, "you put them up the summer you lived here. You wrote a book. You taught Sim to swan dive."

"Who told you *that*?" Gabe asked with a quick, curious look.

"Sim," I answered slowly, smoothing back one of the old maps that had curled in on itself. "A long time ago." Then, of the maps, "Why didn't you take 'em with you?"

But Gabe didn't answer right away, just stood there looking around the room, his hands in his pockets, absently chewing his lip.

"Well, I left in kind of a hurry," he finally said, then strolled along the wall and told us the names of all the battles: Gettysburg and Sharpsburg, Chancellorsville, the Western Theater, occasionally adding a further bit of comment ("Where Jackson was shot by friendly fire," or "Where Pickett got that ass whipped"), speaking of them with a familiar affection, as if they were old friends.

Long after me and Kenneth had gone downstairs to supper, he stayed up there cleaning and rearranging, still at it the next morning when Mama sent me up to get him for church. It was late by then, after nine, Sim and Missy already gone, though when I got to the apartment, I found Gabe still in his pajamas, posed in front of one of the maps, thumbtack in hand.

He smiled when he saw me, called good morning, though I just tipped my head to the house. "Mama says to come on," I told him. "We're all ready."

But Gabe didn't seem to get it. He just stared at me blankly a moment, finally said: "I'm not going, son."

I was the one left staring then, because around our house, church attendance was mandatory, no options, no excuses. Saying you had decided not to attend was like saying you'd decided to quit brushing your teeth. I didn't quite know what to make of it, finally just asked the first thing that came to mind: "Are you saved?"

I don't even know why I asked; I guess I was still trying to identify him; pinpoint exactly *what* he was, though Gabe is constitutionally unable to answer a question in a straightforward manner (worse than Mama, even) and took a seat on the edge of the desk, told me in this weary, patient voice: "Clay, listen: I'm saved, sanctified, Holy Ghost–filled, water-baptized, grew up at Welcome, went to church three times a week the first eighteen years of my life. I know every verse of 'Amazing Grace' by heart and more of the King James Version of the Bible than Jerry Falwell. It's just that Sundays are the only time I have to work on my book. Tomorrow I take my place as, you know, chairman of the board at Sanger, and my book has been lying up here gathering dust for ten years. It's time I got snapping, worked it out—you understand?"

Now, if there was anything I understood intimately at that point in my life, it was a father figure who worked 'round the clock, pursued by the demon of ambition every waking hour. So I just nodded, said something like, "Oh," then trudged downstairs to Mama, who was waiting at the door.

"He ain't coming," I told her. Then, at the furrow that appeared like magic between her eyes: "He's already saved."

Mama, who'd fought the War of Ambition with Daddy for twenty years, didn't look too convinced, just snatched up her purse, muttered: "I wouldn't be so sure of *thet*."

Well, poor Gabe; I knew he was in for it then, because when Mama lapses into her old hick accent, *watch out*. But Sunday was still my day with Grannie, so I really didn't give it much thought, at least not till sometime later, in the middle of the night, when I was awakened by the quiet tread of feet on the creaking old floors of the hallway. I was immediately awake, always on the alert for any phantom slaves that might be lurking about, though the ghostly figure that came through my door didn't confront me with a message from beyond the grave, but just dissolved into the darkness of the bottom bunk.

For a moment, I just lay there, then carefully peered over the edge of the bed, was relieved to see that it was just Gabe. He was hardly visible in the winter darkness, identified only by the dull sheen of his pajamas and the outline of his jaw that was clenched just like I clench mine when I get mad. (Daddy used to call it "jacking that jaw," as in: "Don't you be *jacking* that *jaw* at me, young man.")

For a moment, I just hung over him like a bat, then whispered: "Gabe?"

"Yeah?" he answered in this tired, whipped voice, and just that quickly, I knew what was up: that Mama had waited till they were in the privacy of their bedroom before she gave him his spanking, and *dang*, I was embarrassed, thinking she was getting as bad as Lori, who was as sweet and agreeable a little reneckling as ever decorated the passenger seat of a truck, at least till the moment she got that ring on her finger. After that, Curtis couldn't so much as *fart* without her being on him like white on rice, about taking too many days off work, and not making enough money, and not getting home on time.

I didn't know what to say; finally settled on the obvious: "You and Mama have a fight?"

"Yeah," he repeated with a sigh. "You heard?"

"No," I said, returning to my bunk and speaking into the darkness. "Daddy used to sleep in here when they'd fight."

"Did he really?" he asked with a little more interest.

"Yeah." I yawned. "But he never made it till morning. Bed'd be empty when I woke up."

He grunted at that, a grunt I couldn't read very well, not having been around him too much. It might have been a grunt of interest, or disgust, or maybe tired resignation. I was lying there trying to identify it when he spoke again in this casual, conversational voice: "So, d'you like Rocky?"

There was no one else in the room, so I figured he was speaking to me, though I didn't have a clue in the world what he was talking about. I was thinking about this kid at school named Rocky Smith who I'd known in, like, the fourth grade, was wondering how Gabe would know him, when I realized he was referring to a movie poster of Rambo that I had pinned to the wall above my dresser.

"You mean Rambo?" I asked. "Ain't you ever heard of *Rambo*?"

"Oh, yeah," he answered easily. "Rambo. Yeah, I heard of him." He was silent again for a moment, then offered: "They made a lot of them, didn't they? Two or three?"

"Three," I told him with great authority, for I'm kind of a Vietnam expert, at least where the movies are concerned. "They're making the fourth one in Israel right now."

Gabe made another noise at that, of interest, I assume, and we talked about Vietnam for quite a while, me debating the relative merits of *Platoon* versus *Rambo, Full Metal Jacket* versus *First Blood,* which is how I knew about Vietnam, from the movies. On his part, Gabe discussed it with the same authority he'd talked about Gettysburg, till I finally couldn't keep my eyes open a moment longer, fell dead asleep.

When I woke up the next morning, the bottom bunk was empty, as predicted, though our midnight conversation had caused me to oversleep and I didn't have time to ponder it too much. I just threw on my clothes and scrambled downstairs and out the door, making the bus stop just as old Bus 96 creaked to a massive halt, Kenneth saving me a seat up front like he always did. Local gossip being what it is, a lot of people already knew that Mama had remarried, my fellow students pleasantly weirded out by the fact that my new stepfather was also my uncle, though no word of Gabe's gayness had leaked out, so no one made too much of it.

They probably just figured it was the kind of thing us Rich White Folk did, married our cousins to save on taxes or something, the day passing easily enough, with only one twist: as I walked out of seventh period, Mrs. McDonald handed me a stiff white envelope, told me to give it to my mother. Now, this kind of official notification usually didn't bode well for me and I wanted to rip it open immediately, but contained my curiosity till I was on the bus, when Kenneth (who is my official document reader) carefully opened the flap and read half a dozen legal-looking forms that were signed by all these official people.

"It's an appointment for testing," he finally offered when he made it to the last page, "on January eighth. Gosh, that's quick. It took me, like, two *years* to get tested."

"Tested for *what*?" I asked, though Kenneth just shrugged.

"Gifted, I think. Yeah, it's an IQ test, see? Mrs. McDonald must have recommended you. Cool."

I suddenly remembered Gabe at the door Christmas Eve, telling me he was taking me out of special-ed and putting me in Gifted, though I didn't believe him at the time, because even at a poor country school like

Lincoln Park, being sent out to the special-ed portable had a definite social stigma, like a tattoo on your head that read: DUMB AS A POST.

That's the local term for learning disabled, and let me tell you, I've heard it applied to me on many an occasion, and always in this shocked, incredulous voice, like: How could it be? My brother was an honors student, a four-year letterman, my sister a virtual prodigy—how could one family produce such a sad variety: an achiever and a genius, and then, well, *me*.

It was one of those unfortunate mysteries of life, first detected in kindergarten when I was still heartbroken over leaving the comfort of my sagging old house, and a little puzzled about all those letters and things they were always trying to make you memorize. I mean, I knew the "Alphabet Song" already, or at least the beginning and the end, and it wasn't till halfway through first grade that I realized that memorizing the middle part was a very big deal, indeed.

Such a deal that my failure to recite it meant that Mama and Daddy were called in for conference after conference, and flash cards were bought and many a weary evening was spent with Mama or Missy (or sometimes, Daddy or Sim) holding up letters and numbers and looking at me with these faces of sincere amazement.

"It's an *eight*, Clay, an *eight*!" Missy would positively *shout*. "Gosh, we've done it *fifty* times!"

Even Mama would look concerned when it was her time to hold the cards, even piteously beg: "Baby, just concentrate. Pay attention."

Then she'd hold up some word like BIG or AN or THE, and I'd look at it and concentrate with all my might, but nothing would ring a bell. Sometimes I'd venture a guess, and if I was right there would be universal rejoicing, but most of the time I wouldn't be, and more conferences were called and more flash cards bought, till I was finally packed off to a neurologist in Tallahassee, who gave us the word on the dyslexia.

After that, I was taken out of regular classes and placed in a special-ed classroom that housed disabilities ranging from normal-looking dumbos like myself, to kids with autism and hyperactivity and even one

(Travis Davies) with cerebral palsy. We all knew why we were there: we were the school gimps, the dumbos, the doofuses, the polar opposite of the tiny percentage of the school population that was officially designated Gifted, who wiled away their afternoons in a bright little classroom by the cafeteria, doing fun nonsensical things like playing chess and building Lego cities and studying the Life of Bach.

To even be invited for testing was a big deal, and as soon as I got off the bus that day, I ran home as fast as my little legs would carry me, wanting to discuss it with Mama, to ask how this miracle had come about, and how and oh, how could anyone expect me to pass an IQ test when I couldn't even read? I mean, I could make my way through a comic book or a *TV Guide,* but I still had a lot of errors, and as for my handwriting, it was just junk, pure and simple, just crap. I mean, it embarrassed me so much that I never wrote publicly because I wrote like a total retard, I really did.

But when I got to the house, I lost my nerve the moment I walked in the door, for Mama was hosting a bridal shower for a girl at Welcome that night, and when she is consumed with one of her creations, be it a bedroom or a bridal shower or a rose garden, she can get kind of snappy, all her creativity and attention on the matter at hand.

I didn't even tell her about the testing notice, just attached it to the refrigerator with a magnet and tried to lie low, though I was too wired to stay still, kept wandering downstairs, running into her, getting in the way. I was hoping Gabe would come in, but he was holed up in the old apartment, working on his book, I assumed. I would have liked to have gone up there and showed him the testing notice, and in a perfect world, even confessed my doubts about making the grade. But I was too embarrassed to bring it up, and had gone downstairs one last time to lay in a few supplies for the evening—cookies and mints and a cupcake or two—when I came upon Gabe standing at the counter in the kitchen, eating grapes.

He was obviously about as thrilled as me with the idea of sharing the house with a bunch of chattering women, though before I could make a comment, Mama came around the corner, all dressed and lovely, with that crazed creative gleam in her eye.

"Clayton?" she snapped. "Didn't I tell you to stay upstairs? It's seven o'clock; the ladies will be here any minute. Now, get going—"

I was making noises of excuse when Gabe straightened up and told me in this weary, fatherly voice: "Run get your coat, son. I'll take you to the movies."

I was immediately interested, though I'd already seen the movie that was playing in town *(Lethal Weapon)*; Miss Susan had taken me and Kenneth on Friday. When I told Gabe, he just popped a handful of grapes in his mouth, said, "This is different. It's about Vietnam, showing in Tallahassee. It starts at eight. We'll have to hurry."

Well, he didn't have to ask twice. I flew upstairs and got my jacket, and once we were on the interstate, cruising west at about ninety miles an hour, I got up the nerve to bring up the Gifted Program in a sly way, told him how much fun they had in there with the Legos and the Life of Bach. He was so agreeable that I even summoned up the courage to mention the testing notice, that he was very casual about, only saying, "Really? Good. I think your appointment is on the eighth."

"It is," I said, and wanted to discuss it more, though I didn't want to baldly admit that I didn't think I could read well enough to pass it, just observed that it was quick; that it'd taken Kenneth two years to get tested for Gifted.

"Dumb-asses," was Gabe's muttered reply, though I don't think he was referring to Kenneth, but maybe the school board for taking such a long time to test him.

I just agreed with a great roll of my eyes, as if this was just an evident truth we all lived with, didn't bring it up again as we got off the interstate and navigated the crappy Tallahassee traffic toward the FSU campus that is just huge, enormous, full of snaking side roads and dead ends. Fortunately, it's where Gabe got one of his degrees, so he knew his way around, took us straight to the auditorium where the movie was showing, already in progress when we sneaked in, so that it was kind of hard to follow.

After a while, I realized it wasn't actually a movie, but a documentary, the kind you see on PBS, though I was cool with that. I liked seeing the steaming jungle and helicopters; the automatic rifles and crew-cut Marines. I was casually scanning their faces, wondering if any of them might be Uncle Ira, when I realized the soldiers on the screen were like, naked, lying on the floor with these Vietnamese women who were also naked, or at least topless.

To tell you the truth, I didn't know *what* they were doing down there, at least not until Gabe inhaled sharply at my side, muttered, *"Shit,"* in this tight little voice.

Well, I knew what they were doing *then,* or at least I *thought* I knew, and must say I watched it with a great conflict of emotions, thinking on one hand: My *gosh,* that's the way sex really looks? Because it was so different from what you see in the movies, so less (how can I put this?) active and yipping, the soldiers carrying on conversations like they were having their nails clipped or something.

On the other hand, I was also kind of breathless and tingly, the way you are that first happy moment in any movie when *yes!* The woman is taking off her shirt! Though the tingles passed quickly, replaced by this growing unease, because these women weren't thin and sexy, like Molly Ringwald or Demi Moore, but plump, round-faced farm girls, smiling at the camera the whole time, trying to be agreeable to the soldiers who were just treating them like crap, making jokes about them, laughing in their faces.

I could feel my heart begin to beat hard in my chest, not the thump of desire, but anger, tears of outrage very close to the surface, though I didn't cry, of course. I didn't want Gabe to think I was a *child* or something; didn't want to spoil the fun. I just sat there and quietly sniffed as the action moved on to even sadder sights: toothless old women talking about how their villages were bombed; a family of thin, ragged children crying by an open grave, holding up a photograph of their dead father.

By then, the pressure behind my eyes was so strong it made my sinuses hurt, though I managed to stay dry-eyed to the end, even thanked Gabe for taking me when we got back to the house, then creeped upstairs to my bed like a whipped dog and lay there in silence, tearless and depressed. I guess I'd held back so long I'd clogged my tear ducts or something, because my head hurt like heck, but I couldn't let it go. I just lay there replaying little snippets of the movie in my head, the fearsome implications of Mama's reaction growing in me, knowing that if she found out, then it would be all over but the shouting for Gabe. I mean, he was already in hot water about the f-word, and missing church; what would she do if she found he'd taken me to a dirty movie?

She'd put a hatchet in his back and join Uncle Ira on death row, that's what she'd do, even I knew that, and by morning, had purposed in my heart that I wouldn't tell a soul, though God knows it wasn't easy. For Mama was a great interrogator where movies were concerned, always asking about ratings and violence and whether anybody got naked, a regular Baptist gestapo. I fielded her questions the best I could, and pretty much got away with it, though Kenneth was on to me instantly, the moment I stepped on the bus.

He must have read my face, because he kept at me all day, following me around at lunch and PE, asking if Gabe was okay, if Mama was okay, if they were still fighting, if anyone had thrown any punches yet. I denied it all, but you could tell he didn't believe a word of it, was heading straight home and calling Miss Susan at work, having her call the HRS hotline and report us all. So I finally broke down at lunch and told him about the movie and how *gross* it was, though Kenneth, he just didn't get it.

I mean, he couldn't believe that a mere *movie* could get me so upset, kept asking: "And that's all? Gabe's not, you know, making any threats? Shoving anybody around?"

I assured him he wasn't, and Kenneth seemed kind of disappointed, as was everyone else who eventually found out that week. Sim even took me out to the garage that night and gave me this stern little lecture about how it was time I quit being such a *baby* and *grew up,* all but threatened to whip me if I kept running my mouth about it.

"If Mama finds out, she will pop a *cork,*" he predicted, and made me promise on my word of honor I'd keep my mouth shut for once in my life, though by then it was too late.

For Kenneth, who had long ago heard the gay rumors about Gabe (well, from me, if you must know), had started thinking about this thing, had decided that taking a kid to a dirty movie was just the kind of decadent thing you'd expect from a fag, might just be the tip of the iceberg, if you know what I mean.

So he'd blabbed to Miss Susan, who was about as strict and Baptist as Mama these days, had started attending Welcome shortly after Daddy died, for reasons of faith, she said, and because she'd been so impressed with the way the church had stood by us during his illness and funeral. That was the official reason, though a few catty souls (that is to say: Lori and Missy) privately speculated that her sudden disillusionment with Catholicism had more to do with a secret crush on Carlym Folger than it did with the Doctrine of the Church.

But anyway, she wasted no time pulling Mama aside the next morning after church and telling her all about the movie, naked women and all. As Simon predicted, Mama did indeed pop a cork, going after Gabe right there in the church parking lot, though the shouting was over by the time I got there and I only saw the tail end of the fight: the Mercedes peeling rubber at the corner, with Gabe at the wheel, looking kind of harassed.

For some reason, we'd all come to town in one car that morning, and since Missy went home with Joanna, me and Sim were left stranded with Grannie, who didn't feel like cooking dinner with a family divorce in the works, and walked us down to McDonald's instead. It made for a sad, silent lunch, Sim so disgusted with me and my big mouth that the veins in his neck poked out, and even Grannie kind of quiet, eating her Chicken McNuggets with a far-off look on her face and many a long sigh.

The guilt of the thing was almost more than I could stand, and by the time we started back down the Hill to Grannie's, I had fallen into a haze of apathy, not caring if I lived or died. For I'd spent a whole week turning that *stupid* movie over in my head by then, had decided that Sim was right: that I really was one immortal *sissy* for letting it get to me like that. Furthermore, I had become positively convinced that I was going to make a big old ass of myself on that stupid IQ test, had decided to be sick the next week to save myself the humiliation, because Mama had been too busy haggling with Gabe to even mention the notice, had left it there on the refrigerator, unsigned, apparently unread.

So I really didn't care what anybody thought about me, just wanted to head back to Grannie's, to stake out a bed for a nap, though when we walked in her back door, we came upon Gabe sitting at the kitchen table eating leftovers.

"Where's Myra?" Grannie asked immediately, though Gabe didn't answer right away, just wiped his mouth with a napkin.

"Home," he said finally said. "Where's Missy?"

"Joanna's," Grannie told him, then sent me and Sim to the bedroom to look for clothes, Sim still cold and silent with me, as if he'd sworn an oath to never speak to me again and was living up to his word. But I was beyond caring by then, just fell back on the bed and stared at the ceiling, was wondering why anyone bothered to live, when there was a light knock at the door.

It was Gabe, of course, looking pretty whipped and bloodless in his wedding suit and undone tie. He didn't offer any excuses or explanations, just stood there in the same exact spot Daddy had once tried to clue me in on the facts of life, said: "Listen, Clay—I'm sorry I took you to that *idiotic* movie. It's been, like, a *hundred* years since I saw it. I forgot how intense it was, didn't consider that it might not be, you know, *appropriate,* for children."

Simon made a great noise of disgust at the word, was quick to reassure him: "Clay's seen naked women before," he said in this fast, macho voice, making it sound like we'd grown up backstage at a peep show.

Gabe looked a little shocked at that, paused his apology long enough to ask: "*Where?*"

"*Playboy,* HBO," Sim countered with this proud, defiant face, like no one could accuse *him* of unnatural vices, not old Simon Catts.

I myself couldn't have cared less, just lay there with my eyes on Grannie's old bead-board ceiling, still trying in vain to make someone understand.

"You didn't see it, Sim," I told him. "They weren't just naked. They were just so pathetic. Those soldiers were being so nasty to them, pinching their titties and making fun of them and all they did was sit there and smile. It make me want to puke."

Sim rolled his eyes at that, afraid Gabe was going to invite us to one of his gay-rights meetings, I shouldn't think, though Gabe seemed to get my drift, his face no longer so whipped and apologetic. "That's right, Clay," he said with a sudden return of his old passion. "See, *Hearts and Minds* was virulently anti-interventionist. It purposely showed the pathos of the war: the orphaned children, the crying grandmothers, the women having to resort to prostitution to survive. That's the symbolism, see? Vietnamese women being screwed by American soldiers, like America was screwing Vietnam—see?"

He'd begun pacing around in his excitement, but came to a halt then, stood there with that nutty, earnest look on his face, as if explaining it made it all right—and I tell you what: I just didn't get it. I mean, it was all well and good to report the details of the matter, but that didn't make it any less wrong or bad or gross.

For a moment, I just faced him off levelly, then dropped back to the bed. "It still makes me want to puke," I said, though Gabe didn't seem the least bit offended, but actually laughed aloud.

"Well, good for you, Clay. Good for you. Some things," he added sagely, "are worth puking over."

Then he promised to square things with Mama and I guess he did, for when they came to church that night, they were holding hands in pub-

lic for the very first time, like the morning's fight had never been. I didn't
know what had gone on between them, and didn't ask, Sim and Missy
and Grannie all happy and relieved, though I still had that dang IQ test
hanging over my head. It worried me so much that I could hardly sleep
at night, tormented by dreams where I'd be sitting at my desk at school,
taking the IQ test and doing all right, when I'd look down and find that
I was wearing nothing but a pair of the old Superman underwear I used
to wear in kindergarten.

By Thursday, I was about nuts from the worry and sleeplessness of
it all, flipped out enough to take the notice to school so Kenneth could
pore over it, searching for some loophole to get out of it, though he
could find nothing; suggested I go to Gabe and tell the truth.

"I cain't," I told him. "Him and Mama are just beginning to get
along. I can't go running to him now, telling him I cain't read. Gosh, it's
embarrassing."

Kenneth just sat there a moment crunching Chee•tos (we were at
lunch), then finally finished and crumpled up the little bag, said: "Tell you
what. I'll ride home with you this afternoon, tell him myself."

The relief was incredible; as if I'd lost twenty pounds in the space
of a breath. I couldn't even talk, just nodded, and Kenneth, this Prince
of a Best Friend, was as good as his word, riding one extra stop on the
bus that day and following me up the drive, neither of us bothering to go
inside, but tracking around to the garage and up the rattling old wood
stairs to the apartment.

Kenneth paused at the door and gave me this little look, wondering if he should knock, though I didn't bother, just opened the door and
stuck my head in, called: "Gabe?"

He was there, of course, laboring over an old map in sweats and a
pair of Daddy's old Benjamin Franklin half glasses. "What's up?" he asked
easily, though the glasses made him look so much like Daddy that I was
caught out for a moment, couldn't say a word.

Fortunately, Kenneth was there to take charge, going to the desk and hoisting his book bag on it, then rooting around till he laid hands on the testing notice that was getting kind of wrinkled from so much handling.

"It's this," he said, handing it to Gabe, who glanced at it through his bifocals.

"Oh," he said after a moment, "the testing notice. Am I supposed to sign it or something?"

Kenneth shook his head with great authority, said, "No," then told him in this mild, lawyerly voice: "It's just that Clay, he doesn't want to do it anymore. You know, the test and all."

Old Ken was being just the soul of discretion here, making it sound like a small matter that I'd given some thought to, decided I just didn't want to bother with.

But Gabe was not so easily convinced, just glanced at me, asked in this smooth, oily voice: "Is that right, Clay?"

I nodded, then looked away quickly, for there is something very piercing about Gabe's most casual glance and I knew if I met his eye, he'd read my mind. As a matter of fact, I think he'd gleaned something from our half-second connection, his face taking on this cunning little look of interest. "Well, that's odd," he said, taking off his glasses and leaning back casually in his chair, "because I talked to Mrs. Van Bloklen and she seemed like a nice enough woman. Kind of artsy-spacey, but very dedicated. Solid."

"Yeah, she's nice," Kenneth offered loyally.

"So you're in Gifted, Kenneth?" he asked in that sly little voice, and Kenneth nodded, the big goof.

I knew what was coming next. With no more discussion, Gabe turned back to me and pinned me with a level eye. "So Clay, what's the deal here?" he asked. "You know you want to hang out with Kenneth all day, build Lego cities, study the Life of Bach."

Well, I knew I was busted then, shot Kenneth this thanks-a-lot look, then rolled my eyes and admitted: "I don't want to take that *stupid* test. I cain't pass it. It's a waste of time."

"Sure you can," he countered in a quick, confident voice, and *dang* it makes me mad when someone like him or Missy or Kenneth act so cool and confident about standardized tests. I mean, sure it was easy for them; they're *geniuses,* for crying out loud. They've never sweated a report card or a flash card in their life.

Just like that, I lost my shyness and told him plainly: "I cain't even read, Gabe. I couldn't even read the notice. Kenneth had to, he reads all my stuff."

This was my shocker, my Great Confession, though Gabe didn't turn a hair, just told me mildly: "Well, that's why I called Mrs. Van Bloklen, to arrange for a scribe."

"A *what?*" Kenneth asked, and Gabe was very cool about it.

"A scribe. Someone to read the questions to you, write down your answers."

I had never heard of such a thing in my life, glanced between them to see if they were joking, though Gabe's face was smooth and clear.

"Well, doesn't that, like, defeat the purpose of the test?" I asked.

Gabe just shrugged. "Well, it would defeat the purpose if the purpose was to see if you can read on grade level, which we all know you cannot. But Clay, this is an IQ test and your IQ has already tested out at one twenty-eight, and that was when you were in third grade. Just two more points and you'll be over the magic number and that's where you should be—where you *will* be—if I have anything to do with it."

Kenneth looked perfectly satisfied at this, though I wasn't so sure, was about to shake my head again, tell him thanks but no thanks, when he slumped down even further in his chair, began tapping the desktop with the stem of his glasses.

"You know, boys," he offered in this distant, thoughtful voice, "this situation kind of reminds me of this guy I used to know, growing up on the Hill. He was just the nicest guy you ever wanted to meet, a red-hot pitcher from this dirt-poor family, so poor he never had a glove of his own, had to play barefooted half the time because he couldn't afford cleats."

Such was the magic of his rolling voice that me and Kenneth were immediately drawn in, Kenneth maybe even more than me, his face blank and arrested as Gabe unwound his story in a leisurely manner, the stem of this glasses tapping time to the measured rhythm of his voice: "But he was a heck of a ballplayer, this kid was, best in the county, took his team to state three years in a row, so good a scout from the Reds sent him a bus ticket to try out for the Majors, just like he'd dreamed of all his poor old hick life."

As soon as he said the word *Reds,* I knew who he was talking about: Daddy. He was the one who'd tried out for the Reds, though I didn't know the details of the matter, just stood there spellbound as he continued, his voice as calming as a hypnotist's: "They had him try out at an exhibition game, though he'd gotten the message secondhand, didn't even realize it was a tryout. He went down there in his good Sunday suit, had to borrow a uniform, bum a glove and some cleats from a guy in the dugout, go out on the mound cold, where he pitched like a machine, one ball short of a shutout.

"So they wanted him, the scout did, all but offered him a contract on the spot, but then he messed up—"

"*Daddy* did?" I interjected, though Gabe slowly shook his head.

"No," he said, still tapping the tabletop with those measured little taps. "The scout did. Because he took him out on the town that night, wined and dined him, thought he was scoring points, you know, nailing down the deal. But he overshot the mark with this particular kid, who'd been working in the mill since he was fifteen, wasn't used to being treated that way, felt like an impostor, a fraud. On the long bus ride home the next day, he started thinking that all this talk of money and contracts was just a fluke, that it wouldn't pan out, that he was setting himself up for this massive disappointment.

"By the time he got back to the Hill, he'd convinced himself that pitching in the big league wasn't what he really wanted after all. He became very stubborn, very set about it. Wouldn't return any of the scout's calls, even got a prepaid telegram he wouldn't even open, just ripped it up and threw it away. It was the damnedest thing. I mean, that scout called, I bet, twenty times—was still calling a month or so later, when he tripped at work one night, slipped in a puddle of grease and fell in a saw. He ripped his arm open elbow to shoulder, lost his chances in the big league; damn near lost his arm."

"*Dang,*" Kenneth murmured softly, though this wasn't news to me: I'd seen the ten inches of deep twisting scar that curled from inside Daddy's elbow to the white skin under his arm.

"—and I'm sure it was an accident," Gabe continued in that smooth, careful voice, "but still, there was something very *Freudian* about it all—"

"*What?*" Kenneth and I breathed at the same time.

Gabe just leaned back, repeated in that same smooth voice: "Freudian. A theory of Sigmund Freud, who believed that there isn't any such thing as accidents; that everything that happens is a product of our secret longings. He would have said he fell in that saw on purpose. That he couldn't take the pressure anymore, was permanently closing the door on this huge new life he couldn't trust—and Clay, listen: I'm not reading some kind of Freudian *crap* into you and this test. I just want you to understand that there's nothing wrong or shameful about someone with a language disability using a scribe to take a test—and hell, there's nothing wrong with being scared *spitless* of looking like a fool. Thing is, you can't back down."

He slipped his glasses back on then, was transformed eerily into Daddy's image as he concluded with that level, fatherly eye: "Thing is: I won't *let* you. I mean, I sat there and watched Michael rip up that telegram, walk away from a better life. I'm not gonna sit back and watch *you*. You understand?"

I just stood there a moment, glanced back and forth between him and Kenneth, at their confident, expectant faces, then finally nodded a quick little nod of assent.

Gabe picked up his pencil, smiled. "Well, good. Now you boys run on inside and watch *Batman* or something. I got work to do."

# CHAPTER TEN

The long and the short of it is: after a perfectly sleepless night of grinding fear and panicky anticipation and ten trips to the bathroom to pee, I went down to the guidance counselor's office bright and early the next morning to take probably the goofiest test of my life. As promised, the questions were read aloud by the school-board psychologist, a very nice Cuban woman who made my little heart leap with joy by smiling when we were done, though she sent home a mimeographed note that warned of a huge backlog of testing in the county office, predicted the results wouldn't be in for six months, maybe longer.

I was disappointed, of course, had been nursing this private fantasy of Mrs. McDonald calling me to the front of the class the next morning and informing me in this clear, ringing voice: "Clay, gather your things. You'll need them in GIFTED."

Instead, I was just sent back to special-ed, where my fellow underachievers couldn't quite understand my sudden new success in the classroom, a few of the more conspiracy-minded ones speculating that my *rich deddy* had made a few phone calls, greased a few palms.

"My *rich deddy* is dead as a doornail," I told them plainly, for after five years with these guys, we've grown way beyond sensitivity and tact, will really stop at nothing when it comes to shutting someone up. But aside from that little unpleasantness, The Test, as I came to think of it (as if it was the only test ever taken in the history of man), served other purposes as well. Most importantly, it brought a new warmth to our home and hearth, Mama positively charmed when she heard how Gabe had gone to bat for me with the school board, suddenly less suspicious of his godless Yankee ways and much more wifely and loyal, just as I'd dreamed.

I couldn't help but think that I was responsible for this miraculous transformation, that I was the Shirley Temple who'd stepped in and made this marriage work, everything around the house suddenly more normal and chipper, Gabe even putting aside his magnum opus to attend church on Sunday with the rest of us. He even let Brother Sloan talk him into taking on the men's Sunday-school class, which was made up mostly of old boys from the Hill, none of them under seventy, who kind of reminded me of Mama's old redneck uncles from Slidell, with the same wiry frames and hand-rolled cigarettes and equally contemptuous opinions of Gabe and his liberal Yankee ways.

They were so cantankerous and hardheaded that no teacher would hang with them for very long, though as soon as Gabe laid eyes on them, he recognized his enemy and did everything but dress in drag to get their goats. As far as I know, he never read one Scripture in the whole life of the class, but just stood up there for a half an hour every Sunday and berated them like a drill instructor for their backwoods, racist ways.

At first, me nor Missy or Sim could figure out what was going on in there, for we'd never had much contact with the old boys in the men's class till Gabe became their teacher, when they started going out of their way to approach us in Winn-Dixie or the post office, fix us with a grievous eye and go off on some nutty, irrelevant rant about God knows what: politics or the Civil War; Jesse Jackson's latest outrage. We didn't have a clue why they were suddenly so focused on us, till me and Sim finally got curious enough to press an ear to the door of their class one Sunday, and gosh, you should have heard them in there, ranting and shouting, Gabe lifting his voice to inform someone at the top of his lungs: "Yeah? Well, you're a g-d Nazi, that's why—"

We were horrified and fascinated, as was everyone at Welcome, with the possible exception of Grannie, who didn't give a diddle about the old men, but was increasingly embarrassed about Gabe. Not about his public exhibitions (that she seemed to pretty much expect), but his complete lack of ambition in finding a job once he'd settled into his new role as stepfather. I mean, Grannie is of the old work-till-you-drop school of thought, with a pathological horror (worse than Daddy, even) of shift-less, no-'count men lolling around the house in the middle of the day: trifling, sorry, good-for-nothing.

In her eyes, there was no more detestable a creature, and after a month of waiting for Gabe to make a move, she began dropping all these hints about the value of a good day's work; how it was good to pay in all your Social Security when you were young; stuff like that. On a few occasions, me or Sim or Missy went to bat for Gabe, pointed out that we were rich enough as it was, but God knows that didn't satisfy Grannie, who seemed intent on turning him into this *Father Knows Best* figure who went to work every morning in a suit and tie, dropped by her house every Friday for lunch, just like Daddy used to.

All winter long she kept at him, though the real blow fell in March when he gave up his Sunday-school class after a fight with Brother Sloan (not over doctrine, but the Civil War), and returned to his *book* on Sunday mornings with no apologies to anyone. By then, he and Mama were getting along so well that she didn't bat an eye, though to Grannie, it was clearly the straw that broke the camel's back.

After that, she went after him with a missionary fervor, bringing along a newspaper to the Steakhouse every Sunday at lunch and casually glancing through the Help Wanted section during dessert, reading aloud any good leads, with no job so low that it fell beneath her notice.

"What's lawn care?" she asked one week. When Simon told her it was mowing yards, she just sniffed: "Ain't nothing wrong with thet. Git you a nice tan."

Gabe was used to Grannie and her nutty Grannie-ways and didn't take her jabs too personally, but gave it back as good as she sent (would tell her with a solemn straight face that he already *had* a job: that he was a Trophy Husband and it was a full-time position), their little sniping war going on for most of the spring, till sometime in March—or no, April: the day of the April Fool's dance. That's why me and Kenneth were in the school office that afternoon, we'd left the dance early (ever been the only white kid on the dance floor at a black school at an eighth-grade dance?), were waiting in line to use the phone, when Erica Harper ran up with this incredible news: Mr. Nair had gotten in a wreck on I-10 on the Tallahassee side of the rest station.

Now, Mr. Nair was our American-history teacher, a fossil of an old guy who was due to retire in May and had left school early that day to go to a doctor's appointment in Tallahassee. In the twenty-minute space between the news about the wreck and the last bell, all kind of rumors flew: that he was hit by a semi; that he ran into a tree; that he flipped his car three times and had his head cut off. It wasn't till we got on the bus with the high-school kids that Kemp (who was an office aide and heard all the gossip) straightened us out, told us that no, Mr. Nair wasn't dead, but his leg was broken and his shoulder shattered, that they'd airlifted him to Tallahassee and chances were, he wouldn't be back. He said they'd hired Miss Dales to sub till a replacement could be found, and that was the real tragedy of the thing because she was one picky, goofy old woman, who lectured seven hours a day nonstop, sent home piles of homework.

Kenneth and I just listened impassively till he finished, then turned and looked at each other, said one word: *Gabe*. We didn't even discuss it, just piled off the bus and ran all the way to the house, rattling up the stairs to the old apartment and bursting in on Gabe, who was writing at his desk as usual, surrounded by his legal pads and maps and big fat old reference texts. He looked up when we burst in, but we'd run so fast we were out of breath, me pointing at Kenneth, gasping: "Tell 'im. Tell 'im."

"Tell me what?" Gabe asked, though Kenneth couldn't get it out, just stood there slumped against the desk, fighting for air.

"Mr. Nair," I finally managed, "got in a—wreck."

*"Who?"*

"Mr. Nair," I gasped. "History teacher. Hurt bad, won't be back."

You could tell he didn't have a clue in the world what I was talking about, just sat back in his chair and looked back and forth between us. "Oh," he said after a moment. "Well, I'm sorry, Kenneth. Was he some kin of yours?"

*"No,"* I said adamantly, shaking my head. "He teaches history"—I pointed at him— "like you."

Kenneth finally got ahold of himself then, wheezed: "Kemp had the sub. She's a jerk."

"That's right," I told him, "and Mr. Nair'll be out all year. Come on, Gabe, they'll give the job to someone else. History's the only thing I like in school. I need you."

I must have hit the mark on that because Gabe chewed his lip thoughtfully a moment, asked who was hiring? The school board or the local school? Me and Kenneth hadn't thought to ask, just danced around in this jig of impatience as he slowly came to his feet and went downstairs to the kitchen phone and made a few phone calls. He finally connected with the school-board office, where a secretary told him to come in and fill out an application, that the position was definitely open, and if he was qualified, he could interview that very afternoon.

"Wear your wedding suit," I told him, me and Kenneth about flipped out by then, though Gabe wanted it to be a surprise, made us keep it to ourselves.

All afternoon, we loafed around the house, till we heard the car in the garage and dashed out to meet him, Gabe very cool about it, just getting out of the car and calmly holding a finger to his lips till he saw the coast was clear, when he quietly nodded yes.

Me and Kenneth went nuts, high-fiving each other and dancing around, though he swore us to secrecy, insisted that he wanted to tell Grannie himself. So we just followed him back to the house, showered and changed while he formally invited everyone to supper at the Steakhouse—me and Kenneth, and Mama and Sim and Missy, and last but not least, Grannie.

Once supper was under way, I knew why he'd kept it a secret, for he toyed with her mercilessly the whole time we ate, commenting in this languid, drawling voice about how much work he was getting done on his book, how well it was going, till Grannie finally took the bait, asked him how long he figured it'd take him to finish it.

"Oh, I think I can tie it up in five, maybe six years," he answered with an idle little swish of his tea glass. "I could go faster, you know, but I get so damn sleepy in the afternoon that I just have to take a nap—which is, you know, good for you. Winston Churchill was a great believer in naps. That's how he won the war for the British."

And boy, you should have seen Grannie's face. I mean, DISGUST was written on her forehead, me and Kenneth laughing so hard we were about to pee in our pants when Gabe finally stood, tea glass in hand, and announced in this formal little voice that after careful examination of career options in North Florida, he had accepted a position of enormous responsibility shaping young minds at Lincoln Park Middle School. He did it as a joke, I guess, though Mama stood and publicly kissed him, right on the mouth, and poor old Grannie actually broke down and cried. I mean, she had to blow her nose on her napkin, she was so moved and relieved, filling me with this sanctimonious little glow of satisfaction that I, Clayton Michael Catts, had brought it all about.

I was the one who'd landed the bad boy back in the lap of his family, back into relative masculinity, surrounded by his adoring wife and children, indistinguishable from any other man in the Steakhouse that night, though Mama seemed kind of nervous about him taking a job at Lincoln Park.

All evening long, she warned him to go easy on us, to remember his manners, even walked us out to the car the next morning, left him with one last piece of advice: "Don't give homework the first day and don't talk above their heads—and listen, Gabriel, whatever you do, baby, don't use the f-word in class. Remember, Clayton'll catch it if you get anybody mad."

Gabe just nodded sagely, assured her that he knew how to comport himself in a classroom; that what did she think he'd been doing up north all these years?

Mama just sighed a big Louisiana sigh. "Those were Yankees," she said. "These people know your phone number."

He smiled at that, paused to kiss her lightly on the mouth in that lingering, openmouthed way that still kind of threw me, though I was too nervous to ponder it, me and Kenneth both were. It wasn't that we were afraid he'd slip and use the f-word or insult someone, but quite the opposite: we were worried that someone would make something of his bad hand—or worst still, that rumor of his irregular life would leak out and he would be reviled and persecuted, beat up in gym or something.

I don't know why we were so protective, but we were, meeting for a brief conference in the hallway before lunch, Kenneth (who had him third period) assuring me that everything was cool; that he was funny and interesting and everybody liked him. I was relieved, but still a little nervous because Kenneth was way up on the gifted track with the other school brains, who could understand and appreciate the likes of Uncle Gabe. I was down with the bottom feeders in sixth period in a lower-track class made up mostly of special-ed kids, along with a scattering of dopers and slackers and half a dozen overgrown jocks who sat slumped in the back row in a daze of inattentiveness, their jaws slowly grinding gum, their big old size-twelve Nikes stretched out into the aisle in front of them.

Even the presence of a new teacher only drew a few curious glances as we shuffled in and took our seats that day, no one giving Gabe as much attention as they did a huge, computer-generated sign he'd cooked up with Sim the night before, that he'd taped above the chalkboard, that read: OUR HERITAGE CONSISTS OF ALL THE VOICES THAT CAN ANSWER OUR QUESTIONS.

In smaller letters beneath was inscribed: *André Malraux,* though the name didn't seem to ring a bell with anyone in fifth-period remedial history, Bobo Crain doing a double take when he saw Gabe at his desk, turning back and asking me in this high, incredulous voice: "He yo deddy?" because we did kind of look alike, had the same color hair, the same cowlick, even the same dimple.

I told him no, that he was my uncle, rumor of the relationship making the whisper circuit till the bell rang, when Gabe slid on his reading glasses and called roll with this professional briskness, not calling anyone by their first names, but Mr. Catts and Miss Ross, etc. He'd warned me on the way to school that he wasn't going to publicly acknowledge me, so I wasn't expecting anything, just took out my notebook (so I'd look like I knew what I was doing) as he introduced himself as Dr. Catts, the new American-history teacher.

And it's just as well that he formally presented the official title of the class in that, his first hour, because I do believe it was the last we heard of it, the whole time he was there. I mean, he didn't forsake history altogether, but instead of the worn old path of memorized dates that Mr. Nair had vainly tried to march us down, he began class by coming around to the front of his desk and leaning against it, his arms folded across his chest, and asking how many of us were Americans.

Well, obviously, all of us were, though no one seemed interested in giving up their afternoon nap to discuss so obvious a subject, about half the class bedding down on their book bags in preparation for a nice little rest that Gabe interrupted by strolling down the aisles, roll book in hand (to help him with the names) and asking everyone, point-blank: "Where were you born, where were you born?"

As predicted, almost everyone was from Florida, mostly just down the road at Sinclair. When he finally completed the circuit, he pointed out that we were, indeed, all Americans. Then, without even explaining this pointless exercise, he began wandering around again, spent the remainder of class asking about our families, our histories—or at least he tried, for none of us dumbos were very fast on the uptake and we really didn't understand what he meant by *history*.

The very word seemed to give us brain-freeze, and try as he might, he couldn't draw anyone out, especially the special-ed kids, whose biggest fear in life was that in some moment of misplaced enthusiasm, we'd raise our hand in one of our regular classes and show the world just how far we were beneath them; how we couldn't read; could hardly write at all. We'd long ago learned that it was safer to just sit there and keep our mouth shut, look cool and superior, if nothing else, and after fifty minutes of fruitless digging, even Gabe must have realized the uselessness of his task.

For he glanced at his watch, then returned to his desk and felt around in his pocket for his reading glasses, told us: "Before you leave today, I have a poem I want to read to you, one of my very favorite poems in the world by a man named James Emmanuel, called 'Emmett Till.'"

He thumbed through the book a moment, finally found his spot, and in a ringing, singsong voice, read a short, rhyming poem that was pleasant enough, though I can tell you frankly that I didn't hear a word of it except for the phrase *fairy river boy* that rang out loud and clear, just public as heck. And I tell you what, I could have fainted I was so embarrassed, thinking: Good *God*, does this *idiot* know what he's doing? Mama was right: he'd been up north too long. He had forgotten everything he ever knew about being Baptist or keeping a job or holding his mouth right. He was committing social suicide and taking me with him.

He looked up when he was done and scanned the room for reaction, and my face must have been a sight. For he seized on it immediately, boomed: "Mr. Catts? You look properly moved and provoked. We only have a few minutes left of class. Care to share your enlightenment with the rest of us?"

I just stared at him in horror, thinking that Daddy had sure enough hit the nail on the head when he said his brother was *strange,* though Gabe didn't seem to grasp my predicament, but tried to coax me along, offering: "Mississippi Delta? Tallahatchee River? *Jet* magazine?"

He could have been speaking Swahili for all I knew, a few people gathering their book bags and purses in preparation for the bell that rang almost immediately to my everlasting and eternal relief. I didn't even tell him good-bye, just got the heck out of there, hurried to the bus circle, where I pulled Kenneth aside, asked him if Gabe had read *that* poem in third period.

Kenneth said, yeah, sure; though he admitted that even the school brains hadn't been able to make much of it. In a whole class-worth of discussion, they hadn't gotten much past the fact that Emmett Till was some dude who'd been killed in Mississippi a long time ago.

"Well, what the *heck* does that have to do with American history?" I demanded with some heat.

"Beats me," Kenneth said. "Maybe he was George Washington's nephew or something."

"Well, why's he reading poetry, in *history* class?"

Kenneth just shrugged. "Gosh, Clay, I don't know. He's *your* uncle."

It was the one and only time Kenneth ever ventured to reproach me for favoring my own suspect uncle over his safe and much-loved Uncle Lou—one that cut deep, making me sigh hugely, and hope to God that was the last we heard of that crazy little poem.

But my hopes were unfounded, and as soon as the bell rang the next day, Gabe turned on the overhead projector and put on a transparency that was, by God, that same little poem, written in his own square handwriting, that *word* magnified to six inch letters on the cinder blocks above the chalkboard.

At that point, I was thinking suicide might be an option, though, fortunately for all of us, whatever small interest the sight of a new teacher had provoked the day before had clearly passed, the jocks settling into their bored slump, the nappers returning to their book bags, leaving Gabe to ramble around the room, mouthing nonsense words like *myth* and *symbol* and *empowerment* that went mostly unheard.

After a while, I relaxed enough to sneak out a sheet of notebook paper, was covertly sketching a pretty good Transformer when I realized there was a commotion in the front of the room, Gabe holding up a sheet of paper that had everyone on the front row jerking up from their desktops as if they'd seen a snake, their little cries waking the rest of the class.

"Man, thet's *nasty!*" was their general reaction, Gabe ignoring it to slowly stroll down the aisle so the rest of us could get a closer look, exclamations of disgust following him.

Even the jocks on the back row came to life when he passed, sitting up straighter, muttering *shhhht,* the rest of us all rubbernecking and standing till he turned down our aisle and I finally saw what was causing the commotion: a picture of something, I still couldn't tell exactly what, till he was right in front of me, when I let out a yelp of my own: "Good *God.*"

Because it was a head-and-shoulders photograph of (maybe) a black guy. It was hard to really tell, because the face was horribly disfigured, like a wax figure that had been left on a dashboard of a car in August, was half-melted, hardly human.

"Whut is *thet?*" was the general hum of the room, everyone standing and gawking, though Gabe just motioned us back to our seats and returned to his perch on the front of his desk, where he regarded the picture with a grave, solemn face.

"*Thet,*" he said in deliberate mimic, "is the young man I've been trying to introduce to you for the past two days. *Thet* is Emmett Till."

For a moment, we were stunned to silence, everyone glancing up at the poem on the overhead, though none of us special-ed kids could read well enough to make much of it. But something in the drama and weirdness of that wasted face had piqued our interest, created enough tension that Bobo (who is kind of hyper when he's awake) actually ran down the aisle to Gabe's desk, demanded in this high, curious voice: "Man, whut happened to *him?*"

In reply, Gabe just shooed him back to his desk, though he answered him levelly: "*That,* Mr. Crain," he said, "is a very interesting question." He felt around on his desktop for a manila folder that was lying there, held it cradled in his good hand while he spoke. "For Emmett Till is an unsung hero of modern American history—a young black man from Chicago, only a year or so older than yourself, who lived a pretty ordinary life— went to school, had a lot of friends, and a very nice, very loving mother, who back in the summer of 1955 decided her son might enjoy a break from city life, sent him down to visit some relatives in *Mississippi.*"

Such was his emphasis on the word that even us Crackers knew this was an ominous development, like saying a nice Jewish woman had sent her son to Germany to visit Hitler. We were even quieter then, firmly in his spell as he opened the manila folder and produced another picture: this one of a chubby, smiling black kid sitting next to a prosperous-looking black woman; apparently his mother.

Gabe stood and made another slow circuit of the room so we could get a closer look at the picture, his voice that calm and hypnotizing rhythm: "Now, being raised in Chicago, Mr. Till didn't understand much about race relations in the South, and before he left, his mother warned him to mind his manners, not to get out of line, but he didn't pay her much mind. He had white friends in the North, just didn't get what the fuss was all about. A few days into his visit, on a bet with one of his Mississippi cousins—you know—a double-*dog*-dare—he whistled at a white woman in a country store, the wife of the owner."

We were really quiet then, even the jocks on the back row, some of whom had begun secretly indulging in a little interracial dating, talking to white girls, calling them at home. I think they were afraid that Gabe was about to out himself, not as homosexual, but as a white supremacist or something; that this story was some kind of nutty cautionary tale.

They even quit chewing their gum as Gabe continued his circuit, his voice very smooth and listenable: "Just a silly little joke, you understand—and I'm sure Mr. Till didn't think too much of it, just kept on playing, though when his uncle heard of it, he realized this was a serious thing. He made arrangements for him to be sent home immediately, but before he could get him on a bus, some white men showed up at his door, one of them the husband of the woman he'd whistled at, and took Emmett away. It was the last time he was seen alive."

By then, Gabe had made his way back to his desk, where he assumed that casual, crossed-arm stance as he concluded in a quiet voice: "When they fished his body out of the Tallahatchie River a few days later, he'd been shot, beaten; one eye was gouged out. His own mother couldn't recognize him when they shipped his body back to Chicago, had to identify him by a ring."

I think the part about the gouged-out eye was the clincher, the room so silent it wasn't even breathing as Gabe finished: "And the men who killed him pretty much got off scot-free. Everyone knew who did it, but in those days, no jury would convict a white man for killing a black man, even a child."

He paused to let this sink in, then took a big breath, said: "And I guess that justice wouldn't have been served in any sense of the word, except that Emmett's mother, she wouldn't go easy. Instead of paying a mortician to do an Academy Award–winning makeup job, or shutting him up in a coffin and slipping him quietly into the ground, she insisted on an open-casket funeral, invited all of Chicago to attend."

For some reason, I thought about Daddy's funeral; about his big old expensive coffin and how small and insubstantial he looked in it. I wondered what it would have been like if he'd have been beaten to death; if any of us could have stood to see him.

But it was really just too gross to comprehend. I shook it off with a little chill, returned to Gabe, who met our eyes solemnly, his voice lowered for emphasis: "A *thousand* people a day filed passed that open coffin. *Jet* magazine even published pictures of the corpse—one of which I just showed you—that pretty much did to black America what it did to us here today: it *horrified* them. It awakened the conscience of a nation, did more for the civil rights movement than a decade of legislation, and as Mr. Emmanuel's poem so powerfully illustrates, transformed Emmett Till into a figure of sacrifice, of *myth*—"

Just at that moment, the final bell rang, loud and shrill, making everyone jump a foot in their seats, though we didn't make our usual rush to the door, our eyes still fixed on Gabe, who continued to sit there slumped on the edge of his desk, his voice that hypnotizing rumble.

"The irony of it is that even today, his name doesn't appear in most American-history textbooks, but is still pretty much oral history—that is, *spoken* history—the kind that everyone in this room can produce. Maybe not as colorful, or tragic, but certainly as valid. It is the study of *us,* the history that I'd like to concentrate on these last two months of school, if you're game. I mean, we can study this history"—he picked up our fat old history book—"or we can study *this* history." On that, he held up the manila folder with the Emmett Till photographs. "It really doesn't matter to me, because as I verified the first hour of class, we are all Americans here, therefore our history *is* American history. The school board'll pay me whichever way you choose, we just need to decide to-day: Which will it be?"

There was no immediate response, all of us amazed that we, the dumbest class in the history of the world, were being asked to pick our destiny for the first time in our life. We all knew what we wanted, of course. We wanted to study *us,* it was just that no one wanted to risk a wrong answer, venture a raised hand. The silence drew out for twenty, then thirty seconds, the muffled thunder of the after-school rush echo-ing through the hallways, though Gabe ignored it to sit there mildly on the edge of his desk, manila folder in hand, waiting for our decision.

Soon, Darius and Travis and some of my closer special-ed buds were casting me these beseeching little looks, calling on me to do my duty as Official Nephew. I avoided their glances and shuffled my feet, held off as long I could, but in the end, I finally rolled my eyes and raised a slow hand.

"Ah, Mr. Catts," Gabe intoned cheerfully. "D'you have a vote?"

I just took a breath, then offered in a weenie little voice: "I vote for *us*."

For a moment, there was silence, then all the gimps and dumbos and jocks who'd been too intimidated to speak up finally thought of a way to voice their opinion. They burst out into spontaneous applause, loud and thunderous, making for one of the few bright memories in my whole academic life: of sitting there, face down, very pleased, with Gabe at his desk, beaming on us like a proud old grandpa.

"Well, good," he said, finally coming to his feet. "Tomorrow, we begin the study of our twenty-six individual American histories. Your first project is to somehow finagle your oldest living relative into telling you a story. It doesn't matter how long or how silly; doesn't have to have a punch line or a moral. If you can't get anyone to talk, nose around your attic or spare bedroom and bring in something—an old photograph, a quilt—that says something about your *history*. I'll give a hundred points for any artifact or story, ten points extra if you can get it on tape. Class is dismissed."

# CHAPTER ELEVEN

Now, Grannie was the oldest living member of our family, older than Uncle Case by the space of two minutes (they were fraternal twins). And though she had told me many a good story in her day, when I went to her that night with my newly purchased tape recorder and begged for a family story, one that would reveal our *history,* she closed up tight as an oyster, acted like I was a lawyer in a courtroom trying to catch her in a lie.

It wasn't until I threatened to bypass her completely and go to Uncle Case or Aunt Candace that she broke down and committed a story to tape, nothing particularly historic or telling, but a hokey little bedtime story about a good little Baptist orphan named Little Gene, who was sent to live with his evil aunt. Among other faults, his aunt was so cheap that she wouldn't buy him anything at Christmas but a new pair of shoes. Little Gene is very proud of them, though, and wears them to church on Christmas Eve in a hard snow, where he comes upon a ragged, barefoot little boy sitting on the steps. He feels sorry for him, offers one of his new shoes, then has to walk home through the snow with one shoe on, one shoe off. (Grannie always chanted that part: *hippity-hop, hippity-hop, one-shoe on and one-shoe off.*)

When his cheap aunt finds out he's given away one of his new shoes, she flies into a rage and sends him to bed in the loft without supper.

There, Little Gene cries himself to sleep in the hay, though the next morning, he is awakened by the smell of biscuits and gravy, and sausage and hotcakes (and sometimes a whole lot more, depending on how much time Grannie has). Little Gene can't believe his nose, and slowly climbs down the ladder to the living room, where he finds a huge Christmas tree surrounded by all kinds of toys. While he's standing there, looking around in wonder, his aunt comes out, her face shining, and repents of her evil ways, tells him that the little boy he'd given his shoe to on the church steps the night before was an ANGEL, who came to her in the night, led her to the Lord. Now she was living for JESUS, and would buy Little Gene all the clothes and toys and shoes he wanted!

Well, that's the story, anyway, and such was the power of Grannie's trembling old voice that when I played it in class the next day, even the jocks on the back row were momentarily transfixed by Little Gene's sad plight. Gabe himself (who'd been raised on Little Gene) laughed aloud when it was over, mimicked, "Hippity-hop, hippity-hop, one shoe on and one shoe off," then asked if anyone had ever heard it before.

No one had, and since it really wasn't a family story, I didn't think he could shed much light on it, but he did. Leaning on his desk and folding his arms on his chest, he told us that the story of Little Gene really wasn't original to Grannie, but a Cracker version of an old French folktale, except the little boy in the French story wasn't named Gene and he didn't go to church on Christmas Eve (he went to Mass) and he didn't get saved in the end.

"How did *Grannie* hear it?" I was impressed enough to ask.

Gabe answered with a cool detachment, as if he wasn't kin to us at all, but an anthropologist who'd happened in on our American-history class, found us an interesting study, and decided to stay. "Well, your grandmother is from a county in south Alabama that was settled by the French," he explained, "supporters of Napoleon who had to flee the Continent after Waterloo. That's probably who passed it along— neighboring French immigrants—or maybe your grannie has a little

French blood herself—which, now that I think of it, would explain a *lot*."

The idea seemed to momentarily arrest him, making him stand there and rub his chin thoughtfully, then add in a brisker voice: "In any case, the story has been considerably revised. The sausage and biscuits and the salvation are definitely an Alabama twist."

I was astounded, all of us were, by his amazing ability to trace the most mundane story back to its roots with an accuracy that bordered on the psychic. From the merest wisp of evidence, he was able to tell us all kinds of secret or forgotten things about ourselves: why we lived where we lived, and thought what we thought; why black people sang the blues, and Crackers liked the fiddle. He seemed to take just inexhaustible pleasure in the historical junk people brought in, with no artifact so boring or obscure that he couldn't wrench some bit of social trivia out of it.

Soon, his desktop was littered every morning with all kinds of stuff: old photographs and letters; turpentine cachepots and lye-stained washboards and even a dusty old mojo hand Bobo stole from a nail in his grannie's kitchen (which, incidentally, isn't as nasty as it sounds, nothing but a Ziploc baggie full of dried moss and leaves that none of the kids from Sinclair would come within ten feet of).

"Miz Crain gone put a root on yo ass," they warned Gabe darkly, though he just laughed at their sincerity, clearly finding the po' folk at LPM a fascinating study.

I must say the feeling was mutual, my company at the lunchroom table suddenly very much in demand. Every day, there would be this little elbowing fight when I sat down, everyone wanting to sit next to me so they could grill me about Gabe, who they steadfastly believed to be my father. I mean, there was nothing secretive in their suspicions; there at first, at least twice a day, in gym or the hallway, or sometimes openly in class, someone would dip their head toward Gabe and echo Bobo's high, curious voice that first day of class: "*He* yo deddy?"

I tried to be patient with them; assure them that though we did indeed have the same blond hair and cowlick and dimple, that we jacked our jaws in an identical way when we were mad, still in all, he wasn't my father: he was my *uncle*, my un-cle, my UNCLE. I had to break it down into syllables because it was clear they didn't believe me, something I privately attributed to their own moral shortcomings, their own blasted families. I figured the poor folk around Sinclair had become so tribal and inbred that they had forgotten the concept of a normal family unit: father, mother, brother, sister.

But other than that ongoing annoyance, I did a pretty neat job of PR, told them about Harvard and New York, and how Daddy asked him to come home and raise us when he was dying, how it was The Right Thing To Do. Even the most jaded kid at LPM could not fail to be moved by so romantic a tale, a lot of the girls falling stone in love with Gabe that very first week, their faces in class transformed by a wistful longing, probably daydreaming that Mama would die of typhoid fever so they could step in and take her place as the Second Mrs. Catts.

This was all to the good as far as I could see, my fear of him outing himself fading as the weeks passed and we settled into a happy routine, Gabe driving me and Kenneth to school every morning, his stereo blasting classic rock: the Beatles, Van Morrison, stuff like that. It became the music of the Revolution: "Brown-Eyed Girl" and "Wavelength," "Penny Lane" and "When I'm Sixty-four," the backdrop to all our jokes and optimism and laughter that would follow us to school, church, everywhere we went. Gabe was always ready to listen to our many miseries, Kenneth's usually wrapped up in money woes, and worries for his mother and how much she worked; mine a lot less life-threatening, mostly concerned with Rachel Cole, Sim's girlfriend's younger sister, who I'd been in love with since I first laid eyes on her in second grade.

Gabe commiserated, offered advice and (in Kenneth's case) cash when needed, was such a great and generous support that by May, the whole specter of Daddy's death and illness had passed almost out of memory in a way that occasionally brought me up short, not during the day, but in strange, unforeseen moments at night, when early-summer storms sometimes blew in from the Gulf, rattling our old house to its cracked foundation and waking me from a sound sleep. While I lay there, drowsy and yawning, listening to the ferocious whip of the old oaks, the thunder of rain on the roof, a strange thought would sometimes come to me: that Daddy was dead, he was gone; I'd never see him again.

Once it hit me, I couldn't stay still, but would roll off my bunk and go to the window and open it to the fury of the storm, hoping the clean whip of the wind would blow away that first shock, that sudden, awful sink of despair. And it would, too. After a moment of standing there at the screen, being pelted by little drips and tears of rain, I'd close the window and return to bed, lie there with a clearer head, Daddy back in place, way back in 1986 with MTV and Madonna and *Miami Vice,* back before the Gabe Revolution ever was dreamed of, in my late and unlamented youth.

With that kind of distance between us, I could think about him without that awful sink of despair; could even worry that I was losing him. For aside from my little midnight hauntings, I could hardly remember him anymore: his bossy old voice, his grunts of interest; his wheezing laughter when I said something that amused him. ("Claybird, Claybird, Claybird. What're we gonna do with you, son?")

My failing memory didn't perplex me as much as it filled me with a nagging little guilt over not being more loyal to his memory, though when I mentioned it to Gabe one morning on the ride to school, he didn't seem overly shocked or disappointed. "You were only eleven when he died," he pointed out. "And grief is a strange process, anyway, like the tide on the beach that comes and goes. As you get older, pieces of him will begin to return to you. Then, one day, you'll find that the bad things—the guilt, the regret—are mostly gone, the laughter and the little things are what remain. And that never goes away."

We rode along in silence for a moment, till something seemed to occur to him, making him turn and look at me with sudden interest. "Why don't you make him your final project?"

*"Daddy?"* I asked in amazement, for our final projects were a very big deal, indeed, individual oral histories he wanted us to concentrate on the last four weeks of school with an eye toward entering the best of them in the countywide Social Studies Fair.

This was always held the last Monday in May at the high school in town, though the poor country kids from Lincoln Park hardly ever placed, much less brought home any of the coveted schoolwide trophies Gabe assured us we could win if we played our cards right. To that end, he spent the last three weeks of school giving us a crash course on oral history, hammering us about accuracy and reliability, demonstrating the different ways to collect data. He even bought half a dozen tape recorders for us to borrow, helped everyone pick out a suitable subject, Kenneth doing his on naval stores (that is: the turpentine industry), Bobo on folk medicine, Gabe's enthusiasm so high that even us dumbos in special-ed began to entertain hopes of winning locally, going on to regionals, maybe state.

From the very beginning, I had planned on doing my project on Vietnam, couldn't believe that Gabe thought Daddy would be a more provoking project. "Won't everyone think it's silly?" I asked. "Doing your own father?"

"Of course not," he answered with that old Gabe sureness. "Michael lived and died. He moved in time. He has just as valid a claim to historical preservation as Ronald Reagan, for God's sake."

So I just shrugged, said, "Sure," though I was still kind of apprehensive about it, afraid Daddy wouldn't be nearly interesting enough to place on the county level, much less go to state, because, face it, he was a good man, but he wasn't famous or anything.

But I was so anxious to please Gabe that I didn't argue, just bought a fresh pack of tapes at Wal-Mart, and notebook paper and a big project board, then went to Mama first, figured she'd be a good practice subject,

and not afraid of the microphone. Gabe had lectured us on the importance of a congenial interview site, so I set up my tape recorder on the
kitchen table late one Friday night while she was waiting for Missy to
come home from a softball game, relaxed in her old terry robe, sipping
a cup of hot tea. And though she's not the storyteller Gabe is, Mama does
have an artist's eye for detail, and told me the funniest little story about
the first time she met Daddy when she came back to the Hill when she
was seventeen.

She said that she had come by bus, was just passing through, but
Grannie had talked her into spending the night, had tucked her away in
Daddy's bed while he was working the night shift. Grannie had promised
to leave him a note telling him to sleep on the couch, but apparently didn't
quite get around to it, for sometime in the night, Mama was awakened by
a jiggled bed and a man's voice, right in her face, breathing: "Dang."

"Except he didn't say *dang*," Mama conceded with a fond little smile
(meaning that he really said *damn*).

"Did you *scream*?" I asked, though Mama just laughed.

"Oh, baby, I wasn't much of a screamer in those days. Anyway, your
grannie came strolling in half a second later, her hair in rollers, said,
'Michael, baby, d'you remember Myra Sims? Lived next door? Ira's little
sister?' Introduced us like we were standing in the vestibule of the church."

Mama is also not the mimic Gabe is, but can do a pretty good imitation of Grannie when she wants to, had me laughing my butt off at
Grannie and her nutty old Grannie-ways that were harder than heck to
capture on tape. I mean, in real life, Grannie is full of quaint sayings and
weird convictions, as colorful an old bird as any oral historian could wish
for, but once I set up the recorder, she kind of fell apart on me, started
crying about Daddy dying, her voice all sniffly and muffled, hard to pick
up on tape. In the end, I had to depend on a lot of secondary sources: Uncle Case and Aunt Candace, Brother Sloan, though the best interview, far
and away, was with Daddy's business partner, Sam McRae.

As much a workaholic as Daddy, he was too busy to sit down and talk into a microphone, so I had to tag along with him on one of his bi-weekly trips to Waycross to sign the payroll (he's just a manager in Florida, a co-owner up there). I didn't mind, because I loved the old Way-cross run, the blooming peach orchards nostalgic and familiar, Mr. Sam's voice kind of lulling as we drove along, his story just incredible. I mean, at first it was the same old dry stuff—how they met when Daddy went to work at Sanger; how he'd shown Daddy the ropes because the older hands were too busy to be bothered.

Then, as we creeped along the edge of the swamp, where the gas stations and the interruptions were few, he told me other things: how some of the local guys didn't like it when Daddy made him manager (because Mr. Sam is black; I don't know that I ever mentioned that); how the actual Klan had gotten after them, burned crosses, stuff like that.

I had never heard so much as a whisper of such a thing, but recognized a good story when I heard it, filled tape after tape of notes and details, some of which I had to later cut because they made the report go so long, and I had yet to interview my Star Witness, you might call him: Uncle Gabe. I went to him last of all because he was the Family Expert where Daddy was concerned, though on that particular night, he was kind of quiet; in fact, he let me down.

I interviewed him out by the pool late on a Friday night, everything quiet except for the distant hooing of our colony of owls, and the close, musical piping of the whippoorwills back and forth through the trees. I went about it in just the right way, made sure he was comfortable, led in with good questions, but Gabe just wouldn't take the bait and run. He wasn't weepy and emotional like Grannie, but just sat there slouched down in one of Mama's bayou chairs toying with a glass of tea, not offering any of his hundred hilarious Michael-stories, but just reminiscing in a wandering little voice about the summer he'd left for college; how he'd tried to talk Daddy into coming to Tallahassee with him, but he wouldn't. "Stayed home," he said wistfully. "Stayed home."

His stuff barely made the final cut on the tape and didn't appear at all on the written report that was the hardest part of the whole thing, twice as hard as the interviews or the project board that Mama had helped me design, acted as my Artistic Director, you might say. She helped me go through Grannie's picture box and pick out the best pictures, showed me how to arrange them on the board, then, once they were set, took the whole thing out on the deck and sprayed the margins with invisible glue, sprinkled silver glitter all over it with a light hand.

That left me with a whole weekend to finish my written report, which wasn't as easy as it sounds, because I really and truly have the crappiest handwriting in the world, my squiggly little sentences starting out okay, though after a few paragraphs, they lose their neat margins and begin to slope below the blue line, end up looking like the work of a two-year-old. I must have rewritten the dang thing ten times, finally gave up late on Sunday night and creeped down to Missy's bedroom with my latest draft clutched in my hand.

As usual, she was sitting up in bed doing homework, already yawning when I came in, asking *"What?"* in a not very friendly voice, knowing a favor was about to be asked.

I just stood there by the bed a moment, trying to look as lost and desperate as I felt. "You know my final project, in history?" I asked. She nodded warily, and I shuffled around a moment, finally got to the point: "Could you write it for me?"

Missy rolled her eyes massively on that. "The whole *thing*?" she asked. "Gosh, Clay, why don't me and Mama do it *all,* while you stay home and watch *The Flintstones*?"

She said it with her usual broad sarcasm, though I was too desperate to rise to her bait. "'Cause I don't need you to do all of it," I begged. "I have the interviews on tape and the artifacts labeled. I even have the board ready and the paper finished—but I cain't write worth a crap, Missy, you know I cain't. Look at it," I cried, shaking six pages of my crumpled, uneven hand under her nose, full of erased sentences and misspelled words. "I don't want Gabe to see it like this. He'll think I'm some kind of *retard*."

Now, Missy can be as hard-hearted as the Wicked Witch of the West, but she still has a few old Grannie-bones rattling around inside her, and softened at my sheer desperation.

With a big sigh to show how much of an *imposition* this was, she took the papers from me. "How many pages are we talking about here?"

"Six," I said, "maybe seven. The tapes are the main thing, and the board and the physical stuff. The report is extra, for the judges. I have to beat Bobo, and everybody says his stuff is *good*."

"They'd be more impressed if it was typed," she murmured, though I had no time for that.

"I cain't type," I said, "and anyway, it's too late," then dug out one final page that I handed to her with a red face because it was a dedication that read: TO GABE, WITH LOVE.

"You're doing a dedication?" she asked, as if the evidence wasn't right in front of her nose.

I just shrugged in reply, though her doubt made me suddenly unsure. "Well, you don't think he'll think it's a, you know, declaration of *passion,* or anything, do you?"

She just cast me the edge of a curious eye, murmured: "I don't know what he'll think it is." Then, "When's it due?"

This was the question I was dreading, and for a moment I just stood there chewing my thumbnail, then admitted in a small voice: "Tomorrow."

*"Tomorrow?"* she cried, and all but threw it back in my face, though after a little venting and fuming on her and Sim's favorite subject (how I wasn't a child anymore! I was thirteen! I needed to grow up!), she sighed the sigh of the martyr and promised to give it her best shot.

I thanked her as thoroughly as she'd allow, then creeped back to my room, not at all convinced that she'd come through, though when I woke up the next morning, I found eight wonderful pages on my dresser, with a cover page, a dedication, the works, all in her clear, fat hand. By then, the glue on my project board had dried, Mama's little glitter sprinkles just the right touch, making Daddy's pictures—the old ones from the Hill when he was a little boy, and later, at his wedding, and one at Sanger with Mr. Sam—look magical, as if he'd led a charmed life.

Gabe had to go into town early that day to help the other social-studies teachers set up the fair, so Mama took me and Kenneth to school with our projects and dropped us off at the library entrance. We were supposed to set them up on the back counter for Mrs. Lunt to register and take to town, but once I'd filled out my little slip and hoisted my book bag to leave, I had the weirdest feeling in my stomach, like I was abandoning Daddy to strangers. Even after Kenneth left and the tardy bell rang, I kept standing there at the counter looking up at my project board, thinking about all the stories on the tape: about how Daddy had failed at baseball, but won at money; about his first date at sixteen; how he was too poor to go to the prom, and for some reason, it filled me with the awfulest sadness. When Mrs. McDonald sent Bobo and Darius down to see what was keeping me, they found me standing there in front of my magnificent board, staring up at the picture of Daddy on his wedding day, tears streaming down my face because he looked so much like Sim; he looked so happy.

And though Bobo and Darius are like me, not the brightest bulbs in the pack where schoolwork is concerned, they immediately knew what was up and were really nice about it, patted me on the back and told me how good my project was, how I'd be sure to win a ribbon, stuff like that. I appreciated their support, wiped my face on my T-shirt, and went to class, though I was so nervous all day I could hardly think, me and Bobo both were. As predicted, his project on folk medicine was probably the best of the bunch, his board not so impressive (just a dime-store poster board), though he had *six* tapes and all kinds of physical evidence, not just the mojo hand, but recipes for roots and salves and even a little bag of chicken bones his great-grannie used to tell fortunes with.

Since Gabe was already at the school, Mama took me and Kenneth

to town that night, bought us hamburgers at the concession stand the
Beta Club had set up in the cafeteria as an end-of-the-year fund-raiser.
Missy, who was secretary that year (she'd be president the next), was already there, bossing everyone at the grill with her usual take-charge
manner.

Like Daddy, she's just the soul of competition, and as soon as she
laid eyes on me, she ran over and asked: "Did you place?"

"The award thing isn't till seven-thirty," I told her around a bite of
my hamburger, though Missy just rolled her eyes.

"That's for the school trophies and Living Biography," she said. "The
judges came through *hours* ago. The eighth-grade projects are down in the
gym; go look."

Well, she didn't have to ask twice. Without even finishing our burgers, me and Kenneth tore off out the door and across the courtyard to
the echoing old gym that was packed full of clamoring students and parents and teachers and out-of-town judges, all wandering up and down the
aisles, inspecting row after row of project boards and models and maps.

As we made our way through the crowd, searching for the oral-
history section, I began to have this sinking feeling in my heart, because
some of the projects were doggone good, one gigantic one on the Tet Of-
fensive that really made me jealous. I had stopped to look at it, was staring enviously at its big blue ribbon when Kenneth gave a holler, called me
to the next aisle, where his project on the turpentine industry was pinned
with a red third-place ribbon.

It was a disappointing showing for a hotshot like him, though I tried
to be upbeat about it, was congratulating him on placing at all when Darius and Travis spotted us in the crowd and came running up, making all
these noises of excitement. It was impossible to make out what they were
saying; me and Kenneth finally just followed them to the corner of the
gym, where Bobo was by gosh leaping into the air in triumph, surrounded by a excited little knot of relatives from Sinclair.

"*What?*" I shouted to Kenneth, then saw with a sinking heart that

Bobo's flat little dime store poster was tagged with a big blue ribbon: FIRST PLACE, ORAL HISTORY.

I didn't want to go any further after that. I mean, even if I won second place, I wouldn't go to regionals, must less state. But Bobo had been so nice that morning when he'd found me bawling in the library that I swallowed my disappointment, was pushing through the crowd to congratulate him when Ga'Lisa spotted me from across the room, shouted: "Clayton! Come 'ere! *Clay!*"

All of us—me and Kenneth and Darius and even Bobo and a few of his cousins—raced down the aisle to the very end, where my three-sided project board stood in isolated splendor, a big blue ribbon hanging below Daddy's wedding picture. We didn't know if it was a mistake or what, two projects winning first place, just let out a roar of triumph, not just for me, but for LPM and Gabe and *myth* and *symbol* and *empowerment,* all his other nutty liberal ideas.

Darius and Travis tore off immediately to look for him, to tell him about the wins, finally tracked him down to Living Biographies and brought him back to the gym, Gabe all dressed up in his wedding suit, though his tie was loosened, his hair poking up like usual. When he saw my blue ribbon, he grinned and held out his hand for a shake, raised his voice to shout: "Congratulations, Mr. Catts—excellent job, just first rate. I'd have given you an A even if you weren't kin to me."

"But Bobo won first place, too!" I shouted above the roar.

Gabe just shrugged, "Well, that's all right; this isn't an in-school competition. We can have more than one first place. Matter of fact, the more blue ribbons, the better. We just might take that schoolwide trophy yet." On that, he turned to Kenneth, asked, "Mr. Brown? How'd you do?"

When Kenneth told him third place, the grin disappeared from Gabe's face like magic. He didn't seem to believe us, but had Kenneth lead him back to his project, where he slipped on his bifocals and peered at the red ribbon for a long moment in absolute wonder, then tore off through the crowd, his jaw jacked like he was heading for a fight. We didn't know what to make of it, just stood there with our hands in our pockets till he finally returned with one of the judges, a nattily dressed guy of about his own age, wearing a checkered vest and gold watch chain, who he might have known from Tallahassee, because they were on first-name basis, Gabe calling him Tom, though his name tag said Dr. Some-body-or-other.

Me and Kenneth just stood back and watched in wonder as Gabe acted the part of the outraged parent, browbeating him about Kenneth getting a third place, asking if he'd read the report, listened to the tapes. The judge just rubbed his neck with great forbearance, told him: "Listen, Gabe, there were over two hundred entries this year, we didn't have time to listen to *every* tape—"

But Gabe was having none of his excuses. "Well, you *should* have," he insisted with that chip-on-the-shoulder belligerence that got him kicked out of his Sunday-school class. "This kid has a turpentine song on tape—you ever heard a turpentine song recorded *anywhere*—the Smith-sonian? The Florida State Museum?"

The neat little judge admitted he hadn't, finally took the tapes and physical evidence back to the judges' booth, where he must have con-ferred with the other judges, or maybe took the time to sit down and lis-ten to them. For when he returned to the gym half an hour later, he was carrying another ribbon, a blue first-place one that he tacked on Ken-neth's project board with a little bow of apology.

We couldn't believe our eyes, just stood there staring till Darius and Bobo ran up and let out another shout of triumph that broke our paralysis, made us all leap in the air, high-fiving and hollering like the hay-seeds we were.

The little judge didn't look too annoyed at our enthusiasm, though, but was very gracious, even offered his hand to me when Gabe intro-duced us. "I very much enjoyed your project, Clayton," he raised his voice over the roar to inform me politely. "I never met your father personally, but he sounds like he was a splendid man."

I just shook his hand like a grown-up and thanked him, the thought coming to me that gosh, this must be one of Gabe's *gay* friends from Tallahassee. I mean, who else wore checkered vests and watch chains, used words like *splendid* to describe a man? I must say I was pleasantly surprised, thought how *nice* gay people were; how could people say such nasty things about them?

That really was the tone of the evening: peace on earth, goodwill toward man, Mama coming to the gym when Sim arrived with Grannie (who couldn't drive at night because of her cataracts), all of them so pleased and proud, beaming on me with undisguised affection. When seven-thirty rolled around, we all crowded into the auditorium for the awards ceremony, the Living Biography ribbons announced first, then the trophies by grade. All of us kids from LPM were about spastic by the time they made it to the eighth grade, especially Bobo, who'd been sucking down Coke all night and was about wired. I mean, when they finally got around to announcing the middle-school trophy and the judge looked up and said, "Lincoln Park Middle," he let out a scream like a panther, he really did.

Everyone was pretty good-natured about it, though. They knew we were the poor goobers from the sticks and thunderously applauded as we went up to get the trophy, me and Bobo and Kenneth, because Darius and Travis and Ga'Lisa were too shy to go up front. I probably would have been, too, but had by gosh gotten pumped on all that caffeine and success, beat Bobo and Kenneth to the platform and took the trophy myself, held it over my head in triumph the way Missy did at softball tournaments. And though I had thought of a thousand speeches to make in the miraculous event we won, when the judge stepped back and indicated the microphone, I just leaned forward and grinned: "We'd like to thank the members of the Academy who voted for us," like movie stars do at the Academy Awards.

I think it might have been the funniest thing I ever said in my life, for the whole auditorium exploded in laughter, me and Bobo loudest of all. We would have let it go at that and returned to our seats in triumph, but Kenneth apparently wanted to say something, too. With a timid glance at the judge, he stepped to the podium, trying to be cool, though it was clear that his old Italian blood was pumping, his face scarlet as he took a breath and added in this quivering little voice: "And we'd like to thank Dr. Catts," he sniffed, "for coming to our school, and looking out for us." He paused again, blinked hard. "For helping us remember, who we *are*."

And I'll tell you what: that was all she wrote for any of us, as far as the crying went. I think even the judges were going strong before it was over, and hardly remember the rest of the ceremony that passed in unparalleled victory, twenty-three kids from LPM placing in some category, nine of us getting first-place blue ribbons, one short of a county record. When it was all over, Mama took Miss Susan down to the gym to show her the projects and the rest of us returned to the cafeteria so me and Kenneth could finish the hamburgers we'd left on the counter two hours before.

By then, the crowd was considerably thinned, Missy able to take a break and join us while Gabe stood at the door, chatting with an adoring knot of parents. We were still flying high, told her all about our speeches (that she'd missed since she was working the booth), both of us singing the praises of the little judge who'd changed Kenneth's ribbon. I described his vest and his watch chain in some detail, even speculated that he was probably one of Gabe's *gay* friends from Tallahassee, making Missy look up, breathe: *"What?"*

Just like that, I knew I'd done something very stupid and tried to back up, though Missy wouldn't let me, her face amused and positively amazed. "What d'you mean, *gay friend?*" she insisted. Then, before I could answer: "You think Gabe's *gay?*"

Well, I didn't anymore, and shook my head with great passion and outrage, saying "No, no—"

But it was too late. Missy just stood and called across the cafeteria,

"Uncle Gabe! Come here!"—her face lit with laughter, like it was the funniest thing she'd ever heard in her life.

Well, I saw then that it was time to be leaving and leaving quickly; jumped up and abandoned my hamburger for the second time that night, took off down the hall to the gym, where the womenfolk were still wandering through the projects, basking in the glory of our blue ribbons. When I told Mama that I wanted to leave, she didn't argue, just went on and on all the way home about how proud she was of me, how well I'd done. I just nodded, didn't pay her much mind, to tell you the truth, was too intent on getting to the safety of my bedroom. I hightailed it upstairs as soon as we walked in the house and leaped into bed, pretending to sleep, though it wasn't long before there was a quiet knock at my door.

But it wasn't Gabe; it was Missy, still in her apron from the fundraiser, her hair in a bun. She didn't wait for me to invite her in, just came in and stood by the bed. "You asleep?" she asked in this small, conciliatory voice. I turned to the wall in reply, making her exhale hugely, say, "Clay"—sigh—"listen. I didn't mean to, like, publicly humiliate you, or anything. It was just kind of—funny, is all. Where'd you come up with such a goofy notion, anyway? That numbskull Kenneth?"

"I don't want to talk about it," I muttered to the wall, though Missy just grabbed me by my shirt and hauled me to my back.

"Oh, lighten up, Claybird." She grinned. "Kenneth told Gabe and I'm the one who had to ride home with the raging lunatic uncle—like being trapped in a Volvo with King Lear. You can tell old Missy, I won't tell anyone."

It was always hard to resist her when she was being playful; she sounded too much like Daddy, and looked like him, too, her fair, freckled face lit with his irrepressible grin. After a moment, I sat up on my elbow and told her in an exasperated little voice: "Miss Cassie, remember? After the funeral? I told you she told me."

Missy wrinkled her brow at that, then looked at me with new interest. "Is that the weird thing she told you about Gabe? That he was *gay?*"

I nodded, kind of surprised at the evident shock on her face, that made her draw back and blink at me like an owl. "Well, Claybird," she finally said, "him and Mama have been, you know, happily married since Christmas, rattling the walls about three times a week." When I didn't reply, she offered: "Well, don't you think that says something about his—you know—sexual orientation?"

For a moment, I faced her off levelly, then dropped back on the bed. "Not when you're a retard," I said.

She didn't argue the matter, just stood there a moment, then backed to the door. "Well, I snagged you a couple of free burgers," she said, "left them on the stove."

I nodded my thanks, though Missy didn't leave right away, just kept standing at the door, watching me, finally added in a small, pitying voice: "And Clay, listen: I wouldn't be so hard on myself, if I was you. I mean, it's really not your fault, that you're always so terminally confused." I thought she was talking about the dyslexia, but she just motioned at the dark hallway at her back. "It's this house," she said. "Remember when you and Kenneth were little, you thought it was haunted? You dug up the front yard, looking for graves?"

I nodded, and Missy smiled a smile that was sad and down-tilted, made her very much resemble our mother. "Well, you were *right*," she said with a sudden, small intensity. "It *is* haunted. Our whole family, it's full of secrets; full of ghosts."

I'd been around Gabe enough by then to understand that she was speaking symbolically, though I didn't know what the heck she was talking about, because never in my life had I felt less haunted, less grieved and abandoned, than when I'd stood on the stage that night and made my well-received little quip.

My face must have shown it, for Missy just eyed me a moment, then sighed. "Well, just don't be surprised if you stumble upon one, and soon. Don't flip out on me or anything, 'kay?"

She left on that odd piece of advice, said good night and went to bed, though I didn't get up right away, just lay there faceup in bed till almost twelve, when hunger drove me downstairs to the burgers on the stove. I figured everyone would be in bed by then, the living room hung in gray shadow, but when I came around the corner to the kitchen, I found Gabe sitting at the table drinking coffee, still in his dress shirt from the fair, his shirtsleeves rolled up to the elbow. There was no possibility of retreat, him lifting his face as soon as he saw me, asking: "You all right?"

I just stood there frozen for a moment, then inched my way to the stove, to the sack of burgers that still rested there. "Missy already talked to me," I said, hoping that would be the end of it, though Gabe, being Gabe, wouldn't let the matter pass without discussion.

"So you thought I was gay?" he asked bluntly.

I was so embarrassed I wanted to crawl under the table, though Gabe didn't seem too shocked or horrified, just muttered: "Oh, Clay, git your eyes off your feet—good Lord, you look like your mother." I looked up warily then, hardly able to meet his eye, though you could tell he was letting me off easy like he always did, his voice a good-natured tease. "I don't know why you went tearing out of the cafeteria like that—you shouldn't let these bullshitters around here intimidate you. It was an honest mistake. What else could have accounted for my great good looks and buff physique and artistic temperament? I'm just one of those rare sensitive, good-looking Adonis straight guys, and God knows you don't see many of us around these parts. It was a purely understandable error."

I smiled at that, I couldn't help it, and once he saw I wasn't embarrassed anymore, he quit his teasing and gestured for me to join him. I took my bag of burgers to the table and we sat there and talked while I ate—not about anything serious, but Sim's graduation on Friday night, and whether or not I should risk rejection and invite Rachel to our end-of-the-year dance, stuff like that. When we were finished, Gabe went to the sink to rinse out his cup, said over his shoulder: "Oh—and Missy said there's a snake in the pool. She saw it when we came in."

I nodded, for spring was a suicidal season for snakes in our backyard, all the baby ones hatching and instinctively heading for the water, not smart enough to tell our pool from a lake till they got over the tiles. It'd be dead if I left it till morning, so I went out and searched for it in the dark, finally found it in the deep end under the diving board, bumping its head against the marble, trying like heck to get out. I didn't bother with the net, just offered a palm frond that it wrapped itself around in a fenzy of relief, hardly bigger than an earthworm, only five or six inches long, a baby black racer by the look of it.

Gabe waited for me at the French door, then walked me upstairs, not mentioning my project at all till we were at my bedroom door, when he paused a moment, told me again what a great job I'd done; how I'd interpreted the facts unemotionally, and how that was a hard thing to do. "But my favorite part was the dedication," he added. "That was very touching, Clay. Very nice."

I was too embarrassed to do anything but look at my feet, though he didn't seem to require anything in the way of a response, just stuck his hands in his pockets and commented in a reflective little voice: "You know, I think it's kind of touching and laudable, that you—this fundamental Baptist kid—thought I was gay and took it so well. I mean, you and Kenneth were so protective of me. You took my side a thousand times. You got that from Michael, you know. He had that same natural acceptance. He had a good heart." He paused as if to say something else, but just shook his head, added with a fond little smile: "Calmer of babies, rescuer of snakes—you know, Clay, I think you have the seeds of a great humanitarian in you."

# CHAPTER TWELVE

The seeds of a great humanitarian," he said with all his old pomp and certainty, and such was the depth of my infatuation that I didn't even roll my eyes or laugh: I believed him. That's the pity of it: I really did, the summer stretching out before me, ripe with promise, my oral-history project going on to regionals, where Bobo snagged a first-place trophy, though me and Kenneth only came in second and third respectively, good enough, on that level.

I couldn't complain, for in the meanwhile, I'd gotten my final report card from Lincoln Park, where by some miracle of God, I made the honor roll and got my name in the paper for the very first time. That was glory enough for anyone, though it was only a couple of weeks later that a pale blue envelope from the school-board office finally winged its way to our mailbox, summoning Mama in for a meeting to change my Individual Education Plan.

Now, Mama's about as swift as me about reading legal documents and didn't know quite what to make of it; neither did I. We knew it was Big News, but had to wait for Gabe and Missy to come home from one of her softball games before we found out that this handful of flimsy yellow photocopies was the official results of the IQ test I'd taken back in January.

"Did I make it?" I kept jumping around and begging as Gabe stood there in the doorway and impatiently scanned the legal jargon and sig-

natures, searching for something that he must have found on the top of
the third page.

For he suddenly shouted: *"Yes!"* in triumph, then held out the paper
to me, boomed: *"Clayton Michael Catts,* come and *read* the *Magic* Number!"

He pointed at a number scribbled in a box in the corner that I read
aloud in a hesitant little voice (because I still sometimes read numbers
backwards): "A hundred and forty-two?" then looked up. "What does *that*
mean?"

Before he could answer, Missy, who was standing in the door of the
laundry room, stripping out of her sweaty jersey, let out a noise of disbelief, called in this taunting little singsong: "Uncle *Ga-be.* You *cheat-ed*—"

"Did *not,*" he returned, though it wasn't until Mama snatched the
paper from me that I understood the significance of the enormous number, when she looked up in amazement, asked: "That's his IQ? A hundred
and forty-two?"

"A hundred forty-two, *my behind,*" Missy called from the laundry
room, for being the Resident Genius of the Catts family was her Claim
to Fame, and she didn't much like sharing the glory.

Even after Mama went down to the county offices and changed all
my paperwork and I was officially transferred from special-ed to Gifted,
Missy remained a skeptic, which wasn't what you might call an *isolated*
opinion in the larger Catts family. Even Grannie looked kind of suspicious
when I told her the Big News.

"Well, shug," she asked after a moment, "how come them to send
you to thet special class all these years?"

I tried to explain that I was both dyslexic *and* gifted, that there was
actually such a creature, even brought up Albert Einstein, though you
could tell Grannie wasn't overly familiar with the name. She just gave a
polite little sniff of disbelief, murmured: "Well, I declare."

But nothing they said could steal the glory of the day, me and Kenneth suddenly Brothers in Brilliance, full of plans for high school, where
we'd have most of our classes together now that I was on the Gifted

track. We talked about it all summer, signed up for all these butt-kicking classes when we went to Open House in July—Latin and algebra and honors civics—with Gabe acting as my educational director, Missy, my personal buyer.

For my sister has always been an unashamed popularity hound, and as August drew near, she became increasingly concerned that I'd show up in town the first day of school in my old Wranglers and crew cut and ruin her good name and reputation as a Millionaire's Daughter. All summer long she pored over *Seventeen* magazine and studied the cast of *Beverly Hills 90210*, till she finally nosed out a New Look that was centered around three comfortable items: tennis shoes and knee-length shorts and big surfer T-shirts, preferably with cool slogans on them (RON JON and NO FEAR and the like).

I didn't mind, for under Gabe's liberalizing influence, I was getting kind of tired of doing that *redneck thang* myself and was pleased with my New Look, my blond hair and general chunkiness suddenly more Beach Boy than Mama's Boy, my belly camouflaged by a good-natured bagginess from neck to knee. Even Missy seemed halfway satisfied with the result, standing in the dressing room of an Athletic Attic the Friday before school started and surveying me with a look of unusual seriousness.

"You know, Clay," she mused, "underneath that roll of baby fat and that *cornpone* haircut, I'm beginning to see a glimpse of a decent-looking young man, one that I would not be ashamed to call brother. If we could just get rid of that two-inch *space* between your teeth, we would be well on the way to setting him free."

Because that was my one redneck holdout: unlike Sim and Missy, I still sported a tiny little gap we'd all inherited from Daddy, that they'd had painstakingly corrected with braces and permanent retainers and (in Missy's case) even dental surgery. I probably would have gone the same route, but Daddy died before my first orthodontic appointment came around, and Mama so missed his gap-toothed smile that she let me go natural. This suited me down to the ground, for I'd always liked the stubborn little imperfection in my otherwise dimpled, girlie smile that made me favor Daddy a little (a very little) and, better yet, meant I could spit through my teeth like he used to, in a way I'd always found kind of manly and attractive.

But aside from that, I shook off most of my redneck ways, even grew my hair out a little, enough that it began to curl forward on my forehead, made me look amazingly like the graduation picture of Gabe that still sat on top of Grannie's television, though I didn't mind that, either. In fact, I kind of enjoyed the comparisons, to him and Daddy both; was balanced there between them for a pleasant three months, till it all fell apart in my hands, right there at the end of the summer, on Labor Day weekend, a holiday I've never been really big on, anyway.

To me, it's one of those funky little Monday holidays, so short that you can't properly celebrate or get anything done, just sit around and chew your nails in nervous anticipation of the new school year, which (in this county, anyway) always begins bright and early the next morning. On this year in particular, I was anxious to get this show on the road; get my fine thirteen-year-old self to town and show off my new hairdo and my new *look,* try it out on the girls, Rachel Cole in particular, who was as independent as she was beautiful, had never given me the time of day.

I was hoping that my new urban look might bring her around, got up early that morning and laid out my school clothes a day in advance. For Curtis had called the night before, asked if I wanted to go out on one more run to the river before school started, not fishing, but frog-gigging on the Apalachicola, way down on the edge of the swamp. We probably wouldn't be back till late, so I went ahead and laid out one of my new Ron Jon shirt and socks and Nikes, then went down to Sanger with Gabe to help move a couch.

Sim met us at the office, not in his old work clothes, but pressed khakis and a golf shirt, for after months of lowly menial labor in the wood shop, he had finally been moved to the front office to get in a little hands-on experience in management before he left for FSU next August. The position was purely temporary, didn't even have a title, though the guys on the floor were already calling him the *Heir Apparent* with a hint of contempt for his rich-boy status, making it clear that he would have to earn their respect, and it wouldn't come easy.

Mama and Mr. Sam were worried about it, knew the guys at the plant could be a tough bunch to deal with, though easygoing old Sim had gladly risen to the challenge, his first official act as semimanagement to give his poor old Grannie a brand-new sleeper sofa. Even I knew the gesture was symbolic, meant to send a message, a not-so-subtle reminder that the Cattses' fabled fortune hadn't just fallen out of the sky into our laps, but that we'd all started out right where they had, in a two-bedroom row house on Magnolia Hill.

He wouldn't even let them deliver it, but went down and picked it up himself, and with me and Gabe's help, took it over to Grannie, who pretended to be thrilled to death, though I think she really preferred her old couch, and only took the new one out of politeness to validate Sim's appointment to the front office. In any case, the dang thing weighed a ton, and maneuvering it into Grannie's little living room proved to be a good and full morning's work. When we finally got it situated, we moved the old couch to the back porch, where Gabe wanted to leave it.

"You can sit out here in the afternoon and watch the sunset," he told Grannie, slumped on the middle cushion, sweat dripping down his nose.

But Grannie was the kind of self-respecting Southern woman who wouldn't dream of leaving a washing machine or clothesline or old couch on her porch, and told him in exasperation: "Gabriel Catts, you *git* thet couch down to the Goodwill. It's a good fine couch, a Duncan Phyfe. There's *plenty* of folk'll be *proud* to git it."

On that, Gabe opened an eye. "Good God, Mama, this thing is a hundred years old," he said. "I remember peeing on it when I was a baby. I remember it distinctly."

"You remember no such thang," she said with a little slap to the back of his head. Then, in a more wheedling tone: "You boys run it on downtown. I'm fixing a big nice pork roast for dinner, and potato salad, and making ice cream. It'll all be ready by the time you git back and Myra and Missy'll be here and we can all sit down and eat."

For Grannie doesn't share my prejudice toward Monday holidays, but celebrates them like she does every other holiday on the calendar, with food, food, and more food. On this particular occasion, she had smoked a whole pork loin that she served alongside half a dozen other summertime classics, including her famous peach ice cream that she had just lately begun to make in an electric churn Lori had given her for Mother's Day that she was still mighty suspicious of, complained that it groaned "like a dying cow giving buttermilk."

Indeed, all during dinner, you could hear it laboring out on the back porch, Grannie getting up time and again to check on it, afraid the motor would burn up and set the house on fire. The rest of us weren't too concerned, just sat around the table feasting on pork and discussing the coming year, the room filled with a happy anticipation, though Missy was still worried about me bringing shame on her good name at school, even started ragging me about my table manners.

"If you ever see me in the cafeteria," she warned, "don't bother to speak."

After a whole summer of her warnings and appeals, I had gotten used to her nagging and really didn't pay her much mind, even after Grannie jumped on the bandwagon, began imparting a few tips of her own—how it wasn't polite to talk with your mouth full; how that when one hand is on the table, the other one ain't.

Now, I knew the rule about not talking with your mouth full, but the other one was kind of hard to follow, not just to me, but apparently to Sim, too. He just thought about it a moment, then asked her mildly: "Well, if it ain't on the table, where *is* it?"

I think Sim was actually serious, though before Grannie could answer, I cracked, "It's on your crotch, Sim. That's the polite place to put your hand while you're eating."

Missy let out a roar at that, pointed her fork at me and told me to do her a favor and never *speak* to her again, though Grannie just came wearily to her feet and went out to check on the laboring churn.

"He's a'gitting more like his *deddy* every day," she announced as she went around the table, giving Gabe a little slap to the back of the head as she passed, telling him: "Now you'll see what I went through raising *you,* Gabriel Catts."

I don't think Grannie even realized what she said; neither did I, at first. I mean, if there was anything I was used to that summer, it was people commenting on our likeness, making their little assumptions. It happened so often that it hardly registered anymore, and wouldn't have then, except for two things: Mama, who closed her eyes when she said it, as if she had taken a quiet blow to the face, and Missy, who met my eye across the table, her disgust with my bad manners replaced in an instant by a sharp, poignant expression that I couldn't quite place at first, then realized with a strange little jolt that it was *pity.*

It only lasted a moment, a quick blink of the eye before she turned to Simon and they resumed their bickering, their voices forced and fake, though I hardly heard them, disjointed pieces of evidence beginning to return to me like random pieces of puzzle, falling into place at last. I remembered Bobo's face the first time he laid eyes on Gabe in class: the immediate light of recognition, his high, curious voice: "He yo deddy?" And even earlier than that, Missy sitting up in bed the night we had the stepfather discussion, watching me closely, asking: "Did Daddy ever talk to you about Uncle Gabe? Tell you anything kind of—weird?" And most damning of all, Gabe himself, standing at the wall of the old apartment his first Saturday home, discussing the faded, curling old maps that looked *ancient* to me and Kenneth, though he said they weren't that old; that he'd put them up the summer he lived here, the summer before I was born.

"Why didn't you take 'em with you?"

"Well, I left in kind of a hurry."

Before Grannie even returned with the ice cream, I was already counting forward in my mind: July-August-September, October-November-December, January-February-March—nine months to the day I was born. And just like that, I knew. I understood it completely, all the little hints and confusing winks falling into place, making me close my eyes, take a small, painful little breath.

I wanted to get up then and get the hell out of there, but I didn't, of course. I was like the skeleton who wouldn't cross the road: I didn't have the *guts,* just sat there, my face on my plate, the voices around me coming from a great distance, till suddenly there was a knock at the back door, and Curtis's voice, flat and familiar, calling a greeting through the screen.

I jumped up as soon as I heard him and headed for the door, though Gabe was fast on my heels, caught me just as I made the truck, his napkin still clutched in his good hand. "Clay. Listen," he said, his face pale, his voice trying for normalcy: "I need to talk to you when you get home tonight. 'Kay?"

I didn't answer, didn't meet his eye, just scrambled into the truck and slammed the door between us, though Curtis was polite enough to call through the window: "Sure thang, Gabe. We're just going gigging on the river. Be home by nine."

Gabe backed off immediately, told us good luck or be careful or something, I really don't remember, thrown into shock, I think, my head and neck still hot, so hot I could hardly breathe, had to roll down the window a few inches to get a little breath. I didn't utter a word all the way to the river, just sat there staring out at the peanut fields that were full of weeds that time of the summer, long past harvest.

Every once in a while Curtis would make a stab at conversation, finally offered in a placating little voice: "Well, I got a spare this time, if that's what's worryin' you."

I didn't know what the *heck* he was talking about, just turned and stared at him blankly till I remembered our last fishing trip, way back in December, when we'd run over a nail, had to go back to town before we so much as touched the water. But I hadn't minded a bit, had been happy as a dog when I heard the *pffuf* of the puncture, saw the sag on the end of the trailer. For that was the golden morning Gabe had come strolling back into our lives ("Clay? D'you remember your uncle Gabe, from the funeral?"), his face ravaged with a red-eyed, red-nosed grief that maybe wasn't grief at all. Maybe it was another one of those sagging old emotions that made trips to the graveyard such an ordeal; maybe it was *guilt*.

The very thought brought that heavy lava feeling back to my chest, suffocating and breathless. I rolled the window down even lower, held my face to the rush of warm afternoon air, tried to get a grip on myself as we got to the boat slip, Curtis having me back in the truck, then go and park while he secured the boat.

The little flurry of activity distracted me, though when we were finally settled on the black water, floating placidly along the edge of the cypress, the dark suspicions returned, too close, too insistent to ignore. I finally couldn't take it any longer and broke the stillness of the high black water to ask in a quick, abrupt voice: "Curtis. *Listen.* Who do people say my father is?" He was standing when I asked, gig in hand, searching the river's edge for frogs, his eyes widening with a little jolt of surprise that he managed to hide pretty well, pretending something was wrong with the gig and sitting down immediately, fooling with the tip.

"Whatchu mean by *thet?*" he asked, face down, his voice oily and nonchalant, though I had no time for his games.

"Who do people say my father is?" I insisted, leaning forward a little, trying to see his face. "Do they really think it's Daddy?"

And at first he tried to laugh it off. "Oh, hell, Clay, whatchu dreaming up now? I ain't ever heard of such a thang—"

But he had, too.

You could *smell* it on him, and sitting back on my seat, I worked a little deceit of my own, glanced across the high water and told him in a mild little voice: "Well, somebody told me he wasn't, is all."

"*Who?*" he countered quickly, and the lie came easily to my lips.

"Miss Cassie," I told him, my eyes on the woods that were close and hot, though the sun was past its peak, already behind the trees. "You know—Cassie Campbell—who cuts our hair—"

He let out another bark of laughter, this time genuine. "Well, hell, Clay, you believe everything you hear down at the *beauty* parlor, then you'll be in a sad shape—"

"—and Grannie," I added, turning and meeting his eye. "She said so, too."

At that, his face lost its laughter in an instant, replaced by a look that was akin to the one Missy had shot me over the table at dinner: a look of deep and thoughtful pity, the same kind of look the nurses used to give me and Missy and Sim when we'd visit Daddy in ICU, take him candy and flowers and test papers with good grades that we thought would cheer him up.

He didn't answer right away, just sat there turning the gig over in his hands, the cypress and the water quiet except for the constant piping of the waterbirds and the chorus of the frogs; the late-summer sounds of the river. You could tell he was weighing his options, balancing the merits of a small white lie against the pain of the truth, though his old Cracker honesty finally got the best of him, made him look up and meet my eye evenly, tell me in a flat, honest voice: "Well, I've heard, Clay, that he might not be."

I was the one who couldn't speak then, my mouth so dry I had to swallow a couple of times before I could get out my next question, whispered in a weenie little voice: "Then *who?*"

Softhearted old Curtis, who had been known to cry when one of his hunting dogs got gored in a hunt, looked perfectly tortured at being put on the spot in such a way, though he was man enough to meet my eye and tell me plainly: "Well, everybody says Gabe is."

I must have actually flinched at that, because he was quick to try and soften it. "But, you know, Clay, I just heard that from my gossiping damn wife. Might be something *she* heard down to the beauty parlor, and wide of the truth."

But you could tell he believed it, that look of pained compassion returning to his face when I managed one final question, delivered in a voice of great and utter astonishment: *"How?"*

Curtis just rubbed his neck on that, long and hard, finally reached down and felt around under his seat for the bottle of Jim Beam he keeps hidden there from Lori. He unscrewed the top and took a long swig, even offered it to me, though I just shook my head, waited breathlessly for his answer, that was a shrug and a small, mirthless laugh.

"Oh, hell, Clay, it happens all the time. Gitting a woman pregnant's easy as sliding down a greased pole, you can take my word on *thet.*" I must have looked properly horrified, for he shrugged again, took another swig, then added: "You'll understand, you git a little older."

But he was wrong on that one.

Hell, I didn't need to be one *second* older to understand the name of the game here, the same game that had wrecked Miss Susan's second marriage to a nice-enough air force mechanic from Ft. Walton who was a good-enough deal as far as stepfathers went, a baseball fan who taught Kenneth how to throw a spitball, though he had one fatal flaw: he couldn't keep it zipped. Unlike Kenneth's own father, he wasn't a slapper or a shover, either, but was always stepping out, sleeping around, had given Miss Susan herpes before it was through (and Kenneth said that if I ever told anyone, he'd kill me with his bare hands).

And I hadn't. Hell, I was a Catts. I knew secrets. Knew all about them.

As of last October, I even knew why Uncle Ira was locked up in a little ten-by-ten cell in Raiford, why he'd never again see the light of day. Mama had finally broken down and told Missy, who'd been pretty weirded out by it all, had come to my room one night and told me the gruesome details: how he'd killed a woman, had beaten her to death with his bare hands in a cheap rented room in St. Augustine. Some woman he didn't even know; that he'd picked up in a bar, who'd probably looked like poor old Emmett Till when they finally found her a week later when the landlord came calling when her rent was due. Missy said there were other crimes, too, stuff that even Sim didn't know about, though the woman they'd found in bed was the one he'd fry for, because he'd left enough of his skin and blood and sperm around that the DA in Jacksonville had made a 100 percent match, and that, as they say, was that.

So, yeah, for a rich white kid who'd never kissed a girl, whose mother drove a Mercedes and whose Grannie taught Sunday school, I knew a few secrets. I just didn't know *this* one, and fell into another numbed silence that Curtis filled easily enough, the whiskey loosening his tongue, making him ramble on and on about Mama and Gabe, telling me every little detail that he knew of their Remarkable Romance.

"—they say he always loved yo mama, since he was a kid, never did get over her marryin' his brother. But he backed off when Sim was born, went up north to school and all, but then he come back that summer, moved in thet little apartment over the garage."

He shrugged then, took another draw of whiskey, concluded in a mild little voice: "And I guess sooner or later, nature just took its course."

It was about as much as I cared to hear about that summer, then or ever, but even after Curtis had exhausted every little bit of gossip and innuendo and myth he'd ever dreamed about Mama and Gabe, he kept rattling on, offering little nuggets of advice and wisdom between swigs of whiskey, like: "Way I see it, Clay, is you got *two* daddies, and that's a good thang. Most people these days, they ain't even got one." Or: "You cain't be too hard on people. People," he told me sagely, "are weak."

At one point, one very *low* point, he even commiserated with Gabe over his little *slip*, confided in a mild, swaggering voice: "Yo mama, she's still a good-looking woman, but you should have seen her when she was young." He rolled his eyes, whistled. "Son, she was *fine*."

Drunk or not, this was probably not the wisest move on his part, because there was still a loaded pistol on the seat between us (to shoot moccasins) and I thought about putting a bullet in his head before it was over. Fortunately, the bourbon soon got the best of him, made him blinking and sleepy, mostly silent on the ride home, dropping me off in our front drive as promised.

He was too far gone by then to offer any more advice, just yawned and waved, backed the truck around and went on his way, leaving me standing on the edge of Mama's rose garden in the close, muggy darkness, the front of the house dark, the back dimly lit.

So they were home, I thought, my happy little family, probably huddled around the kitchen table discussing me, Missy the voice of reason, insisting: "Gosh, somebody needs to *tell* him—everybody on *earth* knows but him, it's em*bar*rassing—"

Though she'd be called down by someone (Sim? Uncle Case?) who'd add their two cents with a little shrug: "Why bother? He'll never figure it out. Hell, he thought Gabe was *gay*—"

And worried or not, they'd burst into laughter at that, everyone but Mama—or maybe Gabe himself, who wouldn't think it very funny, would tell them to *hush*—that I was fine. There was nothing wrong with me at all. I was just an unusual personality. *Diffrent,* as Daddy would say.

Like father, like son.

I took off then, back down the drive to the highway that was pitch-black that time of night, the grass verge full of all kinds of nasty stuff you don't notice when you're tooling along in your mother's big Mercedes: dead possum and rabbits and even a smashed kitten or two, dank and corrupt in the September heat, all buzzing flies and matted fur and glassy, staring eyes. I wouldn't see them till I was almost on top of them, would have to step over them in my old fishing shoes, hot and sweating and dizzy, tears streaming down my face the whole time I stomped; strange, independent tears that were quite detached from anything I actually *felt,* flowing down my cheeks and chin and neck, on and on and on.

I didn't even know where I was going—to Grannie's, I guess, to spill it all out, let her fix this the way she fixed everything. To go to bed in tears like Little Gene, wake the next morning to a happy, miraculous turnabout, Gabe restored to his place of honor as my good-natured, hilarious old storytelling uncle who God in His wisdom had sent down as Daddy's replacement, in answer to a hundred prayers.

But this wasn't one of Grannie's hokey little bedtime stories: this was me, Clayton Michael Catts, the runt of the litter, who had never walked more than a block in his life if he could help it. By the time I made it past the courthouse—sixteen miles, at least—I was dragging butt, hardly able to stumble along. I was about to lie down on the sidewalk and die when I saw the yellow lines that marked the school crossing for the high school, and turned there in desperation, made my stumbling way to Aunt Candace's house. I dragged myself down her street and up the narrow steps to her dark porch, stumbling in the half-light, knocking over a wreath and a fern till I finally found her doorbell and rang it, just as the sun was rising on what would have been my first day of high school in town; the first day of my glorious new life.

# CHAPTER THIRTEEN

Aunt Candace herself answered the door, not in a nightgown, but a pair of the baggy teal scrubs she wears to work, apparently just coming home from the hospital or just on her way, I didn't know which. I just pushed inside without a word, was barely able to make it as far as her couch before I collapsed, light-headed and nauseated, though I couldn't puke, I was too tired to heave. I just lay there, eyes closed, head swimming, dimly aware that she had gone into her nurse's mode above me, checking my pulse and feeling my forehead and apparently not liking what she found.

For she started yanking off my shoes and socks and wiggling me out of my T-shirt, her voice rising and falling in a light, excited murmur: "What in the—Clay, does your mother know—good *Lord,* son, look at your feet! Did you walk all the way from the house?"

I didn't so much as open an eye, was content to lie there in bare-chested, barefoot bliss, at least till I heard the click of a phone that brought me back to life with a vengeance, rising up like Lazarus to point at her and shout: "No! *No!* Don't you call them—*NO!*"

I think I must have been a little *hysterical,* for she obeyed without a word, just quietly replaced the phone on the cradle, her eyes very level, though they weren't curious anymore, but tired and resigned and quietly pained, just like Mama's had been at supper; as if a blow had fallen, one long expected.

But unlike Mama, Aunt Candace didn't seem too demoralized by it all, her face quickly regaining its bossy old practicality as she held out her hands, said: "Come and take a bath, Big Man. I think you have a touch of heat exhaustion. A nice cool bath'll set you straight."

I hardly remember anything after that, just followed her to the bathroom in my crippled little walk, yelling aloud when my blistered feet touched the bathwater, though once I got used to it, it did indeed make me feel better, good enough that I think I might have fallen asleep in there.

For when I woke, I was curled up on a strange, frilly bed in one of Uncle Ed's T-shirts and some of his underwear, big old Hanes boxers that almost came to my knees. I rolled to my back and looked around the room with tired eyes, not at all curious about where I was, or why. It was dark, or near dark, and after a moment, I realized I was in Lori's old bedroom that Aunt Candace had left just the way it was the day Lori moved out, almost four years before. The walls were still painted a girlish mauve, the dresser and shelves crowded with a small forest of teddy bears and keepsakes and framed photographs of Lori in these all-American teenage poses: with her JV cheerleading squad, and standing next to Mickey at Disney, and half a dozen of her and a much younger Curtis in high-school formal wear at different dances and proms.

Everything about the place—the hairdos, the tuxes, even the bedspread—was straight out of 1985, a dip back in time that struck me uneasy, for some reason, as if I had woken up inside the opening scene of *The Twilight Zone*. I half expected to hear a voice-over from Rod Serling welcoming everyone aboard, lay there yawning till my empty stomach finally forced me out of bed. Kicking off the covers, I tiptoed down the hall on my sore feet like a little ballerina to the living room, where Aunt Candace was sitting in a recliner watching a rerun of *Designing Women*.

She smiled when she saw me, clicked off the remote, and said:

"Well, good evening, sleepyhead. You nearly slept the day away."

And I'll tell you what: shock is a funny thing. I mean, even after she said that, I still didn't really know why I was there, though I figured it would come to me in a moment. I just sat down on the couch in my T-shirt and big underwear, was about to ask if there was anything to eat when Aunt Candace gave me a look of mild reproach, told me: "I called your mother, Clay. That was a ratty thing to do, running off without a word."

Just like that, the weight and horror of the day descended, making me close my eyes and slump there on the couch, wanting to go back to sleep, or die, or *something*. But it was no use. Aunt Candace had been waiting around all day for me to wake up, had the bright-eyed look of a cat about to pounce.

"So? Are you ready to talk?" she asked.

I just yawned in reply, asked where Uncle Ed was.

"He's at a board meeting at the church," she said. "Won't be home till late. That'll give us plenty of time to work this out. Your mother's very upset, Clay. So is Gabe."

I ignored that, yawned. "D'you have anything to eat?"

Now, I believe I've mentioned that Aunt Candace doesn't cook, nor does she eat, or at least not so that you would notice, her pantry full of the sights and sounds of appetite—gourmet coffees and color-coded Tupperware and expensive cookware—but no actual *food* itself. It took a little scavenging around, even a trip out to the garage, to find a bag of Doritos, the gigantic kind you buy at Sam's for family reunions or church suppers.

I wasn't complaining, just sat on the couch and ate them by the handful while Aunt Candace fixed herself a cup of hot tea, then came and sat down next to me, started talking about Mama for some reason, telling me what a *good* woman she was, and what a tough time she'd had. She finally paused and asked if I knew about her. If I knew what she *was*.

Well, I was all out to sea at that point, had not a clue in the world to what she was talking about, just answered in a tired, flippant voice: "Oh, Curtis told me what she *was.*"

But Aunt Candace didn't catch my sarcasm, asked: "Well, d'you know what that *means?*"

I dived for another handful of Doritos, assured her: "Oh, I know what a *whore* is, Aunt Candace. Even *I* know that."

I don't even know why I said it; where in the world it came from. I think Curtis must have sent it into my head by mental telepathy, though once I heard myself say it, I was sticking with it, my face defiant, while Aunt Candace's was just mild and matter-of-fact as she quietly reached a hand over and grabbed the front of my T-shirt, pulled me about an inch from her face.

"Claybaby?" she murmured in this polite, motherly voice. "If I *ever* hear you talk about your mother like that again, I'm gone go outside and pick a switch and whip yo spoiled little *ass.* You hear me?"

Now, I would have liked to have done something manly in reply, like spit in her face, but the forced march the night before had left me weak and defenseless as a baby. Just like that, I could feel my face begin to crumple up and the tears begin to flow, God, I don't know where they came from. I mean, I'd already cried, like, ten hours, the night before. You'd think I'd be dried out by then, but I wasn't, just sat there clutching my bag of Doritos and sobbing with such intensity that Aunt Candace backed off and dropped my shirt, even made a stab at repenting for using the dreaded a-word, before she, by gosh, burst into tears herself.

I don't think she knew why, either. I think we were crying out of general disappointment with the sheer *wrongness* of life: fathers who died too young and daughters who left home too early, and people you loved so much—you trusted with your *life*—who betrayed you, ripped your heart out by the roots, then wanted so desperately to Make It Right, when there *was* no more Right. When Right was as dead as a doornail— dead as poor Emmett Till, or the woman Uncle Ira killed, or Daddy himself, lying there in his big old coffin, his hair gray, his eyes closed, nothing but a small man in an expensive suit, *gone.*

Aunt Candace got the better of herself before I did, went and got us a big box of Kleenex that she tossed on the couch between us, then sat back down, offered aside in this casual, sniffling little voice: "You know, Claybird, ever since you started going around with your little recorder last spring, looking for family stories—well, there's been this story I've been wanting to tell you. Not about Gabe," she assured me at the quick, panicked lift of my face. "But of me, and your mother, and the first time we met, when she was twelve. Has she ever told you that story?"

I shook my head wordlessly, for despite the flood of family history that had come on the tails of the Gabe Revolution, Mama's childhood was still her own, as veiled and voiceless as the paupers' section at the Riverside, the markers turned to pulp by the weather, unreadable and forsaken. Just like that, something inside of me seemed to stir to life at Aunt Candace's sniffling, hesitant offer, something curious and brave that wanted our family ghosts to show up, to reveal themselves, so I could finally sit them down the way Mama once said she'd like to do, fix them a cup of tea and get a few answers. Not about the century oak, and why they'd planted it so close to the house, but other things—nameless questions I could not even frame, that according to Aunt Candace, all had their roots in the summer of 1959, sixteen years before I was born, when a family of Louisiana Crackers moved in next door to Grannie on the Hill: a mother and father, a redheaded son, and a shy little girl they all called Myra Louise.

"—and God knows we hated them, every one," she concluded with a wry little shake of her head.

*"Why?"* I sniffed, surprised at her vehemence, if nothing else.

For all her fevered religious ways, Aunt Candace is not squeamish about owning up to a fault, and told me plainly: "Because we were hardworking, hard-shell Baptist, and the Simses were everything we despised: redheaded, holy-rolling, snuff-dipping *white trash.* Or maybe not *snuff dipping,*" she allowed, "but you know what I mean."

I did indeed, for there were still a few enclaves of poor white families around Sinclair trifling enough to qualify as trash, with junk cars and rotten teeth and droves of loudmouth, *goof*ball children who were the scourge of the special-ed classroom. It was hard to imagine Mama springing from such a source, though Aunt Candace didn't leave any room for rumination, just forged ahead: "And anyway, it was clear pretty early on that the father over there, well, he was a *monster*—"

"A *what?*" I interrupted again, thinking I hadn't heard her correctly. But Aunt Candace just retrieved her teacup from the end table and repeated herself in a voice of great authority. "A *monster*. Six-foot-three, maybe two hundred and sixty pounds, with a gut and temper, used to beat the living *crap* out of everybody over there, all the time. I mean, all summer long, you could lay in your bed at night and follow the action across the fence like ringside seats at a Golden Gloves match. First, there was the shouting, then the blows and *splats* and shrieks—then, when it was all over, these quiet, shaking little sobs that went on and on, half the night."

She paused on that, her face dim with the memory, her voice lacking her usual hardheaded conviction, though she made up for it in sheer candor, taking a sip of tea and admitting with her dry old honesty: "But I never actually went so far as to feel *sorry* for any of them over there. I was too busy with my own life, in my last year of high school, working for Dr. Winston part-time, already accepted at FSU. I left the pity to Daddy, the worry to Mama, who took Ira under her wing pretty early on, would invite him to supper all the time, give him Michael's hand-me-downs, worried over him day and night, because we knew he was getting flayed over there every week, that some of those quiet little sobs were his.

"She saw some whelp marks on his back at a church picnic and actually called the law on the Old Man, took the bus downtown and signed a complaint, which was just an unheard-of thing back then, turning in a neighbor for domestic violence. It was like a declaration of *war*, though it didn't do any good. The Old Man never saw a day of jail time, just kept strutting back and forth to work every day, and poor Mama, it about unhinged her mind. I actually remember her sitting at the table that summer, discussing ways to discreetly do away with the Old Man—you know, bake him a birthday cake and lace it with rat poison—I really do," she added when I broke out in a grin, I couldn't help it.

I mean, I could just see Grannie sitting there at the dinner table in one of her nice Sunday dresses, sipping iced tea and discussing ways to kill her neighbor and get away with it.

Aunt Candace didn't pause to enjoy the moment, just took a sip of tea and rolled right along: "Then, to make matters worse, Gabe, who was this goofy, extroverted little *nut*—he developed this *huge* crush on the little girl over there, Ira's sister—"

*"Mama?"* I interjected, because Aunt Candace said it in such an offhanded way.

I guess she'd gotten so caught up in her story that she'd forgotten who she was talking to, for she blinked back to the present, agreed in a mild, wondering little voice. "Yeah. Your mother. Myra Louise, they called her, and even that irritated me, it was just so hick and country. I grew to hate the sound of it, and God knows I heard it enough, with that idiot Gabe yammering on about her, day and night. And the strange thing was, though me and Michael *heard* about her all the time, we never actually *saw* her."

Unbidden, a slip of memory bubbled up, of me and Kenneth sitting at the attic window late one summer evening, watching Mama deadhead roses below. "Your mother doesn't go out much, does she?" he'd asked, and I'd had to agree: no, she didn't go out much at all.

Again, Aunt Candace didn't allow any room for reflection, just pushed ahead. "I doubt I would have known the Simses even *had* a daughter, if I hadn't have been a majorette, because she took a liking to my uniform. Every Friday night when I started getting dressed for a game, Gabe would just *beg* me to go out there and talk to her, and there was no denying him. He was just persistent as *heck,* would just nag and nag, follow me room to room, just about drive me *nuts,* because we didn't own a car of our own, and I was always begging rides and running late.

"But Gabe would by gosh get his way, and on the way out, I'd run outside and look for her, though she'd never come any closer than their back porch, would just peer at me from behind a post, her face pale in the twilight, with Gabe dancing between us like a pixie, trying to get us to move in closer. But she never would, and I never really got a good look at her till the night the Old Man turned on Daddy, tried to kill him." She finally paused then, commented in that mild, honest voice: "It was an evil day."

She came to a complete halt on that, just sat there, holding her teacup to her chest, staring ahead with a look of absent thoughtfulness.

I'd gotten too caught up in her story to be left hanging, and sat up straighter. "Killed *who?*" I asked. "Who got *killed?*"

But Aunt Candace wouldn't be hurried, just took another leisurely sip of tea. "Not *killed,*" she corrected, "not *quite,* though he came doggone close—ruptured his spleen, sent him to the hospital for the better part of a month—and we should have seen it coming, because earlier that year, around Christmas, the Old Man had caught Gabe playing in his yard, had broken his wrist, none of us really knew why. I mean, Gabe wouldn't talk about it, neither would Ira, but he'd done more than just break it, he'd actually *crushed* it, Dr. Winston said. Literally ground it to *pulp.* So things were not so great between us there on the Hill, this wall of tension running back and forth between us till sometime that spring— oh, maybe February—I came home from work one night on the bus, was hurrying up the Hill at dusk, when I saw two men fighting in the Simses' front yard."

She narrowed her eyes as if she was picturing it in her mind, try- ing to get it exactly right. "Well, I thought the Old Man had Ira out there, was finally getting around to killing him, went screaming to the house for Mama, but when I got to the fence, I realized it wasn't Ira getting killed over there; it was *Daddy.* He was already unconscious, lying facedown in the grass, the Old Man beside him, just leisurely *kicking* him to *death,* right in front of us all."

She threw up her hands in an odd little gesture of passivity, her eyes still dim, as if she were drawn back in time to that gray February twilight in 1962. "And Gabe was on the porch, his arm still in a cast, screaming his head off, not at Daddy as much as Michael, who came sailing out of the house just as I made the porch, took that fence like a sprinter in one giant bound. He was a nothing but a stripling back then, tried to get between Daddy and the Old Man, but he was too big, too strong.

"He just turned and took him down with one hammer of a backhand, so hard it knocked his feet right out from under him—killed him, we thought. But there was nothing we could do but stand there on the porch and scream—when suddenly, the McQuaigs' screen door popped open and old Brother George come strolling down the porch steps in his undershirt and suspenders, an ancient old shotgun in his hands that he had beaded on the Old Man, promised to blow his head off if he made one more move, just one."

She stopped again, right at the peak of the story, forcing me to sit up again, and repeat like a little parrot: "Did he *kill* him?"

Aunt Candace blinked at the question, as if surprised I'd ask such a thing. "No," she said with an absent little shake of her head, "no, I doubt it was even loaded—probably his old squirrel rifle, or something he'd brought back from the war. But it worked, as far as it went. The Old Man backed off, and Mama called an ambulance, and I went out and helped Michael back to the house, because he was concussed, staggering around, his jaw already swelled the size of a softball.

"I got him as far as the porch swing, went and fixed him an ice pack, was holding it to his face when Gabe came *bursting* out the door, white-eyed and frantic, looking for Mama. Well, I went in one direction and he went the other; we found her in her bedroom getting dressed to go to the hospital, dragged her to the kitchen, where low and behold, there stood Mrs. Sims, and the Mystery Child of Magnolia Hill."

"*Mama?*" I had to exclaim, and she gave a slow, even nod of assent.

"Yessir—twelve years old, standing there half-hidden in her mother's skirts in this ratty old nightgown that hung off of her in *folds,* her arms bone-thin, these dark gray rings under her eyes, clearly terribly ill. I mean, I'd seen children like her before in the ER, with cystic fibrosis or end-stage leukemia, with the same dark rings under their eyes, the same terrible suffering. It was just incredible, *unbelievable,* to me, that this devastation—this dying child was—*intentional*—"

That was about as far as she could go for a few moments, just sitting there beside me with her eyes closed, her hand pressed to her mouth, till she finally got a grip on herself and yanked out a fresh Kleenex, explained aside in a small, sniffling voice: "Mrs. Sims was wanting Mama to hide her—said the Old Man was leaving that night, going to Texas, wanted to take her with him, and Mama, she didn't need any more explanation than that. She just pushed Mrs. Sims out the door, sent her to hide on the tracks, sent me to town to find Uncle Case.

"Well, I took off in a gallop, looked *every*where, finally found him at the café, having supper with Ilene Cato. By the time we got back to the Hill, it was full dark, the Old Man long gone, that old shack standing empty across the fence, the front door hanging open on its hinges. Mama had hidden Gabe and Myra in a closet, wouldn't let them out till Uncle Case went over with his shotgun and nosed around, found Ira crunched down under the porch, hiding from the Old Man, I guess—and it's funny—but he was the sanest one of that bunch, Ira was, really the neatest little kid. I mean, he was skinny as a rail back then, weighed about eighty pounds, used to try to get between Myra and the Old Man—used to try to covey him out to the yard when he was drunk. I've seen him do it a dozen times, didn't know why, of course, none of us did. I mean, we knew the Old Man was a bully and a drunk, but never figured anything else, till—you know—"

She paused the way Missy sometimes did, assuming that I could fill in the blanks, but I couldn't. That was my problem: I couldn't fill in those blanks, and asked her baldly, "Know *what?*"

For a moment, she just looked at me, then told me levelly enough: "That he'd gotten after her, Clay—raped her. That's why she was so sick—why they had to admit her to the hospital that night, for antibiotics and a D and C. That's why the Old Man wanted to take her with him to Texas, because he knew that once a doctor examined her, well, it'd all be over but the shouting, then."

She paused to give me room to ask a few questions, or cry or maybe roar with outrage, though to be perfectly honest, the rape part really didn't register much with me, hardly touched me at all. I mean, I hardly knew what sex was back then, much less forced sex—just sat there blinking as Aunt Candace began tying up the loose ends of her story, her voice no longer so intent, but speculative now, mild and kind of tired.

"In any case, he was gone for good, the Old Man was, and when Myra got out of the hospital, the rest of them left Florida, moved up to an aunt's house in Birmingham, and that was the last we thought we'd ever hear from them. Gabe, he was pretty devastated, as you'd expect, but we all thought it would pass. We thought it was for the best, that he'd soon return to his goofy old Gabe-self, but he didn't. I mean, months passed and his arm came out of the cast and Daddy got better, and I left for college—but still, Gabe wouldn't talk about it, just grew into himself, got quieter and quieter. When I came home the next summer for my wedding, he was this silent, distant stranger. He didn't run with anybody, didn't hang out, just laid around the house all day, his hand held against his chest like it still hurt him, though it had been out of a cast for oh, years, by then.

"But we never heard another word from Ira or any of the rest of Simses, till the autumn Gabe left for school, in October of, oh, maybe '67—when Myra dropped by the house one night on her way to visit that cousin of hers in Milton. It wasn't anything planned, just a casual little drop-in to check out the old neighborhood, but Mama took a liking to her, and when it got dark, she just *insisted* she spend the night—and you know the story—how there was a mix-up with a note, and her and

Michael ended up briefly in the same bed." She rolled her eyes on that, at Grannie and her goofy old Grannie-ways, though she didn't belabor it, her words beginning to compress, a lot of years packed into a little space: "And it wasn't very long after, I was standing at my kitchen sink one morning in Wiesbaden doing dishes, looking out on the first snow of the season, when the phone rang, and it was Mama, all excited, told me Michael was engaged.

"Well, I figured he'd talked Michelle Dunne—this girl he dated in high school—into marrying him, was mouthing my congratulations when Mama broke in, said no, he wasn't marrying Michelle, but Myra. Myra *Odom*. Her mother had remarried in Alabama and that was her legal name then, one I didn't even recognize, and you know how goofy Mama is, she didn't bother to enlighten me. It wasn't till months later, when Michael sent me a wedding picture in my Christmas card, that I realized he'd by gosh married the little redheaded white trash kid from across the fence."

Even twenty years later, the wonder of this event had the power to make her shake her head slowly, in bewilderment, then add with a wry smile at her own curiosity, "So I was naturally dying to meet her, to see how she'd turned out, and the first thing I did when I got back to Florida in '74 was to get my nosy little butt out to your house—and let me tell you, son, it was a spooky old house back then, nothing like it is today. There weren't any roses or garden back then, just a long dirt drive through this wild, ragged little forest, this huge, sagging old house plopped down right in the middle, just weird and isolated as it could be.

"I remember knocking on the back door that morning and standing there, wondering what in the world Michael was thinking, taking on such a project—and when your mama opened the door, you could have knocked me down with a feather. Because the whole time I was in Germany, everybody had been telling me about how *good-looking* she was, talking about Michael's *good-looking* wife—and the woman that opened the door—well, there wasn't nothing *good-looking* about her. I mean, she was so skinny, she was a *bone,* and silent and vacant-eyed, rattling around that big empty house, so drugged and spacey she could hardly remember her own name. It was the strangest thing I'd ever seen in my life, because it had been what—twelve years?—since I'd laid eyes on that woman, and she was the same pathetic, skinny kid Mama had rescued that night on the Hill."

Aunt Candace paused for a breath on that, then let out a big sigh and began tying it up in earnest. "Well, I knew something was wrong," she said, "but it wasn't till we moved back in August that Michael finally broke down and told me the whole story: how that Myra'd had this gruesome breakdown after Missy was born, was seeing this *crack*brain psychiatrist who had her on so many pills she rattled when she walked—"

"Dr. Williams?" I had to ask.

At the very mention of his name, Aunt Candace laid back her ear like a old tomcat. "Yessir, the Wonderful Dr. Williams," she intoned with great sarcasm, and with no more encouragement than that, launched into a thorough, mostly incomprehensible argument against the good doctor, concluding with a great passion: "—but he can hand out the pills and call it what he will: manic depression or post-traumatic stress—but I personally don't think Myra suffers from some kind of *chemical imbalance,* some organic brain disease. It's just part of the baggage she carries from that *hideous* childhood, from that evil time on the Hill. I mean, Clay, it's almost like she didn't make it that night, that she really did die that winter. That's why she's so strong now, why she was so strong when Michael died. That's the kind of strength you get when you spend half your life working on a resurrection."

I had never told *anyone*—not Missy or Simon or even Grannie—about me and Kenneth and our Vampire Theory, and I didn't then, though it made her forceful words very easy to understand, very believable. In that way, it explained a great deal about my mother and her strange, otherworldly ways, though in a larger sense, it didn't resolve the matter of her and Gabe, that Aunt Candace began to warily approach with many little side glances to see how I was taking it.

"That's why, baby, I wish you wouldn't be so hard on her, about what happened that summer, between her and Gabe. She was so spaced out back then, she was hardly responsible——"

"Was Gabe?" I interrupted to ask sharply.

For a moment, Aunt Candace's expression was much as Curtis's had been the day before, as if briefly weighing the merits of a small white lie, though the truth won out in the end.

"Sure, baby," she admitted in a mild little voice. "He knew what he was doing. He wasn't a kid anymore, he was twenty-six years old. But he loved your mother so much, he always did, and when he came back and saw her rattling around that ramshackle old house, half out of her mind, well, he probably thought he was saving her. I really don't know, baby. He was gone by the time I got here, and Myra was already—you know—a few months pregnant."

"With *me*?" I had to ask, some small part of me still hoping against hope that she'd roll her eyes in exasperation at my dim-witted ways, say: "No, *Clay*, with *Missy*. Gosh, did you think I meant *you*?"

But she just watched me a moment with that face of terrible pity, then nodded with a finality that was like a stake through my heart. I was almost numb by then, though I did manage one final question: "What about Daddy?" I whispered, meaning: What was his take on all of this?

If possible, Aunt Candace looked even more pained at the question, though she answered honestly enough. "Well, he didn't like it," she allowed. "But he loved your mother so much, baby, and you, too, from the minute he laid eyes on you—and the fact of the matter is, Michael was a very forgiving man."

She paused then, clearly having a hard time explaining such a thing, till in true Southern form, a story came to her rescue, her face visibly lighting as she switched tracks abruptly, told me: "I mean, the day Myra called and told me Lori had showed up on her doorstep pregnant, well,

I went *ballistic*. I jumped in my car and tore over there to confront her, was chewing her out when Michael got home. He came in the back door, didn't say a word, just took one look at me and pulled me to the kitchen, leaned against the counter and let me rant and rave awhile, till he finally had enough and straightened up, told me: 'Candace? Honey, I know you're mad, but you best be careful what you say to that youngun in there who is your only chile in the world. You remember what Daddy used to say: You take a hard line, you live a hard life.'"

She smiled at the memory, explained, "It's what Daddy used to tell Mama about twice a week when we were growing up, when she'd go off on some tangent about somebody at the church or get in a fight with Uncle Case over his drinking and carousing: 'You take a hard line, you live a hard life.' And you know, Clay, if it would have come from anyone else, I would have spit in their face, told them to go to hell. But coming from Michael, I could take it. And I did. I swallowed my pride and went out there and apologized, and now we have little Ry-man running around, and you know how much we love him."

But I was far beyond that. I was bleeding from an open wound and told her flatly: "Well, *I* cain't."

Once again, she didn't argue, just began gathering the used tissues that were scattered between us. "Well, baby, that's your choice," she told me. "You'll have to work that one out on your own. But you're welcome to stay here while you do. I promised my brother I'd be there for his children and I intend to keep my promise, though I may have to hog-tie your mother and shoot Gabe to do it."

I'd been too wound up in the past to have worried much with the future, just nodded my head quickly and sincerely, Aunt Candace quickly reducing it to practical terms like she always did. "Well, I'll go out to the house tomorrow," she said, "talk to your mother, see what I can do. She and Gabe are just heartbroken and fragile as glass about all this, and the less shouting it comes to, Clay, the better. You understand?"

I nodded again, and she was as good as her word, arising early the next morning and going out to the house to see Mama, somehow talking her into letting me move into town, God knows how she swung it. Knowing Mama, she was probably afraid that if she didn't agree, I'd flip out and run away from home completely; take a bus to New York and end up a child prostitute turning tricks on Times Square. For that's the way my poor old mother's mind works: straight through the mundane possibilities and right to the bottom of the sea.

So she just bowed to the inevitable, packed my new school clothes and my Nintendo and skateboard and let me go without a fight, with (now that I think of it) the same tired resignation she let Daddy go back to the hospital that final time, as if she knew from experience that some battles were lost the moment they were begun. That sometimes, the better part of valor was a quiet retreat to regroup and reconsider, hope for a better day. Or maybe it was a bluff, or maybe she was ashamed to face me, or secretly glad to be rid of me: Who knows?

I believe I've mentioned that my mother isn't the easiest woman in the world to figure, not that I particularly wanted to, back then. I was just relieved to be shed of all of it: the matchmaking and the housecleaning and the peacemaking and the job-hunting, and everything else I'd done for her since Daddy left that night in the ambulance, almost two years before. I was ready for some peace and quiet, and spent my first evening at Aunt Candace's unpacking my stuff in Lori's closet, then went to bed early, still tired from the forced march the night before, my last waking thought that Simon and Missy must be gratified, lying there in their snug little beds out in the country, if they happened to think of me.

For after thirteen years of begging and pleading, I had finally done the thing they'd been after me to do for so long: I wasn't a child anymore. I was all grown up.

# PART THREE
## *The Choices of Clayton Catts*

But the rain
*Is full of ghosts tonight, that tap and sigh
Upon the glass and listen for reply.*

EDNA ST. VINCENT MILLAY

# CHAPTER FOURTEEN

PALM SUNDAY; EIGHT O'CLOCK AT NIGHT

I've lived with Aunt Candace for seven months now, and the whole time I've been here, I've wanted to record my side of the matter, and all the little bits of history and action that led up to my Great Exile, but couldn't. The words just wouldn't come, no matter how much time I had on my hands, no matter how hard I tried. I even bought a tape player. Thought I'd make it into another oral-history project, but no dice. Then one night last week a freak storm blew in from the Gulf, fierce and fast, rattling the windows and waking me from a sound sleep.

I sat up in my tangle of sheets, worried that it might be a storm of consequence: a hurricane or spin-off tornado; something with the power to rip off a roof, upend an oak tree. But as I watched the play of lightning on the dresser top full of trophies and picture frames—mementos of my cousin's perfect life that I've never bothered to put away—I remembered it was April, too late for hurricanes, too early for tornadoes, nothing but an early summer storm, quickly upon us and just as quickly past.

I burrowed back into my covers, was drifting back to sleep when a stark, single memory came to me of waking up the exact same way the spring before to the ferocious whip of the old oaks, the fast, furious rattle of the rain, of being overtaken by that terrible sink of grief. It was the spring of the oral-history project, a spring of great optimism, of endless, baseless hope, and lying there last week, listening to the fury of the storm, I could hardly believe that a whole year had passed: a whole *year*.

The strangeness of it all brought me sharply awake, thinking how funny it was that as you got older, time began to play tricks on you. I mean, when I was little, I never gave a thought to anniversaries or dates or starred days on the calendar. Then suddenly one morning, I woke up a prisoner of time, transfixed by the passing days, marking them, counting them: two years since the day Daddy was first diagnosed; two years since he went in the hospital for his first surgery—and as of December seventeenth, two years to the day I last saw him alive.

And just like that, it all fell into place, and after seven months of stubborn, voiceless silence, I knew *exactly* where I wanted to begin my own personal history: on the icy December night in 1987 when I came home from Tampa in the wee hours of the morning, ran up the steep stairs of our spooky old house so I could talk to my father one last time.

With no more thought or preparation than that, I rolled out of bed and rummaged through all my boxes and bags till I found the portable recorder I'd bought back in October, and the miniature tapes and triple-A batteries. It took a moment to assemble them, then without even testing the tape, I climbed back in bed, sat there in the darkness of the storm, and racked my brain for every single detail I could remember about that night, that seemed so far away—decades past, hardly within memory.

At first, I could only bring up a few stumbling details, till I happened to catch a glimpse of the Busch Gardens picture of me and Kenneth and Uncle Lou that I keep on my nightstand, the tape marks still visible on the back where Daddy kept it taped to his bed rails when he went to the hospital that last very last time. The bright, vivid colors of the little photo unexpectedly inspired me, brought back the day in Technicolor detail: the long drive along the coast, the mermaids and the manatees, then Daddy waiting upstairs in his magnificent bed, his gaunt face breaking into a smile when he saw me at the door ("Hey Big Man").

It was an image I had somehow lost in the bustle and grief of the past two years, and I can't tell you how wonderful it was, unearthing it; bringing it back to life the same way Gabe used to, with his hilarious old Michael-stories—I wonder if he tells them, still. Grannie never says, nor does Aunt Candace or Sim or certainly not Missy, who drives me back and forth to school every day, but is otherwise too consumed with her own busy life to worry much with me and my hardheaded ways.

She hardly mentions Mama or Gabe anymore, though there at first, she was furious at me for moving out, came after me like a pit bull that very first day of high school, back when everything was so new and intimidating. Aunt Candace hadn't even gone over and got my new school clothes yet, so I'd had to wear a pair of Curtis's old Wranglers that were about six sizes too small and made me look like a chunky Dwight Yoakam.

After all her labors to urban me up that summer, I'm not sure if Missy was more angry at me or at my hayseed clothes. I was just standing there at a table in the library thumbing through an encyclopedia, pondering this gruesome paper my honors-lit. teacher had assigned, a paper on our favorite contemporary American author (of which I knew none), when I saw her approaching across the expanse of the room, neat and preppy in shorts and sandals, though her fair, freckled face was dark as a thundercloud.

Without so much as a *hey* or a *hi-ya-doing,* she marched right up to the table, snapped: "Clayton *Catts*? What d'you think you're doing, moving in with Uncle Ed, who'll have you out there mowing and mulching every Saturday till you *die*?"

That's exactly how she put it, all in one fast, accusing breath, so fast that I was momentarily caught off guard, just blinked at her a moment, then asked in this weenie little voice: "Who's your favorite contemporary American author?"

*"What?"* she asked in that snippy little voice. Then: "Flannery O'Connor. *Why*?"

I gestured at the encyclopedia: "'Cause I got a write a paper on somebody, it's due Friday. Who is Flannery O'Connor? What did he write? Is Stephen King a contemporary American author?"

She just stared at me with the wildest contempt, as if she'd caught me peeing in the stacks, though she seemed to be trying to rein herself in, took a deliberate breath and offered in a voice that fought for mildness: "Listen, Clay, we'll go through Gabe's books tonight. He has a thousand of them, has a signed copy of *Wise Blood*—good *gosh*! Why d'you have to be so stinking *stubborn*?" Because at the mention of his name, I started shaking my head: no, no, *no*.

After that, things turned a little nasty, Missy informing me in her bossy, know-it-all voice: "Well, if you move in with Aunt Candace, you can *kiss* those honor courses good-bye. Gabe's the only one who'll get you through 'em and you *know* it."

I just slammed the encyclopedia shut, told her in a sure, shaking voice: "I'll drop out of high school—I'll *work* a *saw* at *Sanger* before I'd live in the same house with *that man*—"

"Oh, you will *not*," she countered, overriding me with sheer volume, "you'll just mope around, whining and showing your butt while Mama paces the floor at night and Gabe goes just about *insane* —your *own* father, Clay! Your own father!"

And just like that, the quiet little fuse Grannie had accidentally lit two days before finally exploded: "He's NOT MY *FATHER!*" I shouted in brilliant disregard for the lifted faces around us, the librarian at the desk who leapt to her feet and started toward us.

"Oh, *hush,* you know he is—"

"I *hate* him!" I screamed, I couldn't help it, it was true all the way down to my toes. "I hate his stinking guts!"

"Well, I *hate* you!" she shouted back, or tried to, because the librarian was on us by then, jerking Missy back by her elbow, threatening to send us to the dean if we didn't leave this *instant*.

Missy was enough of a know-it-all to stand there and try to explain, but I just grabbed my backpack and slammed out the door, not at all hurt or offended, but suddenly vibrant, full of life. It was like every cell in my body was activated, from the tips of my hair to my toenails, making me want to stand there on the sidewalk like a camp-meeting preacher and give all the students milling around the cafeteria a sermon about how much I hated Gabriel Catts. Hated him. Hated his guts. I'd tell them everything: how he came back when we were in a low state, how he slicked us all, won our hearts. How I thought he was God's reimbursement for taking Daddy and used to lie in bed at night and dream I'd marry Rachel Cole and we'd name our first son Gabriel Michael Catts. And how I felt a little guilty at giving Daddy the second billing, but figured Gabe deserved it; after all, he didn't have a son of his own to do the honors—

By the time I'd stomped the three blocks to Aunt Candace's and let myself in the back door, the phone was already ringing, but I just let it ring, knowing it was Aunt Candace, or maybe Grannie, calling to get me in line. To tell me about forgiveness and understanding and mercy, and I didn't want to hear it. No way. Not me. When it finally quit ringing, I lay down on the couch and rubbed my face, but the exhilaration was gone.

Suddenly I didn't feel like making any more speeches, just lay there, kind of overwhelmed by my anger, my deep, dark rage. It occurred to me that maybe I was a bad seed myself, like Uncle Ira or Granddaddy Sims. Maybe I was destined for the cells myself, because even I couldn't fathom the depth of my outrage; it hardly made sense to even me. If they'd just leave me alone, I'd be all right, I thought. I could figure this thing out, decode it the way I had to decode everything: slowly, one syllable at a time, with a lot of errors and fill-ins, though in the end, the gist of the text would finally appear, and I could make peace with it, get the message at last.

I was still lying there a half an hour or so later when I heard a key in the door and sat up, wondering who was home that early. It was Aunt Candace, still dressed in her work scrubs. She didn't speak, didn't put down her purse, just came straight to the couch and handed me the phone, said: "Call."

I looked at her. "Call *who?*"

"Call Missy," she said. "She's at Mama's. Call her there."

*"Why?"* I asked, and she crossed her arms.

"Because Mama called me at work, is about to pull the plug on this thing, gave me specific orders that I tell you to call. So here I am and here's the phone. *Call.*"

She wasn't smiling when she said it, and with a little roll of the eyes to show how *silly* it was, I sat up and dialed Grannie's number. She answered on the first ring, didn't say anything but hello, then handed the phone to Missy, who said: "Clayton." *Sigh.* "I'm sorry I said that I hated you. You know that I don't. And I hope you can appreciate the fact that I love and respect Uncle Gabe even if you don't, and have a natural concern for him when I feel that he is being treated badly."

She stopped then, and I had the definite feeling I was being read to off one of those three-by-five index cards she scribbles notes on for debate. It was something about her voice. A certain stiffness, as if Grannie was standing next to her, making her do it. And the way she said treated *badly*. Not treated bad, the way she'd have said it if she were speaking off the cuff, but treated bad*ly*.

Good grammar. Good theatrics, and I closed my eyes so I wouldn't have to look at Aunt Candace when I answered in a very kind, understanding voice: "Oh. I see. Well, good for you, Missy. And hey, I know you love him and I can respect that." I paused and let a little conciliatory silence build, then added: "And listen, with any luck here, Mama'll go nuts again and kill herself and then *you* can marry him. Then he'll be my uncle and my stepfather and my brother-in-law, too. Just one big *happy* family—"

"D'you hear *that?*" Missy said aside to someone—Grannie, I guess—though I didn't pause.

"—but he will never, ever, *ever* be my father. D'you HEAR *ME?*"

This last was an actual *wail,* so loud that even I was embarrassed after I slammed down the phone and opened my eyes and found myself facing Aunt Candace, who was standing there in her scrubs, watching me with a face of great exasperation.

"Claybird?" she said after a moment. "You got two choices here: either you pick up that phone and call Missy and cry and beg and somehow make it right—or you pack your stuff and move back home tonight. I mean, I can withstand Gabe or I can withstand Mama, but I *cain't* do *both*."

Well, it was logic even I couldn't argue with, and though it took a lot of crawling and apologies, I finally wormed my way back into Missy's good graces, though she is still loyal as a bulldog to Gabe and has never humored me like Grannie and Sim and Uncle Case (who have refused to take sides, pretty much ignore the whole issue). She won't let me make any snide remarks about him while she takes me back and forth to school every day, and still simply *insists* that he is my father.

"You look just like him," she says, and I never point out that *she* looks just like Uncle Ira, but that doesn't necessarily mean she's *his*.

I don't point it out because she'd probably slap me, and I mean, she's buff as Michael Jordan these days, with shoulders like a tailback: Uncle Ira all over again and she hates it. I didn't blame her, for despite my new surfer wardrobe and my even newer spiked hair (not big spike, but surfer-spike), I still look a lot like Gabe, mostly because of that stinking dimple that has set me apart as the family bastard as far as the whole of West Florida is concerned. No one cares to notice that I also have Daddy's hair (not the color but the texture) and his eyes and his brains for money. I also have his religion, which is something I sure couldn't have gotten from Gabe. But see, these things were not obvious. They don't hit you in the eye like that stupid dimple that I have grown to hate so much that I have given up on smiling all together. And of course, Daddy isn't here to claim me and Gabe is, and he's got the kind of personality that makes people kind of bend toward him and see things his way.

Yeah, he has them all fooled: Missy and Grannie and all of my former buds from LPM—Darius and Bobo and Travis—who really did come to love their old teacher and have never quite forgiven me for turning on him, won't speak to me when we pass in the hall, or in gym, as if my rejection of Gabe is somehow a rejection of *them*. Even loyal old Kenneth and I aren't as close as we used to be—not because of Gabe, but girls, mostly, for since we started school in town, he's become positively addicted to them. I mean, what religion is to Aunt Candace, boobs are to Kenneth: absolute obsession.

Maybe it has something to do with his Italian blood, but it's been a strange and swift transformation, one that's gotten between us a little, because I still have a deep and strong love for Rachel Cole and Kenneth is like one of Uncle Case's old hog dogs: he loves females alike, one and all, makes little distinction between tall and short, big or small, black or white, can't understand why I can't do the same.

He's always trying to fix me up with some chick who is best friends with his current chick (and we're talking revolving door here: a different girl a week). When I don't show proper enthusiasm for the job, he gets sulky and insulted, moves his book bag across the room to sit with his old buds from Gifted, who all think I got into the AP track on the back of a bribe and are constantly confounded by my inability to read. ("Are you *stupid* or something?" one or another of them asks me almost every week.)

Fortunately, these classes are so hard that almost everyone (Kenneth included) is failing at least one of them, so no one can point too much of a finger at me. In fact, I'm actually faring better than most, eking by in everything but Latin, mostly because I still have scribes to read me my test, and the Blind and Dyslexic Society, who supply all my books on tape, otherwise I'd be flunking out on a spectacular scale. But aside from these nagging little complaints, and a few close calls as far as running into Gabe are concerned (once at a gas station with Curtis, once at Winn-Dixie the day after Christmas), I've done all right here at Aunt Candace's.

I mean, at first it was hard, with the homesickness, the missing

Mama, but Aunt Candace doesn't run a household that leaves a lot of room for rumination, with every moment of the day filled to the brim with one activity after another. The day after I moved in, she posted a smart little list of daily chores that includes cleaning my room and doing my own laundry and taking out the garbage on Wednesdays, the recycling on Fridays, all of which doesn't sound like a lot of work, but is.

For Aunt Candace is a nurse, and Uncle Ed a building inspector, a career combo that makes for just the pickiest people on earth, with every household task boasting its own little protocol. Take the recycling. Instead of just junking all the newspapers and aluminum cans and paper bags in the little blue recycling bin (and feeling pretty smug and sanctimonious about taking the time to do that), Aunt Candace makes me rinse out all the cans and neatly fold the bags and pack it as tightly as a suitcase for an overnight trip. She also makes me clean my bathroom *every* stinking night, and we're talking clean, here: not a hint of a shadow of mildew or gunk, and all the shampoos in place and the cap on the toothpaste, and God forbid that a sock should land outside the hamper and spend a lonely night on the tile! Chaos! Disorder! Anarchy in suburbia!

At first, I was mighty suspicious of it all, figured Uncle Ed had a secret agenda afoot; that he was too pious to tell me plainly that I wasn't welcome in his house and had concocted a secret plan to run me off by working me like a packhorse. But after months of close scrutiny, I've come to realize that cleanliness isn't a game to these people, but truly a Way of Life, and Aunt Candace is secretly very pleased that she has been given this God-given opportunity to set me on the straight and narrow, right all the mistakes Mama and Daddy made over the years in raising me. I really think that at the bottom of her fervent little evangelical heart, she figures she'll take me on a few years, shape and refine me, fill me with the Holy Spirit and get me in the habit of ironing my pants, then ship me off to college New and Improved and Right in the Sight of the Lord.

At least that's the only thing she insists on: that I go to church with her every Sunday at Living Water Assembly, a charismatic congregation of the name-it-and-claim-it stripe, the kind that subscribe to *Charisma* magazine and watch the *700 Club* and think Kenneth Copeland hung the moon. I don't mind too much, because they're a lot more entertaining than the old folk at Welcome, basically a strange, kooky bunch who dance like Zulus during the song service and come up with these incredible crazy theories that they're always sharing with these innocent, trusting smiles like it's all perfectly normal. Today's sermon dealt with demonic possession, which is one of their recurrent themes. Seed faith and demonic possession—every action on earth can be traced to one or the other.

At first it was so weird that I thought the whole bunch needed deprogramming, but now I just sit back and listen and sometimes it makes a little sense. Anyway, I'd rather sit there next to Aunt Candace and hear about prince spirits than next to Gabe at Welcome and play war on the back of the bulletin like we used to. Those days are over, though Grannie can't help but drop an occasional remark about how that speaking in tongues is of the devil and so forth, which is what Baptists generally think of the charismatics (until the exact moment they become one themselves).

But that's about as much static as she ever gives me when Aunt Candace drops me off at her house every Sunday, one of the few things in my life that has never changed: I still go over to Grannie's every week after church. At first, I was afraid I'd run into Mama or Gabe over there, but apparently Grannie made some kind of arrangement with them, and Sunday is still our day, and though they attend church just four houses away, they never step foot on Magnolia Hill as long as I'm there. And thank God for that, because Grannie is afraid I'm becoming anorexic from living with Aunt Candace and gets up early before church and fixes some of the best food on God's green earth. I'm talking roast in gravy and ham and potato salad, and pork chops and pole beans, not to mention corn bread and biscuits and sometimes even homemade rolls and banana pudding. After seven months' exile in the land of the TV dinner, it really is enough to bring tears to my eyes when I first walk into her rickety little kitchen every week and lift the lids on all the steaming pots, makes me wish my old Grannie had been born Catholic, for if anyone on earth were ever a candidate for sainthood, it is she.

Since the Browns still go to Welcome, Kenneth comes home with Grannie sometimes, and in her presence, he loses some of his babehound gloss and returns to his goofy old Kenneth-self, and the three of us have a big old time. We eat till we drop, then settle down on the couch and watch wrestling on TBS, though I don't like it as much as I used to, I don't know why. I guess I'm getting a little old for wrestling. It's beginning to seem kind of fake and dumb to me, though Grannie, she still gets into it. I mean, to her, these people aren't actors, no way, and when the good guy is getting double-teamed, she gets hot as a firecracker, wants to call Atlanta and tell the police. I guess the television gives it too much of an air of reality for her to handle. Usually she's pretty real herself, but she takes wrestling and *As the World Turns* to heart, and me and Kenneth usually laugh our butts off every Sunday, watching her.

At six, they have to get dressed for the evening service at Welcome, which gives me time to work on my tapes, because Pastor Jim (all these charismatic preachers have regular-guy names like that: Pastor Bob or Pastor Jim) quit having an evening service on Sundays so people could spend some quality time with their families. Well, I really got a witness to that (charismatic term) and have Grannie's little house all to myself for a couple of hours, since Missy's still a good Baptist and Simon is actually living part-time up in Waycross, has rented an apartment up there, where he stays a good part of the week.

I miss him a lot. Sim is good to have around because he's easy on the nerves and good company to boot, has never given me a hard time about moving out, never lays on any little guilt trips. Every once in a while he drops by the high school and takes me to lunch, and if I can swing it, I want to go and stay with him a few days during spring break, which is soon upon us, just next week. We'll have a good old time up there, and if Sondra Cole goes up for a visit, maybe she'll bring Rachel along, and in the light of the Georgia sun she'll lose her disgust for me and something will develop.

I'm not getting my hopes up, though, because Rachel Cole still cannot stand me, even less than she used to, and it's not even her fault, or not altogether. See, the Coles are right on the borderline of poor (not food-stamp poor, but Dollar Store poor) and their three lovely daughters are their primary assets. When Sim and Sondra hit it off in high school, their mother naturally saw visions of rich in-laws and free Sanger furniture, and when I fell in love with Rachel, it was to everyone's satisfaction.

Everyone but Rachel, that is, who is about one hundred seventeen pounds of soft, green-eyed, ginger-haired rebellion, with plans to get out of the middle-class squeeze by her own wits and not my inheritance. A worthy ambition, I am sure, but I didn't ask to fall in love, either, and almost died of it when we used to go to school together at Lincoln Park. Back then, she treated me with a semblance of decency, occasionally sending a polite word or two in my direction, even sitting next to me in the car if Sim and Sondra happened to be giving us a ride at the same time.

Then Simon and Sondra graduated last May, and they decided to forgo any hasty decisions about an early engagement and he moved to Waycross, and they never even talk about getting married anymore, though they still write and visit each other and he still calls her his girlfriend and all. But nothing legally guaranteed to keep the Coles in new couches, so the pressure was on Rachel to perform, and that's when her patience ran out and she has come to the point where she rolls her eyes at everything I say. I mean, I could raise my hand in algebra and ask a perfectly honest, straightforward question about the square root of 42, and out of the corner of my eye, see her face just *wither* with contempt.

Sim long ago advised me to leave it alone, says she's in love with some boy from Blountstown who plays basketball, but I still hang on to her, I don't know why. Maybe because she's not a threat anymore and the sight of her behind in a pair of frayed Guess jeans still makes my chest tighten in a very natural kind of way that I enjoy. I tell you what, it was comfort last year when I thought I was falling in love with Gabe, I'll grant you that.

So I guess I owe her a little loyalty, and maybe if we meet up at Sim's and her mother's not there to exert any maternal influence, she'll forget the jock and give me a little room. Maybe.

There's a car in the drive: not the low hum of the Mercedes, but a jerk of a stop and a quick blast of a horn—Missy, surely. She has this *huge* attitude these days about having to chauffeur me around so much, and really lays on the horn, so I'd better get moving. Grannie always offers to take me home, but she really can't see worth a hoot at night, would probably drive us into a tree—

# CHAPTER FIFTEEN

I got my report card in the mail today. Failed Latin flat but pulled a C in algebra, which is a miracle that I'll have to share with the other mystics at Living Water Assembly on Sunday. Aunt Candace said if I could make a C average I could go stay with Simon, and when she said it she had heard from Missy that I was flunking both algebra and Latin and was pretty smug about it. Then the C I named and claimed came through and she'd like to back out, but since I aced history, my average is a solid 2.0, so she finally gave in and called Simon and he said sure, great, that we'd have a big time and he'd keep an eye on me and all.

Good old Sim, you can always count on him. He's busy as a bee these days, working as a line supervisor up there, though mostly he's just soaking up the business and gaining the respect of the other employees and what have you. Everybody knows he's off to FSU in August, then he'll be back and in charge, though nobody seems to mind or be unduly resentful. Like I say, my brother is easy on the nerves. He just does his own thing and rolls along with the tide and somehow manages to be liked by every man, woman, and dog he meets. But naturally, naturally, no charm involved.

Grannie says he gets it from Daddy, that he's just like him, which isn't exactly the case, for he's not ambitious like Daddy, he doesn't have to be. It's all his for the taking, which, I think, bores him a little. I mean, he's this sixth-generation Baptist with all this carefully bred missionary fervor to do good and right and change the world, but when he looks around, there is just no outlet for his ambitions. I mean, no matter how hard he works or how much money he makes, still in all, there's only so much satisfaction you can get from a well-built couch. And I think Sim is beginning to realize this.

Maybe he considers me an object of Christian charity. He sure has been nice about me staying with him, even called Sanger and made arrangements for Mr. Sam to come by and pick me up, take me up on his weekly payroll run. We took the same route we took last year when I was interviewing him for the oral-history project, even stopped at Jimbo's in Homersville for barbecue, making for a leisurely, nostalgic little drive through the rural twilight. For the first time in a long time, I actually began to enjoy myself, actually began to make a few jokes, told Mr. Sam that the reason all the white folk at Jimbo's looked at us with such wide eyes was that they assumed from his car (a big old black Lincoln) and dress and companion that he was a crack dealer who dealt in virgin white boys on the side.

It's the kind of humor that Mr. Sam finds a little less hilarious than other father figures I've known, but anyway, he laughed, and most of the way to Georgia talked about Daddy, as if I were still interviewing him for a project. I didn't mind, because Sam has a musical kind of—I don't know what you'd call it—*gheechie,* maybe—voice that's hard to understand when you're in a roomful of people, but really does justice to a story when you're rolling through the wire grass at twilight, the narrow county highway mist-covered and silent, broken up by tiny crossroad towns, each with its own churches and trailers and barbecue, just like home.

When we pulled into the Sanger parking lot, Sim was waiting there by his truck, leaning against the tailgate with his arms crossed on his chest, and after not seeing him in for so long, I had forgotten how much he favors Daddy and could have cried or something from the shock. It wasn't his face, really, or even his dark coloring, but his precise way of moving and dressing, which is exactly like Daddy and always will be as long as Mama buys his clothes.

He came over and thanked Sam for bringing me, was kind enough to overlook my watery eyes with no mention that that is *exactly* the reaction one would expect from a son of Gabe Catts. He just helped me get my stuff, didn't mention anything but supper and how I'd have to sleep on the sofa sleeper and it was a Sanger, so not to expect too much. He said this to lighten things up because it's a family joke, how sorry Sanger furniture is. Not the wood stuff they make at home, but the upholstered couches and chairs they make in Georgia. *Trailer furniture,* Mama calls it, and used to cry when Daddy made her buy it for the house, which used to just infuriate Daddy.

So I just laughed, then gathered my stuff and thanked Mr. Sam, and Sim took me out to eat at this sporty little restaurant by the courthouse where all the young professionals eat. It's called Gallahan's or O'Brien's or O'Grady's and is all decorated like an Irish tavern, with neon Bud signs and Heineken lights over the bar. To tell you the truth, I felt just a little bit wicked sitting there at happy hour with a roomful of people who kept going back and forth to the bar, especially after God had come through with that C in algebra and all.

Sim, though, he was pretty cool about it. He must eat there all the time, because the waitresses all knew his name, and a lot of people dropped by the table while we were eating, a few of them said we looked alike. When our bill came I almost fainted because we'd ordered so much: fried cheese sticks and steaks and two desserts because I couldn't make up my mind, and drinks which included beer for Simon. I mean, he just ordered it very casually, this glass of Bud, like he drank it every day of his life, and Grannie would drop *dead* if she knew.

I was talking to this man who'd stopped by the table who is somehow connected to Sanger when Simon ordered it or I would have leaned across the table and whispered: *Simon? Does Grannie know you drink?* Then

I would have been as embarrassed as crud for being such a child, so I'm glad I didn't.

But I don't know. It still seems kind of weird to me. Maybe it's another habit he picked up from Gabe, who is a drunk. Or used to be. He never drinks anymore but he talks about being an alcoholic like it was some great achievement. Some red badge of courage. You'd think he'd have the pride to be ashamed, but no, he'll tell the world. Now that I think of it, that probably *is* where Sim picked it up and I wish he wouldn't. Daddy never did. *We* never did. As far as I know, it's a sin, though Pastor Jim once said Jesus drank real wine. But he never drank beer sitting in a bar with a bunch of other drunks telling him all these complimentary things because they know he's got the bucks and will be a big man around town one day and are all sucking up to him.

Anyway, after we finished eating, he brought me here to his apartment in this huge, six-hundred unit complex on the outskirts of town that is built in kind of a Mexican theme, I guess you'd say, with buff-colored walls and arched doorways and an orange-tiled roof. I was kind of surprised when I walked in, for it's really kind of luxurious for a nineteen-year-old, the living room all color-coordinated and neat, with peach-tinted walls and plush carpet and these big pen-and-ink drawings over the couch. Except that the furniture is that Sanger junk, it's pretty impressive, and kind of a shame that I'm messing up the perfection of the place by sleeping on the couch, but there's only one bedroom and that's Sim's.

I thought we might go out last night, catch a movie or something, but Sim was tired from work and had a softball game early the next morning, so we just turned in, got up early this morning for the game that was held at a softball diamond behind his church. It's a big Baptist one on the highway that isn't small like Welcome, but glass-sided and modern (though the original sanctuary, that does look like Welcome, is right next door, now a Sunday-school wing annex). After his beer drinking the night before, I kind of expected Sim to lie low with the church crowd, though he seemed equally at home there as he was at the bar, the same kind of smiles, some of the same people coming by our seats and telling us the same pleasant things.

Simon didn't seem to see anything hypocritical about it, though I sure did, and on the way home I asked him why he drank beer and he said because he liked it. Then I asked him if Mama knew and he said no, and I asked him why he didn't tell her and he said because she'd tell him not to, and that was the end of that. I didn't say anything else, but I couldn't help but think how flipped out Grannie would be, and how unraveled and unprincipled our family had become in the last couple of years, and all because Daddy had an inherited susceptibility to cancer of the hepatic system (his grandmother died of the same thing).

It really made you wonder.

# CHAPTER SIXTEEN

I'm going on a date. An actual bona fide date in about three hours with the sister of a friend of Simon's. Her name is Keri, but that's all I know about her so far except that she has blond hair like her sister Kendra (who I met at O'Grady's last night). If she favors her sister I'll be doing all right. She wasn't real pretty in the face but had herself all fixed up with makeup and had her blond hair braided. That's about all I remember about her, that white-yellow hair that stayed blond all the way to the roots, and Sim says her sister's is the same.

He (Sim, that is) had to run down to Sanger for a few hours for a meeting, but he's due back soon and I'll have to get him to help me figure out what to wear. I don't look as good in clothes as he does and I bet Keri is getting the lowdown on me from her sister and don't want to be an unpleasant shock. My hair won't spike anymore, it's too long. I should have gone down and had Miss Cassie cut it yesterday before we left. When it just lies flat like this, I look like somebody named Ricky Earl.

# CHAPTER SEVENTEEN

W ell, I've been here in Georgia two days now, and I've seen my brother drink beer and I've kissed a girl without a shirt on, and if Mama or Grannie or Aunt Candace knew, they'd yank me back to Florida so fast that the only thing they'd find left of me here are my footprints in the orange clay.

It all started last night when Simon came home from Sanger and told me to forget my hair, it looked fine. Then he showered and dressed and called Kendra, and off we went across town to pick them up at this house that's inside this brand-new gated subdivision that looks like it was just this year hacked out of the surrounding orange hills. Sim says their father is in some sort of equipment rental business and must pull down the bucks because their house is not only a mansion itself, but is in a whole neighborhood of mansions, the yards all landscaped within an inch of their lives with crepe myrtle and dogwood and mondo grass, all band-box new, right out of a South Florida nursery. Even the live oaks are pruned down to, like, the Essence of Live Oak: a broad, stumpy trunk and a few long horizontal limbs and a touch of Spanish moss here and there for atmosphere, but that was about it.

Simon didn't prepare me for this kind of wealth, and I felt kind of weenie standing there on their stoop waiting for them to answer the doorbell because at home being rich is my ace in the hole. It can't get me the girl I want, who is Rachel Cole, who hates me, but it could get me one of several others if I tried. I felt even weenier when I saw Keri, who not only has real blond hair but also a better face than her sister and a more pleasing shape. But she didn't seem at all shocked or disappointed by my appearance—in fact, both she and her mother (who is also blond, with a south Georgia accent so thick that she sounds like a female Deputy Dog) welcomed me inside as if I was the return of lost but beloved kin.

I didn't quite know what to make of it, was kind of struck speechless, though fortunately Sim was there to do the talking. All I had to do was stand there with my hands in my pockets and look around at their house, which is two-storied and huge, a gigantic blown-up version of Aunt Candace's modest little tract house. Even the living room is decorated with the same kinds of stuff: identical hunter-green carpet and silk houseplants and gilt-framed art prints, all clean and sparkling, evidence of a generous bank account and a full-time maid, and I must say, I was just as impressed as I could be.

After we talked awhile, Simon said it was time to go, that he was hungry, and all the way to the restaurant he and Kendra kept up the conversation, so all I had to do was sit there in the backseat next to Keri and look attentive. This wasn't hard because she held up well under close inspection, her light hair really kind of amazing, but unfortunately, chopped off just below her ears, so there wasn't much of it to see. She was dressed with a kind of MTV theme in mind, with big silver earrings and a lot of spandex and T-shirt stuff—layers of it that made her look a lot older than fifteen, which she just turned, making her a year older than me.

Overall, I felt like I was dating someone's mother, I don't know why, maybe because her and Kendra kept talking so fast, laughing a lot, dropping profanity sometimes, not like they were doing it to impress anyone, but like they were used to it. I didn't much care for it, but other than that, they were so friendly, so smiling and sweet, that I began to relax a little, was even talking by the time dessert came around, making a few jokes of my own.

After we ate, Sim wanted to go to a movie, but Kendra said no, that it was almost ten and that late, the place would be full of niggers, which I found kind of shocking, the way she said it so casually. I mean, a lot of the old people call black people niggers without even realizing it, even the old folk at Welcome (at least till Gabe blew in from the North; now they're probably daresome to say the word *colored* without glancing over their shoulder to make sure he isn't within striking distance). But Kendra didn't say it like the old folk did, she said it with scorn, making me wonder if Sim ever told her about Daddy and the Klan and Mr. Sam being his partner and all.

Probably not, because all he said was okay, then without any consultation with me or Keri, drove us to this airstrip way out in the country. Or I guess that's what it was. God knows it was far from prying eyes, in the middle of this cutover cotton field next to what looked like a deserted hangar. I was just sitting there, wondering what was up, when Simon turned off the car and he and Kendra got out and left me and Keri alone with no instructions at all, just walked off into the dark.

I mean, one minute, I was sitting in a restaurant trying to remember my name on my first date with a girl, the next I was out in a parked car, surrounded by miles of empty field and a quiet Georgia night, without a clue in the world to what was going on. I wanted to get out and run catch up with Sim, ask him what I was supposed to do next, but didn't, of course, just sat there, rambling on, talking about God knows what, till my eyes adjusted to the light and I could make out Keri a little better in the darkness.

At first, I couldn't tell what she was doing, then I realized she was taking off her earrings and putting them in the back dash, then getting a Kleenex out of her purse and wiping off her lipstick, going about it in this very casual, premeditated kind of way.

I must have looked curious because she said: "You don't want to get this on your clothes, it's hard to get out."

I smiled for lack of a better response, and when she was all finished with the lipstick, she reached behind her back and did something under her T-shirt that made a pop, then said: "All righty."

By then I was thinking that God, Kenneth wasn't going to believe this. Not in a million years, because it had finally occurred to me that that pop was the pop of an unsnapped bra. Suddenly I understood exactly what was going on and did my duty as I saw it, though it really wasn't as good as I had imagined because the whole time I kissed her—and that's all I did—a voice in my head kept turning things over and over, wondering if premarital breast-feeling was a sin; wondering when Sim was coming back, and worst of all, wondering how it would be if I was doing this with Rachel.

When I'd think of it that way, I could feel this incredible stab of heat right in the middle of my back, a weight of breathlessness that almost made me faint. Then, right on the tail of that, I'd think what a sleaze I was, making out with one girl and pretending it was another, and try to get my mind out of the car and let my emotions run away with me, but it wasn't the kind of thing you could will into being. I mean, it either happens or it doesn't.

But anyway—I did my duty from her neck up and arms down and she was returning the favor, with none of the aforementioned boundaries, which I found a little distracting. I mean, if I'd have known her better I would have told her to stop, that she was tickling me. But I didn't, so I let her and it went on for long enough that my mouth was getting numb and the bottom of my back was starting to ache when suddenly Sim and Kendra came back at the car, jerking open the doors and filling the backseat with this sudden glare of light.

I jumped like I'd been shot, though everyone else seemed pretty cool, Keri straightening up and rearranging her T-shirts, Sim and Kendra slamming themselves in and putting on their seat belts, talking about a plane. From what I could gather, Kendra was taking flight lessons and trying to convince Sim to do the same, showing him one of her father's planes that he (her father) wanted him to buy, which made me feel like a criminal. I mean, I thought they'd been heading to the hangar for immoral purposes and it'd given me the green light to forge ahead with my own explorations, and here they were, just looking at a Cessna in storage.

"—you could fly up here in half an hour," Kendra was saying as we headed back to town, Sim asking about gas mileage and maintenance costs while Keri put on her earrings and a fresh coat of lipstick, and I tried to get a clean breath of air, even opened the window so the cool night air would hit me full in the face, hoping it'd bring some feeling back to my lips.

When we got to their house, we ran into their father while we were walking them to the door, apparently just coming home from a business trip. He met us in the drive with his carry-on bag still in hand and talked to us a moment, Sim casually kissing Kendra good-bye right in front of him, though I didn't have the guts for that, and took Keri to the door to kiss her in privacy. I did a pretty lousy job of it with her father standing there, not ten feet behind me, then joined him and Sim in the drive where they were discussing the plane.

I tried to throw out an intelligent comment or two before Sim shook the old man's hand and said we had to go, that he'd think about the plane, me following him down the curve of the drive till we were out of earshot, when he glanced at me out of the corner of his eye and in this kind of dry, amazed voice, asked if I knew I was undone. I didn't know what he was talking about, just looked down, where before God, I was unbuttoned from about the middle button of my shirt on down, my shirt tail flapping in the wind, even my belt undone, poking out about six inches in the air. It was like that old awful nightmare I used to have about sitting at school taking a test in my underwear, except this wasn't a dream, it was cold, hard life, and I could have fainted I was so embarrassed.

Sim didn't help matters much, laughing so hard all the way home he kept weaving off to the shoulder of the road, nearly killing us both. I kept begging him to shut up, to pleease shut up, till he finally let up and said good night, leaving me to undress (finish undressing, you might say) for bed, then pull out the couch and lie there awake in the darkness, staring at the ceiling. Every once in a while I'd think about how I was standing there in front of God and everyone, talking about planes with Simon and the old man with my underwear poking out of my pants.

I'd feel a slow wave of heat creep into my face, try to tell myself that he probably didn't notice. He probably thought I was hot or something and had unbuttoned my shirt. By morning I'd almost convinced myself that everything was cool when Simon came out and stood by the bed while he tucked in his shirttail, not saying good morning or anything, but just diving right into a replay of the evening's events.

"—and when we got out of the car and saw her daddy, I didn't look back, saw you walking Keri to the house and thought how it was good, you having the class to kiss her at the door, and then you came out and I turned to introduce you and—" he paused then, laughing so hard he couldn't get it out "—and you're standing there with your shirt unbuttoned, your belt sticking out, a foot in the air—"

"*Please,* Sim—" I begged, covering my face with a pillow, though he didn't quit.

"—but you just stood there making small talk like everything was okey-dokey, saying: 'Yeah, my friend Kenneth's brother just went in the air force, he's in flight school in Pensacola—' Why the heck didn't you button back up?"

I spoke from beneath the pillow: "Because *I* wasn't the one who did the unbuttoning. I didn't know I was hanging out in the wind. Why didn't you tell me?"

"What was I supposed to do?" he asked. "Say: 'Hey, Clay, you forgot to button back up, your drawers are poking out—'"

I burrowed further under my pillow, thanked God that Grannie was a state away in Florida, murmured: "I will never be able to face those peo-ple again."

Sim just laughed harder. "Well, you better," he said, "'cause they'll probably be sitting behind you at church this morning."

I dropped the pillow on that and sat up. "You're *lying,*" I said, but he just grinned.

"Where d'you think I met Kendra?" he asked.

"At *church?*"

Sim just shrugged. "The old man doesn't go, but you can bet your butt Keri'll be there. She's in love."

He made a face when he said it, then went to the kitchen to fix up something for breakfast while I bestirred myself and took a shower and got dressed. I kept thinking he'd come to his senses after a while and come to the bathroom and give me some kind of lecture on chastity or something, but he never said a word, just looked kind of *proud* of me, I don't know why. Maybe for being manly or something, and at that point, all of it began to get embarrassing.

I mean, *terminally* embarrassing, walking into church an hour later and seeing Keri wave at me from an aisle seat she'd saved for me next to her and her mother. I noticed that she was less MTV at church, or at least MTV with a sabbatical touch in dark hose and low heels. I didn't know quite what to make of it, because she was like Sim about the beer, just completely unrepentant, singing the hymns with a lot of gusto, then inviting me to an R-rated movie with her and Kendra and Sim, all in the same breath.

Maybe I'd been hanging out with the Aunt Candace and the fanat-ics too long, but it all began to seem mighty fishy to me, mighty fishy, in-deed. Of course, that didn't stop me from going to the movies with them that night, seeing *Fatal Attraction,* which I didn't think too much of be-cause I sympathized with the crazy woman, wondered if Mama acted like that when she got pregnant with me. Who knows? Nobody ever talks about it, and when the wife killed her, everybody in the audience cheered, even Sim, and I could have cried. I mean, nobody has any sympathy for crazy people. Nobody.

When it was over, Sim took us back to his apartment and me and Keri were left alone in the living room on the couch that everyone *knows* is a bed while they went out to swim in the pool that was pitch-black that late at night. Now, I don't know what they were up to out there in the dark, but as soon as the door shut I was in the spotlight again and asked Keri if she wanted to watch MTV.

I guess I figured from her style of clothing it was her chief form of entertainment, and sure enough, she said yes, so I turned it on and messed with the volume a little, still a little preoccupied, thinking about that stupid movie and how Michael Douglas had gotten the crazy woman pregnant and told her to have an abortion. I was wondering if Gabe had wanted Mama to do that when I realized Keri was getting comfortable again. First it was the earrings, then the lipstick, then, with no permission from me, she just slid her shirt over her head and all of a sudden she was sitting there on the end of the couch with a pretty remarkable imitation of a Madonna-like smirk on her face and no bra at all.

And you know, it had the strangest effect on me.

Suddenly I couldn't remember what had just been bothering me; couldn't have told you what was on the television; might not have been able to remember my name. Suddenly my emotions had sure enough gotten the upper hand, just as Daddy had once warned, and all I could think was how plump and white her breasts were, not as big as the ones in magazines, but for all the world as neat and smooth as a slice of cheesecake sitting there so perky and bare.

There was a mighty pounding in my ears as I went over and knelt beside her and kissed her, not bothering with her mouth this time, but concentrating on unexplored territories. She didn't complain, just stopped to pull my face up and make me kiss her on the mouth every once in a while, and I honestly don't know where it would have ended up if she hadn't pulled my face up a final time and instead of a kiss, said: "Clay. It's Kendra and Sim. They're coming up the stairs——"

She stood up then and gathered her shirt and went in the bathroom, so when they opened the door a half a second later, I was sitting there on the couch watching MTV without a care in the world, all buttoned up and cool, with a face like the sole survivor of a train wreck.

Sim and Kendra didn't seem to notice, just went to the bedroom and dressed and Kendra said they had to go, she had to work the next day (she works for her father). When they were gone, I pulled out the bed and got undressed, needing to sleep since I hadn't slept much the night before, but for some reason, I couldn't.

There was something on my mind, and it wasn't Keri's chest, either. It was something out of place, and when I realized what it was I went to Simon's room and went in without bothering to knock. I found him standing at the open closet in his boxer shorts, picking out his clothes for work the next day just like Daddy used to do, looking a lot like him, to tell you the truth, only taller, heavier in the chest and arms, more like Uncle Ira, like a combination of the two.

He looked up when I came in, asked: "What's up?"

But the question I was going to ask him had been pretty much answered the moment I stepped in the door and saw Kendra's wet bathing suit hanging on the door handle to dry, because that's what had struck me as strange: how they'd gone to the bedroom together to change out of bathing suits. When I saw the evidence right there, dripping water on the carpet, I said: "Oh." Then I almost went back to the living room, except that I really needed to know, and asked in this halting little voice: "Sim? You and Kendra—are you, *seeing* each other?"

Which was a pretty ridiculous way of putting it, now that I think of it. I mean, if they'd changed out of bathing suits in the same bedroom, it was pretty clear they were *seeing* a lot of each other, in more ways than one.

Sim didn't look too insulted by my implication, though. He just went back to picking out his clothes, answering over his shoulder in this cool, casual voice, "Yeah. I been seeing her. You went on two dates with us, remember?"

It was a dodge worthy of our mother and that emboldened me to be more specific. "Is she your *girlfriend*?" I asked. Then, before he could answer, "I thought Sondra Cole was your girlfriend."

"She was," he said, choosing a shirt and tossing it to the bed, "in school. Kendra's my girl now."

*My girl,* he said, making it sound sweet and old-fashioned, like he took her to Sunday-school picnics and gave her chocolate on Valentine's Day. It left me no choice but to baldly strike at the heart of the matter, ask in this incredulous little voice: "Are you *sleeping* with her?"

At the word, he turned and looked at me for a fraction of a second, then said: "Yes."

Well, that's all I wanted to know, I guess—or at least that's what I'd gotten out of bed to go in there and ask. I nodded and said something like, "Oh," then went back to the living room and crawled back in bed, if possible, more awake than I was before.

Sim must have heard me tossing and turning in there and decided a little more explanation was necessary, for he came out a few minutes later, still in his boxer shorts, and stood there beside the bed, not offering any particular excuses, but just providing the details of the matter in this calm, reasonable voice. "We been seeing each other about six months now. That's why I got an apartment, so she could move in, because she and her mother, they weren't getting along too well. If it's all right with you, she'll move back in tomorrow, which'll be great, Clay, because she's a good cook. A good girl. And Keri'll be around more, too."

I must not have looked properly grateful, because he paused a moment, then added with a little more force: "And you can tell Mama if you want, I don't care. I'm nineteen years old, it's none of her business."

And you know, till then, I was still kind of moving through the tail end of the shock Keri had put me in when she peeled off her shirt. But when he said the part about it not being any of Mama's business, I came back to earth with this nauseating thud and saw something so terrible that it made me sick, just absolutely puking sick. Because I knew then that Sim hadn't taken all the Gabe-stuff so well either—not calm and good-natured like everyone bragged. That he'd taken it to the belly like I had, that Gabe had messed him up, corrupted him with his liberal Yankee ways, left him morally pockmarked, just as Mama had feared.

I mean, I knew it so clearly, so suddenly, though I didn't know what to say and just sat there and faced him off a moment till he turned to go back to his room, when I finally spoke, asked the only thing I could think of asking: "Simon," I said. When he turned, I asked: "Do you love her?" He just looked at me a moment, then answered with a flat, level honesty: "D'you love Keri?"

Then I realized he thought I was asking if he loved Kendra when I was really asking if he still loved Mama. And then it really didn't matter, because I had my answer anyway. I just lay back in bed without another word and he went to the bedroom and shut the door. He didn't slam it, didn't seem angry at all, which only made me feel sicker when I thought about poor Mama and how Simon had cheered when the crazy woman got blown away in that *stupid* movie.

And I tell you what, I been up half the night talking into this thing—it's four o'clock in the morning now and I feel like puking *still*.

# CHAPTER EIGHTEEN

I'm back in Florida now. Back on Magnolia Hill, where time is at a standstill, nothing ever changes, or at least nothing changes physically. I myself feel as if I've aged a hundred years in a week, though Grannie's little house is just as I left it, even smells the same, of camphor and butter beans and now that the wisteria has bloomed, of vivid, purple spring. The smell is especially strong here on the back porch, where I've decided to tape tonight because it's pretty private back here, nothing but shadows and birdsong—mostly whippoorwills, though there's an old barn owl in the sweet gum who hovers close once twilight falls, his mournful hooing so loud I'm sure I'll pick it up on tape.

I am pleased to report that finally, after half a dozen tapes of disconnected ramblings, I've come upon a date that has actual historic significance: today is the first time in the history of the world that I've ever missed an Easter service at Welcome Baptist, though from what Kenneth says, I don't seem to have missed much. They didn't even have a sunrise service this year, but are just meeting at the church tonight (this very moment, in fact) and carpooling to First Baptist's huge new Passion Play that has professional sound and lighting and a lead who looks *just* like Jesus, or so Grannie told me a few minutes ago while I was helping her with her coat.

I thought about asking how she could *possibly* know that, but poor old Grannie has had a rough time of it since she found out about Sim and his woman, so I went easy on her, just smiled and said, "Cool," then walked her and Kenneth to the door, told them to have a good time, and Happy Easter.

I stood at the screen and watched them on their way, was glad Kenneth was there to walk Grannie down the Hill, for she looked kind of bent and frail as they went along, one of her bird-thin hands clutching her purse, the other tight on Kenneth's arm, not able to see very well in the dusk. I waited till they turned the corner before I shut the door and gathered my tapes and my recorder and came out here to the porch, where finally, after a week's delay, I have the space and privacy to record the official version of my jinxed little visit to Waycross.

It's hard to know where to begin and even harder to tell it straight, because to tell you the truth, I'm feeling a little pinch of guilt over how I treated Sim. I've tried to call him every night this week to apologize, have left four or five groveling little messages on his answering machine, but he has so far refused to return my calls. I guess he's washed his hands of me, that he and Kendra and Keri really and truly hate my total stinking unequivocal guts—or I assume Keri does.

If I was a girl and had presented my body for the sacrifice to a virtual stranger and had him leave town without a word, I'd be madder than heck—though come to think of it, she might not be mad at all. I mean, I never predicted any of her other reactions, so who can tell? Maybe she never gave it a second thought. Maybe if I saw her tomorrow she'd be smiling and slipping off her shirt again. I just didn't know and that was the problem I kept coming back to that night, tossing and turning on Sim's little sofa bed: how this girl was a stranger to me, and if we continued along at the rate we were going, soon I'd be the father of her children, or could be anyway, and I didn't (still don't) even know her last name. And there we were, hot at it and on the next date she'd be slipping out of more than her shirt and it'd all be over but the washing up and (for me, anyway) the guilt of the thing.

I kept wondering: Why was she doing it? How could she make it so easy? Were all girls like that? Was Simon right—was she in love? I hoped not because he was sure right about me, I didn't love her. Hey, I didn't even know her—and until she got a little naked there, I wasn't even the tiniest bit infatuated, which only made it worse. I mean, I didn't know where Sim came off saying that Kendra was his girl, as in the girl he screws, then just being so straight and good-natured and honest about saying he didn't love her, because—I don't know—it just made me madder than hell. He just wasn't raised to be that kind of cool dude and I don't care what Mama or Gabe or anybody had done.

All night that night in Waycross I tossed and turned and thought about Mama and how flipped out she'd be if she knew and how it was really all that idiot Gabe's fault because until he showed up none of this kind of stuff had gone on. He was the one who'd opened the floodgate with his Yankee ways and his jokes and his cool. Even after Daddy died, we were all right. Mama let me and Missy sleep with her in her big old bed the first few months, we were so scared, while Simon, the Big Man, slept on the floor on a pallet. Back then, there wasn't any of this nasty talk or cursing or R-rated movies or Sim drinking beer or chasing women. It was just us and Welcome and Grannie, and it was so sweet, why did it have to end?

That's the thought that kept me awake all night long, till just before dawn, when I finally drifted off, like two minutes before Sim's alarm clock went off in the bedroom, as loud and obnoxious as an air horn: WAHHHHHH. So I was wide-awake again, my head pounding like it was wrapped in barbed wire, just lying there listening as Sim took a shower and dressed for work then came to the kitchen and made himself something to eat.

He must have realized I was awake, for he came over and stood by the bed while he ate a slice of toast, not seeming to notice that I was on the verge of a nervous breakdown, but talking real casually, telling me how much better we'd eat when Kendra moved back in, how she made better biscuits than Mama, that he'd get her to make them tonight for supper, maybe bring Keri by—

And I said no.

"Why not?" he asked, finishing the toast and slapping the crumbs from his hands. "You wanna go out?"

I said no, that wasn't it, I just didn't want to see Keri anymore. This apparently wasn't part of the game plan, for he looked at me with this face of great curiosity, repeated, "Why not?"

"Because I don't," I said with a shrug, not having much left to say about it. I mean, one more date and we'd be making babies and I just didn't want to chance it.

Sim really didn't get it, though. He just stood there perfectly still, obviously at a loss for words, finally said: "But you've gone out with her two days in a row, Clay. You can't just drop her like that. Kendra says she really likes you."

"Oh," I said, "I see. What's the matter, will Kendra cut off your biscuits if I don't screw her sister?"

I don't even know why I said it. It just came out of my mouth, un-bidden. Before I could take it back, before I could even blink, Sim was up on that bed, knees first, gripping me by my shirtfront, his face about two inches from my nose, and he was not smiling.

"What makes you think you can talk to me that way?" he whispered in this low, level voice that brought a sudden metallic taste to my mouth, a surge of heart-thumping adrenaline, thinking we were about to go at it. That he was going to reach back and slap me and I'd grab hold and pull him down and we'd roll off the bed and get in a few good licks before we came to our senses and everything would be released, and let me tell you, I could have handled something like that. It would have suited me fine.

It's not that I was that mad or anything, I just wanted to fight. To get it out in the open, to scream it all out: Daddy and Mama and Granddaddy Sims and Gabe and all the things that had landed on us like hornets in such a short time. Things that had changed us, had ripped the veil, had torn us apart, that could be released into the wind with a few good solid licks and a lot of nasty names and heart pounding, and I tell you what, I was ready for it, except he didn't make the move.

We were too—I don't know—too cool for that. All he did was let go of my shirtfront with this little jerk of disgust, then went to the kitchen and must have called someone. I could hear his voice on the phone, saying, "—no, don't bother with her or Grannie or Gabe, just tell Aunt Candace to call me there, at Sanger, have 'em page me on the floor. Yeah, I'm sick of it. They can send him to Dosier for all I care. No, I'll tell you later, I'm running late. Yeah. Love you, too. Bye."

This last really got to me, for I realized he was talking to Missy, and they loved each other, and it was like the full-blooded 100 percent USDA Catts children were double-teaming me. I could feel this awful weenie feeling creeping up my chest, closing my throat, making me wish I could apologize to him, take it back. You know, tell Sim to bring on the girls, eat them biscuits, yank them shirts, but it was too late.

He was finished with me, slamming out of the kitchen and leaving for work without even saying good bye, leaving me to lie there on the couch and stare straight at the ceiling for four hours, like I was paralyzed or something. I could have moved if I wanted to, it's just that sometimes when I get overwhelmed by something, I just sit there and can't motivate enough interest to even move a muscle. After I do it awhile, it just builds and builds, till I'm like a breathing mannequin.

That's the way it was that morning till the phone rang around lunch, Simon calling to say that he'd have to come and take me home after work because no one else could get away. He told me to pack my stuff and meet him in the parking lot at five-thirty, and I knew as soon as I saw him that this would be a silent drive home because his face was still blank and seething, not even looking at me as I piled my stuff in the bed of the truck. It was clearly too late for apologies, so I just climbed in the jumpseat and made myself comfortable, using my canvas case for a pillow and stretching out, his face, if possible, even stiffer as he watched me in the rearview mirror.

I had closed my eyes in preparation for a going-home nap when he started the ignition, commenting aside in this voice of just *profound* disgust: "You know, Clay, sometimes I'm real relieved you're nothing but my half brother, you know that?"

It was such an awful thing to say that I actually couldn't believe my ears. I actually sat up and looked at him over the seat, said: *"What?"*

But he wouldn't repeat it, just shrugged and turned up the radio while I kept at it, leaning up on the seat, asking: "Sim? *What* did you say?" Though I was reasonably sure I'd heard him correctly the first time and just had this kind of masochistic need to hear it again, though he wouldn't cooperate.

*"Nothing,"* he snapped. "Just shut up and leave me alone."

So I had no choice but to lie back down, though I knew what I'd heard, and let me tell you, I would have much rather had a cut mouth or a black eye or a cracked rib, because it was like he'd reached down and punched my soul, bruised it, the need to cry so close I could feel it there at the back of my throat, unshed tears, copper tasting and bitter.

I didn't try to sleep then, just leaned against the window, watching the night fall on the endless peach groves and small towns and orange dirt roads of south Georgia, Sim not stopping once, not even for gas, much less supper, both of us kind of groggy when we came to a final stop, not at Aunt Candace's, but Grannie's. I gathered my stuff without a word and followed Sim inside, where he wouldn't even let the door shut before he was running his mouth to Grannie, telling her in an aggrieved voice: "Well, here he is, and it's almost eight and I won't get back to Waycross till eleven, and I have to be up at five."

Grannie, who was standing at the stove in one of the sleeveless cotton housedresses she bought by the dozen at the Dollar Store, ignored his fussing and hugged us in our turn. "Well, thank you, baby," she told him. "Sit down and eat before you get on the road, won't take but a minute."

Some of my hurt and meanness and general confusion and perplexity was immediately cleared by the prospect of real honest-to-goodness food, making me run to the bathroom and pee and wash my hands in preparation for a Big Feed. When I got to the table, even Sim looked slightly more human as Grannie went back and forth to the kitchen, laying out dish after dish of macaroni and cheese (her version, with three cheeses and big fat noodles and sour cream) and fried chicken and potato salad (two of them, because I liked mine cold, Sim liked it warm) and real home-brewed, white-sugared, ice-cold Lipton tea, the quality of which I've never seen equaled outside my grandmother's kitchen.

"You two go on and eat," she told us, as if such an order was necessary. "The biscuits are ready, I just need to pull 'em out of the oven."

I'd already been dipping into the dishes, filling my plate while they were still en route from the kitchen, so I was able to take my seat quickly, was busy stripping my first drumstick when I realized Sim was facing me across the table with a look of mild reproach. "Aren't you going to say the Blessing?" he asked.

In reply, I just chewed and stared, and after a moment, he dropped his eyes and reeled off a lightning-fast God-is-Great, though I didn't so much as blink, just kept chewing and staring, thinking: Boy, what a shit you are.

When he finished the amen, he started eating, but wouldn't look at me again, and with Grannie there, hot-handing biscuits to a plate, looking so relieved and plain happy to see us, I began to see that I had a definite edge here, the upper hand. I mean, old Sim might be the Cool Dude, the Big Man up in Waycross, with his beer and his women, but back here in Florida he was at the mercy of my evilest whim.

And with that nasty, cutting little remark about us being half brothers in mind, I began to play with him a little, like a cat tapping a mouse with a leisurely, fur-covered paw.

"So, Sim, are those biscuits any good?" I asked him with a bland, innocent face when Grannie finally finished her labors and sat down at the table. "You think they'll *make* the *grade?*"

"What's wrong with the biscuits?" she interjected, though Sim was quick to answer.

"They're fine. They're good." Though if I squinted, I could see a faint pink begin to creep up into his cheeks that filled me with this sudden, massive enjoyment.

"Oh," I said. "Well, I thought you might not like these *Florida* biscuits. Not after all the *Georgia* biscuits you been *eating.*"

His face held a definite flush now, little spots of color beginning to flame his cheekbones, though Grannie didn't notice, just poured herself a glass of tea, commented: "I don't like Georgia biscuits. Cathead biscuits. Too doughy." Then, to Sim, "How's Sanger doing, baby? Is the addition coming along like Sam wanted?" (They were building a new showroom.)

"Yes ma'am," Sim answered, clearly relieved at the turn of conversation and taking it on with a vengeance, telling her with a lot of gusto: "It's real nice. I met the interior decorator, Deanna something-or-another, from Atlanta. She's real nice—I think you'll like her—"

"Well, did Sam let you have that couch?" Grannie continued. "The sleeper sofa you wanted for your living room?"

"Yes ma'am," Simon repeated, his eyes still a little nervous, jumping from his plate to Grannie's hairline to the table and back again in these fast little circuits. "It's some of the new stuff, looks real nice, with, ah, tufted arms and all—a lot better built that the old stuff."

Grannie, whose new sofa sleeper had already developed an ominous sag in the middle, was kind enough to let this pass without comment, just asked: "Well, is your apartment nice? Does the landlord know you're leaving in August? Did he let you sign a short lease?"

At the mention of the new apartment, Sim chanced a little glance at me, though I held my peace, just sat there and buttered a biscuit and returned the glance with an innocent, solicitous look of interest, letting him prove what a hypocrite he was with the words of his own mouth.

"Yeah, it worked out all right," he allowed, then got up to look in the refrigerator for pepper sauce, hoping to put Grannie off the track.

But she hadn't seen much of him since Christmas, and was truly interested in every little detail of his life, continuing in perfect innocence when he sat back down: "Well, good for you. Gabriel thought they might stick you for the lease when you left for school. You know he got sued—sued in court—for breaking that lease in New York—had to pay out a pretty penny—"

"Why *did* you rent an apartment in Waycross, Sim?" I broke in to ask, making his face congeal into perfect immobility, not a twitch, except for the blood beating in his temples as Grannie tried to step in and offer an explanation.

"It was too much driving back and forth, wasn't it, baby? It was wearing you out?"

That must have been the official line he'd fed Mama to get her to fork over the cash for the deposit, though Sim didn't jump in and agree, just watched me across the table, acknowledging the challenge with no reaction at all.

"No," he finally answered in a voice a heck of a lot weenier than his cool words back in Georgia. "I needed the, ah, room. I got a roommate."

"A *roommate?*" Grannie exclaimed, amazed that some little part of his life had escaped her eagle eye. "How come you to get a roommate, shug? Is it cheaper? Does he work at Sanger?"

Well, it was time for old Simbo Catts to stand and deliver, though he didn't too much relish the job, just chewed his lip thoughtfully a moment, then answered with the particular stiffness of a man in a dream. "No, it's not anybody from Sanger," he said. "It's a girl, a woman, named Sondra."

"*Sondra Cole?*" Grannie breathed, and at the slip of the tongue, Simon went even redder.

"Not Son—Kendra. Kendra Poyner. She's a girl—a woman—I met in Waycross."

Oddly enough, Grannie didn't look too moved by this extraordinary confession, just sat there and chewed quietly, her eyes not really stunned or excited, but only faintly worried. "Well, baby," she began after a moment, "d'you think that's a good idea? Living with a *woman?*"

At her complete lack of hysteria, of accusation, Sim's whole body loosened, his face taking on a kind of evangelical persuasiveness, assuring her in a fast little voice: "It's fine, Grannie—it's working out great. We talked a lot about it before we moved in together—she knows I'm leaving in August, it's no big deal."

Grannie just chewed reflectively, and I could feel my heart beginning to beat hard in my chest while I waited for her response that came after a long silence. "Well, I hope you know what you're doing, baby," she said, "because, I don't know, shug—it may sound all right, but one of these nights you're gone git mighty lonely and this woman might start looking real good, real good in a bad way, and baby, it'll be a temptation, I can tell you that."

She was so sincere, so truly *clueless,* that it was really kind of horrible.

I suddenly wanted to end it there, to jump to my feet, take Sim aside to the kitchen, and tell him to lie or laugh it off as a joke, anything but tell her the truth because she wasn't goofing around. Grannie didn't goof around about stuff like that. She's a hard-shell, hardhead Baptist, and not the beer-drinking variety, either, but the storytelling, Sunday-school, His-eye-is-on-the-sparrow kind, and it was like a crime against humanity when Simon answered her in a mild little voice: "We are already. Living together, I mean." Grannie just looked at him, still didn't seem to get it, and he tried to clarify it without being vulgar, "Like man and wife."

Well, she got it that time, she got it with a bullet, her eyes widening, though she tried to hide her surprise, wiping her mouth with her napkin and fooling around for her fork before she looked back at him, asked in a small voice: "Why don't you marry her, Sim?"

"It's not like that, Grannie—" he began, then must have realized how cold it sounded, because he shrugged and looked away, added with a lot less conviction: "It's no big deal."

"No big deal," she murmured, dropping her eyes to the table that was piled high with all the food she'd probably been laboring over since Sim called her that morning from the plant. She ran her eyes down the length of it as if checking to make sure everything was on the table: the salt and pepper, the butter and the pickles, then returned to Sim, asked in a voice that was empty of sarcasm, just level and honest as could be: "Has the money done this to you, baby? Was it that? Or Gabriel coming back? Was it him?"

It was such an unexpected thrust into the heart of the matter that I felt my face go suddenly hot, though Simon took it without flinching. "*No,* Grannie," he answered with great force. "Gabe hasn't done this to me, or Daddy dying, or Granddaddy *Sims*—God, Grannie—we all cain't stay held up here on the Hill or out in the woods, polishing floors and tending flowers. Some of us got to get out there and *work*—get out there and *live*—"

Try as he might, he couldn't contain a note of gigantic impatience at Grannie and her funny old Grannie-ways that made her draw back, not used to being spoken to in such a way, especially by her good-natured old Sim. For a moment she just sat there, blinking, then quietly laid down her napkin, and for the first time in the history of the world, my tough old Grannie, who in her prime had withstood the Monster of Magnolia Hill, actually retreated in the face of his grandson, just got up and left. She didn't do it with a lot of fanfare, just went through the kitchen and out the back door and (I guess) down the Hill to see Brother Sloan, to corner him at his desk while he labored over his Easter sermon and warn him that if he ever intended to get a third generation of tithes out of the Catts family, he'd best be praying *hard*.

Sim stood, too, though he didn't run after her, try to apologize or repent. He just stood there with his napkin still clutched in his hand, watching her leave with this white awful face of grief, of perplexity, and I don't know what all else, till his glance happened to settle on me.

And let me tell you: it was a whole different ball game altogether.

"You son of a *bitch,*" he breathed, slinging aside his chair and rounding the table, yanking me up by the front of my shirt and pinning me to the wall like a bug in a science project, shouting "Yer nothing but a shit-stirring little pain in the *ass,*" right in my face, spit flying and eyes bulging, though that was about as far as he went.

I mean, poor Sim, he was really too nice a guy to beat someone up or even cuss them out properly. He didn't even hit me or use the f-word or the Lord's name in vain, just kept banging the back of my head against the old bead-board wall as if he was really and truly trying to knock some sense into me, shouting between knocks: "You thank it's easy working your ass off sixty hours a week? You thank I like it? You thank it's a pic-nic, being Michael Catts's son? You thank it's *easy?*"

It was far from a life-threatening encounter and would have ended without blood loss if I could have left well enough alone. But I didn't much like being shook around like a rat, and when he finally had enough of me and let go with a disgusted little jerk, I came off that floor like a rubber ball. I caught him just as he went into the living room and jumped on his back the way they do in wrestling, trying to tackle him, though the effect was more like bull riding than fighting, for what Sim lacks in fe-rocity, he makes up for in size and agility. He didn't go down under my weight, just rocked forward a little with a roar of anger, and started try-ing to punch me over his shoulder.

For a few sweating, grunting, cursing moments, we whirled around the living room like a two-headed man in a fistfight with himself, knock-ing over lamps and banging into the wall, till one of us finally drew blood. I didn't know who at that point, just that it was suddenly all over the place: Sim's forehead, and running down my chin and shirt, and worst of all, spraying in fat little droplets all over Grannie's brand-new sofa sleeper. When I saw it, I let out a little cry, making Sim pause a moment and look down, and when he saw the spray of dark blood on the broad, pastel cushions, he let out a howl of truly animal rage.

"You *stoopid* son of *bitch,*" he positively *roared,* then in one tremen-dous heave, tossed me to the floor like a rag doll.

He turned on me, was coming in for the kill, when someone shouted: *"Hey!"*

The voice was male and country, so familiar that for one strange, disjointed moment, it sounded just like Daddy, enough to make my heart give this great *thump-thump,* leap to my throat. Even Sim froze, his face suddenly open and scared and full of wonder—though there was no need. It wasn't a ghostly visitation, but just Uncle Case, stopping by for supper like he did almost every night.

I don't know how long he'd been standing there in the dining-room door; long enough to see the blood on the couch, because he didn't bother to ask if we were all right, just snapped: "Clayton Catts, *git* yo ass in thet kitchen and git you a rag and clean up thet mess."

I was so pumped with adrenaline and nerves that I jumped off the floor like a jackrabbit, hightailed it to the kitchen and found a damp dish-cloth, then went back to the living room that was now empty, the front door standing open on its hinges, Uncle Case and Sim nowhere to be seen. I wiped up the floor and righted the lamps and did what I could with the couch, though the red drops seemed to be multiplying rather than disappearing. That's when I realized that I was the source of all that blood, that Sim had busted my nose, the blood still flowing at an amazing rate, *drip, drip, drip,* all over the place.

I gave up on the couch then and went to the bathroom, washed my face and wiggled the end of my nose, feeling for a break. But aside from a strange swelling at the base of the bridge and that fountain of bright red blood, everything seemed intact. I finally just wadded a towel on the middle of my face and went back to the living room, finished wiping down the walls and did what I could with the cushions. When I finally got everything cleaned up, I rinsed out the towel in the bathroom sink, and with nothing better to do, cleared the dining-room table and washed the dishes, had the kitchen mostly clean when I heard Sim's car start up in the drive.

He and Uncle Case must have gone out there to talk in private, for Uncle Case ambled in the back door almost immediately, coming to a halt when he saw me, regarding my swollen face with a look of great distaste. "You clean up that mess in the living room?" he snapped, a heck of a lot more intimidating than Sim would ever be in a million years.

"Yessir," I answered smartly. "Cleaned up the kitchen, too."

He still didn't look too happy, just shook his head in great disapproval. "Then go on to bed. Put some ice on thet face and hit the rack. Don't want to hear another peep out of you tonight—you heah me?"

I nodded meekly, got some ice, and went to bed, though I was too keyed up to sleep, haunted by the crazy look on Sim's face while he banged me against the wall, his fast, frantic cry. ("You thank it's a *picnic,* being Michael Catts's son? You thank it's *easy?*") To tell you the truth, I'd never thought of Simon's life in such a way, and for the first time, I saw a different face on my easygoing brother, the face of a boy who'd had too much put on him too early, who was groping for a footing on a life as stumbling and desperate as mine, and a mad, crazy grief that was driving both of us to the strangest extremes.

My heart really did go out to him, made me feel mighty weenie for deviling him at supper like I had, and after he'd let me stay with him in Waycross, and he'd even fixed me up on a date and it wasn't really his fault that it hadn't worked out, was it? The more I thought of it, the guiltier I got, till finally, after a good ten minutes tossing and turning, I got up and slinked back to the kitchen, where Uncle Case had quite forgotten me, was busy fixing his supper, filling his plate at the stove.

I stood at the door till he heard me and turned, told him in a small, contrite voice: "I'm sorry, Uncle Case, for picking a fight with Sim. I hope I didn't hurt him."

Uncle Case just nodded briefly, then went back to filling his plate, told me over his shoulder, "Well, I'm ashamed of you boys, ashamed of the both of you," and I thought he was going to say: *for upsetting yer Grannie, for taking after yer sorry, good-for-nothing granddaddy Sims and chasing women and trying to settle things with your fists.* But he just added with a little grunt: "Almost grown men, the both of you," then shook his head sorrowfully, "fight like a couple of girls."

# CHAPTER NINETEEN

I meant to record yesterday in the comfortable wisteria shadow of Grannie's back porch, but Sunday has truly become my one and only day of rest. After wolfing down one of Grannie's magnificent Sunday dinners (fried catfish and hush puppies and cheese grits), I fell dead asleep on her couch, didn't wake up till Aunt Candace came and picked me up at nine.

Now that I'm in the middle of baseball purgatory, I don't know when in the world I'll ever find time to curl up with my tapes and faithful little recorder and tell my side of the matter. At the moment, I'm taping here in Aunt Candace's living room and have to go quickly because she's due home any minute, and if she comes in and finds me whispering into a microphone, she'll probably think I've joined the neo-Nazis and am making plans to firebomb the statehouse.

Ever since she found out about the fight, she's been mighty suspicious of me, taking on this air of great and regretful reproach, as if disappointed that despite her best efforts to church me and teach me to iron my pants, my old Sims genes have raised their ugly head and are threatening to undo her good work. It all started when Grannie came home that night and found her couch and living-room walls damp and slightly discolored (not by the blood, but the stuff I'd used to clean it off).

Uncle Case and Sim had left by then, and me and my busted nose were sleeping peacefully in the spare bedroom, so Grannie couldn't quite figure out what had happened. She just went about her nightly routine: watched the Dothan news, then went to take a bath, when she discovered a trail of fresh blood drips in the dining room that she followed through the house to the laundry room. And let me tell you, when she came upon that bloody towel hanging from the edge of the washer, it was like a nuclear explosion went off on Magnolia Hill. Without even bothering to wake me up, she went straight to the phone and called Aunt Candace at work, must have told her that the chickens had come home to roost! The ghost of Leldon Sims returned to get his revenge at last!

For Aunt Candace abandoned all of her patients on ICU just like that, came tearing across town and yanked me from my bed, made me recount my sordid tale in a sleepy little voice, then insisted on taking me to the ER for an X ray to see if my nose was broken (it wasn't). Oddly enough, she wasn't as upset about Sim and his beer and his women as she was with me, for fighting! Right in Grannie's living room! With my own brother, blood all over the place!

You'd think from the way she talked that I'd gouged out Sim's eyes and ripped out his lungs and scattered his body parts all over Magnolia Hill and danced a jig on his bleached bones. Even after Uncle Case called her at home the next morning and assured her that it wasn't much of a fight, nothing but a tussle, really, Aunt Candace wouldn't let it go. It was obvious that she saw Grannie's ruined couch as a dark portent of evil days, the perfect symbol of our family's undoing, and after a week of worry and hand-wringing, finally came upon the perfect cure for my rebellion: baseball.

Try as I might, I couldn't quite grasp the logic of this move, figured she'd run out of household chores to keep me busy and had to fall back on the old standards: sports and practice and round-the-clock exhaustion to rid me of every trace of my latent, Leldon Sims ferocity. If I wouldn't have been so guilt-stricken about ruining Sim's life, I would have probably dug in my heels and refused, but I'm so universally hated these days that I really can't afford to offend Aunt Candace or I might yet end up on the last bus to Times Square, just as my poor old vampire mother still (probably) fears.

So I went down to Kmart and bought a pair of cheap rubber cleats (the kind Missy wouldn't be caught dead in) and joined the Sanger baseball team, which was the only team in Florida willing to take me as a walk-on that late in the season. And after one night of practice, I decided that Aunt Candace might not be so nuts, after all; that maybe baseball in Florida in May really is a soul-purifying exercise, because let me tell you, it's as good a description of hell as I can imagine.

For one thing, the other players are all older than me, mostly guys from the plant who stay in pretty good shape from working on the floor and are natural athletes to begin with. They all played up the ranks in Little League and Babe Ruth, high school, and maybe even a semester or two at college level till injuries or bad luck landed them working on the line at the local furniture factory. I guess baseball is one of their last living links to their youthful aspirations, for they follow the game with a seriousness I remember from Daddy, that I myself really can't quite fathom. That first night at practice, I really thought it was a joke, a sketch from *Saturday Night Live*. I was sure that Coach Bates (this huge old redneck, a dead ringer for the fat guy on *Hee Haw*) was poking a little good-natured fun when he gathered us in the dugout and marched back and forth like a sweating old camp-meeting preacher, told us in this awful old hayseed twang that we only had one more week before our first game, *boiys,* that we'd best work HARD out ther, *boiys,* and play HARD, iffen we wanted to WIN!

I kept glancing around at the faces of my fellow players the whole time he paced, waiting for the punch line, for everyone to throw their heads back and laugh their butts off at this hilarious takeoff, but no, this is serious business. This is salvation without a cross, Living Waters Assembly without the Holy Ghost. I find it all very strange, and they find me likewise, everyone really welcoming and nice at first, for after eight months of yard work and starvation with Aunt Candace, I've become deceptively lean-and-mean looking, with the kind of height and long arms that could (theoretically) hit a ball a country mile. They were all tickled pink to have me on board, though after watching me bat a time or two, a few of them politely pulled me aside and asked if I was recovering from an injury: a pulled tendon, a dislocated disk?

I would have liked to have lied (in fact, I think I did), though no injury on earth could forever excuse my batting stance (or lack thereof) or the fact that so far this season, I've yet to make so much as a hit, not even a foul, tip, or nick; nothing; *swoosh, swoosh, swoosh,* three strikes and you're *out.* I also can't catch very well (that is: not at all) and drop every fly that comes my way, not missed in close, fumbled errors, but as Missy puts it, by a *country mile.*

That was her only comment after she watched me struggle through my first game, along with a shake of her head and a bemused: "Gosh, if Aunt Candace just wanted to humiliate you to *death,* why didn't she make you walk to school *naked* or something?"

The reason it was her *only* comment was that she heard about my fight with Sim by then and was giving me a taste of the old Silent Treatment, taking Sim's side like she always does. She hardly spoke to me for the better part of a week, till Friday, when Aunt Candace had another one of her divine inspirations and somehow talked Missy into giving me a few one-on-one practice sessions to teach me how to bat and catch, if nothing else. I think money might have changed hands in the transaction, for Missy didn't complain too much, just dropped by the house this afternoon while I was doing laundry and told me to get my cleats. Without bothering to explain where we were going, she drove me to the old field behind the church (the same field where Daddy taught himself to pitch) and laid down an official home plate, borrowed from her softball coach.

She was very meticulous about it, carefully flattened it out and brushed it off, then positioned me beside it like a mannequin in a department store and began lobbing me these slow, arching moon balls, yammering advice the whole time. ("*Dang* it, Clay, box it in—no, parallel the base. Drop your elbows—no, not—*there*. Eyes on the ball, eyes on the ball—*swing!*")

After maybe a dozen misses, I finally began grounding them, and she straightened her pitches, began zeroing them across the plate in whizzing underhand fastball that passed two feet in front of my chest in a scary little blur. It took the better part of the afternoon for me to finally, *finally* connect with one, enough to send it flying as far as the side of the church, bouncing off the bricks and narrowly missing a Sunday-school window.

Missy straightened up and watched it arch away, then, like the basically decent human being she is, grinned her audacious old Daddy-grin, called, "Well done, young man!" the same way Daddy used to yell at players during games, bringing fast, sharp tears to my eyes and this sudden stab of pride.

Once the glacier silence between us was broken, her loyalty to Simon must have been overcome by simple curiosity about what had really gone on in Waycross, for when we finished practice, she casually mentioned that she was hungry, offered to buy me a burger if I'd drop by McDonald's with her on the way home. She insisted we go inside, bought a strawberry shake for herself, a Quarter Pounder and fries for me, and as soon as we settled in our booth, she fixed me with a curious eye and asked: "So what really went on up in Waycross? Is Sim really living with some bimbo up there? Did he really break your nose when you told Grannie?"

You might think that after enduring a week's worth of my sister's evil silence I would have given her back a taste of her own medicine, that I'd just sit there and munch my burger and refuse to give an inch, but I didn't, of course. I mean, I really do sometimes think that I'd make a very good Catholic, for if there is one thing on earth I love to do, it is confess. With no more prodding than that, I sat there and spilt my guts down to the very smallest organ, told her everything, from that first dinner at O'Grady's to my dates with Keri, even mentioned that idiot movie, *Fatal Attraction,* and how much I hated it.

"Because the nut cooked the kid's rabbit?" she asked.

"Because everybody cheered when they shot her at the end."

Missy raised her eyebrows at that.

"Some fun," she commented after a moment, then shook her head. "Well, poor Sim. He might have busted your nose, but you sure cooked *his* goose. Grannie and Aunt Candace are on the warpath, insisting that Mama *must* be told."

"Told what?" I asked, and Missy gave me one of her exasperated looks.

"About the chick—Sondra, Kendra—whatever her name is. Grannie thinks they need to tie the knot since they're already in the sack. What does she look like?"

"Kendra?" I asked, and Missy gave me a weary glance.

"No, Clay, *Grannie.*" Then, with another roll of her eyes, "Of course, Kendra. Try to keep up with me here, 'kay?"

I was too happy to be back in the family gossip circle to take offense at her razor tongue, told her what little I knew about Kendra: the big house, the pruned oaks, the incredible blond hair that I thought her finest feature, though Missy just gave a little impatient snort. "Well, of course she's blond," she said. "I think it's a state law in Georgia, for concubines."

"For *what?*" I asked, and Missy grinned her fast Daddy-grin.

"That's what Grannie calls her. Sim's *concubine.*" She laughed aloud, and though I hated to have to do it, I had to ask what a concubine was.

"A mistress," she said. "You know—a kept woman. Poor Sim. Grannie's not gonna sleep till he puts a ring on her finger, and if Mama finds out that she's been footing the bill for a south Georgia love nest, well, old Simbo might be working on the floor up there a few years sooner than *planned.* You know Mama. She can be a little *hasty.*"

It was the first time she'd mentioned Mama in a long time, and something in the way she said it, offhanded and casual, made me think she was opening the door a crack to see how I'd react; whether I'd answer or slam it back in her face. For a moment, I just sat there, fiddling with my straw, then heard myself ask: "How is she?"

Missy just shrugged. "Okay, I guess. Working on a project with Gabe, staying up in the apartment a lot, typing, I think." She paused a moment for my reply, and when I didn't offer one, added: "Got her hair all cut off, shorn for Lent, she says. Looks weirder than *heck*."

I didn't offer any reply or comment, for I actually hadn't seen much of the Mercedes around town lately, at Wal-Mart or Winn-Dixie or even down at the graveyard, which kind of pissed me off. I mean, before Gabe blew into town, she went down every morning, left flowers and tended the roses, kept them watered and trimmed. From the overgrown look of the bushes, I was the only one who ever visited anymore, hiked up there from Aunt Candace's a couple of times a week, a lonely little trip without Mama there to point out the landmarks, tell me some little story about the neighboring graves.

I used to think I'd run into her up there, had long ago decided that if I did, I wouldn't run away or anything. I'd just sit down on one of the little marble benches and be civilized and talk, not about Gabe or me moving out, but ordinary things: about how her roses were doing, or if Missy was really going to school next year in France (as she was threatening). I could picture it so well in my mind, how it would all play out, Mama polite and kind and relieved to see me, hugging me when we parted, telling me she loved me, and I'd do the same, and that would be that.

We'd be friends again, my mother and I, allies in an alien world, though my little fantasy reunion has never come about, simply because Mama hasn't shown up to play her part, I don't know what has been keeping her. I mean, every week, I waited, I paced the grave. A couple of weeks ago, I actually stood up on Granddaddy Catts's tombstone when I heard the hum of a diesel engine below, my heart pounding in my chest. I thought it would surely be Mama, but it was just a car stopping at the stop sign, not a sleek, dusty Mercedes with a catlike purr, but a ratty little Audi that didn't even turn in, just labored into first gear and went on its way.

But I couldn't tell Missy that, of course. She'd run straight home to Mama, tell her to meet me at the grave tomorrow, and she would, too, right on cue, and Gabe might come with her, and it'd all be ruined then, it wouldn't be magic at all.

So I just sat there munching the last of my fries, and after a long pause, Missy made one last stab at connection. "She misses you a lot, Clay," she told me in a mild little voice. "I mean, I know it's strange, how she never went after you when you left—but it doesn't mean she doesn't love you, just that she's too—*whatever*—to force you to move back home. She talks to Aunt Candace every week, follows every little detail of your life. She just can't come out and chase you down—she's too, I don't know: guilty and silent and passive for that. But you know she loves you, always overindulged you, like a thousand times more than me or Sim— remember the little red wagon?"

I nodded, for I remembered that little wagon very well, an ancient old Red Rider wagon that used to be Daddy's when he was a kid, that Mama borrowed from Grannie's shed when I started school because I was a fat little kid, and hated having to walk down our long, twisting drive every morning to the bus stop at the highway. Daddy wouldn't let Mama drive me because she'd never driven Sim or Missy, so she'd get up every morning and pull me along in the little red wagon, would meet me there in the afternoon, too, hide behind a tree so the other kids wouldn't see her and make fun of me, tease me about being a mama's boy.

I myself saw nothing indulgent in the arrangement and would prob- ably be riding to school in a little red wagon till this day if Daddy hadn't have come home early from work one afternoon when I was in first grade and come upon Mama pulling me down the drive, Missy and Sim strolling along merrily at our side.

He stopped his truck and got out, picked me up and stood me on my feet, then squatted down till we were on eye level, told me in his kind old country voice: "Claybird, sometimes in life you git to ride, and sometimes you got to walk. Today, you start walking. 'Kay?"

I hadn't even argued, just nodded, and after that would trudge along on my fat little legs to the bus stop every morning like everyone else, though Mama still hid in the trees waiting for me in the afternoon, always on the lookout for rabid dogs and kidnappers and bullies, poor Mama. I guess when you grow up in a dangerous house, you never get over it. You spend the rest of your life looking over your shoulder, obsessively creating safe havens: polished mansions and rose gardens; landscaped marble pools and magnificent, tulle-draped beds.

"Does she know about the fight?" I asked, and Missy shook her head.

"Nope. There's a big battle brewing over it, though. Grannie and Aunt Candace are wanting to spill it all, though Uncle Case and Gabe are taking to the trenches, trying to protect Sim. So far it's a dead draw, but sooner or later, she'll figure it out. You know Mama. She's a lot of things, but *stupid* ain't one of them."

I smiled at that, a thin, sad smile, commented after a moment in a small voice: "I used to think she was a vampire, when I was a kid."

I don't even know why I confessed such a thing, and braced myself for Missy's roll of the eyes, her snort of derision, though she just looked at me with a face of great amazement. "That is so *weird*," she murmured after a moment in this astonished little voice. "I was thinking the same thing, just last night."

"That Mama was a *vampire?*"

She shook her head thoughtfully. "No—actually, I was thinking about Sim and what makes him tick. He called the house last night, had this long, chatty little conversation with Mama about the renovations at the Georgia plant and how wonderful it was going, how nice the new interior decorator was. Then, right before he hung up, he just casually mentioned that he's bringing a girl to the reunion in July, everything all innocent and sweet. Well, Mama took it, hook, line, and sinker, dropped by my bedroom before she went to bed, told me all about it, and I just thought: poor Sim. I mean, it's gonna be like one of those episodes of *The Munsters*. You know, how they live in this big old haunted house, but they have this one normal child, the blond chick who's always bringing home boyfriends, who're all thrilled with her till they have to drive up that spooky old drive and meet the Frankenstein father—"

"Herman?" I offered, and Missy grinned.

"That's him. Well, I was thinking that Sim was the blond chick of our family—the one normal kid—and Mama and Gabe and Grannie are the vampire mother and Herman and Uncle Fester—"

"That's *The Addams Family*," I corrected, glad to be in the superior position for once, though Missy just shrugged.

"*Whatever*. Anyway, I was thinking that's why old Sim always works so hard to be so cool and perfect and ultranormal, because at the back of his mind, he knows that no matter how rich we are, or how big a car Mama drives—well, sooner or later, he's gonna have to bring people home and they'll figure out pretty quick that we're just a bunch of loony old Crackers. Weird. Violent. Incestuous."

I didn't pay much attention to that, just asked: "Well, who am I?" meaning: Who was I in this strange family portrait she was painting?

Missy didn't dismiss the question, but just tilted her head a little to the side (a mannerism she'd inherited from Grannie), told me with all her old Missy-sureness: "You're the little werewolf boy."

"Eddie?" I asked, and she nodded thoughtfully.

"Yeah. The kind of normal-looking one, except for that weird widow's peak and the howling at the moon and all. I mean, sometimes you can get by with a reasonable normalcy, if you wear your cap backwards and shave your chest. But face it, Clay: your father is Frankenstein and your mother is a vampire, and there ain't much you can do about *thet*, let me tell you."

She was laughing before it was over, she and I both were, breakthrough laughter, you might call it, high and relieved, the first time since our family ghosts had began to emerge that we'd had the distance to joke about them, give them a playful poke like we did everything else. We'd finished eating by then and stood and gathered all our wrappers and empty cups, were piling them in the trash can when I asked her about Sim bringing Kendra to the family reunion, which was news to me, I hadn't heard a word about it.

"Oh, Sim's keeping a low profile," she assured me. "I doubt Grannie or Aunt Candace even know. He just casually mentioned to Mama that he's seeing a girl in Waycross named Kendra, hasn't quite got around to explaining how *much* of her he's seeing, if you know what I mean."

While I ditched my garbage I told her: "Well, if he calls tonight, tell him I said that I was sorry about the fight and all. I've left, like, *fifty* messages on his answering machine, but he won't talk to me."

Oddly enough, Missy didn't argue, just sent me a look of unusual understanding. "Sure, I'll tell him," she said, "but you know what a *hard-head* Sim is. It probably won't do any good, though I, myself, have never understood that kind of spite. I mean, you love somebody, you bend over backwards to protect and cherish them every minute of your life, then you do *one* stupid thing, and *bam*—you're like the *pariah* of the world, no longer welcome in their life, ever again."

I didn't know what a *pariah* was, but figured it was something bad, was amazed and relieved that my sister was taking my side for once in my natural-born life. "You really think he's cutting me off for good?" I asked as we stepped into the warm, grease-smelling asphalt of the parking lot, making Missy turn and look at me blankly.

"Who? *Sim?*"

I nodded quickly, and she said, *"Oh,"* in this smooth, fake little voice, "I thought we were still talking about you and Mama. I don't know about Sim." She added with this smug little smirk, *"Maybe."*

Well, I walked right into that one, and just came to a halt there on the sidewalk and stared at her a moment. *"Witch,"* I finally murmured in a small, heatless voice, not angry or accusing, just tired and honest and so eternally whipped that she didn't even bother to take offense, just grinned her Daddy-grin: smug and happy and audacious as hell.

"Have I ever denied it?" she asked cheerfully, then unlocked the car and drove me to Aunt Candace's, dropped me off about a half an hour ago, just enough time to grab my recorder and get it down fresh, just the way I remember it, before anyone gets home.

# CHAPTER TWENTY

Well, another big fight has broken out in Grannie's dining room (or actually, the kitchen) just yesterday afternoon, and I'm glad to say that I wasn't part of this one, but tucked away in the laundry room, out of sight and out of mind, so no one can point a finger at *me*.

It's the first time I've so much as laid eyes on Gabe since that little glimpse of him at the gas station in December, such a weird and unexpected confrontation that I'm having a little brain freeze here, can't remember where I left off last week. Maybe with baseball, which is still grinding on, humiliation in cleats, though my practice sessions with Missy have finally begun to pay off, and miracle of miracles, last Friday I actually got a hit.

It was an especially satisfying experience, because Mama has started showing up at my games, haunting them, you might say, in her usual Mama way, not sitting in the bleachers with the rest of the fans, but alone in her car, a voiceless, hovering presence. There was no warning she was coming, either. I was just standing out in left field a couple of weeks ago, sweating like a hog and praying to God that no one hit a fly my way, when I glanced aside, and there, just beyond the sagging old chain-link fence, was the shining chrome bumpers of her dusty old Mercedes, an FSU tag on the front bumper.

I looked away immediately, pretended to be fascinated by the action at the plate, though as the inning stretched out, sweating and endless, I couldn't help but chance these sly little glances in Mama's direction, pretty sure she was alone in there, though it was hard to tell through the tint of the windshield. When Aunt Candace came by the dugout to check on me, it was the first thing I asked.

"Is that Mama?" I said with a dip of my head to the general direction of her car.

Like the sly old girl she has become, Aunt Candace didn't answer right away, just turned and lifted her sunglasses, pretended to peer across the field.

"Why, *yes,*" she murmured, "I believe it is." Then, to me: "Is that all right?"

I just shrugged, pretended it wasn't such a big deal, though my mother's voiceless presence there, not thirty feet beside me, had infused the game with new meaning, made me as restless and competitive as the rest of those animals. Not about winning as much as playing well, running hard, looking like I know what I'm doing, proving to the world that beneath my dimple and cowlick and spiked blond hair, there beats the heart of an athlete, a son of Michael Catts.

It's the kind of thing that's easier said than done, though like I say, on Friday night the miraculous actually occurred at the end of the fifth inning when I actually got a hit. It wasn't like the play of the game or anything, the score not close (three to six, I think), though the Sanger team has lost so many games this year that the pressure was on to win and win big—not that anyone was counting on me.

In fact, Missy says the only reason I got on base is that the shortstop bent down and started retying his shoe when he saw I was the next batter on deck, though I saw none of that, my heart beating like a sledgehammer as I stepped up to the plate, two guys on base and two outs, in a position to either make a king-sized fool of myself or (finally) be a hero. I am usually not a fan of that kind of pressure, but handled it all right, oddly comforted by the shining chrome bumpers of the Mercedes that had appeared shortly before the first pitch, and was quietly parked at the corner of the fence, nose in, silent.

Though the tint of the windows pretty much camouflaged Mama's expression, I could feel her in there, sending out vibes of support and encouragement the same way she used to when I was a kid, agonizing over those cursed flash cards. I kept my breath even, my eyes on the pitcher, while behind me, Missy came up to the bull pen to stand with her face pressed to the wire, her voice calling out a fast rattle of instruction to my back. (*"Drop those elbows, Clay. Keep your eyes on the ball. You can get a hit off this guy, he sucks—"*) I didn't turn or acknowledge her, just bent my knees a little and kept my eyes on the pitcher, a relief guy whose face reddened at Missy's (accurate) assessment of his skills, one thought breezing through my mind as he let go the first pitch: Please God, just this once.

It was a lousy pitch, a ball on the outside if I'd have let it go. But I didn't, of course, I swung like I always did, except this time instead of swinging through air, I connected with a hollow *thunk* that vibrated down to my hands and arms with a little shock of surprise.

For a fraction of a second, I watched the ball sail away in a modest little infield fly, dimly aware that the entire Sanger dugout had risen to its feet to a man, the base coaches and wives and other players all pointing at first base, shouting: "There! *There!* Run, Claybird, *run!*"

And that's exactly what I did: high-stepped it down to first, bat in hand, at least till I caught a glimpse of Missy, who was jumping up and down at the fence, crimson-faced and lunatic, positively *shrieking*: "Drop the bat! Drop the bat! DROP THE BAT!"

I probably would have been called out on a technicality if she hadn't, for I'd taken it along as a souvenir, I guess. I pitched it aside in an instant, tagged the base a quarter second before the ball hit the first baseman's mitt to an immediate roar of approval from the crowd that I couldn't hear very well, my head strangely hot, the blood pounding in my ears as if I was about to have a stroke. Later, I realized it was the metal batting cap that was to blame, but I'd forgotten all about that, just thought I was having some kind of out-of-body experience, weirdly separated from the noise and the heat of the game.

I returned to the base and stood posed there, waiting for the next hit, sweat pouring down my nose, my heart beating like a bass drum, not having long to wait. For Coach Bates is the kind of old-school coach who likes to keep things simple, lining his batting order up best to worst (me being worst). So we were right back at the top of the order, our best hitter right behind me, a guy named Ricky Vaughn, who worked in the wood shop at Sanger and was a heck of a ballplayer. He didn't bother humiliating the relief guy or offering any false hope, just reached back on the first pitch and whacked that ball six hundred miles in the air, though no one in the stands paid him any mind.

They must have figured he knew his way around the bases just fine and focused their roaring attention on me, a hundred hands pointing to second, then third, then home plate in a way that would have been doggoned funny if I hadn't been so worried about tripping or falling down or otherwise making a fool out of myself. I just kept my face down and my legs pumping, crossed home to a great thunder of applause from the Sanger people who all worked for Daddy and had watched me grow up, knew I was the family gimp.

Even Coach Bates was all smiles and love, meeting me at the plate and escorting me back to the dugout, his fat old arm draped around my shoulder as if I were an erring sinner, he a kindly old preacher who'd finally talked me back into the fold. But I had paid little mind to any of it, my eyes on the outfield, on the quietly shining Mercedes that was still parked there, voiceless and dim, though I could make out a small, fluttered movement behind the wheel, one that I could identify even from fifty feet away: the sight of my strange old vampire mother, clapping.

At moments like that, I could understand why Daddy loved baseball so much: because it was neat and simple in its way: clear-cut rules, clear-cut goals, nothing gray or uncertain, no mixed motives or heart-wrenching betrayals or tortured might-have-beens. Something I might one day actually enjoy, or at least wanted to learn a little better before the regular season came to an end, not long now, maybe two more weeks.

To that end, I begged Missy to interrupt her last-minute cramming for finals and help me practice my catching game, and after a lot of excuses and whining, she came by yesterday afternoon and took me to the church around six, the May afternoon already full of the sights and smells of summer: sweat and cut grass and a long, lingering sunset. We spent a good two hours out there, her effortlessly popping flies, me running around the slippery grass like a blind beetle, tripping over my feet and almost killing myself while I tried to learn the elusive art of Keeping Your Eye on the Ball.

I finally got to where I could snag a few, and as the brilliant sunset washed out to a flat, dull pearl, we left our cleats and gloves on the hood of her car and wandered down the street to Grannie's for leftovers, burnt out on McDonald's and wanting some real food. We found the house dark, the front door locked, though we didn't let that slow us down, just went around back and let ourselves in with the spare key, were poking around in her refrigerator when there was a noise in the drive, the unmistakable diesel hum of the Mercedes pulling up.

I jerked upright immediately, stood there paralyzed like a possum in a headlight, though Missy kept her head, just turned and hissed at me: "Run hide to the laundry room, *hurry*—"

For some reason, she ran along side me, as if we were escaping from prison, just around the corner to the little folding doors that open into a tiny little room that used to be a corner of the back porch before Grannie made it into an indoor laundry room. I jumped up on the dryer while Missy paused at the folding doors, listening as the back door opened with a clang, the quiet house suddenly besieged with raised voices, apparently an argument-in-progress, one Grannie's and one unmistakably Gabe's.

"—well, I personally don't give a damn *what* Candace thinks," he was saying in a voice of great exasperation. "Since when did she become the Protector of All Souls, the Last Word in this family? Who died and made her queen?"

It was the first time I'd heard his voice in nine months and I was struck afresh with how much he sounded like Daddy, his voice stripped of every trace of New York and fully returned to its mill-town origins, quick and hick and aggrieved, so close that I could make out every word.

*"Shut the door,"* I hissed at Missy, who answered with a quick little nod of her head.

"I'll go get the car," she whispered, "sit tight."

She quietly shut the folding doors, then must have slid across the hall into Grannie's bedroom and tiptoed through the spare bedroom and out through the front door. For no one in the kitchen seemed to detect her presence, the close, hot little discussion rolling on undisturbed, Grannie chiding Gabe about his language, telling him that Simon was cursing like a *sailor* the other night, and she *sho* knew where he'd picked it up.

"At Sanger?" he countered in a needling little voice, trying to get her goat.

"Nosir," she countered stoutly, "a mite closer to home."

He must have come by to take her to the grocery store, was helping her put up groceries, for their ongoing little snipping war was punctuated by creaking cabinet doors and remarks like "When did you start buying instant coffee?" And "Where'd you keep your peanut butter?"

But these were mere counterpoints to the main argument, which was all about Simon and his Secret Life in Waycross, and whether it should remain secret.

"—youngun thinks he knows what he's doing, but he don't," Grannie complained at one point, and later, to a muffled statement of Gabe's: "Well, to hear *some* people talk, you wouldn't thank there was any such thang as sin anymore—"

"That ain't what I said," Gabe countered solidly, clearly on Sim's side, though he didn't try to defend his actions or make any excuses. He mostly just fended off Grannie's sincere moral outrage, on and on, a steady stream of reason that began to lose its tolerance as Grannie continued to insist that Mama should be told, Gabe finally losing his temper, telling her: "*No,* Mama! No, we don't need to tell Myra or anybody else! Sim ain't a child—you cain't just lay down the law, *set* thet boy straight. It's out of your hands—it's out of Myra's hands, and by *God,* it's never been any of Candace's business at all! It's up to Sim! The ball's¹ in his court! He chooses! He chooses! HE *CHOOSES!*"

Which doesn't sound as nutty as it did at the time, because by then, Gabe had worked himself into a frenzy, his voice steadily rising, so it sounded like: He chooses! (in a normal voice); then: HE CHOOSES! (a little louder); then HE *CHOOSES!* lifted to an actual shriek, so loud the folding doors to the laundry room actually trembled as he added: "And he'd better make damn sure he chooses right, 'cause whatever he chooses, he'll by God live with it, the rest of his life!"

None of this was new to me, of course, just a rehash of the old empowerment lecture he used to give us losers at LPM. It wasn't something Grannie could really argue with, for it had a scriptural basis, a variation of what Joshua told the Israelites when they crossed to the Promised Land *(choose this day, whom will you serve)*, though Gabe somewhat diminished the righteousness of his instruction by backsliding and slipping in the f-word *("*. . . the rest of his *f-ing* life"),* which pretty much canceled out the whole point of his message. Just like that, Grannie was on him like *white* on *rice,* the whole argument deteriorating into this fevered little murmur of accusation and excuse that I found mighty annoying, for I could tell it was good and juicy gossip, just pitched so low that I couldn't quite make it out.

I finally realized that Gabe was leaving, and they'd moved their argument to the back porch as he headed for the car. With hardly a stir of noise, I slipped quietly to the floor and wiggled between the washer and dryer to the little four-by-four vent that opened outside. Peering out at grasshopper level, I could see Gabe a few feet in front of me, though his back was turned, one hand rubbing his neck, one cradled protectively to his side in a way I'd never seen him do before, as if he'd just gotten it out of the cast and it still hurt him.

I immediately realized there was something very different about him, though I couldn't figure exactly what, maybe his hair, that was cropped off close to his head, so short it was no longer visibly blond, but mostly gray, as gray as Daddy's was that last month before he died. He even stood like Daddy, leaning there in the doorjamb on one shoulder, listening without comment to Grannie, who was standing beyond the screen, still fighting hard for the Soul of Simon Catts, not angry now, but querulous, asking Gabe what if that girl got pregnant? What would Sim do *then*?

Gabe just rubbed his neck, told her in a tired, spent voice: "Well, Mama, I think I can safely say that at this point in life, Simon knows what birth control is. But I'll take him down to Walgreen's and buy him a pack of condoms if it'll make you feel any better."

"Oh, *law*," Grannie cried, "don't you be doing no such thang."

The very idea seemed to shock her to silence, for she just stood there a moment, shaking her head, offered in a gloomy voice: "It just seems like it was yesterday that li'l ol' Sim was running around here barefoot, building forts and hunting snakes."

"It *was* yesterday," Gabe answered wearily as he straightened up. "Children have a way of growing up on you, or so they tell me."

He was backing up when he said it, about to turn and head down the steps when Grannie asked him how he was feeling; said something about him losing weight. That's when it hit me, the difference I'd noticed the moment I laid eyes on him: he'd lost maybe twenty, twenty-five pounds, his khaki pants bagging on him, his belt nipped in to the first notch.

Gabe didn't seem too concerned, just brushed Grannie off and asked from out of the blue: "Well, did you hear about Clay? Myra says he hit a grand slam the other night, won the game."

This was certainly news to me, though Grannie stood there in her cloak of Baptist righteousness and lied like a dog: "Yessir, he sho did," she said with a proud little lift of her chin. "Him and Missy come down after the game, told me all about it. He's got real good, might play professional ball one day."

I wished to God I could see Gabe's expression on that, but couldn't, his back still turned, his good hand rubbing his neck wearily. "Yeah, that's what I hear. That's what I hear." Then, as he started down the steps: "Well, I gotta go write a final, Mama. Tell Candace to kiss my ass when you see her, tell her if I want her opinion, I'll be sure and call and ask."

"—no such thang!" Grannie called after him, though he didn't answer, just lifted a hand in farewell, then went around to the car without once turning in my direction, which really annoyed me, because I was wanting to see what he looked like; wanted to see his face. But he never turned and it was funny, because Grannie just kept standing there at the screen after he left, her face worried and introspective, an expression I remembered from years ago, back when she used to get onto Daddy for working so hard, for not taking off enough vacation days; for not going to the doctor often enough for annual checkups.

It made me a little nervous, that look of hers, though I just wiggled out from behind the dryer and sneaked out of the folding doors, was making my way through the house when I came upon her in the living room, looking for her reading glasses. I pretended to be dropping by for leftovers (which, now that I think of it, I was) and she was glad to oblige me, went to the kitchen and was warming me up whatever she could lay hands on when Missy came back with the car and offered me a ride home.

Grannie was none the wiser, just fed us and sent us on our way, and when Missy pulled up in Aunt Candace's drive to drop me off, I didn't get out right away. I just gathered my cleats and my glove, thanked her for helping me practice, then, after an awkward little pause, burst out in this goofy little voice: "What's wrong with him?"

To her credit, Missy didn't toy with me or tease me this time, didn't ask who I meant by *him*. She knew I was talking about Gabe and just shrugged, said: "I don't know. He's been losing weight a couple of months now, since Christmas. Doesn't like to talk about it."

I digested this in silence, just sat there a moment, chewing my lip, before I got to the heart of the matter, the thing I'd thought of the moment I laid eyes on him: "Does he have cancer?"

Missy looked a little exasperated at the question. "Gosh, Clay, I don't know," she said with a little roll of the eyes. "If he does, he doesn't know it. At least not yet. He thinks it's an old ulcer acting up."

But I'd never heard of an ulcer making someone's hair turn gray, or lose weight that quickly. Cancer was the reason for that kind of weight loss, that kind of color, me and Missy both knew it, though there was nothing you could do about it. God, we knew that, too.

For a moment, we just sat there idling in the drive, till I finally told her: "Well, tell him he can come to my game next week, if he wants to." Which was the nicest thing I could think of offering him, though Missy just looked at me dryly across the seat.

"You're too kind, sir," she said with her old Missy-sarcasm that, for some reason, just infuriated me; made me madder than hell.

"Just *shut up*, Missy!" I shouted at her across the seat, grabbing my cleats and slamming open the door. "*God,* I get sick of your *mouth*!" Oddly enough, she didn't leap back at me like she usually did, but tried to reach over and grab my shoulder, to apologize, though I shook her off. "This isn't easy for me, either, you know?" I told her in this furious, shaking little voice, appalled when my voice broke, it made me sound like such a child.

But Missy seemed curiously moved by my outburst, not going after me, but telling me in this mild little voice: "I know, Clay. I know. I'm sorry. I'll tell him, okay? About the baseball." When she saw I was calming down, she added with a return of her sly Missy-humor: "If you're sure about that. I mean, we're talking two Tierneys out there in the stands— him and Aunt Candace. There's always the chance they'll rush the umpire on a bad call, get in a big ol' redneck fistfight."

I appreciated her try at humor, had to clear my throat a little before I could speak. "Just tell him," I managed to creak out. "Okay?"

She assured me that she would, though I'm not sure he ever got the message. For the next thing I heard about our nutty old uncle Gabe was that he was in the hospital, had woken up the next morning bleeding from the mouth, lying in a puddle of blood.

# CHAPTER TWENTY-ONE

Aunt Candace was the one who told me, came to my bedroom while I was dressing for school the next morning and knocked softly on the door. I thought she was stopping by to tell me to hurry and called for her to come in, was pulling a T-shirt over my head when I realized she was standing there in the doorway, looking at me with an expression that was stunned and quiet.

Just like that, I knew something was wrong, and for some reason, thought it was Mama. I thought that she'd found out about Sim and the stress had gotten to her and she'd gone nuts again, maybe killed herself. I actually sat down on the bed, was waiting for the confirmation, the tears, the meeting with Brother Sloan and Carlym and maybe Pastor Jim, all of them speaking in kind, hushed voices, telling me the same stuff they told me when Daddy died ("—in my Father's house are many mansions. I go to prepare a place for you that where I am, you may be also—"). It was like my life passed before my eyes the way it's supposed to do the instant before you die, till Aunt Candace finally got it out, told me in this shaken little voice: "Mama just called. Said Myra had to take Gabe to the hospital this morning."

"Why?" I managed in a small, dried-up voice.

"Well, he's been having a little trouble with his stomach," she explained in that distracted little voice. "Started bleeding last night, thinks it's just an old ulcer kicking up. I thought I'd run by and see him before I clock in, but I'll need to leave early, right now. If you hurry, I'll drop you off at school, save Missy the trip. You're still going over to Mama's this afternoon, aren't you? To work in her yard?"

That was the plan, made last week when I was still trying to comfort Grannie over Sim's loss of innocence—that I'd go over and cut back the kudzu and move some azaleas and a couple of camellias that were growing too close to her house. She was paying me five dollars, though I wasn't sure if that was by the hour or by the afternoon, and really didn't care, because I loved the old girl, for one thing, and she was cooking me supper, for another.

When I nodded, Aunt Candace tried to smile, was turning to go back to the phone when I stopped her to ask: "How's Mama?"

"I don't know, baby," she said. "I'm calling Simon in Waycross. He'll come by and get you at school if anything—you know—happens. 'Kay?"

I quickly finished dressing, got to school early, and tried to study for my Latin exam, but it was hard to do, with this new medical emergency hanging over our heads. The whole time I was taking my exam, whenever anyone passed in the hallway or came to the door, I'd look up sharply, thinking it might be Brother Sloan or maybe Carlym, standing there in one of their dark funeral suits, beckoning me to the hall, asking if they could speak to me in private.

But the morning passed with no interruptions, no messages, and when the bell rang for early dismissal, instead of going down to the gym with Kenneth for the end-of-the-year dance to see if Rachel had possibly dropped by, I hotfooted it across town to Grannie's. I hurried along, running the last block up the Hill and bursting in her front door, found her in the kitchen, standing at the stove in a housedress and apron, already working on supper in the middle of the afternoon. She held a finger to her mouth as soon as she saw me, whispered: "*Shhh.* Yo mama's asleep in the front bedroom—you'll wake her up."

I stopped dead at that, glanced around wildly. "Why? Is it Gabe? Is he—?"

I paused, couldn't finish the sentence, and Grannie looked at me mildly. "Is he *what?*" she asked, but I really couldn't get it out.

I just kept staring at her, finally stammered, "Is he —okay?"

Grannie went back to her stove on that, told me over her shoulder: "Yessir, he's fine. The doctor took an X ray, found a hole in his stomach—" But that's about as far as she got, when, to both our consternation, I burst into tears like a big old hundred-and-eighty-pound baby.

I think it might have been the single most embarrassing moment in my life, though Grannie was the soul of comfort, just wiped her hands on her apron and came over and gripped me in one of her tight Grannie-hugs, murmured: "Oh, shug, don't you worry yoursef. Gabriel Catts is like Old Tommy." Tommy was her cat. "Underneath all that fluff and fur, he's a tough old thing. He'll be fine." Though she looked very smug and satisfied when she said it, pleased that at least one of her grandsons hadn't gone the way of all flesh and could still be unashamedly neurotic and emotional and sissy.

"I'm all right, I'm all right," I told her as we parted, wiping my eyes and adding (as if it were the reason for the tears): "I think I failed Latin. It was too hard. And Mr. Neeley hates me."

Grannie smiled at me indulgently, didn't argue or tell me what a *goof* I was, just went back to the stove and finished telling me about Gabe, who'd just come out of surgery, was doing fine, the doctor said, would only be in the hospital a couple of days at the most.

"Sim come all the way from Waycross to sit with him," she added with a significant lift of her chin, as if this were indisputable evidence that my brother hadn't gone *completely* to the bad. "Did it for his mama," she told me, "who wasn't in no fit state to hang around thet hospital all day. I brung her home with me, made her take a nap." Then, in the single re-proach she ever voiced over my treatment of my mother: "She ain't had the easiest life, your mama ain't. I knowed her when she was a chile, living right across thet fence, and let me tell you, son, it wadn't no picnic, growing up over there with that sorry excuse for a daddy she had."

She must have known that Aunt Candace had filled me in on the gruesome details, for she didn't add anything else, just met my eye in that voiceless, chin-out challenge till I assured her: "I know, Grannie. I know."

"Well," she said with a smart little shake her of apron, "you'll speak nicely to her when she gets up."

Her old Grannie bossiness struck me as funny for some reason, made me laugh for the first time that day. "Well, what d'you want me to do in the yard?" I asked, and her face lost its challenge just like that. Grannie's too old to push a wheelbarrow anymore and too poor to hire a yard service, and though she's too proud to let her children pay for it, she really does worry that her neighbors sit around their supper tables every night and wonder aloud at what has become of Sister Catts's nice yard.

So she was quickly all business, took me outside and showed me the kudzu that had taken over the five-acre field behind her house and was making steady inroads on her back and side fence. She put on a pair of leather gloves and showed me how to rip it out and follow it to its roots, big old potato-looking things that she had me dig up and burn (Grannie not being the kind of person who toys with her enemies, but opts for a straight scorched-earth policy).

The kudzu alone took the better part of the afternoon, and once I had the roots and vines smoking in her burn barrel, she showed me the different plants that needed to be transplanted: four azaleas and two camellias, which doesn't sound like a lot of work, but by gosh, was. For we're not talking about fragile little specimen plants here, but big old ancient monsters, the camellias absolutely enormous, six feet high, at least, with taproots, and went on and on, I'm talking to China.

By sundown, I had dug myself halfway under her house searching for the end of the roots, finally gave up and started chopping, hoping to God that we weren't entering one of those cursed summer droughts, or

Grannie might lose one of them and God help us if she did (the old Debutantes were her favorite). Fortunately, she'd gone inside to finish cooking supper, so I got away with my chopping, was moving the last of the camellias, lumbering under the weight of the hideous old thing, when I realized that Mama was standing there on the porch steps watching me.

She must have woken up from her nap and come out without a sound, just appeared there in all her ghostly tranquillity, her hair chopped off so short that she really did look kind of pathetic, like a chemo patient trying to get a little sun before the summer came fully on. I didn't quite know what to say, just manhandled the old camellia over to the fence and dropped it sideways with a little crash, then wiped my face on my arm and sent her a terse little nod, the way rednecks nod when they pass each other on the highway, a brief, neighborly acknowledgment of recognition.

She didn't nod back, just stood there at the top of the steps, one hand on the porch rail, in a timid little stance that was familiar to me for some reason, I couldn't figure why. Then I remembered Aunt Candace's story about how Mama had fallen in love with her majorette uniform when she was a child, but was too shy to come to the fence, would stand on their porch and peer at her across the twilight.

She stood there with that same mixture of eagerness and timidity, till finally, after what—twenty-eight years?—she gathered the courage to leave the safety of the porch and come slowly down the steps.

"Claybird?" she called across the twilight. "Can we talk?"

There was an immediate pound of nervousness in my chest, though I tried to be cool and casual, told her: "Let me finish with this camellia." Then, so she wouldn't think I was putting her off: "Grannie's paying me."

She nodded at that, then went over to the old pig-iron fence next to the sweet gum and sat down in the flickering shade, waiting patiently while I took care of that cursed last camellia, ripping roots and breaking branches in my hurry to get it in the ground, till the gardener in Mama must have gotten the best of her. For she came to her feet, called across the yard: "Claybird. Wait. Here, baby—not so deep."

Then, with no concern for her clothes or nails, she came over and helped me plant it, knelt down on the ground and wrapped the dragging roots in a nice little ball that she fitted into the hole. Once the dirt was nicely patted in, she had me go down to the ditch and dig up some black muck to top it off, then finally came to her feet with the satisfied look of a job well done, her nice khaki pants no longer so nice, her hands and nails a sorry sight.

"Gosh, Mama, you got all dirty," I told her, though she couldn't have cared less.

"That's all right," she said, absently slapping the loose sand off her knees. "Run get the hose and I'll water it in."

But I'd been working in the yard for the better part of six hours by then, was about ready to take a load off my feet. "It'll be all right," I told her. Then, "Did you want to talk?" Because I was tired of waiting, was wanting to get this thing out in the open right now, while I had the courage to face it and was really too tired and whipped to care. But Mama, Earth Mother that she is, couldn't leave that cursed old camellia alone.

"Claybird, the root'll dry out if we leave it like this," she said. "Run get the hose—it won't take a minute."

With a little roll of the eyes to show how much of an inconvenience it was, I went and got the hose and she stood there and shot water on her specially dug hole till it was nicely filled, a mud pond with a camellia bush poking out of it. When she was finished, she washed her hands, though in true Mama-fashion didn't bother to go and ask Grannie for a towel, just wiped them on the butt of her pants, then left the tip of the hose to drip the same way she did with her new roses.

By then, the sun was far down the sky, mostly behind the roofline of the sagging old houses at the end of Lafayette, its last, straining rays catching the top of the old sweet gum, turning its crown a fiery cherry red. That's where Mama settled again, in the sand next to its thick black trunk, her back to the ratty old shack, where rumor had it, she'd once died. She didn't look too disturbed by the close proximity of the scene of her early death, just lifted her face to the sun-dappled old tree when I sat down, said aside in a light, casual voice: "Gabriel and I used to play here, when we were children."

It was actually a strange sensation, having my mother bring up one of her past lives with such casual ease. I didn't quite know what to make of it, just closed my eyes, glad to be off my feet, said, "Really?"—hoping she'd tell me more, but she didn't, of course.

I must not have sounded enthusiastic enough, for she immediately took cover in the mundane routine of current events, asking me about baseball, of all things, then other family matters: how Lori was doing in school, and how Ryan liked preschool; whether Missy would really go to college in France.

I just sat there and listened as the sun sank low in the sky, the old sweet gum losing its burnished glow, disappearing into the twilight, soon nothing more than a dry rustle of leaves above our heads. It wasn't until then, till her old friend, the twilight, had settled upon us, that Mama finally worked up the courage to bring the conversation around to more sensitive waters, told me about Gabe and his surgery, and how she'd talked to the surgeon, and everything went fine.

I just nodded, told her: "Yeah. That's what Grannie said."

She paused then and actually took a breath for courage before she hesitantly offered: "He's sorry, Clay, about what happened."

I just nodded, wondered exactly what he was sorry about (making a fool of my father? making a fool of *me*?). But I didn't ask, just looked across the fence at the nasty old shack that really did have white trash written all over it, the yard weedy and overgrown, the limestone chimney beginning to detach itself from the sagging walls, the porch completely taken by the kudzu, a smooth, sculpted green. I was absently wondering what it'd be like to actually *live* there, to live and sleep and pee in the ratty old outhouse that still stood in crooked, sagging isolation out in the yard, when she pushed ahead nervously, still talking about Gabe.

"I just wish you could accept it—" she began, though when I looked up in challenge, she backed down quickly, stammered: "Not *accept*—forgive. *Forgive* it."

Well, that was hardly any better and I just shrugged to show my disinterest, though Mama wouldn't let it go. You could tell it was killing her to have to directly deal with such an unpleasant subject, her words halting and unsure as she made her point, tried to explain: "I don't mean you have to *deny* it, or say it was all right—because, Claybird, believe *me*, nobody knows better than me that forgiveness isn't saying it was all right, it was fine, what happened. Forgiveness is just saying: that was the way it was, and letting it go. That's all it is, baby."

In another time and place, I might have appreciated the simplicity of her levelheaded advice, but at the moment, I was bone-tired from all my labors: Latin conjugations and yard work and trying to learn baseball and trying to make sense of my doofus little life. I was too tired to be cooperative and just sat there in the lowering darkness, not really feeling up to any more shouts and arguments, the sad, honest truth finally working its way up through my wounded pride to make a brief, unexpected appearance.

"But I don't know how it was," I said in a calm little voice that even surprised me, because by God, it was true. So true that poor Mama looked terribly pained, terribly wounded, sitting there by the fence in her cropped hair and her ghostly paleness, looking shorn and miserable till I added a little clarification of my own: "You don't ever talk about him."

"What?" she asked, and I gave a little shrug.

"Daddy," I said. "Grannie and Aint Candace, and Lori and Curtis—they all talk about him. You never do."

For a moment, she just looked at me in wonder, even tried to argue, stammered, "Gosh, Clay—what d'you mean, I don't talk about him? Sure, I talk about him. I think about him all the time—"

But I had no time for her denial, told her plainly: "You do *not*. It's like he never even lived, you forgot him so quick. You don't even go to his grave anymore."

She looked briefly and sincerely pained at this, just sat there a moment as if trying to find the right words to defend herself, then began in this halting little voice: "Baby, if I don't talk about him, it's just because it's—so hard. I mean, when people *die,* it's like who they really are gets a little lost in the telling. You know how it was at the funeral, when everybody kept going on and on about what a great guy Michael was—how *petty* it all sounded, like we were throwing him a bone because he left us in his will. That's why I don't talk about him, baby—because it *hurts*." She seemed to finally be hitting close to the truth, pausing on the force of the word, then adding in a smaller voice: "And I'm not so good at it, anyway."

She halted on that, leaving us at what you might call an impasse, because I *knew* she could talk about him if she wanted to. I mean, I was the one who'd interviewed her for the oral-history project, and her story, by gosh, it had been the best one on the tape, everyone had said so, even the judges. So I wasn't going to let her off easy, just sat there under the sweet gum, the yard much cooler now that the sun had gone down, a few timid little stars beginning to glimmer at the edge of the tree line that Mama watched with great interest, her face suddenly and mysteriously lighting.

"A star fell the night we got engaged," she told me, her pale face momentarily lit as she glanced down and met my eye. "We were driving home through the flat woods from Milton, and I don't know if I'd have married him if it hadn't, because Mama was dead set against it, pitching a fit up in Birmingham, and I hardly knew him—didn't even know his middle name. But then a star fell like a comet, all the way across the sky, and he stopped in the middle of the road, told me to make a wish."

I smiled then, because Daddy was a great wisher on stars, had done the same thing with me a few times when we were coming home from Waycross, tracking across the flat woods on a cold winter's night, the sky dark and close and mysteriously alive. He'd never actually stopped in the highway, but he would always slow down and point it out to me through the windshield, tell me to make a wish, and I always would, too. Sometimes I'd wish for easy things: comic books or Transformers or the latest Lego invention, but usually it was the same wish, the same prayer that I prayed every night before I went to sleep: that I'd learn to read; that I'd quit being the family dumbo, would grow up to be like Missy and Sim: tall and smart and athletic.

Sitting there in the cool sand under the sweet gum, it occurred to me that by gosh, I'd gotten that wish, and wasn't it funny? It was the one prayer I never had any faith for, that I never thought would come true.

But Mama didn't pause for my ruminations, the floodgates open to her own memories, her own explanations, her voice fast and oddly passionate, as she leaned toward me a little, told me in this earnest, pleading voice: "And Clay, that's what your father was to me: he was that star. He came out of nowhere, he streaked across the darkness. He lit the sky with this terrible beauty, this great love, then, just like that"—she quietly snapped her fingers—"he was gone. And everything faded, back to black."

I came back to myself with a jolt, realized she was actually telling me something here: she was setting the record straight, my mother was, about who I was in this family, who my father was and what he was to both of us, the effort so intense that quiet little tears began streaking down her cheeks that she ignored, might not have realized were even there.

I just watched her a moment, full of this sudden, terrible pity, asked: "What'd you wish for, that night?"

Mama seemed to find the question funny, and laughed a little, even through her tears. "Oh, baby, I don't remember. Happiness, I guess. Or that Mama'd let up on me. It didn't really matter at that point, 'cause I didn't need to be wasting my time *wishing* anymore. I was heading back to Magnolia Hill, to live with Cissie and Mr. Simon—and that's all me or Ira ever wanted, anyway."

It came to me then that by God that was all I ever wanted either: a place of sanctuary, a little peace and acceptance. Maybe it was all *anybody* ever wanted, and after a moment, I moved over next to her, put my arm around her, tried to think of some way to tell her that I understood her tears, and why she loved Grannie so much, and Granddaddy Sims, too—but it was a hard thing to do.

I finally just dipped my head at the nasty old shack behind us that was hardly visible in the full darkness of the early May night. "Aint Candace told me about—you know—when you lived there. Your father and all."

It wasn't the most articulate statement I'd ever made in my life, but Mama seemed to understand, sniffed: "Yeah. It was tough."

"You don't ever talk about it," I pointed out, and she wiped her face and glanced aside at me.

"Well, what d'you want to know?" she asked. I must have looked surprised, for she added: "I mean, I've just come to that point, Clay, that I told you about, where you say: that was the way it was, and you let it go. But if you need me to dig it back up, I will. I mean, I do it for Ira, every time they send me a subpoena. I'll do it for you, too, if you want."

But I was really not into horror stories, I never had been, and just shook my head. "That's all right," I told her, and she looked at me with a face of great compassion

"Because, one day, Claybird, that's what you'll have to do about Gabriel and me. It'll be the hardest thing you ever do in your life."

I was the one who was stuck silent then, kind of embarrassed at her bringing her and Gabe out in the open like that, though I did manage to answer, not with accusation or heat, just the bare truth: "I don't think I can. Not about you," I hastened to add. "I understand about you. But not him. He loved him."

Like Missy the night before, Mama didn't bother to ask *who* I was talking about, just wiped her nose and assured me: "He did. That's what you need to remember, Clay. They did love each other, so much."

"Then how could he do it?" I asked, and Mama just sighed.

"He stumbled into it, Clay, like most people do. Just stumbled into stupidity. Ask him sometime. He'll tell you."

But I still didn't care to hear Gabe's side of the matter, was more focused on Mama, asking her with a small intensity: "Which did you love?" Because that's the thing that bothered me the most: the possibility that she'd loved Gabe all those years, and pined away for him, just put up with Daddy because he was rich and available, and they had children, and it was the Right Thing to Do.

But Mama didn't seem to understand the seriousness of the question. "*Which* did I love?" she repeated with a thread of her only daughter's razor tongue. "Well, what d'you want me to do here, Clay? Flip a coin?"

Now, I am becoming less and less a fan of the rampant sarcasm that has infested our family, and just looked at her levelly, so long that she backed down, told me in a tired little voice: "Clay, listen: I loved them *both*. I loved them *all*: Miss Cissie and Mr. Simon and Candace and Michael and Gabe. You want a division? Everything on that side of the fence, I feared. Everything on this side, I loved. Does that answer your question?"

I had opened my mouth to tell her *maybe,* for in her usual Mama-way, she'd answered everything and answered nothing—but before I could speak, Grannie came out on the porch and started calling us to supper. She must not have been able to see us in the darkness under the tree, for she just stood there at the rail in her apron and hollered: "My-*ra*! Clay-*ton*! Supper's ready!" as if we were fieldhands, and she, the plantation-house cook.

Such was the authority in her trebly old voice that I started to my feet in an instant, though I had one more question for Mama before we went in, the heart of the matter, you might say, the reason I'd been living with my aunt, polishing tile, for nine months.

"People say, he ain't my father," I told her in a small, hesitant voice, though Mama didn't look as pained as she did curious.

"Who? *Michael?*"

When I nodded, she made a face of great weariness. "Well, Clay-bird," she said as she came to her feet, "as you grow older, you'll come to find that, generally speaking, *people* don't know *shit.*"

I have never been a fan of profanity in women in general and my mother in particular, and couldn't help a little squelch of annoyance that made her look even more tired as she straightened up and met my eye, told me plainly: "Michael is your father. He's the one who fed you, changed your diapers, put a roof over your head. He loved you more than he loved me, Clay, and that's saying a lot." She let this remarkable statement sink in a moment, then added, "Gabriel—he loves you, too—he'd have given you his *eyes,* he still would. But I picked Michael, I had to, I loved him so much. There was never a choice for me as long as he was alive. You understand?"

It was the thing I'd been waiting to hear for nine months, confirmation of what I really knew in my heart: that no matter who I looked like, or whatever the arrangement of my genetic code or DNA ladder, Daddy was my father, the best thing, that wouldn't be taken from me.

I can't tell you what a relief it was, overwhelming, almost exhausting, making me take a deep breath, the same kind I'd taken when I'd finally gotten my first run the other night down at the old ballfield. I was about to say something else (thank you, I think), but Grannie had started in on her hollering again, her voice echoing over the Hill, "Myra? Clay? The biscuits are gitting cold!"

We started toward the porch then, Mama taking my arm after a few steps, and when Grannie caught sight of us in the yard below, her face lost its impatience just like that, replaced by the same smug, satisfied expression she'd had when I'd burst into tears that afternoon.

Crossing her arms majestically on her chest, she lifted her chin at me, said: "Look at thet youngun, Myra, six-foot-one if he's an inch. He's grown up on us this year. He's all grown up."

And you know, I think she might be right. I mean, I haven't arrived at any great destinations yet, haven't come to the end of any wondrous journeys, but I've finally quit riding passively along, pulled by my mother's steam. I've finally gotten out on my own little legs and started to walk.

# CHAPTER TWENTY-TWO

It's late, after midnight, and I've had such a strange and fast week that I really should close it down right now, wait till Sunday night so I can tape in the privacy of Grannie's back porch. But now that I'm back in my own little bunk bed out here in the woods, with the swoosh of the old pines and the ghostly creaking of the stairs, I have this sudden urge to tie it all up, get it down fresh while it's still on my mind.

It's funny how quickly it's all turned around, because as of Tuesday morning, I thought my life had come to an end when Kenneth left for his grandmother's a month earlier than usual, with an abruptness that left me kind of numb. I was just sitting there at Aunt Candace's, munching a Pop-Tart and watching a rerun of the *X-Men,* mulling over my conversation with Mama and enjoying a rare morning of leisure, when he called out of the blue, not from his trailer in Sinclair, but the Atlanta airport, of all places.

Apparently, Uncle Lou had snagged a couple of discount tickets to New York that were only good for the month of May, and at precisely eleven o'clock the night before, Miss Susan had decided to go ahead and use them. Before Kenneth could so much as take a shower or tell me good-bye, he had to go streaking over to Jacksonville in the middle of the night, had flown out at six that morning, was at that moment standing at a pay phone, waiting for a connector flight to New York.

He didn't seem particularly apologetic for abandoning me so abruptly, his voice high and fast and excited, raised over the noise of the airport to provide me with a brief, glowing travelogue of his summer plans: "We're flying into JFK at twelve-oh-five, staying at Grandma's till Kemp and Keith come up in July. Then Uncle Lou's picking us all up, taking us to Atlantic City for a week, says I'm tall enough now that he can sneak me in a casino—oh, and he's taking us to see the Mets, too, already has the tickets. I can't remember who they're playing, but it's gonna be good—"

On and on he went, painting the picture of the perfect New York summer, which didn't do me much good, stranded here in hot, humid old Florida. When his flight was announced, he shouted good-bye and hung up, left me sitting there with the dead phone in my hand, overcome by this sagging weight of dread, wondering what in the world I'd do all summer by myself, stranded in town with Aunt Candace. I mean, you could only scrub the dirtiest bathroom an hour a day at the most. What would I do with the other twenty-three? Watch cartoons? Read *War and Peace*?

It was a question that was partially answered a couple of hours later when Mrs. Munden (the dean at the high school) called, looking for Aunt Candace. When I told her she was at work, she regretfully informed me that they'd sent home notices the day before that I'd have to attend summer school to make up for failing both Latin and algebra, and my first thought was: Poor Mama. Since my official address is still out in the woods, she'd be walking down to the mailbox any day now, may receive the little blue notice of failure the same day she finds out that despite a lifetime of vigilance, in Sim's case, True Love Didn't Wait.

I thought about picking up the phone and giving her a little advance warning, but Gabe had come home from the hospital the day before and might answer on the upstairs extension. I'd have to hang up on him, and knowing Gabe, he'd realize it was me and might flip out or something, burst open his stitches. So I just moped around the house all day waiting for Aunt Candace to come home, wondering what she'd do if I didn't pass summer school and out and out failed ninth grade? Shoot me? Send me to Christian school? Go ahead and begin prepayments on a cell at Raiford and spare the taxpayers of Florida the time and expense? When the phone rang at six, I leapt on it, wanting to get it over with, spill it out, but it wasn't Aunt Candace. It was Mama.

"Hey, baby," she said in her slow, easygoing old Louisiana drawl. "Whatchu doing?"

Well, I figured I was busted then; that she'd gotten the notice in the mail that afternoon and was about to lay into me, tell me what a disappointment I was, how I was driving her to an early grave. I rubbed my eyes and prepared for the worst, though she approached the subject with her usual mincing sidestep, not mentioning the notice at all, just asking how baseball was going; if I'd made any hits the night before (she'd missed my game to stay home and nurse Gabe).

I made the most disinterested replies, was bracing myself for a bad moment when she finally got around to the business at hand. "Well, baby," she said, "me and Missy were talking while ago, and we were thinking that maybe it was time you came home."

I was still so flipped out about failing ninth grade that I didn't really grasp what she was offering, didn't know if she was inviting me home to chastise me, or tutor me or what, and tried to hedge a little.

"I cain't this week," I told her. "I'm baby-sitting Ryan. How about Saturday?"

"Saturday's your uncle's party," she answered smoothly, as if this were common knowledge, though I had no idea what she was talking about.

"What party?"

"Well, he's turning forty, you know, and Missy, she wants to throw him a surprise party—nothing too big, just family, and a few people from church. She ordered him an ice-cream cake in Tallahassee and we've got to go pick it up, but you could ride out with Curtis if you want—Lori's coming over early to help decorate. He can help you with your stuff."

It was beginning to dawn on me that Mama was not only inviting me to a birthday party, but actually asking me to move back home in her backwards kind of way, embroidering her offer with a lot of unnecessary detail to make it less threatening. I was kind of caught off guard, and for a moment didn't answer, then heard myself murmur in a small voice: "I don't have a present."

"That's all right," she said easily, lobbing the ball back in my court. "Missy ordered him a book. I'm sure she'll let you contribute."

Again, I paused, trying to dredge the depth of my subconscious to see if I was ready for this, when she added in this desperate, kind of pathetic tag: "Cissie's frying shrimp" (which everyone knew was my favorite food in the world).

Still, I didn't answer, just stood there, not meaning to be obstinate, but mainly just waiting for her to say *something* about that damn notice of failure that she'd probably brought in from the mailbox that afternoon. I gave her a good five, then ten seconds, finally asked: "Well, d'you think Gabe'll mind? Me being there?"

Mama just laughed a dry little Mama-laugh, as if I'd said something very clever. "Oh, baby, I don't think so. I think he'll be *thrilled*."

There was something so sincere, so genuine, in the way she said it that I suddenly realized that the door was truly open, and have to admit that I immediately put two and two together, as in: Gabe + Clayton = Clayton possibly moving up to the tenth grade next year with the rest of his classmates, even the snotty ones in Gifted who thought he was mentally retarded. But I was too proud to admit that to Mama, told her I needed to discuss it with Aunt Candace before I made any definite plans.

She agreed, and just like that, my boring old summer of scrubbing showers and eating frozen pizza was replaced with a whole different scenario: living at home in the woods, waking leisurely at nine, and eating biscuits every morning, pork chops every night. That thought alone was enough to make me call Aunt Candace at work the moment I hung up, interrupt her in the middle of a staff meeting to tell her that Mama had called, had asked me to move back home.

And though Aunt Candace worked hard to sound very cool and nonchalant about the whole thing, I could detect a note of gigantic relief in her voice. I don't think it was vindictive, just that she much preferred being my loving old aunt when I was a hairless little boy. With the onset of puberty, I think I was becoming a little too *Sims* for her taste, though she'd never say anything like that to my face, of course. She just brought it down to practical matters like she always did, told me to go through my stuff and see what I'd outgrown, decide what to take and what to leave behind, and that's exactly what I did: spent the rest of the week baby-sitting Ryan in the afternoon and sorting through my stuff at night.

By Saturday, my worldly possessions were reduced to a brown grocery bag full of the few clothes I hadn't outgrown and a tape recorder and shoe box full of miniature tapes that I spent the afternoon putting in order, meticulously numbering and labeling them with my crabbed little handwriting (*Night Daddy Died*, *9th Birthday*, and even: *Gabe*).

Lori came by at five and picked up Aunt Candace, and since Uncle Ed was away on a reserve weekend, I was left by myself, waiting for the clock to tick down to seven. At six-thirty, I went out and sat on the stoop to wait for Curtis, who showed up late as usual, then had to stop for gas on the way out of town like he always did (because he was too poor to put in more than a few bucks at a time). By the time we made it out to the house, it was almost dark, the sky milk gray from an early-evening rain, the woods so dim that the motion detectors went off in front of us, bringing the sagging old oak and palmetto into sudden, luminous light.

Though I tried to keep up a brave front, I couldn't help but feel a little jitter of nervousness as Curtis hurled down the drive at his usual breakneck speed, jerking to an unexpected halt when we came upon a figure standing there in the twilight, holding up a hand for us to stop. It was Sim, I saw that instantly, though in the dim light of the trees, he really could have passed for Daddy's ghost, standing there in pressed khakis and a Nike golf shirt, for all the world like a PGA pro from Augusta National, magically transported to the heat and palmetto bugs of a West Florida oak hammock.

With his usual efficiency, he was taking on two jobs at once, parking us away from Mama's roses while he paused to chat with half a dozen of the old men from Gabe's Sunday-school class who adored Sim for the same reason they'd adored Daddy (because he was rich and polite and got a kick out of their grumpy old-men ways, never called them on anything the way Gabe did, but pretty much let them go their merry way). They had encircled him in a happy little crowd, were teasing him about his golf shirt and his Rolex, when Missy came out on the porch with the harassed look of the hostess and began silently waving us in, pointing at her watch to indicate that the moment of surprise was soon upon us. It took a little herding to get the old men moving in the direction of the house, me and Curtis and Sim bringing up the rear, though Sim didn't so much as acknowledge me, just walked alongside Curtis, talking fishing.

I took this as a deliberate snub and dropped a few steps so I could walk along by myself, the front yard still damp from the rain, lush and colorful as ever, smelling of wet leaves and mulch. I noticed that Mama's roses were in bloom, vibrant little dots of red and white and pink against the gray-green shadow of the woods, though I paid them little mind, my eyes on the dimly lit house that loomed before me, surprised by its sheer size. I thought that childhood homes were supposed to shrink as you got older, but our haunted old mansion seemed larger than I remembered, the windows and chimneys tall and intricate and strangely opulent in the half-light.

Even the porch steps seemed high and steep, the front door enormous, ten feet tall, at least, Missy halting the old men there and making them pass inside one at a time like kindergartners going to lunch, with many whispered reminders that Gabe was right upstairs, to BE QUIET.

Sim held the door for them, making light of Missy's bossiness by whispering everyone along with many accompanying cackles of laughter, and apparently, he simply hadn't recognized me in the darkness under the trees. For when I made my way into the circle of the porch light, he blinked at me in genuine surprise.

"*Claybird?*" he murmured. "I didn't even—*gaw,* you're getting big!"

This last was in a voice of great exasperation, for it's always been a sore point with Sim, how that after years of towering over me and Missy, he's now in danger of becoming the runt of the litter. I mean, he's tall enough, an inch or so under six feet, taller by far than Daddy or Gabe or any of the other Catts men, but just a couple of inches more than Mama or Missy, which really eats at him (God knows why; it's not like they hand out a million when you reach six feet).

I was amazed he'd spoken to me at all, and paused there in the door and tried like heck to think of some way to apologize for bringing on the Wrath of the Grandmother, but it was hard to do, with the old men shuffling down the hallway, talking among themselves, Missy still hissing for all of us to *be quiet*.

I finally just gave him a little nod of greeting and followed the old men inside, which was kind of a strange experience after a year's absence, like stepping into another world, the house beautiful but dim, unearthly in its ghostly perfection. Gabe's old description (*Storyville Gothic Splendor*) seemed particularly apt, for there was truly a turn-of-the-century New Orleans air about the place, the wood floors shining, the high-ceilinged old rooms lit indirectly with recessed lamps and brocaded lampshades and a two dozen candles that filled the air with the mild, wafting scent of beeswax.

The living room was already filled with family and church people who lifted their hands in silent greeting when they saw me, daresome to utter so much as a *hey,* with Missy stationed at the stereo, strict as a schoolmarm, waiting for a sign from on high to start the music. I just followed Curtis to the French doors and stood there at the edge of the room, taking in the flickering candles, the carved mantels, the marble pool, and the phoenix palms that Mama had wrapped in dozens of strands of tiny fairy lights.

The effect was strangely Florida and strangely magical, and I smiled when I remembered how worried I had been when Gabe came home, convinced that Mama was too boring to snag the Mystery Genius. Now, waiting there by the door, just able to peek around the corner to the dining room, where the white-linened table was piled high with all manner of silver platters and sugared cakes and a huge centerpiece of oak-leaf hydrangeas, I wondered how stupid could you get, thought: No wonder Gabe came back. It was a wonder he ever left at all.

Once Sim had stationed the old men under the stairs that Gabe would soon be coming down, he backed to the French doors and squeezed in between me and Curtis, glancing aside in the hush and whispering "How's that nose?" in a small, amused voice.

I knew then that all was well between us, that he'd forgiven me for outing him and his woman, and can't tell you how happy I was, though I played it cool, just wiggled the bridge, said: "Not broken."

"Well, it shouldn't be," he whispered. "Hell, I think you hit yourself—"

He was cut off by Missy, who sent a particularly potent hiss in our direction, then jerked her head up the stairs, where sure enough, movement could be detected, a small, quarrelsome voice that a year ago I might have mistaken for Daddy, though by now, I knew it was Gabe, being talked downstairs by Mama.

At first, I thought he knew we were there and just didn't want to come down, but as they slowly made their way around the corner to the landing, it was obvious that he didn't have a clue we were there, all his attention on Mama, fussing at her for taking the stairs too quickly. It was a strange sensation, seeing them together for the first time in many months. With their cropped hair and their bickering, they looked more like brother and sister than husband and wife, Gabe still in convalescence, dressed like a grumpy old millionaire in a sleek new paisley robe-and-pajama set that was too big for him and dragged the floor.

It made his progress down the stairs slow and profane, with a whisper of the f-word every now and again, till Missy punched the power button on the stereo, filling the room with a sharp, loud snippet of music. Even then, he didn't seem to notice that his living room was crowded with maybe three dozen well-wishers, all standing around in the dim splendor of the candlelight, punch glasses in hand, making ready for a toast. He just turned to Mama, told her in a clear, irritated voice: "You run tell Missy I ain't sitting down here listening to her nigger music, I don't care *what* kind of cake she bought me."

It was so perfect that at first I thought it was intentional——that Gabe had somehow detected our presence and was making one of his hilarious, audacious cracks. But at the answering roar of laughter, he started, then looked up with a face of enormous surprise and horror, the surprise that his living room was full of people, the horror at the old men, who wagged crooked fingers at him, called, "Now, whut was thet I heard?"——overjoyed at catching him in a moment of weakness, using the Dreaded Word.

For a second there, I thought they'd gone too far; that he was about to flip them off and go back to bed. But his sense of the absurd quickly returned, making him call down something that I couldn't make out over the laughter ("Kiss my *ass*," I think). The old men replied in kind, with another roar of laughter and more catcalls, and Gabe had gripped Mama's arm and was about to continue his descent, when he caught a glimpse of me at the door, the grin wiped from his face in an instant, replaced by the same fixed stare he'd given me the first time he saw me, standing at my father's coffin.

I didn't react, didn't wave or smile, just returned his gaze evenly, a small part of me wondering what had happened to my rage, my disappointment, my storming resentment. I mean, one day it was there, pulsating and alive, the next, it wasn't exactly gone, but it was negotiable. It wasn't something I was scared of anymore, but like reading and writing, something I knew to be a troublesome, but necessary part of life. Uncle Gabe and dyslexia, two strange, incomprehensible gifts that I first denied, then despaired of, then finally, *finally,* accepted, and so became a man.

He was so fixed on me that Mama had to give him a nudge to get him moving again, down the stairs to the living room, where he was engulfed with many hugs and handshakes, the old men ribbing him over his fancy new robe, Aunt Candace wading through them to give him a kiss, Missy's voice ringing out, joyous and needling, calling that she got him! She got him!

I watched from a distance, not feeling up to any face-to-face conversation, just drifting along the edges of the crowd and eventually settling in the kitchen, where I spent most of the evening eating plate after plate of everything in the house: fried shrimp and candied pecans and chicken pot pie (homemade and wonderful) that I found in the refrigerator wrapped in aluminum foil. Even when Sondra and Rachel Cole unexpectedly dropped by to wish Gabe happy birthday, I stayed where I was, watching Rachel circulate with a detached appreciation, noting that she had grown taller and leaner over the last year, had lost a lot of her puppy fat, not that it did me much good.

For she didn't so much as acknowledge me other than a wary glance in my direction when they first walked in, as if I were a slobbering puppy that might run her panty hose if I got too close. So I left her alone, just stood there in the door of the kitchen, noted that Sister Sondra was looking pretty smart and stylish herself in a ruffled black party dress (knee-length, and boy did she have some legs) and high heels and enough makeup to sink the *Titanic.* She was obviously there to check up on Sim, and soon had him cornered by the French doors, genuinely glad to see him, talking to him with a lot of laughter and animation, though Sim seemed kind of nervous and shifty, clearly a Man with a Secret.

The sad thing was that he and Sondra really were close, maybe not lover close, but best-friend close (they'd dated for almost four years; she sat on the family pew at Daddy's funeral). You could tell that it was killing him to have to play her for such a fool; whenever me or Grannie came within ten feet of him, he'd cast us these horrified little glances, afraid we'd blow his cover, though he had no reason to worry about me. I was tight as a clam, I'd learned my lesson.

Grannie, on the other hand, was probably the reason Sondra was there, now that I think of it. Hanging out in the kitchen this morning cleaning shrimp, agonizing over Simon's inalienable right to *choose,* she'd probably started reflecting on how she had a few choices of her own to make, had picked up the phone and called Mrs. Cole and invited the girls to the party. ("Oh, surely, Sim'll be there, he'll looove to see Sondra. No, he ain't leaving for Tallahassee till August. Meanwhile, it's work, work, work—you know old Sim. Sweet as he can be, bought me a couch, *brand-new*—")

As soon as she laid eyes on Sondra, she made a point of hugging her warmly and putting her old Grannie-mojo on her, telling her how pretty she was, and sweet, and how nice her hair looked, and had she lost some weight? Sondra was soon eating out of her hand, no longer so intent on Sim, but just standing there, punch glass in hand, smiling at Grannie with a misty-eyed affection that reminded me of the way the girls in our class used to gaze at Gabe.

Even Rachel softened up before the night was over, made her way to the kitchen and spoke to me over her shoulder while she poured herself a glass of punch.

"Missy says you're doing summer school," she said.

There was no particular contempt or accusation in the question, for one of Rachel's more endearing traits is that she isn't the sharpest pencil in the pack herself, no stranger to blue envelopes and bad news on the school front. So I couldn't take offense, told her: "Yeah. That's what I hear."

"What'd you fail?" she asked, turning and standing beside me against the counter.

"Algebra," I told her. "And Latin."

She nodded easily, as if failing such things was a universal scourge, something every teenager on earth had to endure, recommended I switch to German for my foreign-language requirement. "Mr. Drysdale's a piece of cake," she confided, "and Mr. Neeley is such a *bore,* or so I hear. I'd never have taken Latin myself—too stinking hard—at least for me. Maybe not to you *brains* in *Gifted*."

Well, you can see why I've loved her so long, and probably always will, till I'm a middle-aged old turd like Gabriel, still following her around town like a lovesick puppy. I was tempted to tell her so, right there in Mama's kitchen over a plate of fried shrimp, but was finally old enough to know that some things are probably better left unsaid.

I just told her I'd consider it, was standing there working on my (maybe) fourth plate of shrimp when she added from out of the blue: "I hear you got a girlfriend up in Waycross."

This was news to me, and I looked at her curiously. "Who told you that?"

She dipped her head to the living room. "Missy," she said, and I almost smiled, thinking the old redhead was getting as wily as her grannie when it came to dropping hints and innuendo, creating family myth. But I didn't feel up to playing the game and told her I didn't have a girlfriend anywhere, had just gone out a couple of times with a friend of Sim's.

Rachel seemed intrigued by my honesty. "What's her name?" she asked, the first sign of actual interest I'd ever had from any girl, much less a goddess like Rachel.

"Keri."

When I didn't offer any more details, she picked up one of the shrimp from my plate and nibbled it in this electrifyingly intimate gesture, offered casually: "I hear Sim's got a girl up there, too."

So that's what our cozy little chat was about: a fact-gathering mission for Sondra. I could just see them in the car before they got out, Sondra putting on a fresh coat of lipstick, telling Rachel over her shoulder: "I'll work on Sim, and if he doesn't crack, you corner Clay."

If that was indeed the plan, she was disappointed, for I just shrugged. "You'll have to ask Sim about thet."

She looked stupefied at my lack of cooperation, stared at me in this stunned amazement, as if she were thinking: Who is this Man of Steel? What happened to the roly-poly little boy in the husky jeans who used to follow me around Lincoln Park, used to write my misspelled name on all his notebooks: Rahel, Rakel, Raccel? Who once offered me five dollars to sit next to him at lunch. (Kenneth's idea, I might add. We were eight at the time, and desperate.)

But when all was said and done, she didn't seem any more attracted to the New Clay than she was to the Old One, and left me alone to continue my solitary assault on the shrimp till it was time for everyone to gather in the living room for the birthday song and the presents and the cutting of the ice-cream cake. I was too full to be tempted by the big old Baskin-Robbins creation, just stood there on the fringes while Gabe opened his presents, most of them gag gifts (boxes of prunes and Depends undergarments), though Missy's was the real thing, a biography on Martin Luther King that had cost a pretty penny.

Gabe seemed genuinely grateful and thanked us formally, in turn, though old Brother Kin couldn't resist a little snort of contempt that Gabe couldn't resist challenging, making a point of holding the cover up to him, calling: "Hey, Jack? You want this when I'm done?"

Brother Kin just looked away and muttered *shtt*, making everyone laugh but Gabe, who was by gosh not very amused by that kind of thing, just eyed him levelly, like the eye of the Lord on a malevolent child. But for once in his life, he let it pass, and aside from that little unpleasantness, the night drifted on without conflict, Simon more relaxed after Sondra left, still kind of tired looking and melancholy, but that was the price you paid for the Silence; a lesson that in this family, you'd think he would have learned by now.

Since most of the partiers were over seventy, Missy had planned to wind it up early, but even after the candles were snuffed and the cake reduced to crumbs, the old men hung on tenaciously, ignoring Missy's hints and taking their conversation out on the pool deck, where they cornered Gabe in some sort of political argument, their voices rising and falling outside, showing no signs of slacking off. Missy finally gave it up at eleven and took Grannie home, and I brought in my bag of clothes and tapes and recorder, and last but not least, my Busch Gardens picture that I replaced with a kiss in its old place of honor on my bedside table.

Once it was in place, I went back downstairs to tell everyone good night, found the house mostly empty, Mama wandering in her bare feet, making sure all the candles were snuffed out, about to turn in herself. She paused long enough to ask if I wanted anything special for breakfast, and with no hesitation at all, I ordered everything I could think of: biscuits and gravy and Jimmy Dean sausage and scrambled eggs and grits and not the instant kind, either, but the old-timey ones that took twenty minutes and required a close eye to make sure the pot didn't scorch.

Mama didn't seem to find my order too extravagant, just kissed me on the cheek and told me she was glad to have me home, then headed up to bed, leaving me to wander around on my own, the house still tousled from the party, not as shiningly perfect as it was when I arrived, but quiet and genteel-shabby, as comfortable as an old shoe. It was late by then, and I was heading upstairs to bed when I passed by the French doors and saw that Gabe was still out on the deck, cornered by his entourage of old boys, looking a lot like Daddy, the older he got. It wasn't just his new thinness or his gray hair, either, but something in the way he sat there slumped in his lawn chair, listening to the old geezers and their loud, strident tones, no longer so controlling and know-it-all, but the same way Daddy used to go through life: patient and accepting and mildly amused.

So maybe I wasn't the only one who was growing up around here, and on a whim I opened the door and stuck my head out and told them good night. The old men all turned and answered with a lot of gusto, not showing any sign of giving it up anytime soon, a small look of commiseration passing between me and Gabe when I met his eye, told him: "Good night, Uncle Gabe."

He didn't look at all offended or hurt at the title, but maybe as relieved as me, just lifting a hand in silent reply as the old men quickly rejoined their argument, their muted voices following me up the stairs to the second story that was quiet as a tomb. I looked around awhile, opened a few drawers and nosed around the closet, found everything pretty much as I'd left it.

When I finished my nosing around, I climbed up on the top bunk, thinking I'd go right to sleep, but I couldn't, of course. I was too wired, too full of shrimp and caffeine, wisps of the past few weeks returning to me in odd little flashes: Sim's howl of rage when he saw the blood on Grannie's couch; Missy's shouts at the fence when I hit that first pop ("Drop the *bat!*"); Gabe rattling the wall of the laundry room with his old liberal glory ("*No,* Mama, you don't do anything! It's up to Sim! He chooses! He CHOOSES! *HE CHOOSES!*")

Lying there in my snug little bed, I couldn't help but wonder what old Uncle Gabe would think of his boundless generosity after he met Kendra at the springs at the reunion next month, and she refused to swim because the place was full of niggers. I could just hear her saying it in that snotty, south Georgia twang, openly, without shame, and also see Gabe's face: the outrage! The horror! A neo-Nazi! A Klansman! Stealing our precious son!

The more I thought of it, the funnier it got, making me sit up straighter and laugh and laugh, till I happened to catch a glimpse of myself in the dark old windowpane across the bed, an image so startling that it made me go silent and sit there a moment, spellbound.

Mama must have heard my laughter, for she came to the door and hesitantly knocked, then opened it a crack, her face curious. "Claybird?" she asked. "Are you all right?"

I just nodded, told her I was fine, and after a moment, she quietly

closed the door, leaving me alone in the half-light, still staring at my reflection in the dark old windowpane, hoping to see it again: that brief,
startling image of my father. But the magic of the moment had passed just
that quickly, making me lose my humor, and along with it, that impudent,
gap-toothed Michael-smile. I even tried smiling again, but it was no
good. I was just a big fool sitting up in bed grinning at himself in the
moonlight.

Daddy was gone, no more to be seen, though the memory of that
brief, poignant flash was strong in the room, so strong that for the very
first time, it occurred to me that maybe my father wasn't a ghost after all.
Maybe the best part of him—his optimism, his humor, his sheer good nature—continued to reside in the old house he had so painstakingly re-
deemed by dint of hard work and constant faith. Not in his own flesh, but
in his children's, in their persistence and their courage, their continuing
forgiveness in the face of All Betrayals, Great and Small, which struck me
as funny—ironic, Gabe would say. For I'd spent the better part of a year
searching high and low for him. I'd heard stories, I'd told stories, I'd tried
baseball and spite, ironing and oral history, but when all was said and
done, my father had never left me at all; had never been any further gone
than the closest mirror, if I'd have only thought to look.

# ACKNOWLEDGMENTS

There are a few people I'd like to personally thank for helping bring this book to fruition: my husband and daughters foremost, for putting up with a writer in the house and providing a never-ending source of material. I'd also like to thank Connie May Fowler, the patron of Florida lit., for her early and continual support of my work and (if that weren't enough) for introducing me to our wonderful agent, Joy Harris. Also, thanks to David and June Cussen, who started this ball rolling in the first place and remain Clayton's literary godparents, and Marjorie Braman, who caught the Catts vision on her first reading and made my great leap to New York a smooth transition. Last but not least, I'd like to thank my daughter Isabel and her fellow students at Einstein-Montessori—dyslexics all—who have a little trouble with phonemic sequencing, but otherwise look out at the world with a clear and unwavering eye. You guys are my heroes and I'd have never gotten inside old Claybird's head without you.